DREAM TEMPTRESS

She pressed her lithe form against his long, hard body, and all sanity left him. But it was her eyes that chained a man's soul to her for all eternity. They were fawn-like and beautiful; their enticing indigo depths held both danger and promise. Her golden body was supple and naked, and her legs entwined about his. Roark's hand moved to cup her breasts, to caress their lush firmness, and a slow, smoldering lust ignited within him. His fingers moved over her body, aroused her, and urged a quivering breast to his hot mouth. He kissed her mouth in a haze of desire, savoring the sweetness of her lips and the promises they conveyed. Elusive, wrapped within his dreams, she taunted him, remaining just beyond total surrender . . . .

EMERALD SEA

Tonya Gabriel

With a special love and appreciation to my father,
Rush M. Hicks, who has always been there for me.

Book Margins, Inc.

A BMI Edition

Published by special arrangement with Dorchester Publishing

Printed in the United States of America.

The Emerald Sea

Some quiet evening when the tide is low,
    I shall slip my mooring and sail away,
With no response to the friendly hail
    Of kindred craft in the busy bay.

In the silent hush of the twilight pale,
    When the night stoops down to embrace the day,
And the voices call in the waters' flow—
Some quiet evening when the tide is low,
    I shall slip my mooring and sail away.

    Through the purpling shadows that darkly trail,
      Over the ebbing tide of the Emerald Sea,
I shall fare me away, with a dip of sail,
And a ripple of waters to tell the tale,
    Of a lonely voyager, sailing away
      To the Mystic Isles where at anchor lay
The crafts of those who have sailed before,
Over the Emerald Sea to the Unknown Shore.

A few who have watched me sail away,
Will miss my craft from the busy bay;
    Some friendly ships that were anchored near,
    Some loving souls that my heart held dear,
    In silent sorrow will drop a tear—

But I shall have peacefully furled my sail,
In moorings sheltered from storm or gale,
    And greeted the friends who have sailed before,
    Over the Emerald Sea to the Unknown Shore. . . .

Prologue

A scent, sweet and tantalizing, floating down about his head roused Roark Tillman from the dark depths of slumber. The girl came into his arms with a breathless sigh and a promise of unbridled delight. Without opening his eyes, Roark envisioned her perfectly, welcomed her. It was the same as it had been on so many other nights. His soul's mate, temptress of his dreams, she was no stranger to him. She was a part of him in every way—his destiny. Her waterfall of raven-black hair, the texture of the finest silk, whirled like a cloud around him, floating down over his naked, muscular body. His hands reached to grasp it, to stroke it with a lover's sure touch, then to lace his fingers through it and, with a jerk of his powerful wrist, draw the image of beauty over him.

Roark Tillman, once the fierce ruler of Borneo and Malay, willingly surrendered all to this girl whom he knew only on the other side of his conscious mind. They were of one mind, one desire, and nothing could keep them apart.

The dream temptress pressed her lithe form against his long, hard body, and all sanity left him. But it was her eyes that chained a man's soul to her for all eternity. They were fawn-like and beautiful; their enticing indigo depths held both danger and promise. Her golden body was supple and naked, as her legs entwined about his. Roark's hand moved to cup her breasts, to caress their lush firmness, and a slow, smoldering lust ignited within him. His fingers moved over her body, aroused her, and urged a quivering breast to his hot mouth. The sweetness of the firm, hard nipples began a trembling in his arms. He kissed her mouth in a haze of desire, savoring the sweetness of her lips and the promises they conveyed. Elusive, wrapped within the haze of his dreams, she taunted him, remaining just beyond total surrender. In the spiritual passings of their souls, they had met many times; they were bound by their destiny, not by time—a destiny that had yet to come to pass.

Then, as always, she would withdraw from him, and stand before him with a dagger in her hand.

Later, he would awaken and find her gone, and he would be left with only a faceless, dream-haunted memory.

Morning came. Roark Tillman awoke to emptiness. He reflected upon the meaning of her presence in his dreams. Who was she? Why did she hold the dagger? He tossed restlessly on the tangled sheets, knowing that somehow she was a connection to everything that he sought—or to his destruction.

He knew he would never find peace until he discovered the significance of her in his life. An intense feeling of loneliness suddenly threatened to overcome him. Roark Tillman cast the baffling emotion aside, knowing that for him such deep caring for anyone was impossible. He was the master of forty concubines. No single woman could ever satisfy him or destroy him. . . .

BOOK ONE
Maya

1

The sky was very blue; there was not a cloud in it. The sea joined it in a silver line, incredibly far away, and there was the noise of surf breaking on the rocks at the foot of the cliffs. Riding the limitless emerald sea was a ship, the *Seawolf*.

Inside the ship, Maya was little concerned with the sounds beyond the cabin door, or, indeed, with anything but her own thoughts. She stood alone and silent, watching the flames she had created with an absorbed and quiet concentration. Her face was devoid of expression, yet now and then the light from the fire would catch the hard, brittle gleam in the depths of her dark blue eyes. No man gazing into them now would have found a trace of gaiety to cheer him or any hint of warmth to comfort his heart. The face, so beautiful and young, was made of stone.

A tongue of flame crept up the left breast of a waistcoat, adding for a moment to the brilliance of the bright silk flowers embroidered on it then transforming them into a dark parody of splendor; another flame ate at the curve of the pocket, and after a minute a little shower of coins fell out and hit the wooden floor of the cabin like metallic raindrops. She noted the sound with grave satisfaction.

The flames ate their way higher. The silk shirt caught the spreading fire and exploded with a soft, menacing, upward rush of light. Maya's skin was beautiful in the light; it acquired subtle tones of gold, a translucence under its even tan. There were highlights on her small, slim shoulders, and her firm breasts were given an illusory fullness.

She knelt down in complete patience, watching the flames ascend until they licked at the deckhead of the cabin, and the white paint began to burn.

The flames lit the white lettering on the sea-chest below the clothing. The name "Roark Till-man" stood out scrolled and baroque and assertive. It meant nothing to Maya except as a symbol of power.

There was very little smoke yet, but she knew that in a moment the cabin would fill with it. Carefully, almost with a sense of ritual, Maya poured the last of the whale oil from the base of the lamp over the high boots and over a pair of Chinese cotton breeches that had fallen down when she started the fire, and she watched while the fire discovered them.

The heat began to beat against her, but she ignored it. A drop of oil trickled from the base of the lamp onto her finger and she wiped it delicately on her sarong. At last, with the smoke coming lower and lower and the flames becoming more furious, she permitted herself a smile of satisfaction and, rising in one lithe movement to her feet, began to scream.

The women came first. She heard the bare feet outside the cabin door and the chattering, agitated Indonesian voices. She thought she could distinguish a Chinese woman by a different, more metallic, tone. Then she heard booted feet on the deck above, running, and a white man's voice, an English voice. "Goddamme, sir, the bloody cabin's afire!" Maya could not understand the words, but the note of indignant surprise was unmistakable.

The crackle of the flames was loud now; the smoke stung at her eyes and clutched at her throat. She began to beat the panels of the door with her fists. Now and then she paused to scream.

The bosun broke down the door. It was intensely dramatic. She noted every detail with the same grave satisfaction with which she had watched the falling coins; then she rushed headlong into the bosun's arms. The women screamed at her; men came running with buckets of water; the narrow alleyway became a maelstrom of noise and moving bodies, swearing and shouting, and billowing smoke.

The women pulled her down with them to where they were huddled against the bulkhead at the far end of the passage. They asked, "Why did you do it?" repeating the question over and over again, as if by monotonously repeating it they could make her speak.

For a while she resisted them. Then she said breathlessly, speaking as if she were frightened, "The lamp—I did not know—I have not seen such things. It was hot, it burnt my hands."

She held them up and the woman chorused, "Her hands. It burnt her hands."

"I dropped it," she went on, lying easily and

fluently, "when it fell . . . the fire . . ." Maya made
an uprushing gesture with her hands.

"She comes from the pirate ships," one of the
older women said. "She would not know of such
things."

"I do not know," Maya agreed humbly, filled
with contempt for the other women.

The bosun drove them out onto the deck. He was
still swearing, but he found time enough to
demand, "How did it happen?"

The one woman who had learned enough
English to understand him answered, "The lamp.
It burned her hands. She dropped it."

"Goddamme, bloody little fool!" He stared at
her distastefully. "Shouldn't've bin locked in his
cabin alone."

"It was the Lord Tillman's orders, sir," the
woman said timidly.

"Get that damned pump going!" The bosun
turned to harass the men. There was no need for
the fire pump; he knew it and the men knew it. The
fire was under control already. But he would be
blamed for it in the end and he found a certain degree of consolation in taking it out on the men now.

"Hop to it, you bloody heathens!" he bellowed.
"Hop to it, or I'll twist yor tongues around yor
bleedin' necks!"

Maya, too, knew that the fire was under control.
It had served its purpose of getting her out of the
locked cabin, but she had hoped that the whole
ship might burn. She moved slowly and carefully
away from the other women and stood at the rail,
trying to calculate the distance to the shore of the
bay, wondering if she could swim that far,
wondering if there were sharks.

The bosun saw her.

"Watch that damned girl!" he shouted at the women. "She's goin' to make a jump for it. Hold the wench and keep her from mischief."

The women got hold of her, took her into their circle again. They spoke at her rather than to her.

"She's the pirate's daughter. Naturally she would try to escape. She is the daughter of the Sultan Garuda, the Lion of Ceylon. It would be proper for her to try to escape."

The oldest of them broke up the slowly forming chorus of admiration. "Nonetheless, the Lord said he would take the pirate wench to his bed tonight."

The bosun knew enough Indonesian dialect to understand what she was saying. He looked at her sardonically. "Not in that bloody bed—not now." He turned and went back to the cabin where the fire was almost out.

The fiery ball of the sun began its leisurely descent into the emerald-blue sea shortly after midday, and with its going went some small portion of the blistering heat of the day. Maya clenched her fists in her lap, then unconsciously uncurled them very slowly, like flower buds unfurling, until they were flat. She pressed them against her thighs, as if reaching for something hidden beneath her sarong. Not yet! a voice said inside her head, not yet! Now was not the time. Perhaps there never would be a right time. She gritted her teeth with fierce pride and lay down within the circle of women. If her escape proved successful, she would need all her wits and every second of rest she could get to carry it through.

Anyone who had watched her might well believe she was a witch, capable of casting spells with those mysterious indigo eyes. Those eyes were hooded now and withheld her thoughts and feelings from those around her.

2

Roark Tillman walked heavily down the jetty and men looked curiously at him as he passed. Native fishermen from their net-boats, sailors from the 22-gun slave ship *Grand Turk*, townspeople from the waterfront houses—for the jetty at sunset was a meeting place for Cape Town's inhabitants—all stared after him. It was clear that the news of his expulsion had reached them.

Even though the dusky shadows of evening were about to swallow him, the breadth of his shoulders was apparent under his brown coat, and he held his head proudly, like a Spanish king. His face was handsome, recklessly so, with a straight, thin nose, and a firm but sensuous mouth.

The raging anger he'd felt during his meeting with the Governor had ebbed to a black, deep fury. Already he had arranged for fresh water to be stored aboard the *Sea Wolf.* The clearance papers would be ready by eight o'clock; he had bribed the clerks in the port captain's office to be sure of it.

He looked out to his 20-gun brig, the *Sea Wolf.*
She lay etched with almost intolerable clarity
against the stillness of the harbor. The bay was
glass calm, pale in the first twilight as a sun-
bleached mother-of-pearl. The ship was hard and
dark and black in it, like an irritant on its
perfection. Scattered about her were a small
flotilla of shore boats. He studied the other
ships in the harbor—the 22-gun slave ship,
the *Grand Turk;* and *Amsterdam,* 22-guns,
pride of the Dutch fleet; and the American
20-gun frigate, the *Lady Washington.* Beauties,
all of them, he thought. But the people on
the end of the pier were only looking out towards the *Sea Wolf.* Roark remembered the
Governor's words: "They see your ship when they
walk along the shore in the evening. They
speculate about what ungodly acts happen aboard
her."

A small, dark, turbaned man in a faded sarong
came up the jetty to meet him. He crouched so low
that he gave the impression of kneeling. "Lord,
Lord, there was a fire," he said fearfully. "We
saw the smoke. There was shouting and
screaming."

Roark looked out over the white turban on the
man's head. The shore boats were lying well clear
of the *Sea Wolf.* There was no smoke. "She is not
on fire now."

It was a statement, but the man chose to answer
it as a question. "I do not know, Lord."

"You damned witless fool!" Roark roared.
"Why did you not go to her?"

"I would not have dared," the man answered,
cringing. "I was told to wait for you, Lord. I
waited." He straightened himself, and suddenly,

in justification, he said, "There were many shore boats if help was needed."

Roark stalked past him and went down the steps. The men in the longboat put out the oars, thudding wood against wood. The coxswain gave a melodious cry, somebody pushed the bow out, and the longboat began to move across the water.

At once, by the magic of movement, Cape Town diminished, and by a counter-magic the mountain behind it grew larger. Where before it had been a blue wall, it now was a rampart, an enormous fortress, clean-cut along the parapet, squared at the ends, dwarfing to insignifcance the green-black bastions of the Fortress of Good Hope on the inner curve of the bay.

Roark's mind was confused with mingled streams of thought. It was as if one half of his mind was occupied with the indignity of the meeting in the Governor's house, and the other half with the prospect of new adventure. It is not possible for the Governor to understand me, he thought. No one who has not lived in the Orient can understand why I need my women—not all of those even who have lived in the Orient understand that. I should have told him.

But Roark was aware that he could not have said this, aware that he had gone to the meeting full of arrogance and an aggressive intention to justify himself, and that he had offered no justification. His thoughts were more occupied with his own failure than with Lanford's success. The Governor had outsmarted and outplayed him. Now he would have to leave Cape Town.

I should have told him of the Treasury's delays of my money, he told himself.

Roark reflected upon the intricacies of the East India Company, of the Treasury in London, of the

injustice. He had had no compensation for the loss
of his Borneo land grant; he had still to be paid the
hundred thousand taels of silver for the services
of his ships in Malaya. He should have told the
Governor how their God-damned treaty with the
Dutch had destroyed his merchant business. That
treaty had been the root of the trouble. The
English bastards had used him and now were
casting him away like a leper. Stupid, he thought.
All that waste of time and men and money for
these stinking English. My time, my men, and my
money. Even as he ran over his grievances, he
knew that he had told Langford about them
before. In a different way, with different
emphasis, he had told him of all of them, and none
of them, he knew now, had been settled. Langford
had only been playing with him.

The East Indies had been Roark's home for
more than twenty years. He alone, of all the
Europeans, thought of the Orient as home. All the
others came for a few years and then left. Only
those who died stayed. Even then, if they could
afford it, they would provide in their wills for
their bodies to be shipped back home.

I'll be buried on one of these islands, thank God,
he told himself. Such good times I've had here. But
that's finished. God damn the English.

Everything was working so well, Roark thought
bitterly, but now it's over. Now they've taken
everything.

The longboat moved through the pearl water; to
the right, the earth shadow crept up against the
afterglow, exquisitely blue against its fading rose.
The coxswain was giving the boatmen the stroke
now in a soft-stressed song in a dialect that Roark

only half understood. The mountain grew still greater with the earth's shadow, looming enormous in the fading sky.

Flint, the bosun, met him at the top of the ladder. His blunt face was distraught. He judged everything personally. "We've been on fire. It's out now, but I thought one time that it might 'a been serious."

"Where was it?" Roark demanded impatiently.

"In your cabin." Flint's head was turned away from him; only his eyes flickered towards Roark's face.

"My cabin? How?" Roark swore viciously under his breath.

"That damned wench dropped the lamp."

"What bloody wench? What stupidity is this?"

Flint pointed wordlessly to the group of women standing on the foredeck. Maya stood in the middle of them. Two of them were holding her arms as if they still feared that she would leap overboard to swim to shore. She stood submissively, slender, bare-breasted, with a sarong knotted about her hips, her head bowed.

Roark had not seen her before. She had been brought from the *Grand Turk* at night. It was not a transaction for the light of day, and he had slept the night ashore. Now in the middle of the restless shimmer of the group of women, her small body seemed to acquire stature from its isolation. She was quite still. There was no need for the hands on her arms. From where he stood Roark believed that she was trembling.

"Let the wench go!" he called out in Indonesian. "Let her come to me."

"She will jump!" The women set up a bawling at once. "She will leap from the rail . . . She will kill herself!"

Roark's eyes narrowed in warning. "Be still! Let her come to me."

Flint watched him curiously.

Maya stood motionless for an instant after the women took their hands from her. Then she moved forward. She walked aristocratically, almost with an air of authority. She carried her small body with pride, but her head was still bowed and submissive, her chin down to the hollow of her throat.

"There was a fire." Roark became conscious of her eyes looking up at him, half hidden by the fringe of smooth black hair.

"It was the lamp," she explained patiently. "I do not know about such things. It burned my hands and I let it fall." She made no attempt to express regret or to excuse herself beyond the plain statement of fact.

He watched her gravely. "Let me see your hands, my love."

She held them out palm upward. She had long, delicate, tapering fingers. The palms and the insides of the fingers were a pale shell-pink in contrast to the golden-brown of the backs of her hands. Across the palm of the right hand and across the base of two of the fingers were blisters and a score of small new burns. He was not to know that she had held the lamp and deliberately burnt herself, closing her eyes and her mind to the pain of it so that, if it were necessary, she might have evidence of proof.

"Stupid fools!" He shouted over her head to the women. "Her hand is burnt. See that it is dressed. Take her below!"

Flint looked after her questioningly, but he said nothing.

"Where is Ben Cooper?" Roark demanded,

bringing an end to the scene.

"Captain Cooper went ashore when the long boat came with your note," Flint replied. "We need four hands. Said he would come back with them by dark."

"And Mr. Pitney?"

"Dunno. Hasn't been aboard since they brought the girl last night."

The blood rushed to Roark's face. "Maybe in hell!" he said with a black anger. "Take the boat and find him. Search the taverns along the waterfront first and go inshore if you have to." He lunged his face forward suddenly, his neck lowered between his huge shoulders so that he looked like a crouched vulture. "See that you don't get drunk yourself or I'll hang you! We sail at sunrise."

3

The quiet peace of the starlit bay was broken by the sound of loud voices and noises aboard the *Sea Wolf*—feet overhead, and the thud of heavy objects let down at a run from the tackle on the yardarm, the long boats bumping alongside, and men shouting, and hatch covers dropped on the deck, and canvas drawn swishing across it with a sound like a monsoon in summer-parched reeds. Lanterns shone from every point along the deck, seeming to set the ship ablaze with lights.

The women sat in the half-gloom of the lanterns below deck, divided into small groups. Children swarmed among them, moving incessantly. Babies cried and were instantly silenced with the breast. Maya decided wearily that this was how the women divided naturally, by friendships and special relationships. She wondered which group would try to absorb her into it, would try to use her.

They knew that the ship would sail soon. They knew that the captain was ashore searching for men for the crew. They knew that the man Pitney would come back drunk. They knew everything. The only thing they did not know was whom their Lord would choose for this night and where he would sleep with her, his own cabin being burnt by the pirate's daughter. They came back to this again and again as if it were the magnetic force that pulled at their uncertain and unreliable compass needles. From time to time they talked of Maya openly, without hushing their voices. They were shocked, not because she had burnt the Lord's cabin, but because she had not greeted him with a proper submissiveness, had spoken to him directly and without the respectfulness that they used themselves as a token of their obedience to his will.

The door opened and the small brown man who had spoken to her earlier in the day, before she was taken to the cabin, staggered by her with an enormous bowl of rice. He moved sideways past her as he went back to the door and murmured, "We sail at sunrise." She knew that already, but before she could question him further he was gone.

Where would they sail? This was the thing that mattered. The *Grand Turk*, the slave ship that had brought her to Cape Town, had sailed southwest, away from Ceylon—from her home. This was a ship like the *Grand Turk;* it too would sail west. The few words of English that she had acquired on the long passage across the Indian ocean were not enough to help her here. She could not ask these white devils where the new ship would go. The women knew nothing of the ways of the sea; already she had dismissed them scornfully in her mind. Only this little man with the rice had offered help, and his words were a warning. She had to escape—to escape before sunrise.

She searched the long, low room with her eyes again. Roark had had the partitions between the four cabins on the port side of the ship torn down to make one long room for the younger women. All the doors save one were blocked. There were four small hatchways in the side of the ship, too small even for her slender body. The only possible route to escape she had marked and assessed long since. Over the top of the inner bulkhead at one end was an opening large enough, but to reach it she would have to pass through the women, to pass the gauntlet of their suspicious eyes.

These sluts will sleep, she thought. But she knew that they would not sleep until Roark came. They would squat there in an uneasy rivalry of anticipation.

Another man came in with a large pan of curry. They called her to come and eat, and she went. She was unashamedly hungry.

From somewhere above deck a voice could be heard singing in a rich baritone. The tune was timed to mark the slow, gentle roll of the sea beneath the ship's keel. The breezes would have snatched the words away, scattering them to the sea, but the sweet strains eluded the airy rushes of wind and drifted stirringly below the deck to the women. Some strange quality in the voice held them enthralled, and they seemed bound in its spell of sound as the words were crooned:

Well met, well met, my own true love.
Well met, well met, said he.
I've just returned from the emerald sea,
From a land where the grass grows green.

Well, I could have married a king's daughter there,
And she would have married me;
But I refused the golden crown,
All for the sake of thee.

So come and go with me,
I'll take you where the grass grows green,
To the lands on the banks of the emerald sea.

Well met, well met, my own true love,
Well met, well met, said he,
I have just returned from the emerald sea,
And it's all for the sake of thee,
And it's all for the sake of thee.

When the song ended, the illusion scattered, and
the women went back to their meal.

Later, the same small man came in for the rice
bowl and the pan that had held the curry. With a
puzzled frown troubling her brow, Maya watched
him closely, but this time he said nothing. He was
not supposed to speak in the women's cabin. As he
closed the door, he paused for an instant, looking
at her with enormous, lustrous brown eyes. But
still he said nothing.

Much later, the women began to fall asleep.
They had after all abandoned hope of Roark's
coming. They slept tangled together, some on the
bunks, most of them on mats on the floor. They
were of all ages, the youngest perhaps a year older
than Maya, the oldest—she could not guess—not
very old. The senior wives, the women who ruled
the household, were not here. They were in
another cabin. They no longer even hoped for the
attentions of the Lord Tillman and took refuge in
their authority over the other women and in

spitefulness towards them.

When most of the women were asleep, and only two or three still talked at lengthening intervals, Maya got suddenly to her feet. Awkwardly she brushed a wayward tress from her cheek. She was numb to every emotion save a gnawing fear that feasted heartily upon what courage she tried to muster. She set her mind not to be afraid, yet her legs had a strange tendency to shake beneath her, and an uncontrollable shivering made tatters of her resolve. Despite her show of self-control, however strained, she was terribly afraid, not knowing what lay in store for her if she did not escape, but convinced now that these white savages planned some hideous fate for the daughter of Sultan Garuda.

Unhurriedly, as if secure in the knowledge that no one could touch her, she walked to the door to see if she had properly interpreted the look in the little man's eyes. It was, as she had believed it would be, open. She let herself out into the passage while the women who were still awake whispered uneasily to one another, and slipped through the outer door to the deck.

The deck of the ship, hung with dim-glowing lanterns, was almost as light as the cabin had been. Men moved on it rhythmically, throwing giant, whirling shadows as they moved across the light of the lanterns. Beyond the main deck they were sending up a new foretopsail. The great lashed serpentine shape of the canvas was swaying up in helpless curves. Closer at hand the sheep were coming aboard, petulant and complaining. Men were shouting everywhere, their bare feet thudding on the deck. The bosun was calling up the foremast, and voices answered him, as if out of the dark sky.

The Lord Tillman—she was sure it was the Lord Tillman—was walking back and forth across the poop deck with heavily booted feet. She could sense the anger in his footfalls. She shrank against the corner of the break of the poop deck and the high, scrolled fairing-plate at the side of the ship, merging into the shadow of the ladder and the broken light of the lamps through the rigging. Her sarong was dark, a cloth of purples and browns and dull greens that flowed into and seemed to increase the shadows.

She was sure no one had seen her, and yet, a long while afterwards, fear pricked her consciousness as the little man slipped past her in the dark. He carried a bucket of rubbish to empty over the side. He leant over the bulwark with an ingrained caution to see if the water was clear of longboats below. Then he lifted the bucket to the edge of the rail and threw its contents out into the darkness. Fish swam into the floating rubbish at once from the black depths, trailing spear-shafts of phosphorescence behind them. Only after he had watched them for a full minute did he turn toward the shadowy figure of Maya and say, his voice still a gusty sigh, "We sail toward the sunrise."

She did not answer him. She absorbed the softness of his words, trying to understand them. He spoke a dialect of Indonesian that was all but foreign to her. On her father's ship she had spoken either a Ceylonese tongue or the Malay dialect of

Indonesian that was native to her home of Ceylon.
It was essential for her to know whether he meant
towards sunrise or towards *the* sunrise. She
waited with a curious, unchildish patience, while,
over her head, Roark's boots stamped out his fury
with the English Governor and himself.

A sigh of relief almost escaped her when the
man came again at last. He had another bucket of
rubbish.

"To the east?" she asked in a low whisper, as
soon as he had rested the edge of the bucket on the
rail.

"Timor," he said, "to the east—to the sunrise."

"Then," she whispered despairingly, as if appalled at her error, "it would have been wrong to
burn the ship."

"Praise Allah," the little man said simply.

4

Morning blossomed with vibrant hues that changed the color of the bay, touching and tossing waves with the blues and golds of the breaking dawn. The mountain was flooded with an improbable antique pink, the delicate color of the interior of a sea-shell—a color altogether wrong for something so mighty, so warlike.

A gentle wind rose with the sun, as Roark had said it would. With her anchor secure, the *Sea Wolf* had slipped her moorings at dawn. The sea was calm and the wind east and firm. Men swarmed up the foremast. The new foresail fell away from the jack-stay in stiff folds and creases. It looked startlingly white above the weathered foresail as that in turn was sheeted home. The ship's head swung to the wind ripple that spread in dark blue furrows over the sea, and she began to head softly out of the bay. The high houses on the slopes of Table Mountain began to glisten a

bright white as the sun reached them in the
middle of the tangle of young oak and vines and
up-thrusting pine.

Roark strolled along the deck, then swung into
the foremast shrouds. He climbed easily, the wind
tugging him pleasantly, and he did not stop until
he was braced on the topgallant ropes at the
pinnacle of the foremast.

He searched the sea and the sky, meticulously
seeking the lurking squall or storm, or the hidden
reef or rocks. But there were no danger signs as
far as the horizon.

For a moment he let himself enjoy the wind and
the motion of the ship and the limitlessness of the
sea. He examined all the rigging in sight, checking
for damage or weakness, then climbed down and
went back to the poop deck.

Dawn had brushed the heavens in deep purple
before the sun, rising higher and golden on the
horizon, bleached it to a softer pink and sharply
etched the detail of the *Sea Wolf* in its gilded light.
The morning bloomed into full day. The sky faded
to a subdued blue, and the translucent bluish
green that rose and fell in a languid, heaving
motion became the sea beneath it. Triangular sails
billowed with the full breath of the dawn wind,
and the ship skimmed the waters like a gull in
effortless flight.

Half the women had come on deck to watch the
sailing. They seemed unable to take in the fact of
departure. They looked about the ship vaguely,
huddled together in a knot like the sheep in the
pens.

Maya looked from them to the sheep contemptuously and back again. Once she went to the rail
and stared out over the bay at the shrinking shoreline of the Cape. Nobody attempted to stop her

now. Either they accepted that she no longer
intended to escape or they had forgotten her in the
excitement of sailing.

Once the main topsail was sheeted home, the ship
steadied on course, and Maya looked up the center
line to the high-reaching spar projecting forward
from the bow of the ship and then calculatingly at
the sun over the mountains. The ship was heading
north-west. It would have to go west to clear the
bay, but the north in it woke doubt in her. She had
put the idea of escape aside in that moment of
whispering in the night shadows. Now it was too
late to escape. Even if she tried to swim, these
devils would only lower a longboat and retake her.
If this man was wrong about the ship's intention,
it was now too late to try anything. It might be
necessary to kill him if only to restore her self-
respect. He was standing outside the galley door
just then, waiting for the early morning food. She
watched him somberly. He was an insignificant
person—a Bornean, she judged, a small fisherman
who had taken to seafaring.

As if he had realized her fear, he came aft. This
time he carried coffee. She drifted towards the
poop ladder, and as he came up to her he said,
"There are rocks. She will go north for a little
while and then come round. The rest is God's
will."

She relaxed softly, sagging wearily, released of
her fears. The morning air was crisp, exquisitely
clean, sea-smelling. She felt something of the
immense   exhilaration   of   other   morning
departures with her father, remembering the
motion as her father's ship laid over to other dawn
winds, and the singing and the laughter of the
crew.

There was no laughter on the *Sea Wolf*. Flint

was cursing the men as they worked in the riggings. Behind them the dawn wind freshened, and the buildings along the shore began to shift in relation to the slopes of the hill beyond. They could see as far as the tower of the Green Point light now, but the light was out, snuffed at sunrise.

Maya still found little comfort, even in the knowledge that the ship was sailing east. She dozed fitfully on the deck, rousing whenever footsteps paced near. Usually it was Flint who came to stand above her, his legs braced apart and his hands set on his hips. His dark face twisted in a malevolent smile as his black eyes bored into her. Maya shivered in apprehension as she sensed in him a twisted desire to see her writhing in agony while he had her in some perverted way.

Roark Tillman's men paused often to stare at her with more than a longing glance, but they knew their master and held a deep fear of him. His temper could rise without warning, and his skill with weapons had earned a healthy respect, bordering on fear, from them. Long ago they had learned to stay well away from the huge man and that which belonged to him.

Roark kept his own vigil at a more distant spot, viewing Maya through slitted eyelids while he appeared to rest peacefully, his back braced against a rail, and his legs stretched out before him. For some mysterious reason her presence aboard the *Sea Wolf* troubled him. There was something haunting about her eyes.

The dawn wind failed them ten miles offshore. They lay becalmed in an increasing heat. Even the gulls were too languid to fly in this dead air; they lay in small, snow-white clusters on water that was as lackluster as the blind eye of a cat.

Captain Ben Cooper busied himself with the ship's log on the wheel-box. The gnarled Scotsman at the wheel—one of the new hands picked up the night before—rested his hands listlessly on the spokes, steadying the wheel only when the movement of the ocean swell tugged irresolutely at the rudder. The captain wrote slowly, with apparent labor, yet the script that came away from his pen had a fine engraver's quality about it. He used to say that it was the one thing he had learned in his brief schooling. He filled in the ship's name at the head of the new page: *Sea Wolf.* He filled in his own name, flushing a little, as always, with pride: Benjamin Cooper, Captain. Port of departure: Cape Town, Cape of Good Hope. Then for a little while he waited, staring at the word 'toward', the word that was the ultimate expression of the humility of the seaman, the word that acknowledged that beginnings were with men but that endings were with God.

At length he said coolly, "Mr. Tillman, sir!"

Roark Tillman, pacing up and down the deck, grunted.

Cooper said with a questioning inflexion, "Toward . . . ?"

Roark grunted again.

Cooper repeated the word, stressing the inflexion.

"Toward? Toward where?" Roark exploded irritably.

"Yes, Mr. Tillman"—Cooper's voice was still low, faintly threaded with amusement—"toward where?"

Roark abandoned his introspection. "What d'you mean, Cooper?"

"I am entering the log, Mr. Tillman. 'Left Cape

Town, took departure Green Point light toward . . . '?"

It was old matter this, discussed often over a
drink after dinner in the galley during the long
wait at anchor, discussed before Roark had
brought his people aboard the *Sea Wolf*, discussed
ashore in taverns, in waits on the jetty. Where
would he go? Where would he take his women?

Roark resumed his walk. At the far side of the
ship he snorted, "The Laccadive Islands."

Ben Cooper held his pen poised, not beginning
to write. When Roark had come level with him
again he said, "The new slavery laws, Mr. Tillman
—you do remember them? The Laccadive Islands
are patroled by the British. They are under the
Bengal Government. Your position with the
Bengal Government . . ."

Roark looked at him stormily. "A pack of fools!"
he snapped. "Cowardly, pompous asses! Eleven
months and there is yet no reply to my last letter.
The bastards will pay for my losses in Borneo or
there is no justice in government! I told Langford
that. I told him that I was a prisoner of British
policy." Roark knew that he had not told Langford. He knew that he had meant to use this as his
defense and that Langford had outplayed him. "He
would not listen," he muttered angrily.

Cooper nodded. All this he had heard before. He
had helped to pen earlier letters. It was Roark's
contention that he had been ignored in the terms
of the treaty that handed back his Borneo grants
to the Dutch. He claimed vast compensation. The
number of his letters were already a legend in the
East.

Cooper said, trying to bring things back to
practicality, "Nonetheless, the Bengal Govern-

ment would give you no peace in the Laccadives. The world is changing towards the institution of slavery, Mr. Tillman.''

This too had been said before. Ordinarily Roark exploded in passion, but now he was drained, filled instead with self-pity. "My women are not slaves, Captain Cooper.'' The use of Cooper's rank was an indication of acute displeasure. "They were a present from the Sultan of Malay, a present in accordance with the custom of the time and the place. Sir Robert Hawkins approved of my proceedings. I have the Malay Government document issued under his hand. 'Mr. Tillman was hailed throughout His Highness's dominions as the deliverer of that once powerful kingdom.' ''

Roark Tillman straightened himself. He seemed to fill out, as if the memory of that time had flooded back to restore him to his glories.

"I pacified Malay. I took peace to the country and I maintained it. And the English rewarded me with land grants throughout the islands. Then with their God-damned treaty with the Dutch, they took it all away. And that cold, aristocratic bastard at the Cape''—he looked angrily over at the serrated western flank of the mountain—"what does he know of the Orient? No one who has not lived in the Orient can judge me. No one who has not lived there has the knowledge with which to judge. I was the law in Borneo and Nicobar. I made the law in Malay. Langford was given his task only because of the power his family holds in England. An evil-spirited little man, sir, an evil-spirited little man! What can he know of my needs? A pox on Langford and his bloody king!'' He glowered at Cooper.

"Yet,'' the captain persisted, "the tide is rising against slavery. The Governor has to retreat before it or he is lost himself."

"They are not slaves! I freed them in Singapore before I sailed for the Cape. I have the papers to prove it. It was done with the consent and agreement of Sir Robert."

Cooper nodded, his face half averted from Roark, his eyes cynical. "But do the women know it?"

"They know, dammit," Roark replied bitterly, "that they are my family, my subjects. That is enough for them. I must have a place that is off the shipping routes. I need peace for them. I do not choose to have a place where they will be exposed to men coming ashore after months at sea, men from the whalers." His voice took on a sudden spiteful note and his eyes fixed on Ben Cooper. Cooper had begun his sea life on a whaler with his brother. "The Laccadives are off the shipping routes."

The captain ignored the thrust. "There remains the British Government."

"There are governments that do not care in these matters—the Americans, for example."

Cooper looked up at the flaccid sails as if he were instantly plotting a new course. "South America? North? There are the Portuguese and Spanish colonies."

"I was in Lisbon." Roark's mind flicked back twenty years, concentrating momentarily on memories of corruption and intrigue, but he formulated no objection in words.

Cooper tried a new line, deliberately goading Roark. "Back to Singapore, then? You could present your grievances directly to the magistrate."

"It would be inappropriate until the matter of my money is settled," Roark replied with dignity.

He began to walk backwards and forwards.

Cooper examined the point of his pen. The ink had dried on it, and he took out a knife and sharpened it with the delicate precision of a big man laboring at a minute task.

After a long while Roark came to rest again. "An island—an island outside the authority of government, an island without people." He was momentarily inspired with enthusiasm for the idea. "The Seychelles, the Maldives, Cocos." His mind ran swiftly over the names, savoring them, testing them out. One by one he rejected them without explanation.

"Rodrigues Island!" he exclaimed at last and added, harking back with the curious verbal pertinacity that he sometimes displayed, "Toward Rodrigues Island, Captain Cooper—toward Rodrigues Island!"

Without comment, Ben Cooper dipped his pen in the ink and began to inscribe the name Rodrigues Island in his meticulous script.

The calm endured. At noon they still hung indeterminately in a sea that to the west merged without distinguishing mark, without horizon, into the sky. The gulls still formed little groups that changed their closeness to one another and their shape from time to time but remained elegantly without purpose after the last of the ship's rubbish had floated finally out of their reach into the depths.

The ship's crew ate on deck. Four of the women served Roark and Cooper with taunting murmurs of desire and willingness to please, while Flint watched them with a face blank of all expression, yet radiating disapproval and jealousy. From time to time he stopped watching them for long enough

to walk to the ship's stern and toss over a wood
chip from several that he kept in his pockets. The
chips showed no indication of movement in the
water.

They sat after the meal was finished, a bottle of
wine between them. The women squatted about
Roark's chair, silent and watching him. Roark was
curiously light-hearted, and Cooper wondered if it
were because he had made up his mind at last as
to their destination. For eleven months he had discussed his problems with the English. It was
strange that he had never mentioned Rodrigues
Island before. The captain wondered if this was
because he had always held it in the back of his
mind, not to be brought out unless his letters and
petitions to the Government failed, or until some
other event forced him to make a decision.

Ben Cooper himself had sailed close in to
Rodrigues Island but had not landed. "About a
thousand feet high," he said to Roark. "Fairly
steep most of it, but there's a little bit of a bay to
the north." After a time, in answer to a question,
he added, "Yes, covered with trees, jungle, palms.
Ought to be plenty of fresh water."

Roark seemed satisfied. He asked no more
questions; instead he held his glass up in the sunlight and made a slight murmur of approval. "I
hope we have more of this wine on board."

"Three hogsheads," Cooper answered abruptly.
He felt that he had not had adequate appreciation
for his efforts in getting the ship to sea at half a
day's notice. He had known, of course, that it
would happen like this and had held his supplies
ready for such an occasion. The fresh water had
been topped off twice a week. If it had not been for
the extra hands, he could have got clear of Cape
Town by midnight. There had been no wind at

midnight, but he would have been prepared to tow her out.

He would have been prepared for anything to put an end to the intolerable waiting—eleven months swinging round his anchors, eleven months facing out the north-wester winds (twice he had thought they were going to lose the ship) and then the south-easter winds when the season changed, coming down off the face of the mountain like a cyclone from hell. He would have done anything to get clear of the Cape. Lately he had not often gone ashore; they talked too much there, asked too many barbed questions. The women ashore no longer liked the ship or her crew. He had no place for a town where the women did not like him.

"I must work out a course for Rodrigues Island," he said after a pause.

"Damned lot of work to do, that's certain." Roark said. "And this is typhoon season. Sometimes they come early, sometimes late."

Cooper frowned and thoughtfully considered the liquid in his glass as he swished it slowly from side to side. A typhoon had battered his whaling ship mercilessly a few years ago, and he had been pinned by the falling timbers and masts. A broken piece of the mast, caught by the winds, had flailed him as he lay helpless. His crew had cut him loose, but not before the broken mast had gouged deeply into his left shoulder. The ship had been on her beam ends; he helped them cut the rigging and masts adrift, and by some miracle she had righted herself. Then he had poured rum into the bleeding wound. He could still remember the pain.

And he recalled how he had limped into Singapore long after he had been given up for lost, his fine three-masted whaler no more than a hulk, the seams sprung, masts and rigging gone. And by the time he had replaced spars and rigging and masts and supplies and men, all the profits of the voyage had vanished.

"That's in God's almighty hands," he said finally and emptied his glass. "All we mortals can do is pray for a calm sea."

Roark grunted and nodded his agreement.

When Roark woke there was still no wind, but the *Sea Wolf*'s head pointed out to the open sea; some whim of the current had altered her heading. The gulls trailed abeam of her. Nothing marked the passage of time, for even the shadows had altered with the swinging. Roark lay as he had slept. Only his eyes opened, searching out lazily as if he were trying to discover in the haze the separation of earth and sky.

The four women were still clustered at his feet. They were awake, watching him.

"Bring me the pirate girl!" he said after an interval.

Morgan, the bosun mate, on watch, lifted his head sharply, as if he were startled at the voice.

The *Sea Wolf* rolled very slowly. A swell was making up from the south, somewhere a block banged against a mast, and there were creaking noises and the dry rustle of ropes over wood. Apart from these, the ship slept as Roark had slept, noiselessly and purposelessly.

Maya came up the starboard ladder and walked across the deck, slowly and with an almost unnatural dignity.

Morgan, watching her, thought she was not like the others, she was accustomed to ships.

She met the movement of the deck in the roll

subconsciously, as if she were a part of the ship. She stood before Roark, offering no salutation, silent, watchful, and very straight. Her small body glistened in the harsh afternoon sun. Her sarong was wound neatly and firmly, but it made hardly more than a crease in the flatness of her belly. Clearly her flesh was firm; there was no fat on her. It had the supple firmness of a lioness; perhaps it had the same illusory softness. Her arms and her shoulders were slender, exquisitely proportioned, and her neck was molded out of them with an evident pride. She held her head with a poised and expectant wariness. Her face was softer than her body, its lines less firmly modeled. The mouth was young. The nose, more delicately cut, narrower than was ordinary amongst the women of the islands. Only the dark blue eyes offered a speculative entry to her reality. Now they were hooded, but they gave to the soft contours of the face an improbable, unchildlike beauty.

Roark watched them for a long minute, trying to penetrate them. There was a puzzling glimpse just beneath the surface of her beauty of something to which he could not lay a finger, a hint of sarcasm, a brief flash of savageness, a strange touch of arrogance. He was convinced that had she any other choice she would not have been there. She gave him back the stare, showing no emotion either of apprehension or of fear. His eyes dropped to her firm breasts, suddenly greedy.

"Who are you?" he asked, using the Malay dialect that he spoke habitually with the women.

"I am the daughter of Sultan Garuda." She spoke with an exact economy of tone, loud enough for him and the women to hear, hardly loud enough for the bosun mate. Her voice was modulated, without a quiver.

"Of this Sultan Garuda I have heard," Roark said gravely. "You have a name?"

"I am called Maya." She offered him the exact information that he asked for, neither hesitating nor elaborating on it.

"How did you come to be aboard the *Grand Turk*?"

"We sought to take her," Maya answered evenly. "We lay in wait for her off the islands."

"You sought to take a 22-gun slaver?" Roark's voice rose skeptically.

"We had knowledge." Her breath came out in a rush and her eyes flared with anger, reacting for the first time to his tone. "She had many sick. We would have taken her had Jin-qua not lost his heart."

"Jin-qua?" Roark peered at her questioningly, arching a dark brow.

"A dog!" Maya commented coldly, and spat on the deck.

Roark began to sit up in his chair, the laziness drained out of him; he was fully awake now, as if fascinated by this male attitude of mind from a woman. "And then?"

"She had men enough to man the guns on her port side. Our mast was broken. Before the rowers could get under way, she rammed us. Even then we might have conquered her, but the breaking of the oars destroyed many of us." Her voice was quite passionless.

"And your father . . . ?" With an odd feeling of respect, Roark hesitated before he said, "The Sultan was killed?"

"No, he was not killed," she replied firmly. "My father was knocked into the water as the ships hit. He lives."

"How far were you out at sea?"

"Ten miles, twelve miles perhaps—it is nothing! My father was a great swimmer; he could live in the water."

"Maybe he could at that," Roark murmured to himself. "And you?"

"I would have swum with him, but I was pinned by a broken timber. They could not have taken me otherwise." For the first time the small head lifted back on the neck in a hint of arrogance.

Roark considered her version of the story against the version he had heard from the captain of the *Grand Turk*. According to the captain, he had fought a prolonged engagement, a battle against overwhelming odds, had by his own courage destroyed a pirate fleet. He had hanged five survivors to prove it, and he had the girl. Roark placed the two accounts side by side in his mind: he thought that Maya told the truth. As to her father, there was no answer to that; there were sharks in those waters.

"They found you and they took you aboard the *Grand Turk*?" he asked. "You were their captive?"

"I was their captive," she agreed somberly.

"Now"—he chuckled derisively—"you are mine."

She stared him straight in the eyes, and he lifted his own from her body and answered her look. "I am Sultan Garuda's daughter," she said softly, but with controlled fierceness.

Leaning his head back, Roark laughed into her glare. "Nonetheless, my love, you are mine."

"I am my own, and I am the daughter of the Sultan."

"Who is dead," Roark said cruelly.

Maya stared at him in disbelief. "Who is alive"—her voice was almost insolent now—"and who will find me, and who will judge according to the treatment that I have received."

It was so obviously a threat that Roark flung himself back in the chair and laughed again. Maya remained facing him, but her eyes looked out over his shoulder towards the land, as if she were judging the distance, as if she still contemplated escape.

Roark seized a wine bottle and, raising it high, gave a toast. "To you, Maya, love. Do you know that you are mine until I die?"

He drank deeply and then sat staring at her with amusement. Maya returned his gaze with coldness in her eyes.

The damned filthy fool! she thought to herself. Does he think he could ever best me? His death might be sooner than he thinks.

Morgan, watching her, recognized her fanatic courage. It was implicit in the whip-taut stance of her body, in the poise of her beautiful head, in the instant alertness of her eyes. He was suddenly certain in himself that if Roark made a movement towards her she would be over the side and into the sea before anyone could stop her.

Roark smiled again, then laughed as she glared at him. Three of the women laughed with him, but the fourth looked frightened of Maya.

It took a long time for his laughter to abate. When it subsided finally, Roark leant forward, staring hard at her. "You set fire to my cabin."

Instead of answering him, she said, making for the first time a small gesture towards the bow of the ship, "Do we go west?"

"West?" he repeated, puzzled.

"Do we go"—she groped at the unaccustomed name—"to England?"

He laughed again, shortly this time. "No, we go east—south first and then east."

As frankly as she had admitted it to the little Bornean, she said to Roark, "It was wrong, then, to try to burn your ship."

Again he leaned forward, studying her gravely, as if he felt for the first time the real shock of her personality. "By God, you're a wildcat!" he said in English. Angrily he tossed the wine bottle down.

Morgan, looking at her, thought that the comparison was inadequate; a young lioness was closer to the mark. "I wouldn't tangle with that one in the dark," he said to himself, watching Roark's face.

But Roark said only, "You will be tamed. You are mine now."

"I am my own," she said again. It was at once a warning, a statement of identity, and an expression of her will. She stood looking at him, grave and controlled, her hooded eyes speculative.

The old Indonesian at the wheel spoke, his voice liquid and soft, almost caressing, and Morgan jerked his head away from the little scene with reluctance. The man pointed inshore. On the water was a dark flaw, a wind ripple. The surface of the sea had turned abruptly from a palid, uncertain calm to a growing multitude of continuous aquamarine waves.

Morgan took two steps to the skylight and, bending down, shouted, "Captain Cooper, sir! Wind's coming away from the southeast." Then, without waiting for more than a grunted acknowledgement, he went to the rail. "Both watches!" he shouted down. "Both watches! Jump to it! Look alive! Look alive! Wind's coming!"

Roark, without turning, demanded, "From the southeast?"

"Aye, aye, sir, from the southeast."

The *Sea Wolf* gave every appearance of a ship coming alive, if the number of sailors scurrying about their duties were anything to go by. The decks and the rigging fairly swarmed with men, and Maya was momentarily overwhelmed by their numbers and the size of the trim, black-painted ship and her immaculate appearance. A beautifully carved figurehead reared gracefully from her prow, a lovely mermaid with long, flowing hair painted a dark green hue. The ship's name was written in curlicued script across her bow.

No chance to escape her captor had presented itself during her stay at the Cape. No matter, she thought, she cared not a damn if Lord Roark Tillman had as many concubines as a sultan, nor if he kept them in a harem. The whoremaster would die before he bedded her. She bit her lip anxiously.

A feeling of panic swept over Maya. Despite the coolness of the wind, perspiration had beaded her brow and her palms were slippery. There was to be no escape, none whatsoever, she realized suddenly. How mournful, how bereft the gulls sounded as they wheeled about the masts. Their cries seemed to put into sound the anguish in her heart.

5

Maya crept stealthily along the alleyway to where a lantern hung on a hook to light the pitch-black passage, and hurried up the ladder to the upper deck. She cared not for the hot and crowded quarters of the other women below deck and sought the coolness of the open air.

The upper deck was shadowed and silent save for the slapping of the waves against the bows. She glanced furtively up at the poop deck. The watch's profile was a blurry silhouette against the indigo night sky. She breathed a sigh of relief. The moon, supposed to be full this night, was wreathed in streamers of clouds, and Maya's figure was hidden by the dark shadows. If she were swift, she could pass silently beneath the watch without being seen.

Like a shadow, she wove in and out of the masts and coiled ropes, headed for the bow. Once there, she looked about her. She almost laughed aloud.

She'd done it without being seen!

She crouched down on the damp deck and closed her eyes for a moment, thinking about these European barbarians. They were hairy and apelike. Their manners were repulsive and ugly. They stank beyond belief. They had no culture or manners or graces. Even the lowly Bornean was a thousand times better than the best of these white devils. She shuddered at the thought of their hairy arms and hairy armpits and hairy legs, the coarseness of their skin, and the stench of their sweat mixed with the foul smells of their ship.

And the foods that these barbarians ate—hideous. She had watched them eat many times, almost fainting with nausea—watching appalled at the stupendous quantities of half-raw meats they knifed into their mouths, blood gravy dripping down their chins. And the quantities of maddening spirits they swilled. And their revolting boiled, tasteless vegetables. And indigestible, solid pies. All in monstrous amounts. They were like pigs—like sweating, gluttonous devils.

They had no attributes to recommend them, she thought. None, except their blood-thirsty tendency to kill. This they could do with incredible brutality, although with no refinement. These barbarians were evil personified. And the worst was their master—this Roark Tillman. Maya shook her head in disgust.

She looked about her once more, and seeing that she was concealed by the heavy shadows of the gunwales, tried to sleep.

A few hours later Flint came up the ladder in the darkness with the sureness of long habit.

"You're early," Morgan said.

"First night at sea," the bosun answered self-derisively. "I reckoned it would be light enough at the change of watches." He looked doubtfully across the darkness of the waters. "What happened this afternoon?" he asked softly. "Up here?"

"You mean with the girl?"

"Aye, the girl."

"She defied Tillman," Morgan said, thinking over the words gravely. "She just stood there, five feet of nothing, and she defied him. Spat right in his eye, she did. She's a brave one!" Then, for no particular reason, he added, "She knows ships, too."

"That won't help her with him." Flint was surprised at the sympathy in his voice. They were both silent for a moment or two. Flint looked up into the sails, accustoming his eyes to the darkness.

"What's a Sultan?" Morgan asked finally.

"You never been East?" Without waiting for Morgan's answer, Flint explained, "It's the name they give to their royalty, Malay-way. It would be a title—duke or something, prince perhaps."

"Then," Morgan said slowly, "she's a princess."

"Her?"

"She said, 'I am the daughter of a Sultan.' "

"The Sultan who? There should've been a name. She wouldn't say it without the name."

"There was a name," Morgan agreed softly, searching his mind. "Garuda—Garuda, she said."

"The devil she did! Sultan Garuda? God preserve us!" Flint slapped his thigh sharply, as if he were overcome with inner laughter. "Sultan Garuda! The Lion of Ceylon! She's not a princess, then."

"Why?"

"He's not royalty either, he's a bloody damned pirate. Damn my eyes, he's the bastard who burnt the *Duchess!* He captured the *Jabalpur*—you wouldn't know her, she was an Indian ship. There were others. He's a black-hearted devil. They called him the pirate sultan after he captured a ship with the two sons of the Sultan of Pradesh on it. He cut their throats at the end. That was about all there was left to cut then. That was before this girl was born—must've been. They haven't forgotten it round the China Sea, though. They frighten children with his name."

Flint mused over this for a moment. "Frighten themselves, too. They've got a hide-out up the coast of Ceylon, somewhere up above Jaffna. This brave little guttersnipe is his daughter, you say?" He whistled softly and long.

"She said he would come for her."

"Ha!" Again Flint slapped his thigh. "She said that, did she?"

"She outfaced Tillman. He let her go after that. Would he be afraid of this Garuda?"

"No!" Flint spoke decisively. "No, Roark Tillman's got no fear in him. You misjudge him if you think that." He considered this and went on, "He could lick any man on this ship, except maybe the captain." A little late, he added whimsically, "And me, that is."

Morgan let it pass. "I don't know about him except what I've seen in the two weeks I've been aboard."

"You'll hear a lot of him East." Flint assembled his judgments carefully. "They don't love him much."

"Because of his women?"

"Because of his women," Flint agreed quietly, "but that's not the half of it. He was with Hawkins at Borneo. The Dutch don't like Hawkins; lots of others don't either. Hawkins sent him to Malay—

that was when Captain Cooper's brother took up
with him. Little frigate he had called *The Jawa;*
sweet as a nut, she was. Lost her captain at Bali
and captain's brother took her over."

"Dirk Cooper?"

"That's him—brother Dirk. Mate of a whaler, he
was, and he took up with Tillman runnin' convicts
across from Malay to work his sugarcane plantations in Borneo. Sultan, he'd given him a piece of
land big as Suffolk, more perhaps, but when we
had to give Borneo back to the Dutch he was out of
it. Lost a lot."

"And Dirk Cooper?"

"He was left behind to hold on to what he could.
He had his own war against the Dutch. Built bat-
teries across the river from Banjermasin. Fitted
out the *Jawa* and two other ships as gunboats. I
tell you it was a kingdom! He had his rights. Then
the British said they would negotiate his losses if
Tillman would give up his Borneo land grants and
leave Malay. Any fool knows 'negotiate' to the
British means to play for time."

"Did they fight?"

"No." Flint shook his head as if he were still disappointed. "They hoisted the Union Jack. Dutch,
they wouldn't fire on it. Whole thing went to
pieces. Afterwards they took some convicts back
to Malay. That was when I joined up with Captain
Ben."

"Sugarcane plantations," Morgan commented.
"They were makin' and tradin' rum."

"It was rum all right," Flint agreed. "Damn my
eyes, it was rum! He's been trying to get the
damned British to pay him for what he lost ever
after. By his reckoning he's a rich man with what's
owing to him. Maybe he is—I don't know. All I
know is we brung the *Sea Wolf* to the Cape and for

the last eleven months we be waiting and waiting for the bastards to set pen to paper. Now they're throwing him out of Cape Town to keep from paying." Flint spat.

"Doesn't sound like the kind of a man to be affrightened of the girl's father."

"Not Roark Tillman," Flint replied equably. "You've listened. You don't think he would care, do you?"

"No, I wouldn't. Is she with him tonight?"

"She's right here on deck." Flint's tone was full of irony. "Been here all the time."

"Where?" Morgan looked sharply around.

"In the corner between the bow and the gun-wales."

Morgan took three steps forward and looked toward the bow. He could see in the shadows of the gunwales a more solid shadow. It made no move. "By God's blood, she is!" he admitted reluctantly, as if angry at his lack of watchfulness. He did not attempt to approach Maya, but after a moment he added, "It's against Tillman's orders. He's told them not to come up to the deck. There is supposed to be a watch on the door."

"This one makes her own orders, I'm thinking," Flint said, not far from laughter.

Morgan's stomach tensed with panic. "What will happen?" he asked. It was obvious that he referred to Maya, not to the business of the ship.

"Tillman has the black girl tonight, the Bantu girl." Flint smacked his lips reflectively. "Black velvet! I could do with a bit of that myself. She'll last him for another few days or so. You can't ever tell, but she's a lively one. Then he will send for her." He nodded in the darkness towards the still shadow.

"Will she go?"

"She'll have to," Flint replied dispassionately.

"Will she submit?"

"Aye. What else can she do?" Flint shrugged. "Tillman will have his pound of flesh. She'll like it maybe. You've never been to the Orient; you don't know their ways. She's old enough—big enough, old enough. They don't think like we do."

"I don't know," Morgan muttered. "I watched her yesterday. I watched her face him—out-face him. I don't know."

Roark's refurbished cabin was very spacious but boasted only a few pieces of furniture—a massive chair; a large bunk, bolted to the deck and draped with brocade of deep purple and a matching coverlet; and an ornately carved desk. A window bellied outwards from one wall, framed by still more richly carved wood and paned with stained glass. A cabinet had been built into the wall to accommodate his clothing and personal items, and a huge sea-chest sat squarely at the foot of the bunk. It was bound with leather and studded with brass-headed nails. There were numerous papers and maps strewn haphazardly about.

Tonight the lamps glowed brightly, warmly, within the cabin. The place was alive, pulsing with the scent of the woman. Roark could hear the pounding beat of waves against the ship's planking, the spanking of winds in the topsails, the pounding deep in his loins.

The woman stood across the cabin, awaiting him. She was naked. He had never seen a body so glitteringly black.

The Bantu woman, Zada, remained standing for some moments with her arms at her sides, her head back, statuesque and statuelike.

Roark let the sleeveless shirt slip from his

shoulders. He padded across the cabin in his bare feet, a whispering sound on the floor. The silence of the cabin intensified.

He went close to her. Zada reached out and removed his belt. Then she caught her fingers in the band of his trousers. He stood, feeling himself grow rigid. She drew her hands downward, peeling his trousers off. When he was naked, she remained on her knees, staring, awed, fascinated, at the great shaft quivering before her eyes.

He caught the sides of her head suddenly in his hand, pulling her face against his crotch, pressing her so tightly to his thighs and loins that she could barely breathe. He closed his eyes and put his head back, enjoying this moment of his supreme mastery.

For some entranced moments, Zada remained on her knees to Roark in a kind of sensual obeisance. With his large hands gripping her head, she nuzzled him, exploring him with her hands, hefting his manhood with her palms and, trembling with pleasure, caressing him with her tongue. At last she drew away, her mouth moist, her eyes glittering. Roark flinched slightly. There was about her a look of frantic eagerness, a kind of unleashed insanity.

She stood up, her body pressing against his. "I want . . . I want . . ." she whispered.

"Aye, my sweet, I know," Roark murmured huskily against her hair.

Her clouded eyes flickered, but she did not speak. Her head sank on his muscled arm and lay there, her eyes closed sleepily, her lips parted. He covered her mouth with his, thrusting his tongue deep into her throat. Her whole body quivered, as if convulsed.

He swung her lightly up in his arms and carried

her to his bunk. She lay supine upon the bedding, waiting. He drew his hands from her shoulders, over her firm, orange-sized breasts, along the flat planes of her belly to the wet, hot flooding at her thighs. She had not exaggerated the wildness of her desiring. She lay helpless with passion.

He pushed her legs apart, bent her knees, and moved inside her thighs. She encircled his hips and locked her ankles about his waist. She screamed when he penetrated her, and he clapped his mouth over hers to silence her. He felt the gushing flood of her passion. Her hips battered wildly. She rose to one mindless climax, and another and another. It was as if now that she had submitted to her desire and to him, she was no longer in control of her own body.

"Hellion!" he murmured. "Sweet, wild hellion—love me!"

Roark rode her, at first with measured strokes, trying to draw the fullest gratification from their union, delighted at the fiery floodgates she opened to him. Almost, he had only to touch her to drive her out of her mind, into a frenzied bucking of her hips and then the savagery of her release. Her fingernails dug into his shoulders, clawed along his muscular back. When he tried to withdraw, even for a moment, she caught at him, sobbing with unfulfilled need.

Once roused, Zada was insatiable. She was still in his bunk at dawn after an eternal, sleepless night. He'd known hundreds of women; below deck, forty concubines awaited his every wish, but he'd never encountered a woman of such mindless passion. This one had sucked him dry.

On deck, the ship's bell suddenly shattered the night's silence. Men moved about like shadows, and from below deck the next watch came stumbling out. As if it had been waiting for the bell, the sun began to show itself in the hardening of the eastern horizon.

The long, low room was full of woman smells and child smells. The heat increased every day now as they came up from the low latitudes. They still carried the trade winds, but the water here in the Indian Ocean no longer cooled them.

The three old woman sat together, in a crescent shaped position. Almira, the oldest of the wives, sat in the center. May Ling, the Chinese woman, sat a little in advance of her to the left. The third woman was the Tamil. She was gaunt and hard-featured, and she coughed softly but incessantly. It was believed that she was Tillman's spy. Otherwise, there was no explanation for Tillman's keeping her. She was known always as 'the Tamil.' As if she had never had a name of her own. The three had come from their own quarters to sit, as it were, in judgment. The other women had crowded into the farthermost end of the gutted cabins.

Maya sat cross-legged, with her hands in her lap and her back against a rib of the ship. She sat wholly motionless, her soft skin polished and delicate and shining. She might have been a sculpture, a marble symbol of superiority and dislike and arrogance. She sat in profile, not looking at the three old women.

"In two days at the most he will surely send for you," Almira said softly. Maya made no move. "He grows tired of her."

There was no sign of Zada, the Bantu girl, in the room, but it was obvious that the old woman referred to her. Still Maya made no acknowledgment of Almira's words.

"Hear me, child," the Chinese woman murmured quietly. The sound of her voice, low and honey smooth, ensured that Maya's attention was fully upon her. "He will send for you."

"I do not choose to go." Maya spoke for the first time, quietly, gravely, without altering her pose or turning even her eyes towards the women.

There was a small grasp of shock from the other women at the rear of the cabins.

The old woman's voice took on a note of warning. "You will go!"

"I do not choose to go," Maya reiterated.

If the old women meant to put a fright into her, Maya was having no part of it. She was calm now and knew what must be done to ease her own plight. Nothing would stand in her way after she had come this far.

"Then," May Ling interrupted officiously, "you will be taken by force."

"Who will take me?" Maya asked dangerously.

The Tamil woman spoke for the first time, her voice even. "The man Skinner Pitney."

"Ha!" Maya burst out scornfully. She arched a dark brow towards the Tamil and stared at her until the old woman began to squirm uneasily.

"Nonetheless, child, you will go or you will be taken—" the old woman Almira spoke as if delivering a sentence—"and he will lie with you and it will be accomplished as he desires. It is the law."

"He is not my law," Maya replied, and there was neither disrespectfulness nor fear in her voice. "My customs are other than yours. Hear me!" Again her head turned to the other women, ignoring the old wives. "I will tell you"—her voice altered in pitch and in character, it took on with a surprising exactness the high chant of a story-teller—"I will tell you a tale. Listen to me, all ye women!"

The character of the room changed subtly, as her voice had changed. It ceased to be a hall of judgment; it became instead a place of listening, a place of story-telling. Those at the far end of the room moved, relaxed. They all faced her now, as if the momentary fears that she had inspired in them had been forgotten. She was aware of the women's aroused interest. From beneath her dark brows, she observed them all with close attention, and with quiet patience she paused for a moment, like a cat before a mousehole, waiting to pounce. The shadow of a smile crept slowly across Maya's lips.

"Upon my father's ship there was a young man. He was tall, and his skin was colored like gold so that it shone in the sunlight, and his back was strong. His eyes"—already she had established an almost hypnotic rapport with the younger women —"his eyes were like the eyes of a sea eagle."

"Ah!" breathed a woman's voice deep in the crowd, and somebody repeated the words, " . . . like a sea eagle."

"He fought well with the sword and with the dagger; he was a warrior. We took our ship, my father and I"—she gave herself equal status with an impressive naturalness—"to wait for the merchantman's fleet, and we were a long time from the land, for the winds failed us and the fleet did not come, and we waited alone, my father's ship and two others. The men were a long time without women."

"Ai-e-e-e!" A voice of sympathy came out of the crowd.

"And he took my maidenhood." Again a gasp ran through the younger women.

She waited a long time before she spoke again, while the room grew almost intolerable with tension.

"My father asked him why he did this thing, and he said, 'Oh, Sultan, we have been a long time at sea and I had a desire for thy daughter. I would take her for my wife.'"

She waited for the little explosion of admiration, mingled with astonishment at the young man's boldness, to subside. Then she went on, her voice unemotional and soft. "My father said, 'For taking from my daughter what thou desired, there is nothing that I need to say, for thou art a dead man already; but for what thou hast done there are certain punishments required.'"

A little shudder of fear ran across the women like wind on the strings of an instrument. Again she waited patiently for absolute stillness.

"So they bound him in accordance with the custom of the ship, and they made a line fast to his manhood according to that custom."

This time the shudder that passed through them was emphasized by little moans. Many of the women knew of this terrible punishment used by the pirates.

"When they had put him in the sea they made fast the end of the line, and my father ordered them to let the sails fill." She paused, letting her mind go back to that quiet morning.

"And the young man?" the youngest Chinese girl, Kim Chi, demanded compulsively.

Maya shrugged her shoulders delicately. It was the first movement that she had made except with her eyes. "I do not know. When they hauled in the line the knot was still fast but there was nothing there."

Above the sweep of horrified exclamations, the

voice of the old woman Almira could be heard. "Allah alone is merciful," she said with compassion.

Among the younger women, the voices took refuge in the ritual rites and assurances of their God. "The One God . . . The Sole . . . The Existing . . . The Perfection." But the names of God became lost in a chorus of "Ai-e-e-e!"

Maya sat through it undisturbed. She did not even consider it necessary to repeat her conviction that her father would find her in the end and punish her captors.

Maya closed her eyes and rested her head back against the rib of the ship, smiling like a cat that had just ensnared a mouse.

6

For days Roark Tillman drove the *Sea Wolf* like an arrow northeast, her yards screeching with the fullness of canvas.

He had gone to sea to cleanse himself, to wash away the British treachery and the loss of everything he had worked for.

He went to the bosom of the ocean like a lover who has been gone for an eternity, and the ocean welcomed him with squall and with storm—yet controlled, never endangering the ship or him who drove the ship. She sent her gifts sparingly, making him strong again, giving him life, giving him dignity, and blessing him as only the sea can bless a man, cleansing him as only the sea can cleanse a man.

After he reached the open sea, he had lost all thoughts of his women. He drove himself as he drove the ship and crew, not sleeping, testing the limits of his strength. Watch after watch changed and still he walked the deck, sunrise to sunrise to sunrise, whistling softly to himself and hardly eating. He never talked, except to force more speed, or to order a ripped canvas replaced or another sail set. He drove into the depths of the Indian Ocean, into infinity.

After a week he went below and shaved and bathed and slept for a day and a night, and the next dawn he ate a full meal in his cabin. Then he went on deck.

He stood on the spar at the bow of the *Sea Wolf*, the spray billowing beneath him.

"Do your worst, Sea!" he shouted into the wake of the east wind. "I'm home!"

He stayed on the deck all day and part of the night, and once more he slept. At dawn, feeling he was once more one with the sea, he returned command of the *Sea Wolf* to Captain Ben Cooper and retired to his cabin.

At dawn on the thirteenth day, the rising sun was strong, the wind east and steady—and humid.

There was the sound of scurrying feet on deck, and Roark felt the *Sea Wolf* surge faster through the waves. The whole ship seemed to pulsate with life.

Roark Tillman sat in an enormous oak chair that seemed too large for the cabin. Its rich, splendidly proportioned curves were slashed through with yellow streaks. It was an alien thing in that place, but the fine split rattan of the seat and the back, delicately woven in the Cape style, made it cool and comfortable. He sat on it in many ways; sometimes as a throne, as the seat of a king, or as the seat of a father. Today, he was relaxed. He wore a fine coat of blue silk, and silk trousers. His shirt was open almost to his navel to reveal the abundance of hair on his chest. He lay back in the chair and contemplated a newly filled glass.

Skinner Pitney sat himself back in his own chair. He had, as always, the air of a small, nervous animal—like a sneaky weasel. His too bright eyes peered out over their lower lids in perpetual watchfulness. His own glass was only half filled.

"It would not do to be in a place where ships call frequently," Roark said thoughtfully, "ships that I am unable to control. It would unsettle the women. I require peace." He sat and stared almost menacingly at Pitney, as if he suspected him of attempting to disturb his peace. "For years now, more than I care to remember, I have had to fight intolerance and prejudice against my way of life. I could have been peaceful at Cape Town." The name seemed to remind him of his wine and he drank, sipping it carefully, savoring the full-bodied redness. "I am by nature peaceful. But I'll tell you right smartly, that whole God-damned fly-speck of a colony was bad luck!"

"Quite, quite," Pitney murmured softly.

Before the repetition was complete, Roark swept on. "I offer no hurt to any man. I wish only for the privacy of my own circle. All the reports of Rodrigues Island agree with my wishes. It will be better than the Laccadives."

The bright black eyes watched him. There was a glint of malice in them. "Rodrigues Island has no inhabitants." Pitney offered the statement as if it were new.

"It is that which recommends it to me more than any other thing. I need a place to plant myself, a place where I can expand. I could have built an empire in Borneo and Malay. By God's blood, an empire no less! But I will be satisfied to build a place of peacefulness where I can create a kingdom of my own subjects, my people.''

Pitney allowed his look to become faintly scornful. Roark was no more drunk than he usually was; he was mellow only, surrendering himself to the perfection of his dreams.

"You had better send that bitch daughter of Sultan Garuda on with the ship when she leaves us, then,'' Pitney said, his voice rough and mocking.

Roark put down his empty glass angrily. "Why?'' he demanded.

"The women are terrified of her.'' Pitney did not answer the question directly. "They believe that her father will come for her. She has told them stories of what he has done to men.''

"What men?''

"Men—I don't know. Men he has captured, I suppose. Tortures, brutalities—he is a bloody-minded man, Mr. Tillman, sir. Blood . . . minded.''

"Have you heard of Garuda's fleet coming out into the open sea ever?'' Roark had recovered his temper.

"I have heard of them in the Bay of Bengal.'' Skinner Pitney's manner took on an unaccustomed and careful honesty. "They have sailed the Straits of Java. I have heard of them in the Arabian Sea.''

"Keeping close against the coast!'' Roark snorted contemptuously. "They would not face the open sea.''

Pitney made no reply, not even a shrug of his shoulders.

"They do not navigate. They use known winds, they travel tried courses. Rodrigues Island lies more than fifteen hundred miles to the southwest of Ceylon. They would not dare!'' Again he allowed himself to be a little angry. "You do not know these men, Skinner Pitney. I know them. I destroyed the pirates about Malay." An echo of what was almost magnificence came into his voice. "What I have done once, I can do again. It is time to make an end to this lie. Send the bloody wench to me!"

"Do you wish Almira or the Tamil woman—?"

"Alone," Roark answered royally. "Send her to me alone!"

Pitney, half amused, half afraid, got up from his chair and went to the cabin door. As he opened it, he hesitated, and then, his voice hardly more than a malicious whisper, he said, "And if she will not come?"

"Then bring her!"

Pitney looked for her first on the deck. She had defied the order against it so often that it had established itself as a custom. But she was not on the deck. He made his way to the door of the long, ill-smelling women's room. She was sitting in the place that she had secured as hers by the right of her domination over the other women, her back against the rib, still and self-confident.

He called to her in Indonesian, "The Lord wants you."

The word he used implied needs almost more than wants, and from the other women the inevitable mutter went up, "He has sent for her! He has sent for her!"

"And if I do not choose to go?" The calculated arrogance of her voice cut crisply across the softer pattern of the other women's voices.

Uneasily Pitney straightened himself. His hesitation was brief, but Maya measured it before he answered, "His orders are that I was then to bring you."

She sat watching him with her enormous, fawn-like eyes. At last, when the silence was about to break of its own weight, she finally spoke. "It would . . ." She paused briefly, searching until she found an Indonesian word that had something of the implications of the English word "unclean," and then, giving it proper emphasis, continued, "It would make me unclean if I should be touched by such as you. Therefore I will go." And she rose to her feet and walked calmly out of the room.

Behind her, the air filled with excitement, a cross-babble of voices that drowned out even Pitney's shout. "Shut up, for Christ's sake!"

She walked down the narrow alleyway, out through the door into the sunlight and across the desk. The women and children sitting under the awning turned and stared at her.

"The Lord has sent for her!" echoed across the ship. Women came peering out of the door behind her to stand and watch her straight, graceful figure as she walked quietly across to the other door. She went into the passage on the starboard side, which led to Roark's big stern cabin and, erect and self-assured, went in through its doorway.

Pitney, almost running to keep up, came in behind her a second later.

"Get the hell out, Pitney!" Roark growled. "And shut that damned door!"

As if to make it clear that his anger was directed only against Pitney, Roark smiled at Maya. There was a surprising gentleness in his smile.

She stood in front of him, her hands at her sides, graceful and apparently relaxed. "You have sent for me," she said quietly but, as always, without the submissiveness he was accustomed to.

Roark laughed softly, but he looked at her almost anxiously, as if he were puzzled. "It is time that I sent for you," he replied. "You have been of my household"—the word did not mean precisely "harem" but it implied it—"long enough to know my custom. It is time that you came to me." Maya stood, silent, watching him. "Do you understand me?"

"Yes," she answered, surprisingly, in English.

"Ahhhh!" Roark looked at her with a new interest. "You have been learning English?"

Maya nodded.

"Then you will know that it is time to end this foolishness." His eyes raked her boldly and he smiled slowly. "You are mine, and the women will have told you all that it is needful for you to know. I will be gentle with you." For the first time, Maya looked straight into his eyes, for there seemed to be complete sincerely in his voice. "We will be friends, you and I. Come closer!"

Roark could not read her face. There was no sign of emotion either in her mouth or in her eyes, but she stepped forward until she stood within reach of him as he sat stretched out in the great chair. To him it seemed that she moved obediently, and he smiled again. Yet, even behind his smile there was a slight, fleeting shadow of doubt.

His eyes accepted the rich color of her skin, the dark overtones of her shoulders, the faint golden lines under her bare breasts, the softer shadows of the throat. He could even see a pulse beat in her throat under the fragility of her skin. It beat slowly; she was, he thought, unfrightened. He put up his hand and stroked her, first on the smoothness of the upper arm and then across the softness of her breasts, with the back of his fingers, not fondling them, but nonetheless caressing. He flinched at the inviting warmth and softness he felt beneath them, and at the leaping response that surged through him. Mild astonishment flitted across his rugged face. How could this pretty young woman arouse him so? He shook his head very slightly and hid a smile.

Maya, meanwhile, stood before him quite calmly, not giving the impression that she was enduring it against her will. She was not giving, in fact, any impression at all. Roark was totally baffled.

He found himself thinking that his fears had been unnecessary, that she would have come to him earlier if he had been firmer, that she had already surrendered to his will in her own mind. At last his hand, moving down the silken smoothness of her flat stomach, stretched forward suddenly to the point where the sarong was tucked in. His fingers found the end of it and, with the smile on his lips again, still quite gentle, he pulled at it and the sarong fell away.

He had a momentary vision of her nakedness, its youthfulness, its beauty. But in the very instant of the vision, he saw her arm flex, her hand flash, and instantly and with a sense of outrage Roark was aware of the needle-sharp point of a dagger immediately under the cartilage that joined the first of the floating ribs to his breastbone—and he was aware of fear. He was afraid because he knew it was precisely the point, the classic point, of the murderous upward thrust of the Orientals, the point that was almost to his rapidly beating heart with the shortest penetration of the weapon.

Even as the knowledge brought fear to him, so it brought at the same time a cold logic. Roark knew that if he moved, if he attempted to grab at her arm, the point would drive upwards into his heart. Her strength was more than adequate; her

reactions much swifter than his own. He could
grab her arm, his superior strength could tear it
away—break it, if necessary—but long before he
could do that the thin, weaving point of the dagger
would be three inches into his heart, and he knew
that he would die.

He sat frozen as a man sits frozen in front of the
swaying head and threatening eyes of a cobra. The
point of the weapon had penetrated his body in the
first stab, but he was sure it was not deep. The
small pain of it he disregarded utterly.

Roark waited for a long time. Maya was not
watching his face; she was watching his right
hand, knowing that if he moved he must move first
with that. It was evident to him that she was
remembering a careful schooling carefully
attended.

He could not reach her with his eyes, but only
with his voice. Nonetheless, when he spoke there
was nothing cowardly in his tone. "There was no
need for this between you and me," he said evenly.

The dagger remained steady—he could tell that
by the fact that there was no change in the pain.
Her body was touching his, mainly against his
thigh. He could feel no tremor in it.

Maya waited for a long time before she
answered, and for the first time he perceived
emotion in her. "There was need," she said
clearly, and meant it to the very core of her being.
"I am little. Moreover, I am a woman. Other
women would not do this thing to you, but I am
the daughter of a Sultan. I will not be your
whore."

Again she stood still, and unable to bear the
locked stiffness of his muscles, he shifted his
position slightly in the chair. In instant response,
he felt the point of the dagger dig in a fraction

more. It was no more than a fraction, it was nothing more than a warning—but it was one that he could not disregard.

"Take the damned thing away," he said in a level voice. "I will not harm you."

She made no effort at parley; she did not even question his statement. In one movement, she drew away and stood facing him, holding the dagger in her right hand, her eyes ablaze with a fierce pride.

Roark looked at the dagger, marveling. It was very small, the smallest dagger he had ever seen—delicate, beautiful, an exquisite piece of the weaponmaker's art. The ornamentation of its blade was deeply eroded. It was polished to an intense brightness so that it looked like a silver flame with its waving traditional line. At the end of it a smear of blood caught the light through the window and glowed like a ruby. She had worn it in a sheath bound tightly to the inside of her thigh, guarding it carefully from the too curious eyes of the other women when she bathed. Roark let his eyes drop from the dagger down to the front of his own body, and he saw a spreading stain of blood on his silk shirt and, quite clearly, a small hole in the middle where the point had gone through.

Roark smiled up at her. "There was no need for that, my sweet," he said teasingly, gesturing at the dagger.

"There was need," she answered once more.

Maya seemed quite unconscious of her nakedness or wholly in disregard of it. Roark's eyes moved with what seemed to be a will of their own over the delicate curves of her body. She watched them, balanced like a warrior, waiting for a move. At length his eyes came back, fascinated, to the dagger.

"Fate has decreed that you be mine from this moment in time, my sweet," he murmured gently. "I only want to teach you the delights of love that can be ours. There will be no pain, I promise you. Drop the dagger and come to me."

"If you touch me—" Her threat was gritted in a low voice, but it reached Roark's ears distinctly. "It is possible for you to take it from me," she said carefully. "My strength is small. Also you have many men. But it will not serve you, for there are other knives. It is possible for you to lie on me, this too because I am small and my strength is small. But there will come a time when you will have to sleep—it is the custom of men to sleep after they have achieved that which they desire—and then I will find another knife and I will kill you."

More than anything else the absolute lack of emphasis that she put on the final sentence convinced Roark. "You need have no fear," he said hurriedly, too hurriedly. And then, quite unpredictably, he laughed. This was the first time that he had had been utterly defied; this was the first woman who had utterly defied him. Woman, he thought with a smile. He looked at her again, at the slenderness of her, the smallness of her, realizing the will of iron in her spirit, the courage in her eyes.

"You have no need for fear," he repeated. "We can be friends, you and I."

Maya considered this gravely for a long minute and then, with a quick movement, she slipped the dagger back into its sheath.

As her hand came away from it, Roark's eyes took in the beauty of the hilt. It was of bone of a golden color, and though it followed the traditional oriental lines, it was intricately and exquisitely carved in the shape of a small animal.

"What is it?" he asked involuntarily.

"It is the mongoose talisman for magic. It is Maya. My father called me Maya always, though it was not the name that I was first given. When I was a child my nurse was a Hindu woman, for my mother died within the month. She told me the stories of the magic spells the mongoose weaves to kill the cobra." For the first time a soft smile flickered over her grave face. "There are many stories of this magic. Because I too was small and magic like the mongoose, my father called me Maya."

Roark smiled back at her, his face gentle. "It is fitting."

Stooping down, she picked up her sarong and wound it round her body. "Now I will go."

"You will tell the Tamil woman to give you a new sarong—silk, with brightness in it."

"That I will like." A note almost of childishness came into Maya's voice. She bowed to Roark gravely, and he reflected that it was the first sign of respect that she had ever shown him, but it was respect—it puzzled him to recognize it—to an equal.

As Maya went down the passage, she heard him calling for Almira.

When she stepped out onto the main deck, there was little gasps of surprise from the women. Then at once everybody was still and quiet. They could hear Roark's voice bellowing for Almira now, and the the whining voice of the old woman as she shuffled towards his cabin. The silence became absolute. Even the two bosuns on the poop deck became involved in it.

Across the silence came an appalled shriek from Almira, a shriek that was her instinctive reaction

to the blood on Roark's shirt. It was followed by
lamentations and by Roark's voice, cursing and
boisterous above the woman's. May Ling, the
Chinese wife, ran in and her voice joined Almira's.
They heard the Tamil woman's voice contribute to
the melee and Roark trying to shout them down.
His words were indistinguishable, but the fury of
his pitch shivered across the silence.

Only Maya herself was unmoved. She turned
and climbed the ladder to the poop deck and
walked across it. Her movement was neither
arrogant nor humble, but wholly natural. She
went as far as the wheel-box, lifted herself up onto
it, and sat there, looking at Morgan.

"What in the hell goes on down there?" Flint
demanded.

"It is nothing," Maya replied cheerfully, so
cheerfully that both men turned to stare unbeliev-
ingly at her. "He bleeds a little, that is all."

"What did she say?" Morgan asked urgently.

"She said he is bleeding a bit."

"Who? Tillman?"

"Who the hell else? I don't know what she
means."

"Should we go down?"

"Listen to him! Listen to him! Don't be a God-
damned fool!" Flint turned questioningly to Maya,
but she did not choose to explain further. Neither
of the two men was anxious to ask her more.

She sat swinging her legs for a minute or so
before the two bosuns. "Will we reach the island
soon?" she asked with apparent ease.

"If the wind holds steady," Morgan replied.

"And the wind is with Allah," Maya added
quickly.

The women who had been sitting under the
awning were on their feet now. A small group of

them climbed halfway up the port ladder and were staring at Maya. Flint heard a voice say, "The witch has stabbed him!"

"She has killed him!" another voice added.

"He is not dead. Listen! Listen!" a chorus of voices said. And then all the voices were lost in a babble of excitement and speculation.

Again Flint translated for Morgan's benefit. "They seem to think she stabbed him."

"She's done something, judging by all his yelling, but she couldn't have stabbed him. She looks as innocent as a child."

"I don't know about innocence," Flint said evenly. "They've got different ideas about it in the Orient. I bet she's got a dagger hidden somewhere about her."

"Where?" Morgan asked, as if defending his concept of innocence.

"Where d'you think, you damned fool?" Then, turning, Flint went to the head of the starboard ladder.

Skinner Pitney was about to come up. He looked up at Flint, his eyes wild. "She stuck a dagger in him!" he exclaimed agitatedly. "Stuck a dagger in his chest, by God! Something happened in there—I don't know what. But she stuck it in him all right."

"Does he want her chained?" Flint asked.

"He says not to touch her, not to do anything. He says—he says she is to have a new sarong, something with bright colors." Pitney spread his hands over the rails of the ladder in a gesture of despair. "I don't understand what's going on with her," he added very softly.

Maya sat quietly, still swinging her legs. Morgan thought that she looked happy for the first time since he had known her.

Flint also watched her for a little. By God, she's

a cool one! he thought. He still could not understand what had happened, but there was an aura
of danger about her.

He looked beyond her to the other women clustered around Pitney. Maya had once compared
them to sheep. They were like sheep. Perhaps it
was necessarily like this with the women of a
harem. They seemed to have only one mind
between them, with all individuality eliminated by
enforced obedience to Roark Tillman. They
seemed to move with a single purpose, wanting
the same things at the same time, thinking the
same thoughts. Shrewdly, Flint estimated that this
too was an unyielding law of harems. Without
Roark Tillman they were lost. This was the real
reason for their present panic. This also must be a
law of harems . . . .

7

Flint leant over the rail of the poop, staring pensively down through the gap in the awning where the starboard ladder came up. Maya was sitting with her back against the timbers of the bulwark. Except when she sat on the wheel-box, she seemed to gravitate by instinct to a position where her back was protected against attack. Now she sat fronted by a semi-circle of the children, twelve or fifteen of them perhaps, who squatted, animated and bubbling, on the deck. Her words were punctuated by little shrill ripples of laughter or by groans of fear.

Morgan, standing at the bosun's elbow, said casually, "It's good to hear her playing like a child."

"Ahhhh!" Flint grunted speculatively and stooped low to catch her words. Clearly she was telling the children a story.

" . . . and when he saw him, the tiger was afraid

79

and withdrew to the back of the hut and crouched there, shivering. And the horrid dragon entered, long of fang with fierce eyes and claws, and took the fish and ate them."

"Ai-e-e!" breathed the children with awe.

"Thus the pig had failed and the bear had failed and the tiger had failed."

Her blue eyes danced in the sunlight, and Maya smiled at the look of anticipation that settled on the children's features.

"And the mongoose looked at the pig and said, 'I am small and you are great, but it has availed you nothing.' And he looked at the bear and said, 'I am small but you are greater than the pig, and it has availed you nothing.' And he looked at the tiger and said, 'I am small but you are the greatest of all. Your voice is like thunder and your claws are sharper than anything in the world, but it has availed you nothing. I am Maya, the mongoose. I will stay at the hut and use my magic to make an end of this dragon' . . ."

"Ahhhh!" Flint said again. "The mongoose! Now what's she trying?"

"What d'you mean?" Morgan asked.

"She's telling them one of the Maya stories. Maya's the Hindu word for magic—and it's her name too. The mongoose's one of the smallest things in the jungle just about, and the Hindus reckon it's magic—always comes out on top. I wonder if her dragon is Tillman?"

"And Maya went into the hut and lay down on the floor and tied a bandage round his head and lay there, waiting. And after a little he heard the earth shaking under the feet of the dragon."

"Ai-e-e!" exclaimed the children.

"And the earth shook and the trees shook and the hut shook. And the dragon came to the doorway and he shouted, 'Give me the fish!' And the mongoose groaned.

"The dragon roared, 'Who is there? Who is groaning?'

"And the mongoose said, 'It is I only—Maya, the mongoose.'

"The dragon thrust through the door, and when his giant red eyes became accustomed to the dim light in the hut, he asked, 'Why is your head bandaged?'

"And the mongoose answered, 'It is the stink of the fish. Can you not smell it yourself? It has poisoned my head so that it aches.'

"Then the mongoose used a magic spell, and when the dragon sniffed, he said, 'My head aches too.'

"And the mongoose said, 'Lie down. I will bandage it.'

"The dragon lay down upon the floor of the hut, and Maya took a great length of cloth and wrapped it about his head and made fast the ends of it to pegs in the floor of the hut that he had driven into the ground below. Then the mongoose used another magic spell and said, 'I have a pain in my ankles also from the smell. Do you not have a pain in your ankles?'

"The dragon moved his feet and said, 'Yes, I have a pain in my ankles. Bandage them for me, too.'

"And Maya bandaged his ankles and fastened the ends of the bandages to other pegs in the floor. And then he used more magic and said, 'Do not your legs ache?'

"The dragon flexed the muscles in his legs and said, 'They ache also.'

"And Maya bandaged them in their turn and fastened the ends of the cloth to the pegs in the ground. Afterwards he straightened himself and took the bandage off his head.

"Then the dragon took fright suddenly and began to strain at the bandages, and said, 'What have you done to me?'

"Maya the mongoose laughed at the dragon."

Instantly the children laughed with Maya.

"The dragon roared with anger."

"Ai-e-e!" the children murmured in chorus.

"Maya said, 'Lie still, dragon, or I will take a peg and drive it through your heart and you will die.' And the dragon lay still."

"Then?" one of the boys asked after Maya was silent for a long while.

"Then the pig and the bear and the tiger came back from the jungle, and Maya stood at the door of the hut and they asked, 'The dragon has not been here?'

"Maya answered, 'The dragon has been here.'

"They said, 'He has taken the fish?'

"Maya answered, 'He has not taken the fish. The fish is there and the dragon is there. Do with him what you will.' "

"And then?" another child asked.

"They killed him," she said with simple finality.

"Ai-e-e-e!" exclaimed the children again.

She stood up, and the little semicircle broke like quicksilver and scattered, excited and laughing, across the deck.

Flint straightened himself and walked back to Morgan. "Always on top. She was tellin' them the one about how the mongoose used magic and tricked the dragon into letting himself be tied up."

Morgan looked at him curiously. "What's the harm in that?"

"No harm," Flint answered shortly, "but what's

she up to? Reckon she's tryin' to get the children on her side."

"Why?"

Flint disregarded him.

A voice from the masthead called suddenly in Indonesian.

"Land!" Flint said and called back. The voice floated down again, melodiously hiding its excitement. He reached out for the long glass and hoisted himself up into the rigging.

Before he had settled himself, Maya was past him and already pointing.

Below them the ship buzzed into activity. The captain came up the ladder. Pitney came up a little after him. The women and the children in the middle part of the ship went to the port bulwarks and stared uncomprehendingly into the distance.

Flint shut the glass with a series of swift clicks and dropped down to the deck again. "Captain, sir, Rodrigues Island. Bearing nor-nor'west."

"Good," Cooper said. "Keep her as she goes."

Maya came to them, smiling, clearly happy. "It is an island with a mountain. Of this I am glad. I have too long been without my mountain."

"Your mountain?" Cooper asked curiously.

"The great mountain in Ceylon," she explained soberly, "from which Buddha ascended to heaven."

"This one is less than Buddha's mountain." Flint was surprisingly gentle.

"No matter, it is a mountain."

"Thirty fathom 'n' no bottom," the Scotsman on the bow bellowed.

"Right! Keep it going," Cooper yelled back.

They stared up at the overhang of the cliffs. In the late afternoon light they were dark and shadowy, but at the south point a crevice in the

rocks took the water of the ocean swell and drove
it up in a crystal fountain that caught the sun
beyond the cliffs and blazed for an instant and
died, then rose and blazed again. The east side of
the island was all in shadows, and clouds of seabirds swept out of the shadow, caught the sun,
shone bright for a moment against the blue of the
sky, and dived back into the shadow as if they
were diving into a pool. The air was full of their
screaming. It rose above the noise of the breakers
against the rocks. Everywhere the breakers rolled
in, and crashed, and made long rolls of silver
against the foot of the rocks.

Roark stood beside Cooper, his eyes straining in
the effort to assure himself of a landing place. The
panorama was vast and awesomely beautiful. The
afternoon sun hung low in the blue sky and the
Indian sea lay like a blue-green carpet beneath it.
The small, brown-green mountain of the island
jutted from the sea carpet like an ancient temple.
But there was no landing place.

The wind was from the northwest. This was the
lee side, sheltered from the wind by the island, but
everywhere the water broke in a purposeless,
boiling anger. They passed up the cliffs, and were
pushed away from the island at times as the waves
hit them; and, like a punctuation of their passage,
the cry of the Scotsman came back to them over
and over again. "Thirty fathom 'n' no bottom."

At the easternmost point of the island the wind
grew stronger. They sailed past a small bay with a
sandy beach, but it was filled, like all the rest, with
broken water. Through the long glass, Roark
could see a waterfall and another stream beyond
it, but there was still no landing place. Above the
cliffs the land rose steeply to the small mountain
to the west. It was not a true mountain, but it had,

with the sunset low behind it, a certain splendor.
Trees flagged its summit and grew thick and
tumbled on its slopes. Out of the trees came now a
vast flight of pigeons, first like a grey haze against
the darkness of the shadows, and then, as with the
gulls, flashing into the last of the sunlight—but
flashing more splendidly, thousands upon
thousands of them, catching the light
simultaneously as they wheeled, diminishing and
increasing it with the movements of their wings.

Maya watched it all entranced. Her eyes were
shining, her lips parted. To Morgan she was the
very essence of innocence—until he again remembered the dagger. He watched her, almost ignoring
the miracle of the pigeons.

"Thirty fathom 'n' no bottom," the Scotsman
shouted, his voice weary and disillusioned as they
sailed on.

Cooper took a bearing on the point. "Mr. Tillman, sir, shall we stand off until morning?"

"Bring her about!" Roark ordered, ignoring the
question. "We will return to the bay."

"Won't be any good," Cooper said abruptly,
while Flint watched his face. "With this wind it
would be suicide to try and cross these reefs.
Leave it till morning. Maybe the wind will
change."

"Bring her about!" Roark repeated shortly.

"It will be dark within the hour," Cooper said
stubbornly. "If the wind falls light with the sunset,
we shall be stranded on the reefs."

Roark turned with sudden rage. He seemed to
expand to twice his size. "It is my desire that you
shall bring this ship about, Captain Cooper. The
wind will hold enough for our purposes."

Cooper shrugged his shoulders. "As you wish."

They sailed past the mouth of the bay in the last

of the light. It was silver and grey and purple—
silver where the surf broke in a continuous line
across the curve of it, grey where the beach lifted
in the twilight, purple where the shadowed woods
rose. Landing was still impossible.

Four days later the *Sea Wolf* was still standing
offshore in the open sea, on the east side of
Rodrigues Island.

Flint was standing by the rigging looking at the
island, frowning at the white necklace of the surf.
"Even when the wind fell light two days ago, there
wasn't a hope of a landin'," he said wearily.

"There's a curse on the island," Cooper suggested.

Flint looked at him, brooding. "How long is he
goin' to keep us thrashin' back and forth here?"

"Till he gets tired. His mind don't work the
ordinary ways. Any sign of a break in the surf
yet?"

Flint held the long glass up against the rigging,
steadying it to focus on the mouth of the little bay.
"Not a break. Worse than yesterday. Do we stay
here for a week? Ten days? A month?"

"Ask him!" Cooper snapped. He walked over to
the far side of the deck where Roark leant
morosely against the rail, with Pitney standing
beside him, yielding, always a little awkwardly, to
the motion of the ship.

"No sign of a break," Cooper reported, his
manner cold.

Roark only grunted.

The captain waited for a moment and tried
again. " You will always have this trouble with the
wind in the north. Half the year nothing can land
here. You will have to reckon on being cut off.

Supposing a ship came with supplies that you needed badly?"

"It would wait," Roark replied belligerently.

"If it was your ship—not otherwise. You have got to reckon on that."

"Rodrigues is a good island," Roark said, obviously adhering to his own line of thought.

"It's a good island," Cooper agreed patiently, "but it's a damned bad place to land. A ship would be in danger any time with a shift of the wind— and there is the surf to get through."

"Food, water, fish, timber—there's all that you need there."

"Not all." Cooper contradicted him openly. "Not all. And anything you would want from outside could hang up on the wind for months on end. Four days we've been here now, and there hasn't been a let-up—not a ghost of a let-up."

"Move the ship in closer," Roark ordered without animation. "We will take the longboat in."

"We'll move her as far as the east point only," Cooper said with what was almost open rebellion. "I will not risk the ship again."

It was more than two hours before the ship reached the easternmost point of the island and lowered the longboat.

"I go with the boat," Roark said with a glint of anger at Cooper, who was standing at the rail looking toward the island. "I will take the bosun mate with me. May the Lord have mercy on us." Then he turned and climbed down into the longboat. He was full of foreboding as he drank in the good, clean air and smelled the tang of the sea spray.

They sailed the longboat to the mouth of the bay, with Morgan at the tiller. She handled well, but the course was easy. As they approached, the

palm trees acquired solidity and stood out against
the deep green shadow of their background. The
forest trees on the slope grew tall and magnificent. The rocks took on a solidity and roundness.
Even the spray altered; it was no longer a
tumbling line of snow but separated into
individual crests, into upcurving shapes and
falling cascades. As they came into the mouth of
the bay—sail down and the oars out—it shattered
into individual diamonds, immensely beautiful.
Nonetheless, there was no break in them. Where
Morgan knew the gap in the threatening reef to be,
there was only a later breaking, a less urgent brilliance, and side to side it ran cross-waves from the
edges of the reefs, and eddies, and vicious, jerking
seas.

For a long time Roark watched the churning sea,
his eyes hooded and brooding. When he spoke at
last his voice was angry and low and determined.
"Put your backs in it, pull all together. Morgan,
hold her bow on the dead tree beyond the two big
rocks." He pointed.

Morgan accepted the mark instantly and at the
same time voiced his protest. "You are taking her
through?"

The men had already picked up the stroke and
the boat was heading for the gap in the reef. They
had been waiting only fifteen yards beyond the
breakers, holding their position. Now they were
into the surf almost before they were aware of
what they were doing. The bow of the boat lifted
and fell with a thud as the water broke under
them. Then they could see, towering over them,
the curling crest of a wave. The stern rose with it.
No water came aboard, but they were carried with
the force of it into the center of the breakers.
Instantly the boat was hit by a wave from the reef

on the starboard side. As the bow swung away, a
wave from the port side of the reef caught her. She
was tossed up in the air, tilted to one side, and was
hit again and again and again.

Suddenly they were in the water. One moment
they were wet, but upright and the next they were
floundering, all of them—the six oarsmen, the
bowman, Morgan and Roark.

Even while he thrashed in the bubble-charged
water, Morgan's thoughts were of Roark. He's
acting like a madman, he said to himself. Aye, he'll
land on his God-damned island all right. And he'll
kill all of us doing it.

He came to the surface and found the longboat
floating upright, but completely waterlogged,
alongside him. The five Indonesians of the crew
were already hanging on to the sides. They were
shouting, full of laughter. One of the Scotsmen
was there; the other was nowhere to be seen.

Roark had risen from the water five yards away,
blowing and furious with himself. As Morgan
watched him, he drew a deep breath and dived. He
came up much closer to the dangerous reefs, but
he had the second Scotsman in his grip. He held
the man's head in the air, and the motion of the
water took them towards the sharp, fanglike coral.
Morgan shouted, and one of the Indonesians,
swimming like a fish, headed toward them.

Roark showed no sign of having heard the
shouts. He seemed cool and completely in control
of himself. He judged the distance to the reef and
the strength of the eddy. Pulling the half-
conscious man with him, he moved to take
advantage of the current. It left them, as the flow
of the sea passed, and again they surged towards
the coral, and again Roark, wary and collected,
waited for an outward motion of the water.

"Get in!" Morgan shouted to the bowman. The bowman was small, hardly more than a boy. "Find something! See if you can bail the water out."

The boy understood his gestures, not his words. He climbed up over the bow, and the boat dipped and came back again.

Once more Morgan turned. Roark was almost on the coral now; he still had the Scotsman by the shoulders, he still fought the sea, he was still calm. The Indonesian had reached him; the bosun mate heard him shout words that he could not understand. One last time, Roark waited, and then, with another outward motion of the water, he won away from the coral, the Indonesian helping on the other side.

After several minutes, they finally reached the longboat.

"God damn it!" Roark shouted. "Haven't you got the water out of here yet?"

Another one of the Indonesians climbed into the boat. With two of them bailing, the boat rose in the water. The half-drowned Scotsman hung gasping to the stern. In a little while, the boat was floating high enough for a third man to climb in. Two oars had been salvaged. They got the boat cleared enough to haul the Scotsman in, and one by one the rest of them clambered aboard. The sail and the mast were gone. The boat crept back out toward the open sea slowly, like a tired water-beetle.

Hours after, it seemed, Cooper brought the ship in to meet them. Roark went up the ladder, heavy and tired.

Cooper, waiting for him at the side, looked down at the damaged longboat. "What in the hell happened?"

"Work out a course for the Chagos Archipelago," Roark said, ignoring the question.

Roark and Cooper had gone below to take up the unending argument over the future. Flint leant over the poop rail, watching the crew prepare the ship for sailing. Morgan stood to the side of the men at the wheel, watching the compass as the ship settled on the new course. Only Maya, standing close to the wheel-box, still stared at the slowly diminishing shape of the island.

When she spoke, it was hardly above a whisper, yet it had an urgency in it that reached Flint's ears across half the width of the ship. "Where we go now?"

"Chagos Archipelago," Morgan answered, still watching the compass.

"Where?"

This time there was a fierceness in her whisper that made Morgan look up, puzzled. "To Chagos Archipelago." Then he realized that this would of itself convey nothing to the girl. "Another island," he added quickly.

"England?" The whisper had the same urgency.

"Not England, another island," he answered, almost irritated now. "Eight days from here—ten perhaps."

"I must go east! I must go east! Not go to England!" she said in Indonesian, and the naked desperation in her voice made Flint turn from the rail. Her whole body was taut, gathered as if ready for a spring.

"Watch her, mister!" Flint called. He strode across to the girl. "Get below!" he said harshly, and then he spoke to her in her language. "We're going to another island—northeast of here—to look at it. After that, I don't know."

Maya relaxed; her shoulders drooped. She turned wordlessly and walked to the ladder.

"What the devil is she mulling over in her mind now?" Flint said quietly to Morgan, watching her.

Book Two

Chagos Archipelago

8

The sea bird flew slowly, so high that it was brilliant in the light of the sun that had not yet reached the ship. Beyond it they could already see a second bird, then a group of several.

"We're pointing too much to the north'ard, Mr. Flint—bring her to port a bit more," Cooper ordered, and *Sea Wolf* was turned into the wind. The sails flapped anxiously and the ship lost way and almost stopped. "Keep her head into the wind!"

"Aye, aye, sir!"

Cooper was looking through the long glass at the horizon. "We'll raise the island in a little over an hour. Put a man in the crow's nest!"

To the east of them the sun came up. Suddenly there were hundreds of birds visible in the morning sky.

The full day came and the horizon ahead grew

hard and distinct. The line of the palm trees was a deep green, pencil-thin and clear.

The women on the deck clustered along the port rail, talking aimlessly. Almira, the head wife, and the Tamil woman were on the poop deck. Maya was apart from the other women, engulfed in a surge of children.

Morgan had the watch now. He looked down at her fondly. He was sure that she was becoming a child again, lapsing from the harsh necessity of having to defend what he sentimentally thought of as 'her honor.' Roark had left her alone after they had abandoned hope of landing on Rodrigues Island.

The children jockeyed for position close to her. When the boys climbed onto the rail, she pulled them back; she answered questions; she responded to them. But Morgan noted that she did not smile, and he was sorry. She had not smiled, he thought, since they had set course away from Rodrigues Island. The women had left her alone, too. They seemed to hover in their attitude towards her in a mixture of apprehension and uncertainty. He thought that they could not understand her.

It was possible to see the breaks between the palms trees now. They had no chart of the islands, nothing more than a rough pencilled outline that Cooper had found among his papers—the sort of thing that ships' captains acquired from other captains in the course of quiet conversation over wine—but Morgan was sure that the first break must be the gap between the northernmost islet and the islet that covered the anchorage. Pencilled against this was the name 'Salomon.' He did not know who had given it that name or what it signified. They could see only the windward islands as yet, and only the northernmost of those. He knew that these small islands stretched far down to the south.

Roark came up the ladder and stood staring at the green lines of the palms and inhaling the silky tradewinds that wafted across the *Sea Wolf*. A veritable heaven on Earth! he said to himself. Fish and turtles, bananas and coconuts, wine and game will all grace my board here. I shall live like a king and never want for aught.

He called to the two older women, and they turned submissively and went down the ladder to begin preparing the other women for landing.

Morgan crossed over to him. "We can see between the northern islands now, sir. From the drawing, the course lies a little closer to the port-side island."

"Salomon Island," Roark announced brusquely, as if determined to accept no compromise. He barked the name so loudly that Morgan stepped back a pace. He looked up at the sails as if to judge the wind.

"It's falling light, sir," Morgan said helpfully.

"That I can see," Roark retorted fiercely. "Call me when you can see the surf!"

He went down the ladder, grunting and quick-tempered, and shouted at the group of children that ran to meet him.

All through the morning watch, the palm trees grew in their sight. From a thin line of green they became a rampart, a cliff of jade. The higher crests developed out of a vague raggedness to individuality, to shape, to solidity, and under them at last the eternal white of the reef edge began to play across the blue-green of the ocean. It lacked half an hour before the change of watches. Morgan called Cooper and then Roark.

Over the bow of the ship lay a small island. It was enriched by the glittering emerald-green of the Indian Ocean that lapped lazily at shores of dazzling white sand. Groves of verdant palms with feathery fronds scraping the cobalt-blue sky fronted a lush, jungle-like wall of vegetation. It seemed a fairy-tale isle, Morgan thought with a sudden rush of anticipation, though he would reserve his judgment until he had seen Roark's land of milk and honey first-hand.

Captain Cooper came to deck briskly, measured the distances with his eye, and assessed the speed of the wind and the set of the sails in one quick, comprehensive glance. "Get the longboat ready for lowering," he ordered. "Mr. Flint will go in with her ahead of us, but I want two men in the crow's nest—two good men who can tell a coral reef from a patch of weed. See to it!"

Morgan went down to the main deck. As he passed Maya, she pointed excitedly at the island. "This is the island?" she asked in English.

"Yes, this is it. This is Salomon Island of the Chagos Archipelago."

"A flat island!" she said almost contemptuously. And he remembered poignantly her heart-cry for Buddha's mountain in Ceylon.

Farther down the deck the Chinese girl, who also spoke English, asked him, "What hurts her now?"

"The islands are flat. She was used to a mountain."

"Mountain or flat country, it is all the same,"
the Chinese girl said philosophically. "At least the
palm trees are beautiful."

They crept in very slowly under the fore and
main topsails. Well before they reached the shoal
water, the longboat was ahead of them, crawling
like a turtle. The wind died with the noonday sun,
but there was enough left for the ship to ghost
silently in, the noise of the surf on the reefs rising
from a thin, tenuous thread of sound to a harsh
vibration that permeated everything in the ship
and in their beings.

The color of the water changed abruptly from
the ultramarine of the depths to the first pale
blues of the coral mass. The blues changed almost
as abruptly to a dark green, and then, as they
turned to port to make the anchorage inside
Salomon, it became suddenly, overwhelmingly,
aquamarine. Morgan had never seen a transition
such as this. There was no substance in the water;
they floated in the green of the sunlight reflected
from the bottom. The longboat ahead of them also
floated in light. The lead weight used for
sounding, as it was swung ahead of the boat,
splashed and sent out great circles of ripples that
did no more than vary the gemstone quality of the
water. Morgan watched with a sense of wonder.

Maya stood a little behind him. Once or twice he
glanced at her. She was staring with her inevitable
unchildlike stillness at the inward shore of white
sand, utterly peaceful inside the protective
roaring of the reef. The children had not followed
her up the deck to where Morgan stood; Flint had
frightened them away.

Behind him, Morgan heard the captain's voice

shouting the orders to raise up the topsails. The *Sea Wolf* glided on, as if once in the embrace of the island it no longer required the motive power of the wind. The depth soundings were called back from the longboat, as the water became quickly shallower. Twice the men shouted from the crow's nest, but no change in the steering orders followed. The passage was wide enough, but the ship was scarcely moving now.

Morgan waited, flexed and tense, for the word to drop anchor. "Let go, mister!" he heard the captain's voice shout presently. And he repeated the order to the crew.

The anchor went away with a rush of sound and a violent tremor through the deck. The splash as it hit the water changed the nature of the sound and the quality of the surface, producing two enormous sets of ripples that rushed out from the ship and caught up with the longboat and surrounded it before they disappeared.

Flint, standing in the stern of the longboat with the tiller between his legs, half turned and called something to his men. The longboat began to come round.

The ship gathered for an almost imperceptible backward movement, swinging a little away from the anchor. Morgan could see the bottom clearly now. The head of the anchor had not bitten into the sand but lay flat on the bottom. The ship drifted farther and farther, and he saw the anchor finally come upright and began to bite into the sand.

"Hold that, mister!" Cooper shouted at last. And the men began to secure the cable. Cooper came forward himself to check the anchor.

"I think it will hold," Morgan said.

"It had better!" Cooper answered him shortly.

"I want an anchor watch all the time we lie here—at any rate until we know what the wind is going to do. See to it!" He turned and looked at Maya. "Has she said anything?"

"Nothing. I think she was pleased to come to land."

"Don't think!" Cooper snapped, and went aft to talk to Flint as he came up the ladder from the longboat.

The speed with which Maya moved was fantastic. At one moment she was standing silent and withdrawn on the deck. The next instant her body was flashing down towards the water in an intensely graceful curve. She made hardly a splash as she hit the water, but from her a brilliance of bubbles leaped back to the surface. A few seconds after the bubbles, her sarong came floating up, weaving and twisting as if it had a life of its own. From the deck Morgan could see the golden brown body, delicate and sleek in the water, acquiring added color in the richness of the blue-green light as she lost the impetus of the dive and began to swim under water.

There was no need for him to shout. The women had done that for him, in a violent, agitated chorus. Morgan began, ridiculously, to tug at his boots, while watching the direction the girl was swimming.

Maya's naked figure broke the surface a long way clear of the ship and began to swim strongly towards the sandy shores of the beach.

"Damned deceiving little bitch!" Flint said bluntly to Cooper. "Shall I take the longboat after her?"

"Let her swim!" Roark, leaning over the rail above them, ordered. "She'll come to no harm."

"Sharks?" Flint questioned, and out of the

corner of his eye caught Morgan preparing to swim after the girl. "Don't be a fool!" he shouted.

"We've seen none," Roark replied. "Besides, she swims like a fish."

Sheepishly Morgan began to pull on his boots again.

The women kept up their chorus until Roark came down the ladder to the main deck and strode through them, bellowing. He stopped beside Morgan. "You should not have let her go."

"I couldn't have stopped her. No one could have stopped her. She moved"—he found the words he was looking for—"she moved like a bird."

Already Maya was halfway in to the shallow. She swam rhythmically, leaving behind her a continuous pattern of ripples and eddies and small, bright patches of foam. Anxiously Morgan scanned the water for the fin of a shark. Nothing showed. Behind the dark of her small body the aquamarine grew polished and perfect again.

They saw her reach the shallows and lift herself swiftly from the water. For a moment she stood still, gazing upon everything with avid interest. Then she began to splash in to the beach.

Here the island looked as if an artist had determined to paint a landscape using only the raw primary colors—red, yellow, blue. Even the shadows were sharply cast by the blazing sun, the fronded coconut palms forming an inky pattern on the pale, powdery sand, like the carved pattern of an eastern temple. Gaudy butterflies flitted aimlessly about in the balmy air, like exotic airborne blossoms. Hermit crabs scuttled fearlessly over Maya's feet in the water.

At the very edge of the water she stopped, looking over the sand. There were no footprints on it—no human footprints. There were tracks where

sea-turtles had dragged themselves ashore to lay
their eggs. There were the erratic and intricate
patterns of the movement of land crabs. There
were bird footprints, and worm marks, and the
whorled arabesques of moving shells and
thousands of sand dollars. But there was no sign
or mark of man. All this she took in, in a brief
searching sweep of her head. She saw the tide-
mark with its jumble of debris. She saw the clean
drifted sand beyond that. And she began to walk
up the beach, quite straight, quite naked, quite
unselfconscious, not turning to look back at the
ship or even to see if she had been pursued.

It was very hot on the beach. The glare was
intense after the cool, filtered light of the sea. The
heat of the sun struck down and upwards at the
same time. She walked in it encompassed in a
physical glow of happiness, and the tracks of her
feet, close together and firm and steady, went
straight from the water's edge to the edge of the
shade.

The nearest palms sprawled outwards, hanging
over the sand, the crests of some of them reaching
out over the water. They made a patterned shadow
at first, long feathers of darkness on the whiteness
of the sand, which grew and solidified into patches
of shade, flecked here and there with small circles
of light.

Beyond the thick grove of curve-trunked palms
lay a heavy wall of foliage, a jungle of great, fan-
shaped palms, liana vines and ironwood trees. It
was towards the jungle that Maya headed. Then
even the sunlight failed, and she walked into an
enchanting and perfect coolness. There was a
thick litter of fallen palm fronds between the
trunks, but the trees rose from it straight and
soaring. As she reached the first of them, a pair of

small sandpipers, like delicate, aerial familiars of the place, swept out to meet her, lifted in mock fright upwards, swirled through the palm fronds, and came down again, their wings silent as moths' wings, their movement as light and airy as the mating of butterflies.

She looked up at them, and for the first time in many months she laughed.

The sandpipers followed her as she picked her way through the debris of fallen fronds and rotting coconuts, brushing through young trees, avoiding fallen and moldering trunks, but always heading to the east, as if she were drawn by a magnet. She made no attempt to measure distance; she was not aware of time. She moved in a cool shade that for this imperishable moment was hers alone. She had escaped from Roark Tillman; she had escaped from man's world.

She knew that there was nothing for her beyond the brief half-mile of the heart of the island. On the other side, beyond the palm trees, there would be another beach and the submerged coral reef, and beyond the reef the barrier of the surf. But it was necessary for her spirit that she should discover these things for herself alone and by herself alone.

She walked steadily, neither hurrying nor irritated by the devious path that was forced on her by the fallen fronds and the occasional ironwood trees and scrub bushes that struggled to grow between the palms. The sandpipers flitted through the shade behind and above her, always wholly and perfectly silent, watching her with their curious black eyes.

After what seemed hours, she saw light between the trunks, light that was banded in colors—a long streak of blue that was the clear sky, a turquoise that was the haze beyond the sea, an aquamarine that was the sea, and then the blinding white of the surf, and under it green and white and shadow mingled. Nothing that she knew compared with it. She could only see the indescribable perfection of the beauty towards which she moved.

She came at last to the edge of the palms. The beach here had a different character. Coral boulders lay across it and smaller, rounded stones. The water in the shallows over the slabbed coral of the reefs was of a green so pallid that it was hardly visible until at last, with the deeper pools, it acquired color and texture, and farther on, with the live coral and the shellfish, beauty and form as well. Tiny wavelets from the surf's edge ran across it. It had a life and a liveliness. Small wading birds darted with erratic zigzag movements about it. Gulls cruised along the surf's edge. The very character of the air was different— fresh and salty, the air of the eternal ocean.

Instead of ending in the peace of the lagoon, here the sea ended in tumult. The surf broke in a gusty majesty of sound and brilliance. It was not high, for the wind that had brought the ship ghosting into the anchorage was not now strong enough to lift even the palm fronds. The ocean swell raised the surf, in a movement as regular as breathing, but broken dramatically by the jagged palisade of the reef. It rose, it broke, it tossed up the diamonds of its spray, and it fell away, sucking and roaring, into deep hollows that filled at once again. The same hot sun shone down on a different splendor here.

She stood at the edge of the shadow and stared out towards the eastern sky, towards an absolute and illimitable emptiness, and behind her the sandpipers wove their patterns in and out towards the palms, as if they were afraid to come out into the naked sun.

After a little, Maya wept.

She was safe from Tillman and his men, for the time being, at least, she thought with relief. But would she ever see her home again? Had she yet again jumped from the frying pan only to find herself in the fire?

With a fierce pride and determination, she plunged back into the dense vegetation. Twilight was falling when she at last stopped to rest. Between the curtain of vines that hung like sinuous snakes all about her, and the ironwood trees and the huge, fan-shaped palms, she glimpsed the distant twinkling of the stars. The island creatures rustled and twittered as they settled down to roost or hole for the night, and Maya deemed it eminently fitting to do likewise. She lay on her stomach on a carpet of lush grass and dead leaves, utterly spent. She yawned loudly, exhaustion creeping over her quickly. Her eyelids wavered, her head dropped forward into the grass. In seconds, she had fallen into a heavy sleep.

9

The enchantment had gone out of the island. Maya walked through the palms conscious of the bird droppings and the sour smell of rotted fish. Flies rose and followed her. The jungle lay drenched in steamy heat, made still more oppressive by the choking vines and roots and bushes and trees that grew so closely together that it was virtually impossible to force a path through it without a sturdy machete to hack the way clear. Nor was the place any longer hers alone; she saw carved on the palm trunks letters, writing in the English tongue, and beyond the lettered trees pools of water that had been dug for wells in a clearing and lay now stagnant and covered with a green scum on which bird feathers floated.

Finally, as she came towards her landing place, she heard voices, Roark Tillman's booming authoritatively among them. They are seeking me, she thought with a shiver of dismal apprehension.

Roark strode through the clearing with the imposing authority of a king. The indecisions of the ship seemed to have dropped away from him, along with the weakness and vacillation of the departure from the Cape. Once again he was a pioneer.

"Make a mark here for the beginning of the village!" he called to Morgan. "We can cut a clear path through to the beach in an hour. There will be no need to uproot the seedlings in the other clearing."

He watched as Morgan, awkward with the long machete, sliced a blaze on the trunk of a palm. He measured his paces from it up the clearing, and the men, grasping his intention at once, began to hack away the undergrowth, to clear the piles of fronds, to cut the path. He marked off hut site after hut site, naming them as he did so. He knew precisely what he wished to do, the exact shape of the village that he proposed to build.

"You will find pits dug for the water beyond the clearing—that way, I think," Roark shouted halfway down the clearing.

Morgan took three of the men, wondering. The pits were there—old, silted in, stagnant, but nonetheless there. He set his men to work to clear them out and went back to Roark. A palm tree crashing down almost fell on him. He leapt aside, swearing, and came on.

"You'll learn to watch out for yourself here, mister!" Roark laughed. "Now take these three and clear the path through to the beach."

Roark was elated. The islands were bigger than he had thought they would be, wide enough to live on, and there was a whole range of them to the south. He was sure that there would be plenty of

fresh water. Someone—Ben Cooper's brother
Dirk, he was sure—had planted seedlings. There
were bananas and citrus fruits and young bread-
fruit and papaya. The beach was an admirable
landing place; the width of the island sheltered it
from the northeast trades, and the lagoon sheltered it from the southwest. There were seafood
and fish, oysters and turtle, land crabs and
coconuts. There were large palm fronds for
thatching and ironwood for timber. There was
everything that a man might need. There was
space. There was peace. There were women.

"This place will do," he called to Morgan, who
was halfway down the path to the beach and
hacking away for dear life. "I am not greedy. I
seek no more for a kingdom. This is itself a kingdom."

Maya saw him through the screen of the palm
trunks, striding about with magnificent gestures.
He looked more than life-size. Humanly, childishly
even, she giggled, and without further thought
walked straight into the clearing.

The Indonesians saw her first. They saw and
acknowledged her nakedness and discreetly
turned their eyes away. Morgan, facing her as
Roark's bulk moved out of his line of vision, saw
her and gasped. He saw only her childlike
innocence.

Roark wheeled round at the gasp, following
with a pioneer's wariness the line of Morgan's
eyes. As he turned he saw her. But he saw only the
hilt of the dagger, the polished ivory smoothness
of its carving, the long, flat outline of its deadly
blade under the bandage of silk around her thigh.

"Cover your nakedness!" he shouted furiously.

Maya stood with her eyes alight in acknowledgement of the mischief she had done.

"The water took my new sarong," she answered him directly.

Morgan, inspired by the youthful, angelic purity that he believed he saw, stripped off his shirt, gathered it up in his hands, and, walking up to her, put it over her head. Maya fumbled a little for the unaccustomed armholes, and he felt the warmth of her soft flesh beneath his hands. Then she found the sleeves and the shirt fell, ludicrous and enveloping, about her slim body. She stood quite still, her blue-black, glossy hair parted in the center and falling over one shoulder in a heavy swath, her arms flaccid, her hands not reaching the opening of the cuffs. She allowed her shoulders to droop a little, her head to bow. Her posture aroused an unexpected feeling of pity and compassion in Morgan.

Even Roark for a moment was taken in, then suddenly his giant frame began to shake and he laughed outright. "You look like a God-damned hant."

Maya seemed to realize by intuition that the word meant ghost, and, lifting the ridiculously long shirt sleeves, she flapped them mournfully.

Roark laughed again. "It is apparent that thou art no one else but Maya," he said over his laughter. And Maya laughed with him.

Maya settled herself in the stern of the longboat, clear of the tiller and out of the way of the stroke of the oars. Morgan recognized again how much she knew of the ways of boats. She waited until they were clear of the immediate shallows. Then she stretched over and took a piece of cord from a box of tools in the stern compartment. Straightening her body back up, she wrapped it round her waist. It went round her twice, gathering in the shirt, and she tied it in a knot. Then she rolled up the sleeves and smoothed out the shirt. At once the absurdity of the oversized garment disappeared. The shirt became a long dress, covering her completely and, gathered in by the cord, restoring the slimness of her figure.

She looked up at Morgan with a face innocent of any expression, even inquisitiveness. "When the ship go?" she asked in English.

He jumped as he always did when she used English. "I don't know. Six days—seven days, perhaps. When we've finished unloading."

She disregarded the latter part of the explanation. What she needed was the information as to the number of days. "The ship go England?" she asked after a long wait. To the word England she gave an enormous significance.

Morgan shook his head. "No, east. We go east to Singapore."

"Ah!" she said softly, the word almost a sigh.

After a little she moved and accidentally, he was sure, her body came in contact with his leg. He could feel the softness of it and its supple strength. She seemed to rest against him. She is trustful, he thought.

After a long silence she looked up at him again, her eyes liquid and enormous. "I come with you?" There was just enough emphasis on the 'you' to make it clear to him that the request had a personal significance.

Morgan put his hand on her shoulder in what was meant to be a fatherly pat and that by some change in Maya's position seemed to turn itself into a caress. "He says that you are to stay on the island with—" He was going to say 'with him' but altered it hurriedly—"with the others."

"I go with you," she repeated gently, as if she

had not understood the words.

Within a few minutes they reached the ship, which had dropped anchor some fifty yards off the island.

Cooper was in Roark's cabin lying almost on his shoulder blades in the chair that Roark used ordinarily. Flint had his shirt off. Morgan had not yet put a fresh shirt on. The atmosphere of the cabin was relaxed, as if a weight had been lifted from each of the three men.

Cooper held up his glass and squinted through the red of the wine. "And Roark is going to sleep ashore tonight?"

Morgan nodded. "He wants the Chinese girl and May Ling, and there's a list of bedding and cooking pots and God knows what the hell else." He fished the paper out of his pocket.

"He has settled on the first clearing?"

Morgan nodded again. "It's the best. The seedlings in the other clearing are just coming up. We found initials on a palm tree—D.C. and the date, December, 1824."

"Dirk Cooper, my brother," the captain said. "He must have called here on his way back. There's no telling how long he stayed."

"Long enough to plant bananas and a lot of other stuff. We're to get the ship loaded in six days."

"Dammit, man!" Cooper swore. "How the hell does he think we're going to do that if he keeps half the hands ashore?"

"He said you were to keep as many as you needed."

"And if I do," Cooper grumbled, "he will scream like a wounded tiger. When does he want his women ashore?"

"In the morning," Morgan replied, "to gather

thatching for the roofs. They come back to the ship each night till the huts are ready."

"I'll be glad to be rid of 'em," Cooper said thoughtfully. He yawned and took another drink. "I'm tired of being captain of a floating whorehouse."

Flint looked up at him quickly and smiled. "It's a bit late to be having scruples, Captain. And if he's goin' to stay ashore and leave the women here. . ." He left the sentence unfinished.

Cooper cut across his words. "You leave his women alone! He'll kill you, mister!"

"Ha!" Flint lifted his glass and looked mockingly over it. "He might try."

Morgan fumbled in his pocket for a second piece of paper. "He's made a list." He held the paper up.

"You mean the ones who stay?" Cooper queried, his brows drawn together in a frown.

Morgan passed the paper across to Cooper. "Forty-five altogether, apart from himself."

"And the rest?"

"They go on with the ship. We're to put them ashore in Singapore."

"I'll have the bloody papers freeing them before I'll sail with one of them aboard," Cooper said soberly. "I will not risk prosecution and a prison sentence for slave-trading for Tillman's women. By God, I'll not!"

"Their papers are all in order," Morgan said firmly, "and they've all been well provided for by Mr. Tillman. But what about the Eurasian girl?" he added awkwardly.

All three men knew at once he meant Maya.

"She's on the list," Cooper said, after running his eyes down the paper.

"She is on the list," Morgan agreed. "She wishes to go with us."

"How do you know?"

"She asked me," Morgan answered stubbornly.

"You will be careful about that one," Cooper ordered acidly. "I'll not cross Tillman's bows more than I have to. Keep clear of her!"

"She is a child," Morgan said hurriedly, too hurriedly. "She does not belong here." He waved a wide hand that included everything on the ship. "She wants to go back to her family. By God, she looked like a baby in my shirt!"

"A baby with a knife between her legs." Cooper's voice grew still more acid.

"She is still a child," Morgan persisted with a surprising firmness.

The Tamil woman looked beyond Maya, as if communing with unseen faces beyond her shoulder. "You have shamed us all." Her voice was harsh. Maya regarded her indifferently. "It is not enough that you fled from the ship, but when you were recaptured, you were naked."

Maya smiled gently. "I was not recaptured." Her voice was so soft that it was not possible to accuse her of insolence. "I walked into the clearing that they were preparing for the village. I was naked because the sea took my sarong"—she leant forward suddenly—"and my nakedness is a matter for myself alone. I am my own."

"It is a matter for his Lordship. You are his."

"That is between him and me. He laughed at me." Maya paused and considered the matter. "He laughed with me. Is it your wish that I should go back and tell him that you will not give me my sarong back?"

Reluctantly the Tamil pushed the folded sarong over the floor. "It is here, but it does not resolve your shame."

Maya rested her chin on her hand. "All of you"—

she included all the other women without bothering to collect them with her eyes—"all of you go naked for your Lord. If there is shame in me, there is shame also in you, all of you. You call yourself his wives, but you are not his wives. The Koran says that a man may have four wives, but your Lord is not of the faith. He is a Christian; a Christian has but one wife. You are slaves, the slaves of his body—whores, nothing more."

The Tamil darted her head forward with a look of blind vindictiveness.

After a pause, Maya continued. "You go naked, knowing that you are nothing more than slaves. That is the shame. I go naked because it is my will, and I will go naked when it is my will and not because the Lord Tillman requires it."

Maya rose to her feet and peeled off Morgan's shirt, making of the graceful, simple movements a calculated insolence. For a long moment she stood stripped, knowing that every woman's eyes were fixed on the dagger with its ivory hilt. Then, slowly and deliberately, she arranged the bright sarong round her waist and tucked it in. Stooping, she gathered Morgan's shirt and went to the door, holding her head with the arrogance of an Egyptian Queen.

At sunset the shirt was dry again. She had ironed it with the iron that the old woman Almira kept for Tillman's shirts alone. Neatly folded now and glistening, she carried it to Morgan on the quarter-deck. Her eyes were starry. She emanated an air of happiness and confidence. But when she spoke, her voice had overtones of pleading. She held the shirt on the palms of her outstretched hands.

Every line of her body submissive, she spoke in

Indonesian. "To have worn it is too great an honor. Now I have made it fresh for you. Be pleased to accept my thanks."

The bosun, standing close to Morgan, translated.

"It is nothing," Morgan said awkwardly. "I was glad to do it." He took the shirt, his hands touching hers—by accident, he thought. A small thrill that he could not properly understand ran through him with the touch.

"It was a great thing," Maya said. "You saved me from shame."

Again the bosun translated.

"There was no shame," Morgan said hurriedly.

He is a fool, Maya thought as the bosun translated back to her, but he is a kind fool.

"I will go with the Lord Morgan on the ship," she whispered in English, bowing gracefully. She had given him the same title as the other women gave Roark.

10

Roark had decided to make the final landing an official ceremony. The village was complete now. It had taken fourteen days instead of the six of his first estimate, but that, of course, was inevitable.

The long main clearing ran deep into the heart of the island. A straight path ran through it from the beach. The Lord's house, Roark's house—it was no more than a long, high roof balanced on the cut-off trunks of palm trees—was on the eastern side of the path. Before it and beyond it were storehouses and sheds for the simple presses that he had brought for the manufacture of oil from the coconuts.

There were houses for the seven married men. Their wives were to live with them again now—they were no longer segregated as they had been to protect them from the crew of the ship. There was another hut for the unmarried men. The three old wives had a hut to themselves. Next to it was a long hut for the younger women and beyond that a hut for the children; they were opposite Roark's own quarters. Skinner Pitney had a hut near the beach, away from the rest. The village was Western in design and looked out of place in the shadow of the palms; yet it was cool and easy to keep clean, and for the time being, Flint believed, it would serve its purpose.

He had watched the procession of Roark's subjects ironically. The children came first, crowned with little white scented flowers, and the young girls next. Maya walked in the center of them between the two Indian girls from Rangoon and the youngest of the Chinese girls. She walked with an air of ease and acceptance; Flint thought that her ease was somewhat exaggerated. Behind her walked the black girl, by herself, then the older women with babies, and, last of all, the three old wives—Almira, May Ling, and the Tamil.

Between the huts the men were playing gongs, drums and cymbals. Roark had always kept enough men to make an orchestra of some sort. The colorful, happy music drifted gently among the palms.

Roark sat on the big oak chair that had been brought ashore at last, watching his parade with the air of a Roman emperor at a village festival. His god-like aura was benign and bountiful. The children greeted him as the joyful, fancifully costumed procession reached his chair. They made the traditional greetings to their master and Roark accepted them easily.

Flint, watching with a skeptical eye, was convinced that Roark was quite genuine in his acceptance, that he thought the greetings and salutions were his due and by his acceptance of them he was conferring a real and meaningful favor on his people. The older girls made their salutations in turn, and Flint realized with a quick tingle of excitement and delight that Maya was no longer with them. Somehow, in the excitement and pageantry of the parade, she had slipped away. He wondered what devilish plot she was hatching now, what mischief.

The young women made their bows. The older women followed them. Almira passed last of all before Roark's chair, made a low bow to him with the palm of her right hand held to her forehead in a greeting of respect, and moved to sit on the woven matting by his side.

And then, as Roark turned to speak to the old woman, Maya walked softly to the chair. The laughter and conversation hushed. As if by a single impulse, the eyes of the group turned towards her. She fell gracefully to her knees and stretched forward in an elaborate prostration before Roark.

Her voice came up to them clear and distinct and innocent of mockery, yet the whole gesture was a mockery.

"My Emperor, oh great Emperor!" she said. "Lord of this mighty kingdom!" There was a quick catch of breath in the ranks of the women. Without lifting her head, Maya went on in imitation of a servant giving a flowery greeting to the Emperor of Salomon Island—with Roark the object of her amused adoration. Somewhere she had acquired a complete knowledge of this respectful but foolish greeting. Now, without exaggeration, she made this simple ceremony and Roark himself appear ridiculous.

Flint watched Roark growing red with anger and unable to do anything without making himself look even more ridiculous. "If she was my daughter, she'd have her bottom smacked so hard she wouldn't sit for a fortnight," he said softly over his shoulder to Morgan.

Roark rose suddenly from the chair, his face almost purple with rage. "Enough! Enough!"

Maya rose to her knees, checked herself, bent forward just enough still to look humble, and gazed at him with enormous, liquid eyes.

In the shadow of the trees, a man sniggered.

"Not the last boat," Morgan had said, "but the one before the last. The last they will search for a certainty."

Maya crouched under a layer of canvas and sacking that was going back to the ship. The long-boat was afloat already, held steady by two of the Scottish hands. They knew about her; that too had been arranged. She had seen Roark less than two minutes before and had accepted a tongue-lashing meekly. She was certain that no search would be made for her, certainly not before dawn. Every-body was sated and sleepy with the food and the liquor. The long festivity of the first day had gone on all through the moonlit darkness. Maya's head was ringing with the rhythm of the music; her eyes were tired.

Through the night, the frightened birds had kept up a canopy of beating wings above the palms, their voices boisterous over the music. They were silent now. This was the silence before the dawn, the silence before the seabirds began their morning flight. It was time that the boat went out.

The tension grew in her. From the low moon there was enough light for Maya to see under the canvas and make out the dim side of the longboat. She was lying under the second oarsman's seat on the starboard side, as still as the oars that lay on the seat above her, motionless, fragile, a shadow among the shadows.

Suddenly hands plucked her out from under the canvas before she had time to get at her dagger. They wrapped her in the canvas, rolling her in it like a cocoon to keep her still and powerless. They seemed to know precisely where she was. Someone must have betrayed her—one of the Scotsmen, she was sure, the tall, gaunt one. She could not think why he would have betrayed her; there was no reason for it except that he might be thinking of a reward. She was carried roughly to the shore between the two men.

Roark was waiting for her on the beach. He looked down mockingly at her face, furious in the moonlight.

"You would have done better to swim," he snarled, "but even then I would have searched the ship for you. You did not think that I would let you go thus easily? There is still much between you and me." His scowl darkened.

Maya lifted her nose disdainfully and watched him with hostile eyes, recognizing that words were useless.

Roark flung an arm wide, encompassing the sea that stretched endlessly to the dim horizon and sneered, "Who in the hell do you think you are? Some Hindu goddess, raised upon a pedestal of your own construction, who does what she damn well pleases? The haughty Maya, beautiful, untouched, pure, who strolls this earth for but a passing whim and sighs for some great hero, that perfect man who will snatch her from this squalor and take her back to her homeland and there serve her every wish. Ha!" Roark snorted. "Beware, my sweet. That perfect man might also seek a perfect woman."

Struck dumb by his words, Maya stared at him.
"Bring her!" he said at last, and stalked away
towards the path.

In a sense, it was an imitation of the parade and
ceremony that she had mocked earlier. This time
there were no flowers and no songs and no music.
They dumped her unceremoniously in front of
Roark's doorway. The low moon made no light in
the clearing, but there was light enough in the sky
above to distinguish the outlines of the place. She
could see with her furious eyes the roof of the hut
of the elder wives, and beyond it the hut of the
young women, and beyond that still the hut of the
children, and over the other side of the hut the oil
press and the storehouses. She sought them out as
if it could somehow ease her powerlessness.

Roark came out of the doorway. He carried a
bullwhip in his hand. Maya had seen him beat the
Bantu girl with it before. He beat her now. The
first slash of it stung through the canvas in which
she was wrapped.

The pain Maya felt was unimportant. What mattered was the assault on her pride. She writhed
desperately, her arms held close to her sides by
the wrapping of the canvas, and the whip came
down again and again and again. With each slash,
her anger grew. She was infused with it. It permeated every area of her body and soul. It contained humiliation, and an awareness of ridicule,
and shame, and a determination on revenge. She
moved after each blow, hardly aware of the
physical contact of the lash, aware only of the
diminishment of her dignity. She made no sound,
no observable acknowledgment of what was
happening. Twice she brought her knees under her
and attempted a convulsive movement towards

where Roark stood, cold and oddly impassive. Each time he moved backwards just far enough, and the whip descended again and again.

She could not see faces in the darkness, but she was aware of eyes. The other women ringed her somewhere in the darkness, watching her and rejoicing in her degradation.

Roark stopped beating her at last, with no more preamble than he had begun. He tossed the bull-whip behind him, back into his hut, and stood looking down at Maya, grave and powerful. And while her right hand clutched frantically at the hilt of the dagger under the pinning folds of the canvas he bellowed, "Take her to the children's hut!"

Men drifted out from under the darkness of the huts and picked her up. The hands were impersonal on her. The door of the children's hut was opened, and she was thrown inside, landing in a tangle of childish limbs and bodies. Then the door was shut again, and the chain pulled round it and the padlock snapped shut. Maya lay quite still, listening to the small, sharp, metallic noises outside.

Then she heard Roark call out sarcastically, "You are now mine forever, my sweet. Sleep well!"

Now, finally giving vent to all her pent-up rage, fear, and humiliation, Maya screamed with a piercing shriek that trembled the hut. "I am my own! I am my own!" She paused only to draw breath, then raised her voice once again. "I am my own!"

In the quiet that followed, she heard the gale of loud laughter that filtered in from outside the hut.

Inside the hut the children unwrapped her, fumbling in the darkness. They made little liquid, cooing noises. They patted her arms, her legs, her head, trying to comfort her. They made a space on the mats for her and half lifted, half pushed her to it. They were full of pity and solicitude. It was like a whispering of sympathy for one of their own.

In the darkness of the hut, it was impossible to know who was helping her, except when she could recognize the whispered voices. It did not matter. They had all known that she would try to escape. They had not known the plan, only that she believed that she would sail with the *Sea Wolf* when it left. They waited for her to cry, but she lay quite still on the matting, and for a long time they sat around her, some of them still touching her to comfort her, some keeping away, afraid to have to share in her sorrow.

The song came to them as they sat. It was very far off—deep, a song of men's voices, slow and rhythmical—while the *Sea Wolf* prepared to get under way. Now and then, as the drift of the night wind came in to them, they could hear even the clicking of the anchor winch beating out a rhythm to the singing.

> Far arovin' I go
> Far arovin' goes me
> Far across the deep
> Blue sea,
> Sad I'll be without
> Thee.
>
> Far arovin' I go
> Far arovin' goes me
> Far across the deep
> Blue sea.

Then the song ceased, and they heard shouting

and wood banging against wood, and faintly, almost indistinguishable over the seabirds' cry, the squeak of the ropes in the unoiled blocks hoisting the sail. Another song came, with a quicker tempo as the topsails went up, and then a third song that grew faint in the distance as the ship began moving farther away from the island.

In the absolute darkness of the hut, Maya turned on her side. Even then she did not weep.

11

The light of the children's hut was soft and gentle. No sun reached it so early in the morning. The dawn clamor of the birds was silent, the seabirds long since gone on their outward flights to sea.

Maya became conscious of herself as one slowly stirring to life from a total void, knowing of no previous existence beyond the present indeterminate moment. She was an embryo floating in darkness, living and breathing but somehow set apart from the world by a hazy mist surrounding her. With a natural buoyancy, her mind rose slowly to the surface of awareness, but as she neared the indistinct border where the first weak rays of reality penetrated, fiery claws of pain began to emanate from her back. She recoiled from the harrowing torment and hovered just below the elusive level of awareness, not willing to break her bond to that uncaring, painless oblivion and accept in its stead the sharp pangs of being fully awake. Voices drifted to her as if through a long tunnel, reaching her with words that were at first blurred and muted, entreating her to make an effort to hear.

The children sat around her in two little groups, oddly intertwined, each group centered on one of the two oldest of them, two small, gentle pyramids of mingled colors—the pale yellow of the Chinese children, the light brown of those with Indian blood, and the dark golden color of the Indonesian children.

It was one of the Indonesian girls who was speaking. Her name was Ana, the diminutive of Rohana, and she was round, soft-looking and sly.

"The ship is gone," she said, certain at last that Maya was finally awake. "What will you do now?"

Maya turned her head a little with acute discomfort and studied her. She could, of course, frighten her into silence without trouble, but she wanted the children on her side. "I will wait," she answered coolly.

"He will beat you again!" The girl Ana brought the talk swiftly to Roark.

"He will not beat me again. Such talk is foolish."

"And if he sends for you?"

Maya had her opportunity. "I will go"—she put her hand down with a quick movement to the inside of her thigh—"as I went before." She allowed the words to be full of menace. "I will not again be wrapped in the folds of a canvas."

A delighted shiver ran through the other group.

"But if the ship never comes back?" Opal, the center of it, said softly.

Maya sat herself up and stretched cautiously. The canvas had protected her, but there was still pain from the beating. "It will come back, or if it does not, there will be other ships. Three have been here already. You have seen the names; I myself have shown them to you. More will come."

"But our friend Morgan has gone."

There was a little murmur through the children.

"You love Morgan?" Ana asked boldly.

"No." Maya smiled a smile of an odd, communicable wickedness. "I did not love him. I allowed him to grow to love me so that I could use him. But he was a fool; he was not worth love. I should have swum out to the ship."

There was a flutter of admiration through the children.

"It was the Tamil woman who betrayed you," Opal whispered. "The Scotsman told her—the one she slept with on the ship."

Maya's slim shoulders made a little upward shrug. "It is no matter. The plan itself was folly. It was his plan—Morgan's. And he is as the rest, a barbarian."

"And now there is neither ship nor lover!" Opal was incurably romantic.

"He was not my lover. I have no lover, nor will I have a lover until I choose. I am myself alone. I do not need a lover. I am the daughter of a Sultan." The children swayed away from her in respectful terror. "I am my own. I am not a slave." She looked at Opal with her eyes narrowing. "You are his slave."

The girl had a beautiful face. Her neck and shoulders were brilliantly molded. Her hair had strong red highlights in it. She held herself with a certain pride. "I am his slave. It is our custom and—"

"And when the white devil sends for you, you will go."

"I will go," Opal answered without emotion in

her voice.

"Would you not rather go to a man whom you love?"

"There is here no man to love," Opal answered reluctantly.

"Ha!" Maya exclaimed derisively.

The children seemed to weave themselves closer in, as if in need of protection against her contempt.

"It is the law," two voices said simultaneously, seeking refuge in tradition.

"Other ships will come," Maya repeated, "and other men with them. What can he do to you?"

"Beat us," five of the voices said simultaneously.

Ana looked at her faintly puzzled. "You are sure that other ships will come, but you do not know. They may not come ever. No men have lived in this place before."

"They will come," Maya asserted simply. "I have arranged it."

Again the gasp of respect ran through the children. It was the measure of her domination over them that they believed even this.

"How?" Ana alone asked.

"I knew that it would not be easy for me to escape. Therefore I spoke to the men. I told them that at Singapore they should say in talk upon the other ships and on the waterfront and in the eating places that the daughter of the Sultan Garuda was upon an island at such and such a place and desired that her father should come for her."

"I do not know where Singapore is," Ana said stubbornly. "How shall that help you?"

"They will talk," Maya replied patiently, as if explaining obvious truths to a witless one. "They will talk to the people who sail the water. They will talk to the merchantmen and the merchantmen will carry the word. There is nowhere in the islands where the merchantmen do not go. My father will hear of it, for he will capture a ship and someone will save his life by telling him that I am alive." She was silent while they watched her with wide, enormous eyes. "It cannot fail," she said positively and, standing up, began to rearrange the bright sarong. She had already offset much of her loss of prestige, and she had almost forgotten her pain.

The liquor had given Skinner Pitney courage. The weasel was becoming the wolf. He slumped at ease in his chair.

Roark had called him to celebrate. "We are on our own now. Drink to it!"

The women waited respectfully in the distance, uncomprehending, anxious only to serve the evening meal when Roark called for it.

"God-damned French ideas. The noble savage!" Roark said with a sneer. "They don't know these people as we know them. They're nothing more than cattle."

"All the same," Pitney said obliquely, "you should have sent that wildcat on with the ship."

Roark looked at him threateningly. "Are you saying that I cannot handle a child?"

Pitney waved his glass in an imitation of saluting. "There is nothing you cannot handle, your lordship, but that ball of fire is a troublemaker. She terrifies the other women."

"Good!" Roark returned obscurely. "They will be the more docile. There is nothing she can do to them."

"Two things," Pitney said forebodingly, putting

down his glass and holding up two fingers, "two things." He bent one of his fingers over. "Her father—"

"Her damned father is dead!" Roark broke across his words.

"They do not know it."

"And there is no way she can get a message to him."

"There is a way," Pitney replied craftily. "You do not know everything that happens. I make it my business to know. There is a way." He put his feet up on the table.

Roark stretched out and kicked them off with sudden anger. "How?" he roared.

"She told the Indonesians on the ship to spread the word at Singapore, to tell the merchantmen that the daughter of Sultan Garuda was here."

"How do you know this?" Roark demanded harshly.

"She told it to the children this morning"—for the first time Skinner Pitney's voice was quite simple—"and the children told me."

"Garuda is dead," Roark said with finality. Then he pounced. "Your second point, mister?"

Pitney moved finger and thumb to his index finger and bent it slowly over. "She has the look of death." His voice was thick now. "With that dagger, she will kill. The women know this."

Roark began to laugh. "She will not kill. It is a threat only. In a little she will come to me of herself. She has spirit; she has more spirit than all these women put together." He waved his hand to indicate the women sitting silently at the far end of the great hut. "With her, we will not grow dull on this godforsaken island." He leaned forward and glared at Pitney. "You will have nothing to do with her. You understand this? You have your own women." His eyes clouded and became brutal. "If you touch her, I will have you tied to a tree and castrated by the women. You understand?"

Pitney emptied his glass before he answered. "I have my own women and I would not relish a knife in my ribs. I will leave her alone."

"Drink!" Roark ordered drunkenly. "No one spies on us here. We are our own masters. This is no longer the Cape with Jesuits, and the missionaries, and the Governor who is too good to live. Drink, Pitney!"

"Pitney sleeps like the pig he is," the Tamil woman said softly.

There was a little ripple of unease among the other women. They were afraid of Pitney, not physically, but because of his devious mind and because of the brutality of his revenges. They watched him for a while in silence as he lay passed out on the table.

"Where has the Lord Tillman gone?" Kim Chi, the Chinese girl, asked doubtfully.

"To seek the daughter of Sultan Garuda." She made the name seem like a sickness. She spat largely and eyed the great brown-stained pool of tobacco juice. "She is a witch!"

"She is not a witch," Almira said calmly, "she is a willful child, nothing more. She should be beaten again."

"He should have sent her with the ship," the Tamil answered harshly.

"There will be no peace until she goes," another voice said.

"Therefore," the Tamil woman nodded, "we must make a plan."

Imperceptibly, three of the younger wives edged

away from her.

"You are afraid," the Tamil woman said scornfully. "What are you afraid of?"

"They are afraid of the dagger," Almira, contemplating the pattern of the mat on which she sat, murmured. "They are afraid of that pig there, they are afraid of the Lord Tillman, and they are afraid of her father. These things are enough for fear."

"She is but one child," the Tamil woman returned angrily.

Kim Chi looked up hurriedly. "You said yourself she is a witch and of that too I am afraid. She has told me to withhold myself from the Lord Tillman. She says that we are slaves and whores to give ourselves to him."

"That she has told me, too," another voice said.

"And me also."

"This is all foolishness." Almira's amazement was complete. "We cannot withhold ourselves, those of us whom he still wants. It is the law. We have been happy in the past."

"And yet"—the Chinese girl's voice was eager—"I would have liked a young man."

"What can a young man do that he cannot?" the Tamil woman demanded contemptuously. "His back is still strong. It is this devil child who has put these thoughts in your heads. This is a place of peace. We could be happy here again. Therefore," she repeated, "we must make a plan and rid ourselves of this witch."

"But how?" Kim Chi questioned, watching the malevolence in the Tamil woman's face.

Roark walked down the path with a lumbering dignity. He was drunk, but still had total control of himself. The women's guess was right; he was

looking for Maya. The voices of the children had
been noisiest from the northern side of the island.
They were silent now, but he knew that they were
still there. They would be with Maya; they
followed her everywhere, accepting her leadership.

He heard her voice before he reached the edge
of the screen of young palms on the sea beach
above the constant murmur of the surf. It rose and
fell in the singsong of the village story-teller. She
would be telling another of the Maya stories, he
thought. She had an inexhaustible supply of them.
He went quietly to the edge of the screen and
looked down. The beach was in shade, the sun so
low that the shallows and even the edge of the reef
were dark in the shadow of the palms. Maya was
seated on a coral boulder, cross-legged on a pad of
leaves. The children sat below her with upturned
faces. They followed the intricate, delicate movements of her hands with an enraptured attention.
She was telling the story of the mongoose in the
pit.

"And then"—she laughed, her eyes shining—
"the tiger stood upon the back of the bear, and
Maya the mongoose stood upon the back of the
tiger, and from there he could leap easily to the
rim of the pit. And so he leapt, and easily, to the
rim of the pit. And he left the others in the pit
behind him. And they were angry, and with their
claws they dug against the sides of the pit until the
earth came down, and they dug and they dug till
they were weary and their paws were sore and
bleeding. But at last they pulled enough earth
down to scramble over the rim and onto the
ground again, and they pursued Maya. All through
the night they followed in the tracks that he had
made, and at dawn he heard them coming and he

climbed into a great tree where hung a hornets' nest."

Maya broke off suddenly. "Look!" Her voice quivered with excitement. "They come."

At once the children turned away, the enchantment broken. They stared out to sea, following her pointing finger. Far away, like white specks in the low sunlight, they could see the sea birds coming back to roost. They stood watching them with an intensity of anticipation that Roark could not understand. He watched them also, swaying slightly on his feet, fascinated.

After a few minutes the birds came closer and closer so that they were now winged specks and very clear against the pale light of the east.

"Look!" Maya said abruptly.

Instantly the children turned to her. The degree of control that she had attained over them was incredible. She was holding her hand up, pointing high, and Roark, slightly impeded by the palm fronds, looked up into the sky where she pointed.

The sky was full of frigate birds wheeling on long, black wings, superb and graceful, making wide arabesques against the turquoise. The gulls came in. They were so close now that they could be seen as gulls. They flew slowly, gorged, flapping their wings to sustain the enormous weight of fish that they carried in their gullets.

Maya had risen to her feet. She stood on the pad of palm fronds, poised as if ready to take off in flight herself, and, once again, she flung up her arm. "Now!" she cried.

As though she commanded the evening ambush, streams of frigate birds dived on the leaders of the gulls. In an instant there was a turmoil in the air. The gulls swung off to left or to right or dived away from the raid, but always the thin-winged, exquisite precision of the frigate birds forced them to the moment of panic. Their gullets expelled the undigested fish. Now and then it could be seen flashing in the sunlight, and the frigate birds, turning in miracles of elegance, swooped in and took the fish as they fell.

Maya stood clapping her hands and laughing, her face turned up and eager.

Roark stood watching her from the screen of the trees. She is like a frigate bird herself, he thought, and then, grinning ruefully, thought that she was like a mongoose also. At last he turned and walked back along the path. As he went he thought, Is it possible that this utterly ruthless child is the temptress of my dreams? Her eyes still haunted him. As he reached the big hut, he answered himself out loud.

"Yes! It is possible! But if she is not, she will still be mine. She will be tamed!"

Then he clapped his hands and called for his food.

12

The long spring day whimpered under the cruel heat of the sun. The sand on the beach was too hot to walk on; even the children had withdrawn into the cool shelter of their huts to play. The island grew quiet as its inhabitants sank into the apathy and exhaustion of a long nap. Heat waves rose from the roofs and shimmered on the distant horizon. A languid lapping of the sea on the shore was the only movement that could be seen; no breeze stirred the palm fronds. The sky was devoid of clouds and seemed bleached of its normal blue by the sheer heat of the day.

That morning, the boy Rahmzi had seen the canoe first, but only by a fraction of a second. Maya knew at once that it was important to her as it lay, half covered with seaweed and palm fronds, on the tide line. It was a small canoe of the type used by boys in the Maldives Islands to learn the lore of the sea and the techniques of fishing. It was sea-battered; the float of the outrigger was gone, and one of the struts as well. The other still cocked up from the canoe as it lay over on one side, with ends of ropes drooping dejectedly from it. They pulled it over until it was upright, and with quick hands cleared it of rubbish and leaves.

"It is broken," the boy said.

"There is nothing broken that cannot be mended," Maya answered with a discerning eye. "This is mine."

"I saw it first," Rahmzi protested. She did not even answer him; she merely turned her head and looked at him for a moment.

"It is as you wish," he said hastily.

"It is mine," she repeated, "and it is my secret. We will hide it now in the bushes. Afterwards I will see what can be done with it."

Between them they carried it away from the beach. There was an ironwood tree just inside the line of shore palms and a flurry of young trees and scrub and East Indian palm beyond. In the middle of this they placed it and covered it with fronds.

"Now," Maya said, "you can go where you choose, but see that you say nothing of this now or hereafter—nothing."

"I will say nothing, Maya," Rahmzi went down the beach reluctantly.

Maya swung off the opposite way, her head down, thinking. She was light-hearted, elated even —not that she could see any immediate use for the canoe, but it was still a symbol of her independence, a symble of freedom.

They had been on the island three months now. Roark had organized a manner of life that suited him absolutely. The women looked after him with an enhanced devotion; they schemed for a place in his bed; they quarreled among themselves; they were lazy and incompetent, but they were also obedient, yielding to Roark's every desire. He was the master—more now than ever. He moved from the big hut late in the mornings to bathe and the women followed, adoringly, to bathe with him. They hung flowers round his head, and he looked like an inappropriate bearded imitation of the Greek god Pan with a powerful mixture of a fool thrown in. Food was ready for him if he clapped his hands; drink was always there.

The calm and peaceful days went by in timeless succession, each day precisely like the last except that the shower of cooling rain at times changed its hour of coming. It was seldom too hot or too cold at the Chagos Archipelago. It neither blew too hard nor grew too stiflingly still. The water was always warm, but not too hot to be refreshing in the midday sun, and all through most of the hot afternoons the cool trade winds blew.

Roark did no work now. He had expended all his inclination for work in the building of the village. Now it was no longer necessary for him to work; he had his women to do everything for him.

Skinner Pitney worked. He drove the eight Indonesian men whom Roark had brought ashore with an endless nagging energy. They fished, they sent down coconuts, they cleared scrub; and the women who Roark was not using at the time worked with them, under the lash of the bullwhip when they complained. The oil presses were set up. Roark had told him that they must have a cargo of palm oil for the ship when she next passed through, and in the pressing of the oil he could work out his obscure revenges with the whip. He drove his own two wives more harshly than any of the others. Oddly enough, they loved him. Even the children worked, carrying in the

coconuts to the husking, carrying the white
coconut meat to the presses, gathering shellfish.
The older boys went in the boats to fish with the
men. The whole village turned out to use the long
fishnet in the shallows. Everyone worked on the
island, Pitney hardest of all, a slave to his need to
establish his own superiority.

Only Roark did not work at all—Roark and
Maya. Maya had the quality of invisibility; she was
never there when work was necessary.
Sometimes, to please herself, she would go out
with the boys in the boat. She gathered shellfish
when she wished to wander in the shallow. She
would go up the leaning palms that hung out over
the water to get young coconuts if she was thirsty.
But she did these things when she chose and in her
own time, and she completely ignored Pitney.
Short of beating her, which he did not attempt
because of the dagger, there was nothing that he
could do.

The wives had tried to starve her—that was the
first of the Tamil's plans. But when Maya was
hungry, she sat herself down at Roark's table, and
he laughed, guessing the plans of his wives, and let
her eat. They had tried not talking to her, and she
had appeared unaware of it. They had made the
children keep away from her for five whole days
once, but the children themselves had brought
that to an end.

Roark sometimes sent for her in the afternoons.
He had developed an inquisitive passion for her
stories, always sensing the personal emphasis that
she put on the legends that her Hindu nurse had
woven into her being. He knew that she thought of
herself as the mongoose—weak, small, infinitely
resourceful, and magic. He knew that she had a

profound conviction of her ultimate triumph over him.

Occasionally he fondled her a little, and she would allow it with a humorous gleam in her eye, as if she knew perfectly well what his thought was and was prepared to allow him so much indulgence and no more. Improbably, a real friendship grew up between them, but when he tried to evaluate it, he knew that it was a fragile thing indeed.

Each morning, as a ritual she went, he knew, to the northeast to look into the sunrise.

No ships came.

On the evening of the second day after the finding of the canoe, Maya went back to the shore from the nightly sport of the frigate birds. The fishing boats were not in yet and, with the children, she went down to the landing place to watch them approaching. They were working towards the south end of the cove now, and they came drifting it with the light evening breeze in their sails, silhouetted and very beautiful against the sunset. Looking beyond them, she knew suddenly what she would do with the canoe. Underscoring the fishing boats, very dark against the last glow of the light, the line of the palms of the west island became a promised land. The canoe would make it a reality, would make it accessible.

The next morning, after her ritual search of the horizon to the northeast, she went to the hiding place. The canoe was safe.

It had dried out by now. One triangular piece was smashed out of the side almost amidship, but there would be no difficulty in putting a patch on

that. An ironwood branch would serve for the
broken strut. She could steal enough cord from
the stores to make the lashings. There remained
the float. She considered asking the boy Rahmzi to
help her, but decided at last that it was beyond
him. It would have to be shaped out of a solid
block, streamlined, and balanced so that it would
not make the canoe too heavy or unmanageable.
The whole thing had to be light enough for her to
handle, and she knew the limits of her strength.
She would appeal to Ameni. Ameni was the
shipwright, the skilled carpenter, the man on
whom Roark relied for all the woodwork of the
colony. The wife of Ameni would object, of course,
but that was unimportant; the wives always
objected when she asked their men for anything.
Ameni would do it, but how could she stop him
from talking?

She thought for a little, then went and found the
boy.

"Rahmzi, you would like a small boat to sail in
the shallows?" she said to the boy.

"I have a small boat."

"Nonetheless, you would like another—a bigger
one." She stretched her arms to indicate the
length. "A boat as large as this." He grinned at her
suddenly, grasping her meaning. "Ameni would
like to build you such a boat."

"He would not!"

"But if I asked him, he would."

Rahmzi laughed outright. "What devilment do
you do now?"

"No devilment. I need a canoe so that I may be
by myself when I wish to be."

"You will not take me with you, then?"

"Sometimes," she replied graciously. "There
will be occasions when I need company."

"Who is to ask Ameni?"

"You," Maya said firmly, "but I will help you when he says no."

It took two weeks for the float to be made. She and the boy bored holes through it for the lashings of the struts. They had to make a fire to heat an iron, and it took ten days for them to get through the hard wood, but there was no hurry.

Maya had not yet learned that the Tamil woman was advocating the use of arsenic, of which there was a canister in the stores, to rid themselves of her. The Tamil was especially angry with her now, for Maya had prejudiced Roark against her by her ridicule—the Tamil woman's breasts drooped shamefully and the skin of her neck was scrawny and dry-looking—and she had become the subject of Maya's inexhaustible supply of stories. How much Roark understood, she did not know, but there had been several bursts of trouble between him and the Tamil, and that was sufficient for Maya.

The lashing of the canoe was easy enough; Maya had done such work on her father's boats. She took pride in it, working out the traditional patterns with care and memory.

When it was all finished, the canoe was too heavy for the two of them to carry to the water.

"I will fetch Nessumontu and Senwadjet," Rahmzi said.

"You will not!" Maya said firmly. "This is our secret only, Rahmzi. We do not share it!" She began to undo the lashings so that they could carry the heavy wooden float separately.

A month after they had first seen the canoe, they carried it in the moonlight to the cove beach and hid it, the canoe and the float together, in a safe and well hidden patch of scrub and palm fronds. It required much effort.

Three nights later, with the lashings renewed, they launched it, and in the still brilliance of the night they paddled over the bay shallows with the mysterious luminiscences of the water following in their wake until they were sure that the canoe was seaworthy and that she could handle it alone. Then, grunting and gasping in the darkness, they dragged it back to the security of their hiding place.

The Tamil used the arsenic two days later. It was a remarkable coincidence. She had been awaiting an opportunity for a full month. Maya ate one mouthful of the curry that hid it, but only one. She recognized at once that there was something evil in it.

The Tamil had a daughter named Djanah. Watching her mother, Maya pushed the plate across to the daughter. "I am not hungry. Eat, Djanah!"

The Tamil woman snatched the plate away from her daughter.

"I am Maya," Maya said, a smile flitting across her face. "Next time, she will eat it or she will feel my dagger."

Nothing more was said. None of the other women, not even the three who knew about the plan, offered comment. They sat quietly eating, and Maya sat placid with her beautiful hands in her lap and gave no sign either of anxiety or of anger.

That night, with the boy Rahmzi to help her, Maya dragged the canoe down to the water again. She had brought things with her—rice, dried fish, a line and hooks, a machete, a small grass mat, a length of cloth, tea and a cooking-pot, flint and tinder.

As they dragged the canoe, the boy kept whispering, "Where are you going, Maya? To where are you going?"

At last, when they had dragged the canoe into the water and it floated, she wetted her lips and looked at him. "To be by myself. This time you do not come, my friend. But brush out the marks of the canoe in the sand before you go home, and if the Lord Tillman grows too angry about my leaving, tell him that the Tamil tried to poison me."

"Then she will poison me," Rahmzi said reasonably.

Maya shook her head in the moonlight. "No, she will not try to poison anyone for a time now."

"Nonetheless, I am afraid of her."

"But you are afraid also of the Lord Tillman. You must choose."

A gleam of light showed through the palm trees, but only for a little; then it disappeared and the palms themselves diminished. From a dark cliff, they sank slowly to the dimensions of a wall. The water became very lonely. It was not still this night. The wind blew softly and easily across it, making ripples that beat against the bow of the canoe with gentle liquid noises. Maya was not afraid. Often enough in the past she had moved at night in the dark hiding places where her father's ship had anchored. She was aware of the special qualities of darkness and of water.

The canoe was not easy to handle. It took time to discern its rhythm and its character. At the beginning she discovered, looking back over her shoulder at the light, that she was moving southward. One time, looking back over her shoulder, she found that there was no longer a light, and she chose a bright star in the arc of the horizon where she knew the west island lay and steered by that.

The star paths were broken on the water but, as she looked down through the outline of the out-rigger struts, she could see other lights—the pulsing glow of the jelly-fish, the vague, creeping green of unidentifiable creatures in the coral, the darting flash of a startled fish. She came to a stretch of water that was milk-white in the moonlight, from the white sand bottom of the baby. Fish paths crossed it at intervals, but for the most part it was as if the sea bed itself shone up at her and the canoe floated on a pool of milky light, the float and the outrigger very dark against its brilliance.

She was aware of the west island first as a strengthening of the horizon. Then it was like a low edging, a fringe of darkness, a barrier, and at last a cliff stretching out wide at either hand, losing itself in ultimate and mysterious darkness. She came to dark water and broken coral, and finally to the insubstantial clearness of the shallows, and the canoe's bottom struck softly on sand.

The tide was falling but she knew that it would rise again with the sun. She dragged the canoe far enough onto the beach to grip firmly, then went ashore with the bow line of the rope in her hand. It was long enough to reach to the trunk of a small tree, and she fastened it there.

She was very tired. Her arms were aching, there was a burning pain in her joints, and her back was stiff and sore. She took the cloth and the tinder and the flint and a little bundle of coconut husk, and in the warm darkness of the beach palms she lay down to sleep.

Here in the cover of the palms the wind was

still. There was a rustle only in the uppermost leaves, and over it occasionally the night squeak of an uneasy bird. In the fallen palm fronds below the trees, she could hear rustling, and over the sand the soft, all but inaudible, whisper of the land crabs moving down to the water to moisten their gills. She lay quite still.

She was almost afraid.

The light of the morning sun woke her, for she lay with her face towards the east. She had planned exactly what she meant to do, and she woke clear-eyed and ready. It took her no more than a moment to gather the cloth and the unused tinder; then she tore off a branch and wiped out her footprints on the beach.

The canoe was turned sideways in the shallows, already afloat. She went down to it walking backwards, bushing out the footsteps of the night and of the morning and, as soon as she was in the canoe, moved down the coast towards the south. The men who had gone over to loose the pigs on the west island had told her of a deep bay, a small interior lagoon, halfway down the length of the island. As she paddled, she looked out over he shoulder, but there was no sign of searching boats.

The sun was well up when she came to the mouth of the inner lagoon, and she slipped into it at the top of the tide. They had told her that most of it was covered with soft mud, but that there were deep pools in it. She headed north again and found what she was searching for, a stream that led in through the arching palms, to a place secret and unviolated by men. Moving her things from the canoe, she tipped it until it filled with water, then added large pieces of coral to it until it sank. Then she covered it with weeds and fronds until it no longer had the shape of anything that floated.

While she worked at it, she became aware of the sandpipers. As on the first day on Salomon Island, they floated silently like moths, watching her with their curious, bright eyes. The sandpipers on Salomon Island had deserted her after the first few days, frightened by the clumsy insistence of the children to chase them, scared by the older women, intimidated by the axe noises and the cutting of the trees and the building of the village, and, above all, afraid of Roark's enormous, noise-filled progress in building his new kingdom. It could be that these were the same sandpipers, but it did not matter. The birds had come back to her; it was a good omen.

She made a bundle of the things in the cloth and moved back towards the lagoon beach, looking for a mark by which she could identify the place. The jungle growth was denser here than on Salomon Island. There was more ironwood, more bushes, and flowers, more small palms; but close to the lagoon beach, it was clearer and she found almost at once a configuration of rocks that was enough for guidance.

She moved lightly now. A happiness overtook her and occasionally, on the open ground beneath the trees, she skipped like a child at play. Sometimes she sang in a sudden outburst of energy. An immense and indefinable gladness encompassed her. She was alone. She possessed herself. She was her own!

After enjoying the sights and sounds of her new surroundings for a long while, up to the north at the edge of the pool that struck suddenly blindingly blue through the pillars of the palms, she made herself a camp of sorts. She was utterly confident. They would not search for her this morning. They would not discover that she was gone until the day was almost done. After she had eaten, she would look out to identify the sails of the fishing boats, but they would have put out long before her absence was discovered. Not until tomorrow would they search for her. When she had eaten, she slipped out of her sarong, unwound the silken bandage of the dagger and stood, naked and wholly relaxed, as if freed of a burden. Yet, when she went towards the water, she took the weapon with her and laid it on a log by the waterside. The water was cool, and only faintly brackish. The bottom was brilliant white sand, but the blue-green color persisted. She swam in it naked and free, her skin outlined in tiny silver bubbles. Now and then she laughed. And the sandpipers wheeled and floated over the water.

The search did not reach the west island until the third day. A furious Roark had harried the men relentlessly down the islands of the eastern side, certain that she had waded or swum across the shallow channels. They had found nothing. He had sent the boats to Peras Banhos, the northernmost island, and there too they had found nothing—only their own footprints on the wind-smoothed sand and the marks of their own boats from when they had gone there to release the first of the pigs.

The boats reached Eagle, the west island, late in the afternoon, and Maya watched them, lying on her stomach in the fringing scrub, her eyes brilliant with mischief and her whole small body like a leaf on the wind with the intoxication of freedom.

They searched carelessly. Twice men passed within touching distance of her. She watched them with stifled laughter, and when they were out of earshot she laughed aloud. Once, as Skinner Pitney came plodding along the beach, the sandpipers swooped down low and flashed through the bushes that hid her.

"Do not betray me, my friends," she whispered. "Go!"

Pitney plodded on, unseeing. The men went away in the end, Pitney calling them back to the boats. His voice was rasping and irritable.

She had an impulse to go out on the beach as their sails filled for the homeward run, but the remembered caution of her father held her safe. She lay still, laughing, and the sandpipers came down again and perched on a bough above her shoulder.

In the days that followed, she explored all the island. Three times she saw the pigs that had been loosed. There was a boar and four young sows. They were rooting amongst the fallen coconuts, but already they had acquired the instinct of wildness; they fled when they heard her coming. For the rest, she had the company of the indignant gulls, the frigate birds that eyed her from the palms and the ironwood trees, and always and incessantly the silent friendship of the sandpipers.

On the outer beach there was wreckage—a mast, a cabin door, carvings, and a broken spar. There were tree trunks, one of them with a bright lizard basking on it in the sun, and sprouting coconuts, and crabs' backs and shells and sand dollars, and the fragile puff-balls of the Portuguese men-of-war. The island was a treasure chest of wreckage from ships and marine life.

She carried her bundle with her wherever she went, and she slept wherever the sunset found her. She made her fires deep in among the palms where no light could betray her to the outside, and even the smoke was reduced by the branches and the wind. She sang and she laughed and she was completely free.

But on the twelfth day—she had not counted, but it was the twelfth day—she took the cooking-pot and the cloth and the few things that were left to her, and she went back round the head of the inner lagoon and searched for the stream where she had left the canoe. That night she slept close to it, and in the morning, after she had gone to the eastern beach for her bright ritual of the sunrise, she began to free the boat of the pieces of coral and the rubbish and the weeds.

At sunset she headed back for Salomon Island, the wind behind her, helping her this time. The sense of freedom persisted in her. It had been vital for her to get away from the schemings of the other women and the demands of the children and the acrid bitterness of the man Pitney, but that necessity was now past. She could go back with a sense of victory.

She landed in the night close to the southern tip of Salomon Island. She could make it out clearly by the darkness of the palms against the low stars. It took an hour to get Rahmzi silently out of the family hut, and another hour of cautious maneuvering to beach the canoe, through all of which she bubbled with silent laughter as if her whole entity were full of bright colors and lighter than air. When Rahmzi came whispering with inquisitiveness, she drew him down to the canoe.

Only when they had pulled it into the depths of the beach scrub and brushed over the sand to the water's edge would she answer his questions.

"I went where I wished to go," she whispered. "I wished to be by myself. There is nothing more to tell." As they went back towards the village, she stopped the boy and asked, "Was the great Emperor of Salomon Island angry?" Her voice was light and indifferent.

"He was more angered than I have seen him," Rahmzi replied wonderingly. "The Tamil woman was beaten, but she has not done anything to me. My mother says that she will not try anything again."

"Ha!" Maya said, skipping a little.

Her mind darted from the Tamil to the community as a whole. "Has the child of Mai Yazid come yet?" she asked.

"A girl," Rahmzi said affirmatively. "It cries much. I think it will not live. It is Pitney's child. Pa Pahzen thinks it is his, but its hair is the color of Pitney's, and the women say that they know."

"This they would know," Maya agreed equably, "the matters of the bed and the cooking place. They have no other knowledge. Their minds are like the minds of sheep."

A great weariness had come over Roark in the quiet of the hut. His lust for this child-woman's body was driving him close to insanity. The labors in the heat of the day, as well as the search party for her, had sapped his strength, and his mood plunged into the darkest depths of despair. He lay naked across his cot in the unlit hut and stared upward into the darkness. His mind was numb, and the very air he breathed seemed heavy and oppressive. His eyes, closed, and wispy, foglike tendrils of sleep drifted about him. It was as if he stood in a dense mist while colored lanterns moved about beyond his sight; then, a single bright light flamed before him, and he hastened toward it until he came into a clearing in the midst of a jungle, sunlit and empty but for a woman wrapped in veils of such beautiful colors as to make him halt for breath. As he stared, the bright veils began to float free in a rainbow of colors that obscured all else. Then a pair of lips, moist, gently parted, appeared. Then above them, indigo-blue gems became a pair of haunting eyes, with a depth that beckoned to him. The swirling mass of veils became a face of fragile beauty formed with the skill of an artist expending all his talents in one effort of beauty. The eyes held him entranced. The lips formed voiceless words that enthralled his very soul.

"Reach out your hands. Take me. I am yours."

When he stretched forth his hand, a long, sharp dagger thrust into his flesh, and in searing pain, he withdrew. The face laughed and tossed brilliant tresses that flowed about it in wild disarray, as black as a moonless night.

The voiceless words increased and became intense, blinding his will to all but the beauty that beckoned, calling, crying out for his touch. He lunged forward carelessly again, and with evil eagerness the dagger plunged deep into his body until he sobbed in agony and the burning whiteness of the pain wiped away his vision. He tried to withdraw again, but each movement freshened the ecstatic torture of the plunging dagger.

Roark's eyes flew open, and he stared into the darkness again as his senses returned. Cursing his weakness for this woman, he rose, lighting a candle beside his cot, and donned his short breeches. He would send for one of his wives to ease his mind and his loins, and he'd be damned before he would let Maya's little games torture him again. This noble little savage would in the end be bent to his will, just as the others had been.

But Roark's thoughts were still confused. He had yet to see the face of the temptress of his haunting dreams, his soul's mate. Was it truly Maya? Why did this child fill him with such unease?

13

Rahmzi flung the small net in a wide, beautiful curve and stood for a moment in the frozen pose of a Greek statue. The net sank, and he drew it in to him and the fish leapt, furiously enmeshed in it, in a splendor of bright colors.

"Put it with the others," Maya said.

As he waded into the shallow holding pool, Maya stood meditative.

"I have said all the prayers to the gods for the safe return of the ship," she murmured when he came out again, hardly bothering whether he heard the words or not. "I have made the sacrifices."

Rahmzi, gathering the net to make another cast, caught the word 'sacrifice' and cocked his head up. "It was you, then, who stole Ma Pythia's lamb."

"It was I," Maya agreed, as if the matter were of

no importance at all. "Also I took rice and roots and sugar from Fatima's hut."

"The sugar also!" Rahmzi nodded, as if things were beginning to add up. "And the sweet-meats . . ."

"From Tillman's hut." Maya smiled at him delicately. "But those were for myself."

"For that I was beaten!"

Maya nodded slightly. "I know," she said softly.

"Ai-e-e-e! You are a devil, as the Bantu girl says."

"What is she to you?"

"Nothing," Rahmzi replied. "Only she is angry because after you talked to her at the full of the moon, she did not go to the Lord Tillman, and he was angry with her and she was beaten."

"With each unjust beating the soul acquires reward," Maya misquoted from the Chinese saying.

"Ai-e-e-e!" Rahmzi said again and made a fresh cast with the net.

"I made the proper sacrifices, but nothing has come," Maya said. "Therefore, I must try other things."

Rahmzi looked at her suspiciously. "What?" His voice was uneasy.

"All that my Hindu nurse taught me I remember," Maya answered obliquely, and waited while her memory moved back into her childhood.

"What did she tell you?"

"That a woman can become a mana. This she told me, but it requires rituals."

"What is a mana?"

"A sorceress, a priest, a healer, a vessel for the spirits of the ancient ones." She poured out the words as if they interferred with her thought processes. "I do not know the rituals. Morever, it

requires the help of another mana. But if I had a
head . . .''

"God alone is real!" Rahmzi dropped the net,
his eyes bulging. He made the familiar praise into
an oath.

The Tamil woman crouched on the matting, her
shoulders bent and inconsolable. Occasionally she
picked at a ragged thread of palm frond. She
looked old and weary.

"This is your own damned doing," Roark said
sharply. "These things you bring upon yourself.
Leave her alone!"

"She says that she will kill me."

"You have tried to kill her." Roark's voice was
brutally frank. "It will be no more than just."

"I do not wish to die!"

"Nor did she," Roark's voice rasped. "But you
tried to kill her with poison—my poison!"

"That she-devil will make trouble—always she
will make trouble! She must be killed!" Her lips
trembled as she gazed fearfully at Roark.

Skinner Pitney stood against the other chair,
brow twisted in agreement as he listened to the
old woman. "She's right there! That little bitch
will make trouble always. Give her the God-
damned papers and send her on when the ship
comes back."

"We would have been content without her," the
Tamil woman said morosely. "Now we are against
her, all of us, but we do not trust each other. The
young wives scorn us and talk against us, and . . .
and . . ." She stopped and looked up pleadingly at
Roark. "And they do not always come to your bed
when they are called. It is her doing, all of it!"

"God's death!" Roark grunted. "That is because
you are fools, and the young wives are fools also.

In the end"—he shrugged his huge shoulders—
"they will come. It is no matter here on the island.
We have time; other things we may lack, but we
have all the time that there is under God."

The old woman muttered something piously,
and in almost the same tone went on, "But what of
this word that she will kill me?"

"Who told you?"

"The boy Rahmzi."

"Ah!" Roark exclaimed quickly. "If he told you,
she told him to tell you. And if you were told, she
will not do it. She does not give warnings, that
one."

"That is true, Mr. Tillman, sir," Pitney said,
anxious not to be left out of the discussion. "That
is true."

"Why has she said this?" Roark asked sourly.
"Why do you think she has said this?"

"Because," the Tamil woman answered naively,
"I told the black girl to put poison mushrooms in
her rice."

"That's why she's run away again," Roark said
reflectively. He scratched his chin. "I thought we
would get to it sooner or later. Did you know this,
Skinner?" He glared at the man.

"The Bantu girl told me."

"Did she do it?"

"She said she would not harm the girl for the
Tamil." He nodded down at the old woman on the
mat. "She told Maya of the plan instead."

"And Maya took the canoe and went. Where is
she this time? Peras Banhos? Eagle? Diego
Garcia?"

"God knows!" Pitney replied, intimating his
opinion that God also did not care.

Roark shrugged his shoulders. "It may be"—he
stood directly over the Tamil woman, his face bent

over her head—"that she will kill you this time.
That is in her mind, and it is in her hands also. If
she does, I will not punish her, for you have
brought this thing upon yourself, woman. It is no
more than justice. I will not this time have you
beaten, for it may be that you are about to die."

On her hands and knees, the Tamil backed out of
the great hut; as she went, he heard, floating back
over her shoulder, the words of the old woman.

"I am forsaken! I am forsaken!"

"I don't understand you anymore," Pitney said.

Roark glowered at him. "I do not require your
understanding, fool. I should have sent that one on
to Singapore."

"I don't understand you," Pitney repeated
defiantly. "The old woman is right; that girl has
destroyed the peace of this island. She has tried to
destroy your authority over the others."

"What do you know of peace or authority?"
Roark roared at him. "What do you know of her?
She is worth all these women. She has spirit, she
has fire, she has life. These . . . women!" He
dismissed them with a gesture of contempt. "You
could not understand her. You are from the
gutters of a London slums. She is the daughter of a
leader of men. You could never understand the
mind of an aristocrat."

Six days later, when the boys came running up
the path to shout that the canoe was coming—
Maya no longer crept back in the darkness—
Roark himself went down to the beach. She
handled the canoe beautifully now, her shoulders
moving with the paddle in an exquisite economy of
effort. The upper half of her body was bare, her
sarong adjusted below her breasts. Roark felt a
rich, impotent fury of desire sweep through him.

As she came up the beach, she lifted the paddle in salute. "The turtle are laying on the northern beaches. It would be well to collect the eggs. I have a score myself." She offered no apology, no explanation of her absence.

Roark laughed at her. He was always surprised and impressed by her candor and her contempt for authority.

The children rushed in and hauled the canoe up, taking the turtle eggs from her.

"If you want them, you had better send the boats before nightfall. There is a big wind coming."

Roark nodded to her as an adult. He no longer treated her as a child or even as a young girl. "I have seen the cloud."

He looked over the line of the western breakers. They were high and very brilliant in the sun, angrier than usual, a continuous line of white from which leapt brighter summits of breakers. Beyond them on the horizon there was a small flower of cloud. It was hardly bigger than the sails of a ship. It was very distant, so far that he could not even judge the distance, but it had an evil light, a mingling of purple and silver wholly different from the clouds that built up day after day in the hot, upward currents of the air. Roark watched it carefully, according it a large measure of respect.

The children lifted the canoe from the water and began to carry it up the beach to its usual place.

Maya stopped them in mid-stride. "No, take it there!" She pointed to the place where a clump of ironwood came close to the sand edge. "Push it in as far as—wait! I will show you."

She walked down the beach with it and Roark watched her curiously, sitting on a boulder of coral. On the horizon, a screen of gigantic thunderclouds grew out of the sea and towered, peerless, to fifty thousand feet, closing in on them.

Before the children returned, Pitney came down to the beach. "Have you seen the barometer?" he asked.

Roark nodded curtly.

"Bottom's falling out of it," Pitney went on with a ill-humored relish. "Best make peace with our maker. It's going to blow."

Roark grunted again.

Pitney picked up the direction of Roark's eyes. "Ha! So that's it." Sobered by Roark's look, he sat down on a smaller boulder.

Maya came back. "It is a typhoon," she said over her shoulder almost indifferently as she passed them. She sat down behind them in the shade, her eyes also fixed on the rising clouds.

The children played noisily for a while in the shallows and then appeared to catch the contagion of apprehension. The air was lifeless; no leaf moved in the palm trees. Even the birds were still. The water was glass-smooth. Only the roar of the surf was unnaturally loud and distinct. They came up from the shallows and sat with Maya, demanding a story.

Maya silenced them and sat still, silent herself for a moment, still watching the clouds.

"I was with my father in a typhoon south of Sumatra," she finally said.

"What happened?" one of the children asked.

"Be still!" she replied harshly. "It took our masts and our sails, and four good men drowned."

Oppressed by the silent tension, the children left them at last, drifting quietly in through the palms.

"It will miss us," Roark said, an hour later. "It is moving across the north. We will get the edge of it, though." By a physical effort, he broke himself out of his lethargy. "Get everything lashed up! Get the boats in! There's no telling what this devil storm might do. We have not got more than ten feet above the water at the highest point of the island." After a pause he added, "We could be swept."

"Never been swept before with all these palms," Pitney said.

"Palms grow fast," Roark said, more to himself than to the other man. "The ironwood and the dadap are a better guide. I'd say the island has not been swept in fifty years, but that's not to say that it could not happen now. Now get the bloody damned men to work, mister!"

Maya stood behind them in the shadows. "It is wise," she said softly. "This will be a very great wind. A supreme wind!"

The first of the supreme winds swooped across the island an hour before darkness. All through the afternoon the wind had risen, beginning with gusts from every point of the compass, settling to a steady blast from the west that bent the trees over and held them there almost without relenting, the palm fronds streaming downwind like the hair on a woman's head as she swims through breakers. There was nothing to fear in such a wind. Here and there the crown of a palm snapped off with a sharp pistol shot and went whistling, but these things had no importance. It was an honest, steady gale of a wind, and under it there were even sudden brilliances of gold and indigo and purple from the sunset.

Then, with the sunset, the Devil Wind hit them. It came almost from the north across the island from the outer sea. It came so suddenly that it was impossible to note the lull that there must have been between the steady wind from the west and this new brutality.

They were not prepared for a wind from the north; they had no expectation of it. They had come to believe that the gale would come only from the west. In its steady and relentless path through the palm trunks, it had lulled them into a false sense of security, so that the new direction affected them with a sense of shock.

At its first onslaught, the Devil Wind cut a wide swathe through the trees, as a sickle cuts through standing corn. The swathe was clear of the village, beyond the last of the Indonesian huts. They could just see in the final silver of the twilight the approach of the cyclone's spume that came with it, blotting everything out. Then they were enveloped themselves and could hear only the crash of the trees, the snap of the trunks, and the shriek of twisted wood. Water came with the cyclone. The hut roofs went with the very first onrush.

In the half-dark, Maya and the children could hear Roark roaring, and to his voice they crawled, unable to breathe against the wind, their eyes full of sand and tears.

Another devil gust rocked the trees, and another, and a third, and it seemed as though they could hear the huts blowing apart.

It was not possible to remember afterwards in detail what had happened. Maya could recall only the shriek of the birds as the Devil Wind hit them. They had been insanely restless all through the early evening, had cowered, bemused and unseeing, in the steady rush of the western wind. Now it seemed that they exploded in an instant of despairing fury and disappeared with the brutal rush of the cyclone.

Roark was in a corner where six trees close together made a sort of windbreak. He had four of the smallest children with him. As the others reached him, he grabbed at them, packing them into a tight, compact bundle in the small shelter. All the while he kept up a tremendous shouting, unintelligible most of it, some of it abusive and vulgar, using his voice as a guide to safety. The women began to come in towards it. Maya felt the Chinese girl next to her and one of the Indian girls. There were others beyond. Once, when the fury of the noise for a moment relented, she heard Pitney's voice shouting beyond them. After a while no more women came, and even as she was certain that no more would come, the wind dropped.

"What happened?" Maya asked, her voice sounding unreal in the overpowering hush.

It was possible to hear Roark's words also. "The eye of the storm," he shouted. "This is it. The center! Come on," he said urgently, "we must get to the ironwood trees. We will have the sea over us if there is another wind like that."

It was hardly possible to believe that the sea was not over them already. Wind-driven water under the cyclone had flooded the belt between them and the reef beach. They crouched in a streaming flood that even in the hot tropic air chilled them to the bone as they waited for the Devil Wind to return.

Roark moved when he thought that they understood his intention, and they crawled with him and behind him, touching one another in the darkness, a bruised, terrified, rippling line of children and women. None of the men had reached them.

The lull in the storm held, a lull in relative terms only. It was stronger than the wind from the west had been earlier. It was punctuated by the snapping of tree trunks; twice, as they crawled, crowns from the palms crashed to the ground close to them. The thud of coconuts torn away from their stems was unceasing.

The fiery lightning blazed for the first time as they reached the edge of the clump of ironwoods. It produced a high, simultaneous shriek from the children. In its blue glare Maya saw Almira, looking old and terrified, and the boy Rahmzi, and Roark, moving crouched with four small children in his enormous muscular arms.

Suddenly everything was easier. Even the wind seemed lighter. The lightning flashes were continous. They moved on their feet now, hurrying towards whatever protection Roark had in mind. Their trust in him was absolute; his stature among them seemed gigantic. He went ahead of them in the intermittent light, and when they came up with him, he was lashing the small children into the forks of the gnarled and arched branches of the ironwoods.

He gave the boy Rahmzi a length of cord and another to Maya. "Get up! Make yourself fast to the trees!"

"Praise Allah!" Rahmzi said in a high exclamation of relief.

Roark was helping the old women. One by one he got them into place. He began to shout again, bellowing for Pitney and the others. There was no answer. They could hear nothing above the wind and the deep, shuddering pounding of the surf against the reef. While they still stood with their feet on the ground, they could feel it trembling underneath them. The whole island had acquired an impermanence, as if it might at any moment disappear from beneath them and join the ancient Atlantis below the sea.

And then the Devil Wind fell upon them again. The second blast hit them, still from the north, an hour after they had fastened themselves into the ironwood, an hour of cold and exhaustion and fear. Its roar was more terrible even than that of the first because perhaps their ears had permitted them to hope. The water came with it, blotting out even the nearest trees. They could hear the crash and collisions of the broken palm trees, the terrible wood noises again, and then, behind them, another and altogether different noise—a noise that had the deep thunder of the reef itself in it and that came roaring up in a slow, intolerable volume of sound. Then they were aware of deep water sweeping under the foam beneath their feet, broken and split by the tree trunks, ghostly white and racing. It passed under them, lapping some of the lower places where they clung.

Quite suddenly, it was gone, and the roar of the wind with it, and the foam was gone too, and they could see the nearest trees straightening themselves. Through the ruined palm trees, Roark saw a ragged patch of sky and a few pale stars in it. They were left with only the immeasurable crash and thunder of the surf.

After a long time they heard voices shouting. Roark, already down from his refuge in the ironwood tree, shouted back, and the voices came towards him—Indonesians voices, men's. They came slowly, picking their way across broken tree trunks and palm fronds and the wreckage of the village. They were very close before their words came clear above the thunder of the reef. They were shouting that the Tamil was gone. When they came up finally to the safety of the ironwoods, they seemed to transfer their terrors and their responsibilities to Roark. The fear went out of their voices when they saw Roark.

"The Tamil is gone," they said to his questions, shouting still, for they had to shout to be heard. "She was with us when the water swept us and after—she was gone!"

"And where is Pitney?" Roark roared, his voice forebodingly angry.

"He is in the shelter of the stores hut with the rest of the women."

"Has he sent to search for her?"

"He has done nothing," one of the men said simply. "Therefore we came to seek for you."

"Stay with these!" Roark ordered the leader of the men. "If the wind comes again, tie them in the branches as they were before. Ameni, Zurim, you come with me."

He began to fight his way through to the cove beach. Flashes of the now distant lightning gave enough brilliance still for the women to see him. He appeared heroic among the shadows, sure and powerful in his movement through their splintered world. They took hope and courage from him.

He crashed his way through to the beach, the two Indonesians following him. At the edge of the water he stood shouting. Maya could not make out what he was shouting; it must have been the Tamil woman's name, which she had never heard. After a little, he worked his way down the beach to where the pathway had led to the village. Everywhere was cluttered with wreckage. The path itself was choked with timbers from the huts, rafters, even broken furniture. Roark thought that he saw the ruins of his great oak chair, but the lightning flash did not last long enough for him to be certain. He

moved up the path, shouting all the time. There
was no answer, except that when he came closer to
the village he could hear an unintelligible babble
of hysteria in women's voices and children's; they
seemed to be berating the man Skinner Pitney.

In the twisted wreckage of their refuge, the
others heard his voice again, mastering the
thunder of the surf. He was calling to them to
make their way to the village. The women stirred
uneasily, their movements slow and indecisive, as
if they no longer had power over their own wills.

Maya climbed down first. She loosened the end
of the rope that Roark had given her and that had
held her to the ironwood branch through the
worst of the wind. Stiffly, she felt down with one
foot, found the shoulder of the boy Rahmzi, used it
as a foothold, and dropped to the ground. Her
movements had no spring. The boy watched her,
silent, and fumbled at the knot of his own lashing.
After a moment, he felt for the knife that he
carried, and cut the knot. They moved off together
towards the village.

Maya's body was slack, her shoulders drooped,
her head bent forward. She was still frightened.
For the first time in her life, she had recognized
real fear, the fear of something that man had not
made and that man could not control.

She had little memory of the night except the
explosion of the birds, the first roar of the Devil
Wind, and the heart-shattering thunder of the sea
that swept across the island. Superimposed on
these was the image of Roark Tillman. It seemed
twice life size—Roark, with his enormous
muscular shoulders, carrying a fountain of
children; Roark standing against the lightning like
a latter-day Hercules, securing their lashings and
shouting coarse, obscure words of comfort; Roark

managing the hysterical women, slapping them into sober caution, helping them into security; Roark plunging through the dawn light and the wreckage, searching for the Tamil woman on the rubbish-strewn beach. He had acquired a new stature in her mind, a heroic dimension, though she could not put it into words even to herself.

When she saw him again in what had been the village, with the morning sun flooding down through the ravished palm trees, it frightened her once more to see that he was only his own size, that he was stooped with weariness, that his face was grey and haggard. For the first time, and with a sense of having come into collision with a fundamental truth, she realized that Roark was a man like other men, in no way immune from the limitations of mortality. She was aware of a feeling for him, though she could not have given it a name—something that transcended the limited friendliness and respect that had grown irregularly since they had come to these islands. Only the hoarse, bull-throated voice remained of the night's illusion of a god. Today he was once again just a man.

He was furious with the man Pitney, who still lay in the shelter of the boulders that they had used as a foundation for the now vanished stores hut. He lay there, wet and bedraggled and almost invisible under a tangled heap of women—his own two wives, May Ling, Astram the Malay, and Zada the Bantu girl. The children who had been with his group sat apart, watching them. Pitney was paralyzed with fear. Gradually, under the savage lashing of Roark's tongue, he lifted himself from the ruckus. There was something inherently comic about him, but Maya could not bring herself to laugh; she was still too shattered herself.

Eventually he sat up.

The other Indonesian men had come up from the beach. Roark made a swift count. They were all there except the Tamil woman.

"You yellow-spleened son of a whore!" he bellowed at Pitney. "Sit up straight and look at me and tell me what happened!"

"She was with us and the wave came," Pitney answered under the lashing. "We had a rope and we hung on to it. And then she screamed, and after that we saw nothing more of her."

"It was the girl who did it," the woman Astram said quietly.

Roark took three quick strides forward and stood over them as they lay on the ground. The water had washed all resistance out of them. "The girl? What girl?"

"The girl Maya."

"Fools! Imbeciles! The girl Maya was not here. She was with me over at the ironwood trees."

"She hated the Tamil." May Ling hardly breathed the words.

"She wished her dead and now she is dead," Zada, the Bantu woman, added.

"Be silent! Get up from there—stand up! The girl had nothing to do with this. She was with me. I will not have this talk. She could have done nothing."

May Ling rose to her knees and held her hands forward in a gesture of supplication. "She called up the Devil Wind. She has the magic."

"She is a witch," the other women said in chorus.

Even Roark hesitated for an instant, as if appalled by their complete agreement with each other.

"You are half-wits, cowards, all of you. You

have not all of you together the strength of this one girl. This is not to be said again, or I myself will beat the woman who says it." He turned and looked at Maya.

She stood there as she had stood from the very beginning, her shoulders stooped so that she looked, in the pulsing flicker of the lightning, even more childish, more fragile than she was.

She was still frightened.

14

Maya found the body on the third day after the typhoon. It was caught between two coral boulders in the shallows just below the south point of Diego Garcia Island. For a long time she stood quite still, the water halfway up her thighs, staring at it. The sarong, secured round the old woman's waist with a length of rope, had reversed itself like an umbrella blown inside out, and now covered the upper half of the body. One leg had been torn off at the thigh, either by sharks or on the sharp spikes of the coral. Fish had nibbled at the flesh elsewhere. It had a macabre cleanliness, tide-washed.

"Is it true, then, that I am a witch?" Maya asked it, her voice expressionless. When she got no answer, she bent down at last and pulled the sarong back.

The fish and the crabs had kept away from the head. The face was almost undamaged except that one ear had been torn, perhaps by the coral.

She looked into the dulled eyes of the Tamil. "You hated me because I was young and you were old," she said in judgment. "I never hated you. But you made the women believe that I was a witch. Now I will be a witch, and for that I require a head —your head!" Again she paused as if waiting for a reply, her head cocked a little to one side. "Wait while I fetch the machete."

She stalked back gravely through the shallows, the limpid water splashing in little bright gem sprays from her shins.

The canoe was at the northern point of the island across the shallows. It had survived the Devil Wind. At some time in the early gale of the evening, it had been thrown into the ironwoods to which she had secured it and it had been jammed there by the wind and water; one outrigger strut had been broken, but the rest of the canoe had escaped the grasp of the great wave. One of the four boats that Roark had brought from the ship had disappeared altogether, and the other three were badly damaged. The canoe, when the outrigger strut had been spliced, was the only thing that still floated.

For three days now she had worked, searching for equipment and stores that had been washed out to sea and to the other islands. Mostly, the boy Rahmzi had come with her, hanging on to the canoe and swimming. They had found a net and three paddles, one of the boat sails, badly torn, and one mast, unscratched. There was a trunk that had belonged to Roark, washed clean of its contents. They found clothing and bales of cloth. These things she had carried back to the landing beach or had stacked in safety on the other islands.

This afternoon Rahmzi had not come with her; he was wanted to help with the roofs of the new huts. The village was coming to life again. But she would not work there herself with the eyes of the other women following her about as they made thatching for the roofs or cooked or tended the children or husked coconuts from the unlimited store in the wreckage. They seemed to always be whispering as she passed.

"She is a witch! She is a witch!"

"Therefore I will be a witch," she said aloud now, striding through the shallows.

The machete they had found with the other heavy tools, half-buried in the sand two-thirds of the way to the beach, where the giant wave had washed them. Only this morning she had made Ameni sharpen it.

When she returned to the body, she stood silent for a moment of respect as she had stood before, staring down at it. The crabs had come up while she was away and were exploring tentatively at the neck and shoulders. "Go away!" she shouted. "This is mine. After I have done you may take what you wish." And suddenly, with no more hesitation, she slashed down at the neck.

Instantly the water became tinged with red. She had not expected this. It was inconceivable that the body could still hold blood despite the gaping wound of the thigh. But there was blood congealed in the great arteries of the neck. The scarlet spread through the waters, and small fish came up and explored the body and its color and swam away again.

She chopped the neck with the unhurried, accurate strokes of a samurai warrior. Despite the sharpness of the machete, it met with unexpected resistance. The flesh seemed to have acquired a solidity in the water.

She chopped on. Each time she slashed, the water spurted up, thinly red. It was difficult to get at the vertebral column because the flesh flowed back after each cut. In the end she was forced to lift the shoulders and prop them with a piece of coral. The head fell back then, opening the whole of the neck. Two more swift strokes sufficed now, and the head rolled clear, the long hair streaming through the red water.

She stood very still, staring at the stump of the neck, sorting things out in her mind. Then she put the machete down and withdrew the dagger from its hiding place. Deliberately she began to cut round the stump of the neck in little stabs.

"This will look as if a shark took her head as she floated in the sea," she said aloud to herself. "The leg beyond doubt was taken by a shark." She studied the nature of the wound on the thigh and made one or two tentative cuts to match it. The water gurgled obscenely in the open windpipe, as if the corpse of the old woman were answering her at last.

"Be still!" she said. "I am all but done."

She made three more cuts, obscuring the transverse chopping of the machete, and then, removing the piece of coral, let the headless shoulders sink back below the surface.

The blood had almost ceased to dissolve now in the sea water. The streaming current of the tide took the red patch to the south; she could see it growing always more faint. In a little, the water at her feet was clear and the head lay, grotesque in profile, the long black hair streaming and alive in the movement of the sea, alone on the sand.

From Maya's memory came, abruptly and without warning, sentences of the rites that men used when they took the head of an enemy. She knew that it did not matter what head was taken; this her Hindu nurse had told her over and over again. It did not have to be a man's head—a woman's would do. It could be taken by simple murder, a knife thrust in the back—anything. The head was the one thing that was important, not how it was obtained. The stories of the courage, the singleness of purpose of the headhunter warriors were stories for the white men. White men seemed always to be looking for ways to glorify murder, to make heroes of the murderers.

The crabs came back slowly. Two of them, bolder than the rest, attached themselves to the stump of the neck. A third went towards the head.

"Do here as you wish, but that is mine!" she said, and, taking two strides forward, she bent down, grabbed the head and lifted it.

It was astonishingly heavy, but she walked through the shallows with it towards the stripped palm groves at the north point of Diego Garcia.

It was the middle of the afternoon now. Maya rested in a patch of shade, sitting cross-legged with her delicate hands in her lap, and remembered the Hindu woman. There were certain chants to be said and certain rituals to be done in the preparation of the head. It would have to be smoked. Certain woods were better than others, but she could remember only that hard woods were necessary. Some of the rituals she would have to do without; it would not perhaps matter. The main thing was the head.

When she was rested she began the grisly task of cutting through the thick muscles at the base of the skull. The dagger was not a good cutting weapon, the machete was too clumsy. After a long while, she separated the first of the vertebrae, and then, cutting more freely, slashed the remainder of the neck clear of the skull itself. Walking deep into the battered palm grove, she threw the flesh containing the bones away. The rats and the land crabs between them would deal with it quickly.

Her hands were bloodied with the work. She looked down at them distastefully and decided to go back to the water. Again the water performed its miracle, transforming the flesh from a red anger to a pallid acquiescence. The dagger seemed to work better in the water.

It became obvious that she needed a more flexible tool, and she went back to the high-water mark to search for a piece of bamboo. As she stalked back through the shallows to the beach, she saw that a cloud had come up. Now, as she crouched down over the head again, the cloud hesitated on the edge of the sun, edged itself with unbearably bright pinks and golds for a moment, and then overran it. The green light of the cove went out as if snuffed. The water surfaces became leaden, and Maya heard behind her the onrush of rain, great drops stabbing at the water and raising return droplets greater than themelves.

She did not even bother to look around.

"It is well that the rain has come," she said to the head. "Now there will be water for all."

The great wave that had overrun the island had turned the wells brackish. The new wells that Roark had ordered dug on the morning after the storm had been only a little less brackish. The whole water supply of the island was ruined. It was Pitney who had remembered the South Sea Island trick of tying a bunch of leaves round the trunk of a palm so suspended as to direct rain water from a heavy shower into a jar or a basin. There were few jars left on the island. For the

most part they had had to be content with gourds
or giant clam shells, but even so she knew that this
shower would give them drinking water until the
wells cleared again.

She felt the coolness of the rain on her bare
shoulders and against her head. Her hair became
limp and bedraggled, but she worked on,
preparing the head. All through the rain she talked
to the head, and sometimes, as her hands moved or
the water caught at it, the mouth seemed to open
in a terrible imitation of speech.

The crabs collected in rings around her,
stepping with little sideways movements, holding
up their claws as if to beg for something from her.
Occasionally Maya talked to them, telling them of
the power that the head would bring her.

All the while, the sun sank in the western sky. It
was late in the afternoon before she prepared,
deep in the tangled scrub of the island, a three-
legged stand and build a fire below it. She hung
the head from the top of the tripod, calmly and
without a tremor, on a knot of its own hair. She
had the flint and tinder that she always carried in
the canoe. With its paddles and her fishing lines
and the small hand net, it had remained safe in its
lashings through the cyclone. Now she lit a fire,
using dry palm fronds that had been sheltered
from the rain by the trees, and coconuts husks.
She piled chips of ironwood to make the smoke.

For a long time she sat silent, watching it. A tiny
handful of birds that had survived the storm
circled her, inquisitive, but at last they settled,
and she knew that it was almost evening. The fire
was low enough to leave now. She built up a
screen of branches and leaves that would hide the
tripod from an accidental eye and at the same time
keep the smoke in as long as the fire smouldered.

Then she went back to the canoe and tipped the rain water out.

The sun set when she was midway between the high sand island and the village. The tide was full now. An unaccustomed loneliness assailed her. Some of her self-sufficiency seemed to have drained itself in the bloody work of the afternoon. Once, in the red of the last of the sunset, she had looked herself over with immense care to see if blood was left anywhere on her body or her clothing, but she had bathed before she started for home and everything, even her sarong, was clean.

The canoe was heavy to handle and she moved very slowly, for behind her she towed a barrel, another oar that she had found, and a little raft of odds and ends of shaped timber. In the canoe itself she had another bale of cloth and four gourd dippers with handles that she had found, oddly enough, within a few feet of one another.

The soft and exquisite light of the afterglow faded and the deep blue velvet of the night covered the sea. The stars blazed in it. In a windless silence, broken only by the dip and splash of the paddle and the occasional rap as it knocked against the side of the canoe, she came at last to the beach.

Roark himself was waiting for her.

"You are late!" His voice was rumbling and almost kind.

"I had much to do," she answered. "I have a barrel and another oar. Also there is yet another roll of cloth and a part, I think, of your great chair."

The canoe grated on the sand, and the boy Rahmzi and two of the other children rushed forward and dragged it firmly in.

Roark stared at her in the starlight. "What

else?"

"Four dippers. They floated together and I found them together." And then, as she turned to go up the newly cleared path to the village, she added casually, "And the body of the Tamil."

"My God!" Roark exclaimed, startled. "You found her body?"

"It is her," Maya replied with her voice still unconcerned, as if she were discussing only another piece of wreckage. "It lacks one leg and the other is torn, nor is there a head on it, but it is the Tamil. I knew it by the color of the sarong." She felt Roark staring at her, but she continued to drift slowly up toward the village.

"How did this happen?" he said from behind her.

"The coral," she answered indifferently, and then after a long pause she added, "or it might be that it was a shark." Deliberately she had chosen the less dramatic possibility first.

Roark seized on the alternative. "Aye, it would be a shark."

"Or it might be the coral." Maya repeated herself with calculation. "It is not possible to tell, for the fish have taken what they would and the crabs also."

"Wait! What did you do with it?"

"I did nothing. It was too heavy for me to lift. Moreover, it is stuck between the boulders of the coral. There was nothing that I could do."

He relaxed, suddenly satisfied. "You will take us to the place tomorrow."

"I will take you, but what will you go in?"

"The boat will be ready by noon—not finished, but patched enough for that."

"I will take you. Now I am hungry and tired."

* * *

The women were making thatching with a furious, quarreling energy. Maya sat with her back against a broken log, soaking in the morning sunlight and wriggling her toes in the sand. May Ling regarded her ominously. On her seemed to have settled the responsibility for trying to discipline Maya, the responsibility that had been the Tamil's.

"It is not in my disposition to make thatching," Maya explained lightly. "That is women's work. It is required of me that I go out with the men."

"It would be better if you went to a beating," May Ling said.

"Slaves are beaten," Maya observed cheerfully.

"Where do the men go?" Zada demanded.

"We go to bury the Tamil woman." Maya addressed herself directly to May Ling.

Almira, working five yards away from May Ling, let fall the two segments of the palm frond that she was beginning to plait for a screen. Her hands went up to her face. May Ling herself stood frozen, with one arm ridiculously misplaced behind her. Roark had said nothing of the discovery. Maya herself had kept silence. The shock spread through the whole village, even those too far away to hear the words. The babble of talk and argument that had filled the clearing was abruptly silenced.

"She is found, then?" It was Almira who spoke first.

"She is found," Maya agreed indifferently.

"It was you who found her," Zada said. The note of accusation was almost palpable.

"I found her."

"How?" Almira's voice was deeply shocked.

Maya turned to her. "Walking on the beach I saw her sarong. It showed above the water. The pattern and colors, I knew."

"Why was it that it should be you?" Zada asked in her dreadful, twisted Indonesian. "What black art did you use?"

Maya rubbed her back delicately against the palm trunk. The scratching effect was delicious. At last, with a lazy insolence, she rose to go and turned to Zada.

"I am a witch. You have said it."

The women gathered self-protectively a little closer.

"There is no God but God," Yin-hsi, Pitney's head wife, said. "It is true that she is a witch."

Maya led the boat in her canoe, five yards or so ahead of its clumsy progress. There was not enough water inshore on the western side of Diego Garcia for it to make the beach at this stage of the tide, and she took the canoe down well below the northern point of the island before she turned into the shallows. The boat grounded before she reached the rocks that held the body.

The sarong still floated, patterned, on the surface.

Roark stode up through the shallows, making a tremendous noise in the afternoon hush. Pitney had not come. Roark had three men with him. One of them stayed with the boat, the other two followed him. He stood looking down at the battered body. It had swollen evilly since the previous day. The abdomen was distended and ugly, and the stump of the thigh was opened back so that the broken bone jutted whitely through it.

"My God!" Roark said, his voice shaking. The tone had nothing in it of his customary complacency. "Pull the boat up!" he called without turning his head. "Bring a blanket!"

He disregarded Maya absolutely and stood quite still as the men rolled one of the rocks back, lifted the ruined body enough to work the blanket beneath it and folded it over the top.

"Take her to the beach!" he said.

"Do you bury her there?" Maya asked.

"Not bury." Roark's voice was slow and reflective. "I will burn her upon a pyre. She was a Hindu. I know nothing of their rites, but I know that their dead are burned, and she deserves at least that of me."

Maya considered the words carefully. She could not understand the meaning behind them. "Deserves?" she whispered tentatively.

Whether Roark heard her or not she could not tell, but he went on.

"She was from Malay," he said, his voice still low, so low that she could hardly hear it above the booming of the reef. "She came to me before the others, except Almira. She was young then—not as young as you, but as graceful. She had the beauty of a reed in the wind." There was an immense sorrow in his voice. "She had soft eyes, like a young deer's—like your eyes—and her voice was soft as the night rustle in a tree."

Roark was quiet for a long time, watching the men. They had dropped the body on the sand and were walking along the tide line, picking up driftwood.

"Afterwards she grew old and shapeless and her voice became hard," he said gently, "but I remember her as she came to me a long time ago." He began to walk heavily in towards the body.

Maya stayed where she was, holding the canoe steady.

They made a bed of palm fronds and on it they put dry sticks from above the high-water mark, and then dried driftwood logs, and branches and broken wood. On top of it they put the body.

"Leave it! Leave it!" she heard Roark's voice angrily shout as Ameni started to take the blanket out from under it.

He lit the pyre himself, blowing the tinder into a small bright flame with fragments of dry leaves. There was something spiritual about the way he lit each of the four corners of the fire, passing ceremoniously around it to do so. When it was ablaze, he stood away from it at what would have been the head end if there had been a head, his hat in his hand. There was no wind. The smoke rose with a greedy uprush into the still air, elongated itself with its own interior heat, and stretched up and up and up.

Maya, sitting low in the canoe, saw these things happening as in a dream. On the small elevation of the beach, the men were silhouetted against the empty sky. The palms began twenty yards back from them, leaning over in sorrowful curves. Splintered trunks reached high above the beachward crests. The three Indonesians stood in a group, self-supporting; Roark stood alone, and in front of him the fire blazed, red under the grey and blue of the smoke.

Maya could not tell how long she waited. Time stood still; there was nothing by which to mark it by. Only the creeping tide took notice of the passing of the hours. It moved in toward the pyre as if it conspired to put out the flames, but before it reached them the thing was done. The Tamil was gone, dismissed into the still and uncomprehending air.

When only the ashes glowed and smoldered, Roark came back to the boat, leading the three men in silence. A little shiver of apprehension

went through Maya. This was the moment of challenge; this was the time when, if he had noticed
the difference between the wound of the leg and
the wound of the neck, Roark would deal with her.
She waited with her courage slowly failing, her
hands tense on the handle of the paddle, but
Roark had not even looked at the neck. He walked
past her blindly, but even as she thought he was
past, she heard his low whisper.

"We will go back now to the village."

She shook her head, though he was past her and
could not see the gesture. "I do not go back now.
Your women believe that I did it. They have called
me a witch again. I will stay by myself until their
minds are at rest."

"Little fool!" Roark said brusquely. "I will talk
to them."

"Speak to them with a whip," Maya suggested
mischievously. "I go now, but I will come back."
This was the first time she had ever committed
herself.

She swung the canoe. The men could have stopped her, but they made no movement. Roark knew
that it was impossible to pursue her either in the
boat or by wading through the shallows.

Only when she was round the farthest point of
Diego Garcia did she shake off the faint,
unidentifiable depression that had settled over
her. The smoke of the cremation still hung in the
sky, very thin and almost incandescent in the glare
of the late afternoon. She grounded the canoe and
went up onto the beach. The boat was still in sight,
but only as a minute speck already crossing the
bay across from the village.

She lay in a patch of shade, giving it time to get
out of sight. Once again, as in the aftermath of the
storm, she saw Roark as a man, subject also to

sorrows. It was the tone of his voice that stayed with her. It had a sad quality, a lament for the fleeting grace of youth and beauty. She did not recognize that it was also for love that he grieved —for he had loved the Tamil in his own way.

When she was sure that the boat was out of sight, she paddled lazily north again.

The head was safe in the tripod. Neither crab nor rat had got at it in the night. A rank smell hung about it. She wrapped it in leaves, making a large, untidy bundle, and placed it in the stern of the canoe. Then she set off on the long passage across the large bay between the islands, paddling fast and strongly. The sun was low now, and it was urgent that she should get there before it set.

The west islands had also suffered the blast of the Devil Wind. She could see, as she approached it, that the northern mile of the island was a wilderness of splintered trunks. No green thing lived there. To the south, the damage was slightly less. She could not tell yet if it had been swept by the great wave, but the wave had come from the northeast.

Already it was too late to use the inner lagoon; the tide was too low. She made for a point on the beach level with the blue lagoon, steering by the rocks that lay off it. As she made the canoe secure, she could see that the wave had hit. Judging by the driftwood and the debris caught in the beach bushes, it had not been as high as on Salomon, but it had been high enough. There was no sign of her hiding place, no sign of the pots that she had so carefully stolen, no sign of the bed place that she had made.

With the red sun breaking in splendor through the palm trunks, she set to work with the machete to make another tripod. It was deep enough in the

unruined trees here for the light of a fire to be
hidden. Now she worked with a steely desperation. She cut ironwood saplings for the tripod. She
gathered the chips of the cuttings for fuel. The
head she tied up by the hair again. This time she
improvised a basket of ironwood creepers around
it. And at sunset it was ready for the fire. She lit it
with the experience of the previous day, fed it with
driftwood until it burned clear, and fueled it with
green chips. Finally, she wet it down and covered
the outside with greenery. Only after that did she
make a rough bed.

That night the land crabs bothered her and she
slept lightly, changing her resting place from time
to time, waking herself up to fuel the fire with
fresh chips. Once the light night wind changed,
and the smoke of the burning and the stench of the
scorching flesh overpowered her, and she woke
crying.

At dawn, hollow-eyed and desperately tired, she
woke again and fed the fire afresh, and lay down
in the clean unfrightening light to sleep once
more.

The fire was insatiable. All through the day
she fed it, while, without interest, without
enthusiasm, she made a sleeping place where the
land crabs could not reach her, and roofed it
roughly with palm fronds against the rain. She
had a great confidence in building, born out of her
shipboard knowledge of lashings and spars and
the sharpness of the machete that she had stolen.
With the disappearance of the pots, she had no
cooking utensils, but there were giant clam shells
and the fish that she caught could be broiled over
the ashes. There were fresh coconuts and even
bird's eggs from the handful of sea birds that
remained.

Except for food and the canoe, the fire absorbed
her energies. With her servitude to the fire, she
had acquired a fear of the head. Even when she
had to replace the green palm fronds at the top of
the tripod, she did it with her eyes averted. The
very hair knotted above the structure offended
her.

She became a slave to the fire, wholly absorbed
in it. She did not attempt to explore the ruined
north side of Eagle Island. She did not bother to
keep watch over the lagoon, though she guessed
that the second boat must be all but repaired by
now. But she bathed herself scrupulously—it was
difficult to keep clean with the work of the
fire—and she slept exhausted, interrupted only by
an inner compulsion that woke her to go back
every few hours to the smoldering heap.

On the evening of the fifth day, she opened the
protecting screen. There was still enough light
from the low sun to see. The face had shrunk. The
cheeks were drawn, in a mockery of the soft
hollows of the Tamil woman's face. The eye
sockets were wide, but one of the lids dropped a
murderous wink. The lips were thin and tight and
drawn back from the protruding teeth. The nose
had receded, shrinking back, elongating the
nostrils upward. It was terrible and inhuman—
but it was, beyond all doubt, the Tamil. It
expressed all the evil of which she had been
capable, the jealousies and vindictiveness, the
cunning and the cruelty and the bitterness.

All through this day with fanatical energy, Maya
had worked at the permanent resting place for the
head. It should, she knew, hang above the fire in a
lodge-house—a baang. But she had no baang. It
should be the center-piece of a community; but
there was no community. She made a small,

strong shelter, shaping it according to her memory of what the Hindu nurse had told her of the little hut used in the ceremony of welcoming the head, anchoring it against the trunks of two broken palm trees. It had a pitched roof, the gables sealed with strands of palm frond, the roof itself heavy with thatching strongly tied down. The floor was made of flat slabs of coral dragged painfully from the beach.

Now she took the head and, repeating the chants that the Hindu woman had taught her and that came of themselves out of memory, she carried it to the shelter. She knotted the long black hair to a peg in a cross-pole of the roof. The eyes seemed to follow the movements of her hands even above the head, though there were, in fact, no eyes now. She replenished the basket of creepers and lashed that to the cross-pole. She passed a fresh lashing of cord from the canoe round it all.

Then she brought leaves to it.

"They should, I know, be holy leaves, but on this island there is no priest to bless them. It is enough, I think, that I do you such honors as I can. Also, there is the matter of the tree. This is a small island, very far in the sea. There is here no cedar tree. The tree that I will bring you is a good tree and should house a good spirit. It is a rare tree also; it is the only tree of its kind that I have seen on the island. You will accept its spirit?"

She shaped the words like a question, but asked the question cautiously. The cedar tree, she knew, was necessary—perhaps even essential. It was a part of the origins of the cult of the heads, the holy tree in which lived the spirits of the gods.

Last of all, as the brief twilight swept past the island, she lit a fire on the flat coral slabs. The fire gave enough light to illuminate the underside of the fresh thatching, the clean green-gold of the palm leaves, the fresh surface of the wood. Gradually, the smoke thickened. In the utterly still night air, it collected under the canopy of the leaves until the surface of them became misted and insubstantial and the rafters were swallowed up. Last of all, it swallowed the head. She could see it only when the swirls of hot air made clear patches about it and it seemed to stare down out of the mystery of the smoke.

She sat in her customary position, her back against a trunk, her hands motionless on her lap, contemplating the head as it danced in and out of the smoke. She remembered Roark's words, "Not as young as you, but as graceful." She repeated them softly.

"I do not care," she said as the clean air swept the smoke away from the head. "You were old when I knew you, and ugly."

She waited while the smoke swallowed the head again and remembered Roark's next words. "She had the beauty of a reed in the wind." Again she waited until the clean air revealed the head to the flickering light of the flames.

"What is it to me how graceful you were? You are now dead, and you are mine!" Again she thought back to Roark, remembering and rejecting the sorrow in his voice. "Your eyes are not like a young deer's now," she said to the head.

The clear air went up, and in the play of the fire the eye sockets seemed to come alive and move.

"You cannot frighten me!" Maya was startled into a sudden anger. "I have said the right words and I have prepared the right place for you so far as I am able, and there is nothing that you can do to me, whatever you were when you were young."

The fire grew brighter as the hardwood chips

dried and became combustible. The hut had a ceiling of smoke. All round the eaves it escaped, like the veil of an inverted waterfall. Inside it breathed up and down and the head appeared and disappeared with an hypnotic, malevolent effect.

She moved away from the trunk, crouching closer to the fire, her head forward, staring to detect the Tamil's head at the precise moment when the smoke freed it. It seemed to change expression.

"It is nothing to me what you once were," she said over and over again. "You are what you are now, and I need certain things of you. Be still while I ask you!"

There was no moment of stillness. The smoke still billowed up and down. The head seemed to move up and down through the smoke.

Finally the fire grew too hot, and she moved away uneasily. The hut was full of small noises—fire noises and noises where the thatching was drying and where the ironwood creepers were tightening and where the rafters were stiffening in the heat, making little whispering sounds. They flowed into the malignant hypnotism of the head, the commanding power of the eyeless sockets.

Maya grew more and more uneasy, moving father and father away till she came to the edge of the hut.

"I will light another fire outside," she said suddenly, as if to re-establish her own powers.

The flames of the new fire leapt up and lit the underside of the palms. She had made the shelter at the edge of a patch of the storm's destruction. The palms had fallen here to make a natural clearing, and the night sky was open to the north, its velvet encrusted with stars. The fire lit the little cove in the trees brilliantly, and she stood by it, staring at the hut through the soft cascade of sparks.

"You are tied fast in there," she said softly, "and I have no fear of you. When the smoke has cleared, I will ask what I have to ask you."

Then, quite still, she waited.

The wing hit her with the instant shock of a lightning flash. She had heard nothing coming. Only after the thing hit her and swept up did she hear the whistle of the wind through feathers, and almost instantly another wing brushed past, not hitting her but so close that the wind of its passing fanned against her. This time she saw the flash of it in the firelight, a sudden whiteness that was instantly lost in the darkness. Another bird came from a different direction, and another and another. As she looked up, she could see wings flashing as they caught the firelight, diving towards her, sweeping upwards in a rustle and sometimes a snap of hard-braking feathers.

She was not sure that they were birds. In the trance induced by the head she had lost her sense of ordinary things. These were like emanations of the head, like demons called up by it from the spirit world, like legions of allies for its eyeless, evil intelligence.

She could not know that the great flock of the sea gulls, blown far out over the open sea by the typhoon, had come back at last to the island. She could not know that, attracted by the fire, blinded by its improbability, they were diving on it, not on her.

The rate of the diving increased. More and more birds seemed to be pouring down in a constant attack. The fire itself was leaping under the beat of the wings. Maya was brushed again and again. A bird began to scream and other birds took up the

cry. The air was harsh and ungraceful and terrible
with its sounds. Still they came, more and more
birds, dodging one another at the bottom of their
dives, brushing against each other, colliding,
quarreling, screaming, demon-riding and demon-
ridden.

She put her arms around her head to shelter
herself, still standing there, and when they hit her
arms she crouched down to the fire. She became
terrified, hysterical, but she did not scream; her
voice would not have been heard above the clamor
of the birds. She gathered herself at last on her
knees, her body arched over, her head against the
ground, her hands over the back of her neck—
sobbing, incoherent, utterly in despair.

She could not measure afterwards how long she
endured there. She only remembered that,
abruptly, she told herself that the Tamil woman's
head was hers, and that the demons of the head,
therefore, were hers also. Rising to her feet, she
stretched out her hand, found the stems of a
couple of dried palm fronds, thrust them on to the
fire, waited till they caught, and then swirled
them above her head. The brilliant flame of the
new blaze lifted high into the darkness of the
night. Looking up into it, she could see a mass of
bird wings, wings that went up in an endless flow
to the night sky, that moved in incredibly
beautiful arabesques against the stars.

She waited while the dry fronds blazed to their
end. Then she stalked through the still-diving sea
gulls to the shelter of the hut. She sat down again
with her back against the tree trunk, laid her
hands on her lap, and looked up. The inner fire
had diminished but there was still light enough to
see. The smoke had risen so that the head hung
clear of it. There was almost no flicker from the

glowing embers. The head appeared to be subdued and waiting.

"They were no more than birds," Maya said to it after a long pause. "It was a trick only. I am not afraid anymore. You will do now what I ask of you. You will bring my father's ship to this island." She watched the head earnestly. It made no sign either of acceptance or of rejection. "It is a new ship. I cannot tell you how it will look or what its name will be. I can tell you only that it will be the fastest ship on the coast. If, because of this and because of the fact that you are a woman and know nothing of ships, you cannot find my father's ship, you will bring another ship to the island so that I may go away and find my father by myself. Hear this!"

She stretched out her hand and flung a chip or two on the fire. As they caught, the shadows seemed to give motion to the lips and to the eyes in a monstrous, macabre imitation of life. Outside the whistle of the still-diving birds had something of the character of whispering.

"My father's ship," she said again, "or at least another ship."

Book Three
The China Clipper

15

The clouds raced over the face of Salomon Island, seeming to herald the billowing sails of a mighty vessel that glided effortlessly through the tossing sea, curling the blue-green crystal water beneath her lofty prow. The azure sky was vivid beyond the fluffs of white and, against the indistinct horizon, the ship was like an eagle in flight, soaring gracefully on outspread but motionless wings.

The boy's voice was at the topmost level of the register of excitement. "Ship! Ship! Ship!" he was shouting over and over again. The voice was coming up the path now from the landing place, growing in shrillness and volume as it approached.

"Now indeed it is true that I am a witch," Maya said with utmost complacency, sitting in the shadow of the big hut.

197

Her instinctive knowledge of sea matters told her before the boy reached the village that it was the second part of her request that had been fulfilled. This ship was not from the east. The boy must have seen it from the lagoon beach. With the wind that was blowing, it must be sailing up towards the entrance. Therefore it was not her father. But it was a ship.

"Is it from the east?" she asked, to make quite certain as the boy reached them, sobbing for breath.

"No, from the west."

Roark was up at the oil-pressing shed where they were trying to rebuild the presses. He came down now. Excitement enveloped the place. The children came running from the vegetable patches, the women from the wells and from the coconut gathering, the men from the endless, intolerable work of clearing away the wreckage of the storm. They surged down the path towards the beach, Roark moving in the middle of them like a shepherd enveloped in his sheep.

Maya waited till they were all on the path before she walked, skipping a little, at the end of the procession, hugging to herself the knowledge that she had done this thing. For six days she had waited, six days since she had come back from the west island thin, worn, and spriritually exhausted by her experience.

Roark, meeting her on the path as she returned from the west island, had said, "God! What have you been doing to yourself, woman? Go and get some food." And as an afterthought, "The women will not trouble you now."

She did not bother then or after to ask what
Roark had done to ensure her safety. It was not important. She might, of course, have asked the head to
look after her, but she was wholly certain that this
was within her own power.

The ship was there all right, but despite the
shrieking of the children and the buzzing chatter
of the women, there was almost a sense of anti-
climax about it. It was no more than a minute
pyramid of white sail on the horizon, just clear of
the northernmost point of Egmont Island. It hung
there while Roark adjusted the long glass that
they had recovered, half buried in the sand,
halfway to the sea after the Devil Wind. Water had
got into it and a small area of the lens was
clouded. He fiddled with it, growling angrily.
Pitney came up the beach, hearing the commotion.

After a long while, Roark got the glass adjusted.
"It's a schooner. It could be the *China Clipper*."

"There's plenty of schooners," Pitney said.

Roark disregarded him. "Seems as if she's heading up towards us, but there's no telling. I want a
big fire built up at the end of the island. We'll light
it when she gets close in."

The children raced up the beach, shouting,
laughing. The men began to drift up, and women
followed them. It had become suddenly a holiday;
all thought of work was abandoned. Pitney went
up behind them to direct the placing of the fire.
Roark stood watching through the long glass.

"I told you a ship would come," Maya said
casually when he lowered it again.

He put his head on one side and looked at her.
"Aye, you did. And how the devil did you know?"

"I knew," she answered distantly, "and now it has come. There is no need for a fire. It will enter the lagoon."

"If it is the *China Clipper*, it will be Dirk Cooper come to see his seeds."

"Whoever it is," Maya said calmly and with absolute confidence, "it will come."

She began to stroll leisurely up the path the join the others, holding back the flame of a secret victory. The head had worked for her. A new world was opened.

The boat was close alongside the schooner. There was much shouting back and forth. People lined her rail from bow to stern. There were women on the quarter-deck. The schooner had a festive holiday air to match the wild excitement along the beach.

Maya lay farther away in the canoe, her paddle poised and glistening in the bright sunlight, her eyes taking in every movement, every sound, every new shape, as the *China Clipper* glided through the calm water and the men on her deck stood ready to drop the anchor.

"You're about right now," she heard Roark bellow. "I'd let the anchor go." She watched the schooner's head swing into the eye of the wind with the last drifting movement that was left to her. Then she saw the splash grow under the prow as the anchor dropped heavily into the lagoon.

Roark was aboard before the splash had died down, Skinner Pitney with him.

Maya dipped the paddle and moved slowly in towards the schooner. She had from the deck something of the appearance of a water insect, tentative and skittish.

Along the mid-ship rails was a line of young
men's heads and shoulders leaning over the
bulwarks.

"My God," a deep voice from among them
shouted, "it's a wee lass!"

Maya sensed rather than understood that the
words were meant for her; she looked up and
smiled, and there was a wide outbreak of smiles
along the rail and craning of necks and a chorus of
calls. She put her head back and laughed delightedly.

One of the young men threw her a line, and she
made it secure and allowed the canoe to be pulled
alongside. She went up the ladder and hesitated at
the top of it; she did not want Roark to see her for
the time being. The young men crowded about her,
but she stepped onto the deck with dignity and
downcast eyes, and she found at once a corner
where she could settle down with her back against
the bulwark.

She was less than ten feet from Roark. It was
apparent from his stance that something had gone
wrong. He faced a tall man, taller than himself,
broader, even more powerful, his face weathered
by a hundred storms. His black frock coat was
silver-buttoned, and his tight white trousers were
tucked carelessly into seaboots. He was armed—
knife in the crease of his back and sword at his
side. He was in his thirties and redheaded, and his
eyes were emerald green.

This, Maya knew, must be Dirk Cooper, brother
of the captain of the *Sea Wolf*—that much she had
gathered from Roark's talk with Pitney during the
hours of waiting—and it was clear that Dirk
Cooper was angry. The first words that she heard
as she settled herself on the deck were his.

"By God's blood, Roark! I established rights to the island. I planted it."

Roark's shoulders were squared and already angry. "Rights be damned! They're uninhabited islands. Did you expect me to up anchor and sail a thousand miles because of a few God-damned withered seedlings?"

"They are my islands!" Dirk Cooper said stubbornly.

"Nobody's islands! Anyway, there is room enough for both of us—room enough for five of us with a big island apiece, if it comes to that."

"It's not the room. It's the principle."

"Principles be damned!" Roark retorted. "A stinking pox on principles!"

The young men had fallen back a little. They stood in a small, compact group, watching. Maya allowed her eyes to consider them once, but the fascination of the meeting of the two giant men held her.

"You were determined to take them from me," Dirk said savagely.

"God damn it!" Roark roared. "I didn't know that you'd been to the islands. If you had kept to the time you promised—"

"I promised no time," Dirk broke in angrily. "My orders were to pick up a load of rum and call at the Cape on my way to London."

"And you spent months piddling round these islands on your own private business. If you had come when I expected you, I'd have known you had plans for these islands."

"Liar!" Dirk Cooper's voice rose indignantly. "You damned well knew. It was on my list."

"Lists! Lists! You made lists of every damned island group in the Indian Ocean, and the Atlantic, and the Pacific. Maldives, the Falklands,

Rodrigues, Chagos, Cucos—there was no end to
your lists. How in the hell was I to know which one
you had chosen?"

"Why did you set out for the Chagos?"

"God damn your obstinate hide, Dirk Cooper! I
never set out for the Chagos! I set out for
Rodrigues Island. Ask your brother Ben when you
see him! Ask him to show you the log. 'Cape Town
towards Rodrigues Island, it says. We stood off
that damned island for days before we gave it up. I
near lost a boat's crew in the landing place."

There was a brief silence as Dirk Cooper considered this. The ship's company, the young men,
stood gaping.

And then, from above them on the poop, a voice
came down, acidulous and rebuking.

"Mr. Cooper, is it not your intention to intro-
duce your wife and me to Mr. Tillman, if this
indeed is Mr. Tillman?"

Roark looked up as if he had been utterly
unaware of the presence of women. He lifted his
hat in one of his splendid gestures. "Your servant,
ma'am. I am Roark Tillman, of whom no doubt
you have heard."

"I have heard," the woman replied, thin-lipped.

"Mrs. Finch, may I present Mr. Tillman?" The
second woman came forward. "My wife—Mr. Tillman." Cooper's tone seemed to hold not only a
rebuke, but a warning.

Roark turned away from him and went up the
ladder. Maya watched him from her position on
the deck, craning her head upwards. He moved
quickly and easily with the young man's grace that
he always assumed when there were strange
women present.

On the poop deck, he took off his hat again,
almost sweeping the ground with it. "It is a

pleasure to be able to offer you the slender resources of Salomon Island, ma'am." He addressed himself particularly to Dirk's mother-in-law. "After months on shipboard, you must be eager to rest yourselves ashore."

"I will make my own arrangements for my own people," he heard Dirk's voice say belligerently over his back.

Roark disregarded the interruption. "Such as we have, it is yours, ma'am, but we have, as you must have seen, been swept by a typhoon." He turned to Dirk lightly, all trace of anger gone even from his eyes. "When we saw your sails, we were deeply thankful, for Salomon was swept by the sea." He turned to Mrs. Finch again. "One giant wave in the night, ma'am, but it took our stored foods. You would not have rice to spare, I doubt?" The last question was addressed to Dirk Cooper.

"We come from the west," Cooper replied shortly. "We have no rice."

Roark shrugged his shoulders. "No matter. My people will survive until the *Sea Wolf* returns. We expect her daily."

"I can let you have flour," Cooper said grudgingly. "Something in the way of dry stores perhaps. The meat has gone."

"We have no need of meat," Roark answered grandly. "The ocean and the seabirds give us a livelihood. They have come back to us, the birds. They returned six nights ago."

Below on the deck, Maya shivered. Presently she tuned away from the picturesque scene on the poop, where Roark still exerted his charm on the two hostile white women, and considered the young men. There were nine of them. They formed a group quite separate from the crew of the ship, which was partly Indonesian and partly international. They were young, all of them, the eldest not more than twenty-one, she judged. Most of them were fair-haired, sun-blistered, red, but they had an air of energy and purposefulness that was non-existent in the scheme of island things.

She heard Cooper's voice again. "I shall settle on Egmont or on the south island, as I judge to be most suitable."

"As I have said," Roark answered, directing his immense animal magnetism over Mrs. Finch, "there is ample room for all. The islands look small in this sea of waters, but they have a richness of their own. We will help you with our boats and our people."

"I require no help, sir," Cooper said furiously, his anger stirred up again by Roark's attitude. "I have nine young men who settle with me and I have my own boats."

"There is water in plenty on Egmont," Roark said equably, "but it may yet be brackish. Ours is still affected by the wave. There is little damage on Egmont—a few palms, hardly more than that. The west island suffered worst of all. It was a cyclone that wreaked the damage, something that swirled off the main typhoon, circling back to strike us."

"Do they strike the islands often?" Mrs. Finch asked.

"No, ma'am." Roark bowed slightly. "There cannot have been one like this for a score—for fifty years perhaps."

"Ah!" Mrs. Finch's voice was relieved.

Dirk Cooper coughed angrily, his face a flaming red.

Mrs. Cooper spoke for the first time. "That child?" she asked, looking over the rail to where Maya sat quietly, a small light-brown image of total purity and innocence.

Roark looked down after her, though he had no need to do so. "She is the daughter of a famous pirate in the Orient. She was rescued by another ship after a battle. I brought her with us to return her to her own people." There was an oily-tongued smoothness in the tone of his lie.

"Poor thing!" Mrs. Cooper hesitated for a second, then leaned forward and called down to the deck. "Chris, bring the child up to us!"

A boy detached himself from the group. He looked younger than the others, no more perhaps than eighteen. He was fair, but his skin, unlike the others, took the sun. And he was beautiful, Maya thought reluctantly as she watched him, if a man could be considered beautiful. Every inch of his body was well-muscled and lean, and against the brown of his hair his skin shone like burnished gold in the sunlight. He moved with the lithe, virile grace of a Greek athlete.

He held out his hand to Maya. "The mistress wishes tae speak with ye."

Maya steadfastly stared at the deck, refusing to look at him, afraid that if he saw her eyes he would be able to read her thoughts.

She took his hand with the trustfulness of a little girl. From the first, she had singled him out in the group as being nearest to her age. Even in her quick side glances, she had assessed the molding of his head and the strength of his young body. She allowed herself to be helped to the poop ladder and she went up it childishly, giving the impression that she needed support.

Pitney, waiting below on the main deck, watched her open-mouthed.

She moved very delicately across to the women, her head down, her eyes hooded, her hands lax.

Opposite Mrs. Cooper she stopped, youthful and naive.

Even Roark was shocked.

"You poor child!" Kathleen Cooper said in her deep, maternal voice.

And inside, Maya bubbled with a sheer and beautiful wickedness.

Roark continued to watch her through slitted eyes.

16

The boy Rahmzi was busy trimming a new strut
for the outrigger. The hasty repair after the
typhoon had served its purpose, and Maya needed
a more permanent fixture. Moreover, she had used
the last of the cord that had bound it for the
support of the Tamil's head. She herself was
working, repairing a hole in the fish net. The hand
nets were her own special province, and she would
allow no one else to touch them except Rhamzi
and herself.

While they worked, they watched the longboats
moving back and forth from the *China Clipper* to
Egmont Island. It was a long haul down to the
central island.

The schooner herself lay head to the wind in the
wavy surface of the anchorage. She looked
graceful from where they watched her. She was a
six-masted schooner, longer, lower, and slimmer
than the English ships. Dirk Cooper had built her

himself, in the wild days in Borneo, from timber that he had selected and seasoned, with workmen that he had trained, to his own design. And when at last he had sailed her to Malay, where Roark had moved with his harem, she was a thing of beauty. Dirk Cooper had had few prouder moments in his life than when, at the end of her first passage to England, she had been surveyed by Lloyds of London and classified A1. By some financial trickery that he did not understand James Tillman, Roark's brother, owned most of the vessel; Dirk himself owned one-eighth; Roark Tillman one-tenth only, and yet he was still the dominant partner—the influence of the Malay and Borneo appointment still hung over him like a crown of nobility.

"She is deep in the water," Maya said.

"I heard the man Pitney talking," Rahmzi answered. "She has cargo for Singapore and for Hong King. Afterwards she collects spices and pepper and some tin for trade in the west."

"She will take me to Singapore," Maya said confidently. "In a little, the women of Egmont will send for me—you shall see. Meanwhile . . ." She dropped the net across her lap and stretched back against the palm tree, looking up into its fronds to see if the sandpipers that had come back after the typhoon were still sitting companionably there. ". . . Meanwhile there are nine young men who will stay in the islands, all of them devils."

"Ha!" Rahmzi muttered noncommittally.

"The oldest of them has hair upon his belly and upon his chest—black hair, much of it. We shall call him tun-mai."

Rahmzi laughed, remembering the hairy caterpillar so called.

"He has been at sea for a long time without a

woman," Maya murmured dreamily, still watching the curious eyes of the sandpipers. "Except the foolish one with the deep voice"—she meant Kathleen Cooper—"and the old one with the voice like the juice of a lemon." She puckered her lips meditatively. "So," she said positively, after a short pause, "he would be suited to the Bantu girl, being, as he is, half black himself—at least as to his hair."

Rahmzi looked at her in alarm. "What witchcraft is this?"

"It is not proper that young men should endure too long without women," Maya replied demurely, avoiding all words which might have a sexual implication. "Also Zada has herself had no satisfaction since the Devil Wind. The Lord Tillman has not sent for her. It might be that they would find favor in each other's sight."

"Beyond all doubt," Rhamzi said, as he had said it so often, "you are a witch!"

"But you are not afraid of me." She lowered her eyes from the birds and stared fixedly at him.

"I am nothing in your eyes. You will not take the time and trouble to destroy me."

For the first time in a long while, her smile was complete and natural. "You are my friend, Rahmzi."

The boy laid the strut on the ground and looked at her gratefully.

On the morning of the fourth day, Kathleen Cooper sent for her. In the intervening period Maya had kept close to the landing place. Rahmzi, wanting to go fishing on the reef, had had to go by himself. Maya had found something to keep her busy always within sight of the *China Clipper* and the boats that worked from her. Early on this

morning the boat headed in towards the village.
Roark had broken down Cooper's first hostilities.
His boats were helping to put the gear ashore, and
half the Indonesian men were on Egmont Island.

The first mate of the *China Clipper* was with the
boat. He came ashore and strode up the path to
find Roark. Maya drifted up the path behind him.
He was a shifty, brutal-looking man, and she kept
a wary distance from him. But she was close
enough to the big hut to hear his voice as he made
the request and to hear Roark's amused answer.

"To look after the children—Maya? To look
after children?"

"Why not?" demanded Gunn. The first mate of
the *China Clipper* was nearing fifty, a huge, one-
eyed man as hard and as permanent as an iron
anvil.

"No reason."

"Mrs. Cooper said that the girl seemed gentle
and was kind with the children when she took her
below. She wishes it for a matter of days
only—until the huts are built."

Roark snorted. "She has seen the girl once, and
she thinks she knows her. It is by her own choice. I
will send for her." He called over his shoulder to
his Chinese wife. "May Ling! Tell Maya she goes to
Egmont Island to be of help to the white women."
Even the impassive face of May Ling creased into
a look of surprise. "Fetch her, woman! Fetch her!"
Roark ordered testily, and began to pour a drink
for Gunn.

"Early in the morning," the mate said, and
tossed it down.

"When do you sail?" Roark asked.

"Ship sails as soon as the huts are finished,"
Gunn replied shortly.

"I want the girl back before she sails."

"I'll tell Mrs. Cooper."

May Ling had found Maya. They came into the hut together. Maya walked soberly, her eyes downcast.

"You will go to the other island to help the white ladies," Roark said. "There will be no devilry."

She bowed submissively, putting her hands together in a gesture of absolute obedience.

Gunn looked puzzled at both of them for an instant. "All right, we'll go, then. Does she need anything?"

"I will go in my own canoe," Maya said quickly. "I will not go with him."

Roark did not bother to translate what she said to Gunn. "She will go down with the canoe," he said simply. "She can fish then." Privately he chuckled at the thought of the possible situations that could develop.

They were enchanted with her. In a single morning she accomplished the conquest of the seven children. To the women she was gentle, submissive, and entirely willing. To Dirk Cooper she was always respectful. To the young men she was laughter. An unquenchable gaiety seemed to emanate from her. The children—it was their first full day ashore—she taught the ways of the birds or showed the shore crabs and the little fish that darted along the shore. She found turtles' eggs for Mrs. Cooper and shellfish for Mrs. Finch. She taught the young men the art of climbing the easier palms to the accompaniment of gales of laughter and lost time. She helped with the proper placing of the thatching, and the Indonesian men watched her with awe and suspicion.

The young men were attracted towards her in the rest periods, but she was immensely careful.

Always she had a protective screen of children around her or moved towards Mrs. Finch as if to seek the shelter of her skirts. She made an exception only of the youngest of the young men, the fair-haired Chris Lovel. Occasionally she gave him a shy smile for his own that was quite different from her laughter. Once or twice she spoke to him. She could understand his English when he spoke slowly and carefully.

"She is a friendly little soul," Mrs. Cooper said, "gentle and kind." And Maya, understanding less than half of what she said, nonetheless laughed inwardly.

The days passed swiftly.

At sunset, they made a fire large enough to illuminate the new clearing of the Cooper village. Mrs. Finch sat on a chair that had been brought ashore. Mrs. Cooper sat close to her with the baby and two of the youngest children beside her. The other four children sat with Maya a yard or two away. The men sat all together in a little group while Mrs. Finch read an evening prayer. Dirk watched her uneasily out of the corner of his eye, holding a lantern to reinforce the flickering light of the fire.

Maya, with her instant imitativeness, followed the movements of the others, clasping her hands when they clasped their hands, bowing her head when they bowed theirs. She even managed an unidentifiable but acceptable sound at the deep 'amens.' Mrs. Finch held on too long with an unmemorized and unplanned prayer for the benefits of heaven on the new settlement. The lantern in Dirk's hand wavered several times. It was altogether different, Maya decided, from the first day on Salomon Island, the day on which she had mocked Roark with the title of Emperor. Nonetheless, she preferred that day. She had enjoyed it immensely.

Mrs. Cooper, not able to read her thoughts, regarded her benevolently.

When it was over, Cooper told the young men to sit. He made a short speech—a rehearsed speech, clearly. Maya understood almost nothing of it, for he spoke quickly and his accent differed from that of Roark; but she caught Roark's name from time to time and saw his hand point up to the northern island, and read enough into the anger of his voice to know that he was talking of the other village.

Dirk Cooper had, in fact, evolved a series of rules to control the new situation. None of the young men were to go to the northern island on any pretext whatever except with him or with Gunn. None of them was to have contact with anybody from the northern island—particularly not with Tillman's women. None of them was to take any orders from Roark Tillman if Roark Tillman should come to Egmont Island. They were not to interfere with boats from Salomon or allow boats from Salomon to interfere with them. They were not to fish close into Salomon or chase turtles into the cove of the island. They were to keep clear of all trouble at all times. They were to come to him—or to Gunn when he was gone—with any news, however slight, that concerned the people of Egmont, and they were to watch Roark Tillman whenever he came to the island. Above all, they were to keep away from the women. Above all, they were to keep away from Roark Tillman's women!

Maya was aware of eyes looking at her.

"Dae we have a celebration tommorrer?" a voice from the group asked.

"Why?" Cooper demanded abruptly, jerked out of his contemplation of the wrong that Roark Tillman had done him.

"St. Andrew's day!" two voices answered loudly.

Cooper suppressed his temper for a moment. "Are you sure?" he asked, at a loss.

"We're good Scots," replied the first voice.

Maya, watching the group in the glitter of the fire, identified the tall man whom she had christened Tun Mai.

"I'm a good Scot too, Duncan Campbell. But this is no time for celebrations."

"There will be no drinking," Mrs. Finch said.

"Hell's fires!" exclaimed an unidentifiable voice in the deep dusk.

Cooper looked at her hesitantly, uncertain whether to assert his authority.

"God's blood, Mr. Cooper, it's aye been the custom!" one of the sailors protested.

"There will be no celebration," Cooper announced firmly.

Several voices began to protest in a chorus of cursing.

Maya could not understand it, but her eyes darted from voice to voice, identifying the speakers, storing their identities in her mind. It was obvious that there was disagreement here, a crack in the solidarity of this other village. The young man Chris, she noted, took no part.

For a minute or two, the argument went on until Cooper ended it. "That's enough!" he said bluntly. "Away to your beds now!" And then he took a sidelong glance at Mrs. Finch for approval.

Maya stored up the fact that Dirk Cooper was afraid of Mrs. Finch. She stored up the fact that the obedience of the young men, at least in this

matter, was reluctant. She went to bed with the
children, snuggling into the first shelter that had
been put up on the island. The big huts were
nearly completed now, but they were not yet ready
for occupation.

Mrs. Cooper was almost as gentle with her as
she was with her own children.

Morning blossomed with vibrant hues that
glistened upon and changed the color of the
waters, touching the tossing surf with the yellows
and reds of the breaking dawn. The very air
seemed laden with a golden mist, and the greens of
the trees and the vegetation spread until they
joined the emerald green of the gently rolling sea.

In the exquisite perfection of this morning,
Maya took the children down to bathe. They
splashed, happily naked, in the shallows. The
young man Chris passed them, going down the
beach to fetch a load from a pile of gear. He
laughed gently at her as she drew her wet sarong
with a modest urgency about her body.

A pair of sea eagles flew along the northern
shore of the island. Maya had often watched them
hang on motionless wings as they rode the
currents of air high above the crashing surf. Her
spirit soared with them. She felt in tune with her
world; she felt an over-riding sense of peace and a
strange aura of confidence that all was going to be
as it should be. The realization that this state was
somewhat due to this young man's presence on the
island did not seem to disturb her as it had at first.
She was like a flower unfolding under the warm
rays of the sun as she bathed in the glow of Chris's
eyes. It was a feeling completely new to her. A
feeling she must understand.

Cooper himself came down the path later and
stood watching and laughing too.

"You had better put your clothes on before your grandmother sees," he said, when his laughter ended, to the eldest of the three girls. And they sobered and came out of the water quickly.

At the first work-break of the morning, she moved the children close to where the men were resting. Chris Lovel sat at the edge of the group, nearest to her. She heard almost at once the phrase that she had heard the night before.

"St. Andrew."

"What is this thing?" she whispered to him.

"St. Andrew," he answered softly, "is the patron saint o' Scotland." And then, with a simple understanding, he recognized that she could not possibly grasp the meaning of his words.

"He was a saint. D'you know what a saint is? Na, ye would not. He was a great man."

That at least she understood.

"On his day we drink tae him." Chris raised his hand in the gesture of holding a glass and tipped his head back and gurgled in his throat, and Maya laughed delightedly.

This too she understood. Her quick intelligence linked up the hints that she could gather. There was a great man and it was customary to drink to him, and from what had happened last night and from the tone of the voices now, there would be no drink. She arrived at this in a miracle of perceptiveness, basing it all on the young man's single unmistakable gesture, and her mind raced ahead to the glimmerings of a plan. She said no more, but sat there with the children circling around her, listening and thinking.

"It's the old bitch," she heard Duncan Campbell saying. "She doesna know the needs o' a Scotsman —or even a man, come tae that. And I've got a dryness in ma throat. A pox on the old bitch!"

Gunn came down on them finally. "Stop your damned belly-aching! You sound like a bunch of old women yourselves! Now get on with it! You've got the goddam stores to bring up and get stacked." He spat deftly to windward.

"He's not your saint," a voice said.

"Supposin' the bastard ever had a saint," an English voice added softly.

Maya gathered the children, smiled companionably at Chris Lovel, and went away. At least she was certain that they were thirsty men.

In the middle of the afternoon, someone sighted a boat coming down from Salomon Island. Maya, making a pool in the falling tide to hold starfish and hermit crabs and a baby turtle that she had triumphantly captured in the morning, heard shouts and stood up. It was the best of Roark's two remaining boats and it crawled slowly, deep-laden, in the water. Skinner Pitney was sitting in the stern. Two of the Indonesian men paddled; it had not been possible to make a new set of oars yet. The middle section of the boat was piled high with something that was covered with palm fronds and leaves.

Cooper himself, warned of its coming, came down to the beach. He stood waiting for Roark.

Pitney climbed out of the boat uninvited and came up the beach to him. "Mr. Tillman, remembering that it is St. Andrew's Day, has sent an offering."

Duncan Campbell fished down into the boat and pulled up the leaves.

"Roast pig!" he cried before Cooper had a chance to refuse. "St. Andrew himsel' would ha' appreciated it."

"They are three parts cooked," Pitney said. "An hour over a slow fire will have them ready, and there's a keg of rum.''

''Rum did you say, by God?'' One of the English sailors strode towards the boat.

''Leave it!'' Cooper roared.

Campbell, already alongside, snatched at the leaves and a small keg of rum stood exposed. ''It's just a wee barrel!'' His eyes were wide.

Cooper surrendered. The mischief was done.

''It is all that we can spare,'' Pitney said smoothly, facing him. ''We lost the great part of our stores when the sea swept us. Mr. Tillman regrets its inadequacy and ask your forgiveness.''

''It will be more than adequate, I have nae doubt,'' Cooper answered gratingly, his anger overcoming his accent.

Maya judged her moment with a fiendish precision. Campbell upended the empty keg and squinted into the hole with an air of comic despair. Even watered, the rum had barely lasted three full rounds. Cambell had gathered to himself the rounds of two of the non-drinkers, but he was not drunk—no more than highly stimulated.

''Not a drap an' the nex' St. Andrew's Day a full year awa'! It's a dry worrld.'' Campbell saw Maya laughing at him. ''Lassie, tis no' matter for laughter,'' he admonished her.

Her eyes held his, and he frowned for a moment, puzzled. Then he saw an almost imperceptible gesture of her hand towards the north and his wit, thirst-sharpened, leapt at a possibility.

''Is there mair where this came from, lass?'' he asked very softly.

She answered his eagerness rather than the actual words with a nod.

''Hey, lads! We'll tak' her away up the beach an' put her tae the question.''

She grinned at him in a companionship of utter mischief and shook her head.

"Chris," she said. She could understand him, and he could understand her alone of them all.

It took time for her to make Campbell understand. She sat serenely quiet until he did.

"She's not fer us, lads," he said drolly. "That wee devil Chris's out ahead o' us. Chris, ye bloody young ram, tak' her awa' and sift the matter of the rum oot o' her!" She rose as Chris rose, and Campbell slapped lightly at her bottom. "Hey, lads! She's got a neat wee arse, too." His enormous hand gathered in her firm buttocks and squeezed.

Maya's hand brushed lightly over the resting place of the dagger, but it was not a threat, for the young men knew nothing of the knife. It was a personal gesture of reassurance. She shook herself, remembering, and went out into the fresh darkness.

Chris followed.

17

The wind churned up the promise of a storm in small, confused whitecaps as the darkness settled on the surface of the water. Night had descended with its cloak of black, and warming breezes settled across the islands; its warmth streamed over them.

Chris, lying in the bows of the boat with his head peering into the darkness, felt the night wind ripple through his hair like a teasing hand. He watched the translucent wake of the canoe ahead of them, the phosphorescence swirling in light, delicate whorls. In the moonlight he could see Maya, her body silvered on the eastern side. She leaned forward, paddling with a strong easy stroke.

"Pull, laddies!" Campbell said behind him. "Pull! She's fetchin' awa' from us again."

"Quiet! The sound carries over the water. I can see th' island." Chris could see it as a dark bank against the moon haze over the reef. It lay in a aura of soft light.

The canoe altered course, and Chris passed the information back in a low voice. Maya was apparently heading for the open sea. He judged that she was keeping to deep water as long as possible before turning in for the southwestern horn of Salomon Island. The current caught them a little here, and the pulling was heavy. The light canoe skimmed ahead with the assurance of a night bird. Then, quite suddenly, they were grounded at the very edge of the beach. The distance in the moonlight had been deceptive. Maya was already standing motionless in the shadows, waiting. They pulled the canoe and the boat up on the sand, clear of the rising tide.

"Only three come," she said, holding up three fingers. "You"—she indicated Campbell—"you" —her finger picked out Tom Hunter, the Englishman—"an' Chris."

"What aboot us, then?" one of the others asked, his voice instantly distressed.

Maya patted the ground in a gesture of sitting down.

"We'll bring the stuff here," Campbell said. "It's no' a party we're goin' to, mon!"

"An' the women? I dinna trust ye the length o' a knife, Duncan!"

"After three months at sea I dinna trust myself, mon!" The big man began to laugh.

"Come quickly!" Maya said.

She led the three up the horn of the island's crescent-shaped shore and along the seaward beach to the west. They walked in silence, Maya picking the way through the piled wreckage, the logs and the broken timbers that had been left by the last of the typhoon. There were new boulders piled up, broken from the edge of the reef and rolled in by the force of the seas and the Devil Wind. But she picked her way unerringly through it all, the light of the moon more than ample for her purpose. At the end of ten minutes or so she found what she was seeking—four big boulders in a conspicuous group at the edge of the beachward palms. She had half feared that they might be missing, but she knew that they marked the end of the short path that led to the site of the hut of Ameni.

Now she would pay Ameni back for his lies.

Four full months back, three jars had disappeared—big, roomy jars. Inevitably she had been accused; every disappearance was put down to her. One of the jars she had seen already one early morning at the rear of the hut of Ameni, insufficiently covered with palm fronds. Three times since she had seen Ameni drunk, not stumbling drunk, but gently, happily drunk. She had stored up the useful knowledge that Ameni was making palm liquor. He had, of course, denied all knowledge of the jars, had made no attempt to shield her from the wrath of Pitney—not that she cared for Pitney or was afraid of him, but her friend Rahmzi had been beaten several times by Pitney for no apparent reason. Maya guessed it must have had something to do with the jars and that the weasel Pitney was beating Rahmzi because he feared her dagger.

The hut itself, like the others, had gone in the typhoon. Ameni, she judged, had been too busy since to investigate his cellar. Now he was safely on Egmont Island with the other men whom Roark had lent to Cooper.

She led them up to the rocks, turned in along the path that was partly obstructed by fallen palm

trunks, and found the clearing. Two of the upright
supports of the hut were still there to fix the
correct position. She stooped and began to pull
fronds and palm leaves away to get at the sand
below. They found the first jar in five minutes. She
cleared the sand from the stopper, opened it, and
put her nose to it. It was beyond question full of
matured palm wine. She laughed and beckoned
Campbell to put his head down to the jar.

He drew in a long, deep breath. "For Godsake!"
A smile of enormous admiration and awe split his
face. "You're a cunnin' wee devil!"

She pointed her finger at Hunter and made a
motion of digging, throwing sand away from the
side of the jar.

"Come!" she said to Chris and Campbell.

Campbell took her meaning instantly. "Ye stay
behind an' dig oot the jar, Tom Hunter, an' if a
drap is spilled, I'll have yer balls!"

Since the typhoon, the women had slept in three
small shelters; the children and young girls in one,
the younger women in the second, the older
women in the third. Maya, on her stomach on the
ground, worked her fingers through the thin,
temporary palm-frond screen.

Zada, the Bantu girl, always slept in this corner.
Maya was resting her luck heavily on the black
girl's inborn and unrestrained curiosity. Presently
she had a hole big enough to put her hand through.
She groped delicately in the darkness until she
found the warm, polished ebony skin. She found it
with no more than her fingertips, but at once Zada
stirred. She stroked delicately, trying to give to
her fingertips a touch of reassurance. After a
moment Zada stirred again, more awake. Maya
gave to her fingers a feeling of urgency, almost of

imperiousness.

Then, sure that Zada was awake enough, she stopped.

"It is I, Maya," she whispered. "Come outside!"

Zada stirred once more. "Who?" she murmured sleepily.

"I, Maya."

"What. . . ?"

Maya shushed her into silence, withdrawing her hand from the hut. She knew that curiosity and perhaps a degree of fear would bring Zada out now. In a moment, she saw a shape darker than the darkness under the eaves of the hut. She stretched out a hand, caught Zada's arm, and pulled her beyond the edge of the clearing.

"The Lord Tillman has not sent for you; I have a young man for you tonight."

Zada backed away quickly from Maya. "Beyond doubt, you are a witch!"

"The man I bring," Maya said smoothly, "is nonetheless a man. A young, strong man. Come!" Again she took Zada by the arm.

She led her down the path a few yards. In an open clearing, Duncan Campbell stood in the moonlight. He looked enormous, intensely virile. Zada walked towards him, wholly fascinated. Her movement was like sleepwalking. As Campbell opened his arms to her, she almost threw herself into them.

"By God," he muttered, "there's an armfu' here!"

Maya gave them only a minute to establish contact. Then—small, commanding, and eager—she separated them. "Go back now to the hut and waken Sabina—and softly! If you rouse the others I will indeed use my witchcraft. Go now and quickly, for there are more men at the horn of the island, and they have been at sea too long."

This at least Zada could understand, though she understood little of the rest of the what was happening. She gave a deep laugh, itself an expression of her sexual hunger, and hurried up the path.

"Chris!" Maya said, suddenly nervous.

"I am here," he answered out of the shadows.

"You want girl?"

She saw him shake his head in the dim light. "No," he said, "not one of these."

They arrived back at the horn of the island in an hour. Campbell and Hunter carried the great jar between them, slung on a pole over their shoulders. Three women walked with them—Zada, Sabina, and Astram, who had wakened and by necessity had been brought with them.

They were greeted with complaining whisperings from the four men who had been left behind.

"Like a lot o' bloody old women!" Campbell exclaimed witheringly. "Ye should have trusted the wee lassie here." He put his arm across Maya's shoulders. This time she slipped from under it with an abruptness that contained a warning.

They unslung the jar and collected halves of coconut shells from the boat.

Campbell poured, holding the whole weight of the jar in his muscular arms. "It's no whusky, but on a wee island like this in the middle o' yon vast, unthinkin' sea, it's in the nature o' the nourishment that the good Lord brought to the Hebrews i' the wilderness. Drink, ye goat-smellin', lily-livered sons of whores!"

The taste was wholly foreign to them. It was deceptively mild, and it required all the assurance of Campbell, the knowledgeable one in the field of alcohol, to make them drink enough of it. But in a short while, it established its own authority.

The women drank hardly at all, so that the whole thing started slowly. They were shy. Even Campbell was shy, standing with his huge arm about Zada's shoulders and unwilling to acknowledge that he was shocked by the appearance of her bare and splendid breasts in the soft moonlight.

Maya withdrew herself, first within the confines of the group and then physically away from it. Chris followed her; he had drunk only a little.

The lighting of the fire sparked all the trouble. It was the Englishman's suggestion. They built it rapidly and efficiently out of driftwood and dry rubbish, and it lit in a single, leaping, bright blaze.

"It will bring him down on us!" Chris protested anxiously, remembering Roark Tillman.

But Maya had considered the position carefully before she spoke.

"It is not matter now," she said. With her inevitable, unchildlike judgment, she had arrived at the conclusion that these young men, introduced once to the possibilities of alcohol and the willingness of the women on Salomon, would thereafter harass Roark in their own ways. Her part was accomplished. Roark was paid for the beating.

She sat watching the simple drinking develop into boisterous festivity.

The young men became lightly drunk, excited, competing for the attention of the women. As if the light of the flames had fired them, the women became part of the celebration. They moved about the fire. Sabina slipped away from a passionate embrace and was chased and brought back screaming with laughter. Zada began to dance in a slow, unmistakable rhythm. They all laughed.

They rushed backwards and forwards. The women's voices were shrill. They drank more and more. They piled the fire higher. The tempo of passion and lust leapt upward with the flames.

There were six men and three women. Early, there was almost a fight. It failed because of drunkenness, but they pulled the women between them and the women screamed with laughter. And then, with almost no anticipatory fondling, Campbell fell on Zada, spreading her thighs and penetrating her, thrusting harder and harder, faster and faster, while Zada wailed louder and louder in her ecstasy.

Campbell read her uncontrolled desire, her unbridled passions, and gave her what she wanted. She wanted to be used in every way known to sensuality, and he used her. He put her on her hands and knees and kept her there until her arms and legs were too weak to support her. He was getting everything he wanted, and more.

Maya, sitting quietly with her hands, as always, still on her lap, watched the primitive, urgent copulation while the rest of the men and the two women stood around and cheered and shouted.

Hunter, the Englishman, pulled Astram's legs from beneath her, and they wrestled on the ground. The watching group split and came together again. Somebody began to sing. Chris, watching intently, the furrowing of his forehead accentuated by the firelight, recognized the words.

> ". . . an' I were never too weary;
> To lay thee on an open field,
> And plow thy virgin furrow,
> Bonnie Anne, my dearie. . . ."

The other voices caught up the loud, boisterous melody. The laughter punctuated it.

Campbell rolled away at last and lay gasping and crowing with laughter. Somebody carried him a drink, and he propped himself on one elbow and lay back again, shouting unintelligible obscenities between the gusts of laughter. Sabina dropped on him where he lay and his massive arms folded around her. The other men started to cheer again.

"The ill-mannered bastard means to have them all!" a voice said.

Two of the men fell on their knees beside Sabina and tried to pull her away. Campbell struck out, still laughing, and the girl laughed with him, and they clung together.

The men began to sing again, a song that this time Chris did not recognize. The two who had been kneeling next to Sabina moved to Zada, who lay outstretched and still inviting, moving her hips upward sensuously as they approached. She chose one of them with a single clutch of her arm.

Maya watched entranced, her eyes dancing with malice. From time to time, she stole a side glance at Chris, who sat still, his eyes and thoughts seemingly far away.

After a little, Campbell was quiet again.

"Whar would the young lass be?" he said softly in the ear of Sabina as he lay there. And then, when he got no understanding from her he began to look around the clearing. "Whar's Maya?"

"With the boy," Sabina answered him in clear English.

"God's blood, and ye speak English as weel! Whar's the boy?"

"Leaver her 'lone! She carries a dagger."

"A dagger?"

"A dagger," Sabina explained savagely. "Between her legs she carries it."

"That's no' a place for a knife," he laughed.

Somebody poured more drinks. They sat up. The singing went on through the drinking. Somebody else threw more dry wood on the fire. The night was full of the sound of flames and laughter and wildness.

Then Roark came out of the night with a ghostly suddenness. One moment there was only the light of the fire against the tarnished silver of the palm fronds and the white of the beach and the nothingness of the dark shallows off the shore; and then there was Roark with a gun in his hands, and Pitney a safe ten yards behind him, and one of the Indonesian men behind him.

It was Sabina who saw him first, and shrieked. The reality of her fear was instant and communicable. The other women scrambled to their feet and ran blindly into the darkness.

Roark began, as always, to bellow.

Campbell rose quickly. He was not so drunk that he couldn't see the gun in Roark's hand and assess its danger.

"The boat!" he shouted. "Push out the boat!" And the men ran in one confused pattern of arms and bodies, lit by the flames against the darkness of the sea.

"Stop or I'll shoot!" Roark was bellowing.

They saw him raise the gun, and Chris rose on one knee, staring with an almost painful intensity. As he rose, he felt Maya's hand on his arm. He heard her voice in a long hissing warning.

"Ssssh!"

The boat was half afloat already. The men pushed her into the water in a flurry of firelit spray. Their own legs flung up more spray. They were tumbling aboard her. Under the shadows of the palms Maya could hear the thuds as the men scrambled aboard. The last man, Duncan Campbell himself, pushed ferociously and, as the water reached his waist, flung himself upwards over the bow and lay with his legs kicking.

Maya could hear a roar of laughter, and above it all Roark's thunderous voice again.

"Stop or I'll shoot!"

"He must no' shoot," Chris said, panicky.

"He has no gunpowder," Maya whispered softly. "Now we will go to the canoe."

She had beached the canoe farther down, almost at the exact point of the southern horn of the island. She slipped through the beach palms like a small ghost, and Chris, still shocked, still half hypnotized by the riotousness of the night, followed obediently behind her. Over the water, as they ran, they heard the thud of the oars between the peg holders and the splash as the men began to row. The boat drew out of the firelight, out of distance, out of range of the unloaded gun. The men began to sing again.

> "The cats like milk;
> The dogs like broth;
> The lasses like the young lads well,
> And th' old wives too."

And then came the amusing chorus, filled with laughter:

> "And we're a' noddin',
> Nid, nid, noddin',
> We're a' noddin' full and even,
> Nid, nid, noddin'. . . ."

Maya stopped level with the canoe and surveyed

it cautiously. Less than half of it was in the water. She turned back and watched Roark. He was raging at the water-edge, Pitney behind him. Their heads were drawn to the singing. Maya judged that it was wholly safe, and walked quietly down to the water's edge.

"Lift!" she said.

Chris grasped her meaning at once, and between them they walked the canoe out until it floated. She sat herself in it and motioned him to go in between the outrigger struts; she placed his hands at the point where the struts grew out from the hull.

"Swim!" she said, and he laughed softly, achieving an instant understanding.

He walked the canoe out until he too floated, and then he began to kick as he felt the paddle dig into the water. They slipped swiftly out of the ring of the firelight. At any moment Roark could have seen them, but he was still facing out toward the other boat, shaking his fist after the retreating song. The ballad had changed now to a vulgar bawdiness.

18

The soft, bluish red hues of the breaking dawn swept outward in undulating rays from the eastern horizon and skimmed over the tossing surf, touching the white, foamy crests with a pinkish cast and awakening the inhabitants of Egmont Island to the beauty of the morning.

Dirk Cooper had been up for hours; he walked down the line of men with his head low, thrust forward with something of the appearance of a bull preparing to charge.

"You—you—and you!"

One by one, he picked out the six who had taken part in the drunken celebration on Salomon that night.

He had no difficulty identifying them. They were bloodshot, bleary-eyed, tousled. It had taken them four hours of blind rowing to find their way back to Egmont without the canoe to lead them. Maya, already snuggled down between the children, had listened to their whispering, stumbling, still half-drunken return. Chris was already in his sleeping quarters.

She had landed him at the north point of Egmont to allow him time to return to camp before he was missed. But he had decided to wait and help her drag in the canoe, and in the darkness he had walked softly up the path to the huts lightly holding her hand.

Cooper separated the six from the others. He passed Chris by without a glance.

"I warned you yesterday morning. By God, I'll not warn you again! I'll set up a triangle and I'll flog the next man who goes to Salomon. I'll flog the next man who gets drunk. Goddam, I'll flog the lot o' ye! How did ye find the drink? Come on, how did ye find it?"

They stood silent, not answering. Campbell at least was sure that the rage was assumed. He watched intently for an opening. Before it came, Cooper was aware of a figure on the lagoon beach. The boat from Salomon had come down unsighted. The whole settlement was concentrated in this scene of accusation.

Pitney came up to him without greeting and held out a note.

Campbell relaxed slightly.

For a moment Cooper read in silence; then suddenly he spluttered and read aloud:

> "Mr. Cooper,
> I thought when I sent rum and roast pig
> to your sailors that they would stay
> away from my wives. . . ."

"His wives—his wives, by God's mercy! He calls them his wives. Those women are whores and his island's a brothel, no less, and he calls them his wives!''

Campbell relaxed completely. He was sure that he knew enough of Cooper to know that the crisis, so far as it concerned them, was over. He watched Dirk Cooper towering over the wretched Skinner Pitney.

"Who is he to send me letters like this? Who does he think he is? Damn, man, these are my islands! My men will go where they will. If he wants to keep his women, let him keep them. I'll no' help him.''

Maya, with the children gathered round her half fascinated, half terrified by the excitement, watched with her eyes glistening. Her mischievousness was a particular joy to her.

Cooper went on and on, and Pitney cringed and made no attempt to answer him.

"Get back and tell him that," Cooper said when he was almost exhausted. "No, by God! I'll go up to Salomon and tell him mysel'. You"—he turned to the group—"get the boat in the water, damn your stinking hides!"

Pitney finally found his voice again. "Mr. Tillman requests that you shall send back his men with my boat. He no longer wishes them to be of assistance to you.''

"Take them and be damned to them, the pack o' lazy, skulkin' bastards!''

"And the girl," Pitney said with surprising firmness, "the girl Maya.''

Somewhere behind him, Cooper heard his mother-in-law clear her throat.

"Take her and be damned to you!" he said.

Again Mrs. Finch cleared her throat. This time it held a warning, but it was Mrs. Cooper who came forward.

"Don't send her back!" she begged. "She is so young, so gentle."

"Mr. Tillman insists!" Pitney said in his most irritating manner.

"Can she not stay, Dirk?" Kathleen Cooper asked gently. "She has been good with the children. I think they love her already. She is such a little thing. She does not need to go back there with those ungodly heathens."

Cooper turned to face her. She stood with her hands clasped, her face anxious and pleading. "I do not like to think of a child with a man like that," she added softly.

"Child be damned!" Cooper returned abruptly. "She has been in his harem for the best part of a year. Do you think she is still a child?"

Mrs. Cooper put her hands to her mouth. "No, no, Dirk! You cannot mean—?"

"What do you think Tillman brought her for? I have told you enough of him."

"So young," Kathleen Cooper murmured.

"Roark Tillman's had 'em younger," he said indifferently, and suddenly, he wheeled on Maya.

"Where were you last night?" he demanded.

She looked at him with her enormous fawnlike eyes. "With the children, Lord," she answered softly, immensely enjoying the situation. It was even, in a sense, true—or partly true. She had been with the children for the last part of the night.

"Send her back if it is as you say it is," Mrs. Finch said from behind. "You cannot keep her here. You should not have allowed her to come here. It was monstrous, Mr. Cooper!"

"Ma'am," he muttered abstractedly, staring all the while at Maya. "I believe you are finished here, little devil," he said at last.

"At least put her in safety on the *China Clipper*,"

Mrs. Cooper said sorrowfully, "and take her east with you so that she may find her father."

Pitney had somehow reacquired his customary self-assurance. "You are right, Mr. Cooper, sir! She is a full-fledged devil, and a witch to boot. I would myself gladly see her go to hell. She is at the root of all the troubles on these islands. Ask your children where she was last night!" And then, as if he had gone too far, he paused for a moment to collect himself. "But Mr. Tillman would not permit it, sir," he added, "in no way would he permit it. He is in a sense bewitched by her, sir—"

"Goddam Roark Tillman and goddam you! Get your men and get the hell off my island!"

Maya lolled back in the canoe, calm and idle. She saw no reason that she should paddle when her canoe was tied to the stern of Pitney's boat. Pitney had taken his orders literally. "Keep a tight hold on her till you get her back here!" Roark had said.

Pitney's boat was sluggish, well astern of Cooper's swift longboat. She could, of course, escape. It required only a slash of her dagger at the line and a few strokes of the paddle. Pitney's overloaded boat would never catch up with her. The knowledge was itself a strength, but her curiosity as to the outcome of this affair was enough to overcome it. She lay lazily, occasionally putting a foot over the side and trailing her toes in the water. The glittering spray ran up under her knee and trickled down her thigh. Once or twice she dipped a hand into the water and patted her forehead with its coolness.

The young men in Cooper's longboat were sweating. He drove them remorselessly. They worked out their hangovers in a fierce, pounding rhythm, hammered out by him on the gunwale with a fish club. At times he swore at them, but there was no malice in his swearing. He was driving them only so that he could get to grips with Roark.

Maya heard his voice long before she had thought it necessary to raise herself enough to sight the island. There was no one on the beach, but Cooper was shouting in the thunderous voice that he had used in the old days of the whaling ships, the voice of the harpooner.

"Ahoy, there! You, Tillman—don't you know that what a sailor considers heaven is more than rum and roast pig?"

Campbell laughed and, when Cooper glowered at him, he laughed again. The sweat was racing down his face and over his chest, but that was little enough to pay for a celebration that would have not disgraced a tavern in Glasgow on St. Andrew's night.

They lay on their oars, waiting, and presently, as Pitney's boat went past them, Maya, looking beyond it, saw Roark come out of the path from the village, his gun cradled in his arms, and stalk, furious, to the water's edge.

"Keep away!" he shouted out. "I'll shoot the next one who tries to land!"

"Shoot and I'll burn your village down over your head!"

Maya listened, convulsed with inner laughter as Roark's voice grew stronger and Cooper's diminished with the progress of the boat. The shouting match went on—old accusations, recriminations, new insults, sheer fury. It was not worth while attempting to separate the meaning out of the thunder of the words. She was content with the knowledge that she had stirred this up.

She steered the canoe to one side as the heavy boat grounded and, clambering out, pulled it up on the sand. Then she walked demurely, childlike, wholly submissive, to the thin shadows of the path.

Roark watched her with suspicion out of the corner of his eye. He had recognized the marks where her canoe had been dragged up, when they searched the scene of the orgy at sunrise. He became distracted in his exchange of obscenities with Cooper. Over the water, Cooper redoubled his efforts.

Maya went on towards the village and the battered palm trees swallowed her.

The hut into which Roark thrust her had been reinforced. New uprights had been driven in all around it, filling in the spaces between the original posts. To her eyes it had at once the appearance of a prison. It was, in fact, a prison. They had saved the padlock, and she was locked in—and she knew at once that escape would be very difficult.

She lay there, alone. At noon Kim Chi brought her food.

"Never has he been so angry," the Chinese girl whispered, "but never, never!" She slipped out again.

An hour after the meal, she heard Rahmzi's voice, low and apprehensive. He was lying on his belly on the far side of the hut from the path. "He is more angry than he has ever been. The hut is watched. I will bring what I can, but there is no escape from here. Almira watches now and the men will watch at night. It is his order, and they are afraid of him."

She smiled and saw that the boy's eyes looked

shocked.

"I have been working on a plan," she whispered. "Now I will take a rest. He will not beat me again."

She settled herself comfortably, and one by one the older children came up on the path side and talked to her through the bars of her cage.

Maya slept well that night. In the early morning the birds woke her. She was acutely sensitive to the birds now, and when the gulls had gone, their cries diminishing in the distance, she thought back over the madness of the night and the splendor of the morning quarrels. From time to time, little gusts of laughter shook her. She was completely happy.

It was not until the evening of the second day that she began to have doubts. Roark had made no move. Since he had thrust her into the cage-hut, he had not come near her. She had heard him from time to time giving orders, berating the women, crashing once through the undergrowth, but she had not seen him.

Her food came when the others had their meals. The children drifted up and were chased away and drifted back again. There was always someone to talk to if she chose, but the watch was constant and effective. It was clear that everyone was terrified of Roark in his present mood. Once or twice, Pitney came and looked in through the bars, smugly satisfied.

It was Pitney perhaps who aroused her doubts. She began to wonder if she could not have stayed on the other island. Mrs. Cooper—she thought of Mrs. Cooper as a foolish woman—had said something about the *China Clipper*, about the ship, but she had not understood it completely in the quick-fire exchange. Perhaps, if she had chosen, she could have stayed with Mrs. Cooper.

Perhaps, if she had stayed, Mrs. Cooper could have helped her to sail with the *China Clipper*. It took a long time before she formulated this idea, but when she had accepted it, the depression was instant and absolute. She knew now that she had made a mistake. To get aboard the *China Clipper* by herself would require immense cunning and her best magic, and she was locked in this stupid prison. For the first time, she began to consider escape seriously.

In the early evening when Anpu Yi, May Ling's child, drifted up to the cage to talk, she sent her for Rahmzi. The boy came a long while after, in the darkness. She heard his whispered greeting close to her head as she lay, her mind pounding over the possibilities of her mistake.

"I must get to the *China Clipper*!" she said.

"You cannot," he answered softly. "He will not let you go. Tonight the men watch, and you cannot break out of this place without noise. They will not dare to sleep. He has told them that he will lash them against a tree and beat them to death if you so much as break one pole of the hut."

"And you?"

"What can I do? I am a child. I could bring you a knife, but you have a knife already. If you need a machete, I will bring it, but it will not help you because of the noise. I have heard the men say this."

"I could dig my way under the posts."

"You could not. They go too deep. He made it that way, thinking of this."

"What am I to do, then?" She began to feel a stirring of panic.

"It is not for me to say," Rahmzi replied softly.

All through the night she lay restless and afraid. She knew now that she had mishandled the affair.

It was humiliating to admit even to herself that she had been wrong; it destroyed her confidence. If she had used Mrs. Cooper, she could have stayed; she was sure now of that. Cooper himself would have given in, in the end. And now she was in this accursed cage, and the men were terrified of Roark—and there was no chance of escape.

Unless . . . unless she could do something with the men themselves.

She spoke to Zurim when he came to the hut to make certain that she was still secure.

"I must get to the ship. If you aid me, there will be great reward."

"There will be unmeasured beating and death," Zurim said soberly. "For myself, I would let you go, for I believe that there is endless mischief in you, but he has punished Zada and forbids her to leave the women's hut, and he has beaten Sabina and Astram, and I will not make a fourth in the beatings."

"You will not be to blame . . ." she began, the persuasive note coming into her voice.

"It is not a matter of blame," Zurim broke in with finality. "If you escape, I will be beaten. Even if a god came down from the sky and lifted you out through the roof, I would still be beaten. Therefore, I will not help you."

"Coward!" She spat the single word after him, but it did not seem to weigh particularly heavily on him.

When the watch was relieved a little before dawn, she tried again with Ameni.

"Who revealed to them the hiding place of my jars?" he asked.

"I did, but a jar of palm wine is a small thing against the reward that you will get from my father."

"We have been here the most of a year, and your father has not come," Ameni pointed out firmly. "I do not any longer believe in this reward."

"Then, because I am a witch, I will bring a curse upon you."

"I fulfill his orders," Ameni said uneasily, but still determined. "I know how he will punish me. I do not know about your curses." And he walked away.

On the morning of the fourth day, she heard the singing. She heard shouts, and the creaking of the blocks, and the rhythmic, repetitive clacking of the pawls as the anchor was raised.

As the *China Clipper* put out to sea, she lay her head on a pile of leaves and wept with deep, shattering sobs. It was not simply that the *China Clipper* was gone. It was not alone that her chance of escape had vanished with it. It was that her faith in herself was gone.

19

Rahmzi flung the fish net. It hung for a moment lightly and playfully brilliant in the evening light, then attained its full and perfect circle, and dropped. Maya remembered the morning when she had stood with him fishing in the lagoon—months ago now—in the almost forgotten period before the Devil Wind. He had been more persuadable then; it was time to make him persuadable again.

She waited until he had gathered in the net and was ready to make another cast.

"It was my error," she said. "I did not ask my head for help."

He grasped her meaning in a flash of time. Precisely as he had done on that other day, he dropped the net. "Merciful Allah!" Then, gasping, as he crouched down to recover it, he asked, "What head, in the name of God?"

"You surely should know," she answered loftily.

"It was the head that brought the ship, but I did not ask it to permit the ship to take me away. This was my error."

"And now?"

"Now I must go to it and make the prayers and the spells."

"Why do you tell me this?"

"Because I do not wish to go alone."

"I do not go!" The boy gathered up the net and clasped it to his chest. "I do not wish to hear of this."

"You have heard," she said smoothly. "Last time she called the birds down on me, and I wish to have someone to stand at my back."

"I will not come!" Rahmzi was frankly terrified now.

She shrugged her shoulders. "Then I must go alone. At least the canoe will float now."

Roark had put a hole through its bottom as a secondary guarantee against escape. It was not a very big hole and, with the help of Ameni and the boy, she had repaired it, Roark raising no objections once the ship was safely gone. She had been let out early in the morning of the departure. No one had said anything, not even Pitney. All the village had heard her sobbing. The women at least were afraid of what would happen next.

It had taken her a full ten days to re-establish her confidence in herself. For the first of them, she had crept around the village like a wounded bird, and Roark, his own anger appeased now, had watched her compassionately. As much as anything, it was the smugness among the women that restored her faith in herself. It became necessary to deal with them.

She cast her mind back over these things for a minute.

"I will go tonight," she said to Rahmzi. "There is no moon, but it does not matter; there are at least the stars. And I am not afraid." She did not add 'like you,' but Rahmzi accepted the reproach.

"It is true," he said after he had meditated over it for a little, "I am afraid. I was afraid of her in her life, but in her death I am many times afraid. I thought when they said that a shark had taken it . . . but I put the thought away."

"That was wise. It will be wise if you put the thought of talking about this away also."

Roark came down the path as she went back towards the village. He grunted at her, and she could not tell from his bearing whether he were angry with her or pleased.

"You are coming back to life again?" he asked.

She decided to say nothing, and Roark seemed bemused by her silence.

"Rahmzi passed me like a frightened rabbit."

"Rabbit?" she asked, turning to stare at him for a moment.

He bent down to look into her face and actually laughed; her innocence was so exquisitely fabricated.

"You don't know about rabbits. Any kind of small animal in your stories, then, when Maya the mongoose has frightened them. What are you planning now, my little mongoose?"

"I plan nothing," she replied airily. The story of the mongoose and the dragon fleeted across her mind, and she smiled. "It is only that things . . . happen."

"You had better get it into your small head that you can't escape me," he said, half menacing, half humorous. "It is time that we were friends."

She opened both hands in a gesture of appeasement. "It is my wish to be friends with all."

"It was in friendship, then," he said as if trying to follow her line of reasoning, "that you brought the young men from Egmont to the beach, that you uncovered the palm wine of Ameni, and that you persuaded my women from their hut?"

She looked at him full in the face, her voice disarming. "The young men had been many months without women, and for what I know without drink also."

Roark exploded with laughter. "Beyond doubt, you were born in the pit of Hell itself!" He went on down the path, still laughing. "Sleep well, my little mongoose!" he said back over his shoulder.

"I will sleep well," she called back musically, and added softly so that he could not hear, "when the time comes for me to sleep, my mighty dragon." And she went on her way to the village.

The birds grumbled and complained in the darkness as she crept beneath them. They could hear her passing, though she moved as softly as was possible. They could see the small flame of the coconut stem torch that she carried in her hand—more for comfort than for its dim light.

She found the shelter, lonely at the end of its storm clearing, untouched, silent, forboding, and waiting. It took no more than five minutes to gather fuel for the fire beneath the head—this night there was no question of a fire outside. As she blew up the spark of the stem torch to light the fire she saw the head for the first time—vague, undiminished, and malignant. Then the fire caught, and the eyes began to move with its flickering, and the mouth to change its shape as if to speak. When the fire had taken, Maya moved back to her place against the upright, settled herself, and contempated it.

The Tamil head had suffered a little since she left it. The skin had cracked in places and the corners had lifted up in a mockery of wounds; the eye-sockets were deeper and darker, and some small bird had perched on it and there were droppings. Strangely, the cracking at the corners of the mouth had altered its expression. It had seemed malignant in the first red glow of the torch, but now, in the full light of the fire, it took on a macabre cheerfulness. The mouth had almost the appearance of laughter.

"You may laugh at me," Maya said. "This is your right, for it was my error. I should have come to you." She thought of adding in explanation, 'But I am young and foolish,' and rejected it.

The lips appeared to move with the play of the flames, but no sound came.

"Laugh, then!" she said. "Laugh! But now I shall say the words that the Hindu woman taught me, and then you will again do my bidding. So laugh while you may."

She leaned her head back against the post and closed her eyes, digging deeply into her memories. The words came to her of their own volition. She found herself pronouncing them without conscious formation of the sounds. About her, she could hear the squeak and protest of the birds, but this she could disregard, for there was no whistle of diving wings. For a long time she sat quite still, allowing the little streams of words to come together and issue forth from her mouth. Half of them she had never understood; of half of the rest of them the meaning was forgotten. The words were the thing that mattered. When at last her mind became utterly empty with effort, she sat in silence. Far away, the surf boomed; the bird sounds and the rustle of wings, and the occasional clap of feathers in clumsy take-off came under the eaves to her.

The smoke had filled the inverted bowl of the roof. The head once more was swooping in and out of it, most of the time invisible or at best half-seen, and once again she waited for the fire to die and the level of smoke to rise.

When at last it did so, she bowed in soft supplication to it.

"I need another ship to come," she said. "See to it." And almost as if she were not saying it herself, but the phrases were formed independently of her as some of the spells had been, she went on, "Also I have been afraid and am sad, and I need happiness." And a long while afterwards, drowsily and about to sleep, she looked once more at the head. "See to it!"

Chris came down the narrow stretch of the high-tide beach, disconsolate. Once he kicked at a shell, started to kick at it a second time, then abandoned the intention. More than anything else, his cheerless mood betrayed both his unsettling feelings for the girl Maya and his unhappiness.

Duncan Campbell had been at him continually. Campbell was not cruel. It was only that he lacked perception of other people's feelings. Since the night on Salomon Island, he had maintained a constant harassing of Chris.

"Ah! But where were ye, ye wee bugger, when we were in trouble? Awa' in the bushes with the lassie—and you the youngest o' us all!"

He meant it in laughter. Another man might have held a grudge against Chris for escaping from the violent rage of Cooper, for not admitting that he too had taken part in the adventure. Campbell, however, bore no malice; Gunn,

however, the first mate of the *China Clipper*, who
had been left in charge of the men and Egmont
Island when the *China Clipper* sailed, had long
since discovered Chris's part in the affair. And
Gunn had a sour and a brutal temperament.

Chris walked on, lost in his thoughts, not even
bothering to kick another shell that lay directly in
his path.

Maya watched him from her place in the shade
of the shoreward palm trees. She sat, as always,
utterly still, completely absorbed in his approach.
She was not sure that she had asked the head of
Tamil to bring Chris to her. In the moment
between waking and sleeping, she might have
asked anything of it; her memory had stopped at
her sad and lonely appeal for happiness. Had the
head brought Chris to her, or had she come to him
of her own free will? Did she want him, or had the
head ensured that she should have him? She was
unsure of her own feelings and of the reasons that
had brought her here. What was this malady she
was feeling? Maya moaned softly to herself. What
was this unknown affliction deep inside her heart?
She had had the attentions of much more lordly
men before and found no softening of her heart;
yet now her mind seemed to seek out this young
man, this Chris.

She knew only that she had woken early, long
before the first light, and that she had come
straight across the water to Egmont and hidden
the canoe in the trees at the northernmost point of
the island. It was as if she had moved like a puppet
of the traveling minstrel shows, given life by
invisible hands. She had left the canoe and had
waded down through the shallows towards the
Cooper settlement. And all through the day she
had sat here waiting—and now he had come.

He walked framed under the arch of the outward-leaning shore palms. The blinding glare of the afternoon sun seemed to make a halo about him. The thin emerald green of the shallows lessened the glow hardly at all, and he walked in a glory and in the center of the glory. He had the look of a lost child, sad and lonely. She was aware of compassion; but it was an emotion she did not know how to deal with. She had once felt compassion for Roark; only she had never before had the need to show it.

Chris came under the last half-arch of the palms and walked straight past her, unseeing and self-engrossed.

"Chris!" she said softly.

Chris stopped instantly, as a man would stop at a gunshot; he turned and ran, half stumbling, towards her. With a completely childlike gesture, he dropped to his knees in front of her and held out his hands, reaching uncertainly for her hands.

"What are ye doin' here?" he said, his eyes on her eyes. "Oh, Maya, that man Gunn will be angry if he finds ye! What made ye come?"

For the first time in her life Maya was at a loss for a positive answer.

"I wished to see . . ."

"Oh," he said, momentarily disappointed, certain it was not he she had come to see. "But I am happy to see you!"

There was something important in the touch of his hands on hers, something more intimate than friendship; it was new to her, different from anything that she had ever known or felt with Rahmzi, a new and perhaps irrational feeling.

"Chris, I have left the island . . ." She removed her hand and swept it up to indicate Salomon Island. "Now I live . . . there." She pointed towards the thin line of the palm tops of the west island. "You come with me!"

"Tae the west island?" The words themsleves were not important; the willingness to believe them was.

Chris sat back on his heels and studied her face. "Ye mean, ye want me tae go to the west island with ye tae live?" he asked after a long pause.

Maya still made no reply but kept her eyes steadily on his.

"Lassie, ye dinna know what ye are saying," he said. "And then, after a still longer pause, "Aye, but by God, ye do!"

He realized that he was still holding her hands, though in the act of sitting back on his heels his arms had had to stretch out to their full length. He released her hands, and then, as she put them back into her lap, he reached forward and took them again—and in that moment she knew that she had won.

For a long time, nonetheless, he argued against it, thinking of Mrs. Cooper, the children, this duty to Dirk Cooper; and then, balanced against these good things, Gunn and his violent temper and brutality, and Mrs. Finch and her thin-lipped disapproval, and Campbell and his endless crude joking. Once, he got up and walked to the water's edge and picked up a flat piece of shell and skimmed it over the shallows. She waited patiently, quite certain that he would come.

The journey down the western shoreline of Egmont and across the channel to Eagle Island was desperately long, five miles the way she took; waiting for the tide to flood the shallows, wading with the canoe till they found water deep enough for him to swim, going back into the shallow water to give him time to rest, standing in the enchanted combination of new moon and starlight. He swam well with the canoe now, hanging on to the forward outrigger at the point where it was attached to the hull, kicking in the rhythm that he had learned on the night of the escape from Salomon. Maya made the rest periods long, as they moved silently towards the western island. He grew cold, though the water was warm and the night air soft. He looked very young in the delicate light, and when he stood in the shallows he faced away from her always. It had taken the best part of ten minutes to persuade him to take off his trousers and put them in the canoe before they started.

It was past four in the morning before the bow of the canoe grated on the lagoon beach of the west island. The tide was too low to take the canoe round to the inner lagoon; they themselves were too exhausted. They dragged it with a slow weariness onto the dry sand, and she took the bow line in and fastened it to a tree.

When she came back, he was struggling into his trousers, wet with the bottom water of the canoe.

"Give," Maya said sharply, and took them from him.

Chris was too tired to argue and too cold, and yet he was still very aware of his nakedness and was blushing uselessly in the darkness.

Maya led him by the hand through the palms, sure even in the night of her direction. Inside the shelter of the trees, she struck flint and lit a torch of coconut husk, then went forward again. In time, they came to the small hut that she had made beside the blue pool.

Chris walked like a man asleep, his will power gone, utterly exhausted with the swim and the necessity to avoid the sharp spikes of coral, and the difficulty of walking in the uncertain shallows. He saw the place where she pointed the husk torch and accepted it as a place to lie down. He accepted the cloth that she spread for him and he accepted, perhaps because he did not even comprehend what it was, the cover of her sarong when she spread it over him and lay down beside him and pressed her body against him for warmth.

As the morning sun rose on the western island, it was as if a tall, billowing cloud had given birth to a spot of emerald green. Several low sand hills crowded close upon a light, brownish yellow strand of beach, which separated the living green from the tumbling surf that licked the naked shore with white-crested tongues of foam. The deep aquamarine of the open sea gave way in the shallows near the island to a brilliant iridescent blue that matched the shade of Maya's eyes.

Chris woke first. He was conscious that he lay in a green pool of light, the sides of which were made of the silver of the palm stems. The surface of the pool was the bright blue of the morning sky, and from time to time the white of the wing of a drifting seabird skimmed across it. There were the four colors only—white, blue, green, and silver— four colors, except where Maya lay, still asleep, the honey-brown of her skin glowing.

He stared at her for a long time before he was fully aware of the implications of the closeness of their bodies and their nakedness. Maya was still totally asleep, her eyelids closed and pale, her mouth relaxed and inviting. He could see a pulse beating in her throat, slow and regular, and the beat of it reminded him of breathing and the thought of breathing drew his eyes, against his embarrassed will, to her bare breast, and at once he saw not the slow rise and fall of her breathing but the disturbing swellings of her breasts. They had matured since she had first been brought to the *Sea Wolf*. They were no longer the beginning buds of that time, but were developed and rounded and firm. Beneath them the skin was lighter in color, so that at this angle and in this light they looked more mature than in fact they were.

He felt himself becoming aroused by her beauty and blushing hotly; as if it were against his will, he put out a hand to touch her. His fingertips received a shock. He had touching nothing before that was like this swelling softness; it had a quality of unreality. It was difficult for him to adjust it to his own responses. He stroked her timidly, apprehensively, ashamed of what was happening to himself and yet proud of it. And presently and very slowly, Maya woke, and a slow, lazy arm curled round his shoulders, and pulled him down against her.

Maya was still a virgin, but she was full of knowledge, remembered knowledge of the rapes of captured women on the deck of her father's ship and remembrance of the necessarily public sex on the crowded ship. She had no inhibitions, no personal shyness. For almost a year now, she had had no controls on her except her own.

"Hurry," she giggled noisily in his ear and traced it teasingly with her tongue.

She took him joyously, giving him the knowledge that he lacked, softly telling him about the art of love, for he was almost harshly ignorant.

He lowered his hips between her thighs, and she guided the burning heat of his maleness into her. With anyone else, he would have been awkward and shame-faced and conscience-ridden, but she brought laughter to it.

Foolishly, under the reassertion of his Scots upbringing, Chris insisted on putting on his trousers when they went down to take the canoe round into the inner lagoon to sink it out of sight in the blue pool. He took on a consciousness of guilt with them. Maya left her sarong in the hut, splendidly indifferent, and as she walked ahead of him, her buttocks firm and beautiful, he remembered something that had troubled him vaguely throughout their lovemaking—there was no knife between her legs. Remembering Pitney's warning and the vulgar joking of Campbell, he could see, or thought he could see, on her left thigh the marks of the silken bandage in which she habitually carried it. But there was no dagger now, and there had been no dagger in the early light when he had first overcome his morality enough to look upon her young body.

Willfully, Maya put the entire episode out of her mind, remembering the path she had already chosen. It was the fulfilling of her revenge against Roark, nothing else.

Now she walked with a jaunty gaiety, quite unconcerned with what had passed between her and Chris. There was no time for such thoughts. When she allowed herself to think coherently again, she thought only that she had won a victory against Roark. Nothing that he could do could touch her now. She had escaped him. For a moment, she wondered vaguely if that were why she had conceived the idea of bringing Chris to the island, but that thought appeared to be unimportant also and she abandoned it. It did not matter why she had brought him, whether it was herself or her necessity for revenge against Roark or the head's interpretation of her need for happiness. The one thing that was important was that he had come, and that, having seduced him, she was very happy.

Chris walked in an increasing oppression of spirit. It was dark out of the clearing of the hut. It was depressing in the deep thickness of the palm trees. He was conscious that he had broken all the strictures of his upbringing.

Occasionally Maya skipped a little as she walked and sang a few lines of a song. Chris moved gloomily behind her. When she called back to him in words that he could not understand over her shoulder, he answered with a grunt, and she turned and laughed at him and held out her hands, and suddenly his depression lifted. The spaces between the palm trees were wider now, and they could walk hand in hand, and hand in hand they came to the edge of the tree line and could see the bright colors of the lagoon.

At the edge of the palms she halted cautiously. From inside the shoreward fringe of the trees, she scanned the surface of the lagoon. There were no sails on it. She had no fear of Roark's boats, but she thought it was possible that Gunn might send a search party for Chris. Nothing moved on the water. It was too early yet for his absence to be noticed, although it was difficult for either of them to grasp this fact; so much had happened since nightfall. It seemed as if they were immeasurably removed in time from the quarreling and the harshness of Salomon and Egmont.

They took the canoe into the inner lagoon when the tide rose, brought it right up to the blue pool, and sank it, covering its outline with palm fronds

weighted down with rocks. They made a game of
the sinking, rocking the canoe until it filled with
water, swimming out with the stones to sink it,
diving down into the blue luminescence of the
pool to fix the palm fronds that would mask its
outline from the casual eye. They bumped against
each other in the water and laughed, and bubbles
exploded in silver to the surface. The water was so
warm that they had no sensation from it except
that it was another element and that they moved
differently in it, gracefully in the swirling patterns
of their naked bodies. When they had weighted
down the last of the palm leaves, his eyes met hers,
and they clasped together wordlessly and without
the necessity for words and without fear, and
rose, clinging, through the blue water to the
brilliance of the day. A huge sea eagle on motionless wings came over them and hung there,
drifting close to better view these odd sea nymphs.

When at last they went ashore to the strip of
white sand beneath the palms, he picked up his
trousers and carried them back to the hut.

That day they enlarged the small hut. It took
time for Chris to learn the different uses of the
machete, but he was quick with tools and he found
its sharp edge suited to the task of making the
rafters. They searched for timber along the beach,
hard driftwood posts that had come from
unguessable continents. Maya did most of the
work without complaint, splitting the fronds,
plaiting them swiftly and skillfully into matting.
She made baskets to hold their small store of
possessions. She showed Chris how to bind the
thatching down and helped him, and by the time
the sun was low they had completed three-
quarters of the work.

They laughed then and went out to the lagoon beach to bathe. Afterwards they ate the last of the little store of food that she had brought with her from Salomon and supplemented it with young coconut meat and drank the milk. But when the sun set, she put the fire out and would not tell him why, and because he needed her he did not press for an answer, and they lay together on the bed of leaves and made love again.

Much later Maya lay on his chest, her cheek resting against his neck. She was again her bright and cheerful self, though since reaching the west island the amount of sleep she had gotten had been meager indeed. It was as if a great burden had been lifted from her, and truly she conceded that the fulfillment of her womanhood and the restoration of her honor had accomplished wonders. Roark Tillman could do no more to her. His control of her was past—done! She was free of him. She could set her mind to more important matters. Her need for revenge against Roark began to fade.

She was gay and lighthearted and went to sleep naturally, like a kitten that has been at play. But Chris lay awake in the darkness, and in the darkness his upbringing crowded in on him again. He could remember denunciations from the pulpit of the small white church in which he had sat out long Sunday mornings, against the sins of the flesh, of fornication. For the first time he could visualize the word; it had a faintly ridiculous quality, yet it had overtones of threat and doom. He thought of what the succession of preachers who had clouded his boyhood would have said to even this present innocence, and he put his arm across the sleeping Maya; she stirred and turned towards him.

"Ye're a noble one, young lassie," he whispered, and knew that these were not the words that his preachers would have used to describe her. His mind, running in a sudden change of direction from his boyhood teachings, began to examine whether his feelings of guilt were real or whether he felt only what the preachers would have said that he ought to feel. He succeeded only in achieving a high state of metaphysical confusion. It was wicked, but it was also beautiful. It was sin, but it was also happiness. It was guilt, but it was also innocence.

Maya stirred again and pressed against him. Her eyes were still closed, her long thick lashes like black fans against her golden cheeks. Her breasts rose and fell with joy, and her expression was rapturous. He held her close and felt irrationally valiant and protective. The white church at the head of the loch was three oceans away, and this island was perhaps out of the eye of God. And, as if to punctuate the thought, Maya in her sleep smiled softly.

They woke into a patternless succession of days. They finished the hut, and they raised the bed on a low platform that they floored with bamboos from the high-tide mark—to keep them clear of the land crabs while they slept, Maya said. They dug a well and, finding the water faintly brackish, searched for giant clam shells and put them at the base of palms and tied bunches of leaves above them, as Pitney had done on Salomon after the typhoon to collect rain water.

His trousers hung from one of the rafters of the roof like a banner of defiance against the church. He discovered that it was a simple matter to slip back into a state of nature, that it required only the kindliness of an island climate. He tanned slowly but steadily, and his muscles hardened with the work. He learned to use the fish net almost at a single lesson, but he could never match Maya with the fish spear, could never challenge her instant and darting eye or the lightning response of her muscles.

Maya showed him all the secrets of the reef—the young clams that were good to eat, and the great clams that lay with their mantles open, ready to close like a trap on an unwary foot. They lay sometimes teasing one, and they teased also the octopus that hid in the darkness of the coral rock and whipped out long encircling arms at the unsuspecting fish. He learned the value of the birds as food, and though he would never succumb to her passion for eggs boiled with the young inside them after the manner of the Orientals, he developed an immense appetite for the fresh ones.

Between the fishing and the foraging, they swam. In the heat of the afternoon they lay in the hut with the wind blowing through the open walls and made love, discovering and inventing. They were lost in an enchanted and magical kingdom of their own.

Only Maya kept a hold on reality. It was because of this hold that they saw the search party. She would break off the idle fantasies of the island to cross over to the lagoon shore from time to time to scan the ocean. Always, once at least, in the morning she went down to watch for a little. It was about the twelfth day that she saw two of the Egmont boats coming across to the island. It was too late to slip out and obliterate footprints across the beach, but the chance of a strong wind from the northeast during the night had sent little waves up almost to the palms. She measured and judged this and nodded, satisfied, and they lay on their stomachs, buoyed up with mischief and freedom, watching.

The boats ran in steadily on what was left of the northeaster. They were steering for a point close to the cove, a small lake that lay inside the beach midway down the northern section of the island, and from their concealment Chris and Maya watched them come in on land.

Chris spoke first. "It's that blood-thirsty devil Gunn in the first boot an' Duncan Campbell steerin' the second."

She laughed at his tone of anger.

A wonderful sense of security enveloped them. They knew that they could escape this search. The island was theirs. It brought a contempt for the plooding ignorance of the searchers. They laughed as they saw them splashing out of the boats to stand uncertain on the white sand. They knew there were no footprints up there; they had not been to the north of the island since they came.

The men from the boats fanned out uncertainly, moving up first a little to the north, then coming south. Gunn plodded to within a quarter mile of where they lay, and Maya and Chris watched him, laughing. They knew that they could get away, that they could never be caught in the thickets of the palms because of their intricate knowledge of the terrain of the island. At the worst, the enemy— they thought of the Egmont men as their enemy now—might find the shelter, but if they had to withdraw they would withdraw by way of the shelter, and take the irreplaceable things with them—the machete, the flint and tinder, the dagger and the clothes. They could retreat to the southern stretches of the island, they could double back, they could swim across the island's inner lagoon. They could get away from anything.

It was all unnecessary. Long before the search became close, it was abandoned. The virgin whiteness of the beach seemed to satisfy Gunn. When three of the men started in through the palms, he called them back. After they had been ashore for perhaps an hour, they took to the boats again. The wind had fallen to an absolute calm, and it was necessary to row back all the four miles to the settlement on Egmont Island.

As the boats pushed off, Maya's arm curled around Chris's neck. In a moment she had fired his blood and they fell to the ground together, her legs and her arms twined around him in what was more a gesture of defiance than love.

Chris's arms slipped around her beneath her buttocks. He felt the heat of her soft body under him, and all other thoughts fled his mind.

Maya pressed herself tightly against him, caressing the hard, bare firmness of his body.

When it was over, Chris stared down at her, smiling. "Tha' was immoral, lassie," he said, and laughed at his own boldness. "But I doubt if you hae any notions of morality in this part o' the world."

Maya frowned her bemusement, for she could find no sense in his words.

His mouth sought hers again.

No search came from Salomon Island. Roark had known that Maya would disappear after the departure of the *China Clipper*; her behavior had developed a pattern over the months she had been with him. He guessed that she was on the west island, and he believed that she would come back as soon as she was tired of her independence. She had always come back before.

On the sixth day, however, a boat had come up from Egmont, carrying a glowering Gunn, to ask if they had seen the boy Chris. Roark ordered him off the island and went back to the big hut to think. There were the canoe marks at the southern horn of Salomon on the night he had caught Cooper's men with his concubines. There were two pairs of footprints where the canoe had been pushed back into the water. All day he raged like a wounded animal in the big hut, taking out his uncontrolled anger on the whole camp. If the boy was with her, he would pray a thousand times for death before Roark was finished with him. But he sent no boat in search. He knew enough of Maya now to know that it would serve no purpose.

On the west island, the beautiful life went on. For Chris it slowly cast off all its overtones of sin. For Maya, the feeling that with each time she made love to Chris she plunged another knife in Roark diminished until she achieved only an exquisite pleasure and happiness. Their whole existence was only innocence and youthful passion.

Their days divided themselves into the necessities of the search for food, the brief and simple ways of cooking, the need to cool themselves in the water, and the pleasant hours of love. They made an expedition once to the far south of the island to hunt for pigs, but the pigs were sly and suspicious and they had no luck, and their traps were sprung in vain and their pitfalls filled with water, and they laughed and gave up. After four days they went back to the hut and took up the simple pattern of pleasure again. Almost their only link now with the other world was the morning ritual of the scanning of the main island lagoon and the channel for search parties.

It was on the morning of the twenty-fifth day that they saw the ship.

Maya was a little ahead of Chris. She came to the fringe of the trees at the shore and stood immobile, her slender naked body conveying at once an impression of fear and a sense of warning.

"Wha' is it, love?" Chris called anxiously from deep back in the palms.

"A ship." Her voice was low and thin, almost tremulous. She drew a deep breath, and then, less clearly, as if she spoke to herself alone, she whispered. "She has sent it, then. First she sent happiness, and now she has sent a ship—and I do not know that I want a ship anymore."

"What were ya sayin'?" Chris asked, coming up to her.

"It is nothing," she answered. Maya cringed inwardly and sought to ease her shaking. She could only stand and look at her trembling hands, though she knew his eyes were on her and that he waited.

Chris looked at her with the first stirrings of fear.

20

The ship looked lonely on the still water. The island also seemed lonely and forlorn. No boats moved between the ship and the island. Maya had rested her plan on this, certain that Roark would be taking his afternoon nap; it had been his custom in the past.

It was beyond question the *Sea Wolf*. She had been certain in her heart of this at the first moment of the sighting, but now she could see the odd angle of the fore-topgallant mast of the black-painted vessel and the beautifully carved figurehead of a mermaid rearing gracefully from her prow. Maya had planned to reach her in this hot afternoon hour and now, as she approached the anchorage, she watched the island beach rather than the ship.

She had put Chris ashore at the Egmont landing place, itself lifeless and empty in the noon hush. It had taken all the early hours of the morning to raise the canoe from the bottom of the blue pool. They had accomplished it without laughter, and there was no love-making as they waited for the tide to come in so that they could take the canoe out through the shallow passage into the channel. They had sat silent and oppressed, looking like children found out. But they made the run back to Egmont more swiftly than in their first reckless crossing. In the daylight the passage was easier. Chris was stronger, his muscles more accustomed to the water. She had cut the rest periods down heedlessly, driven by an indefinable compulsion.

Now she felt an equally indefinable reluctance to approach the ship. She moved in fear. The masts and the yards grew larger, and presently they towered above her. The hull stood like a cliff, though the ship was low in the water with a full cargo of spices. No one saw her, no one challenged her. The anchor watch was asleep like the rest of them in the heat. She went aboard by the ladder, letting the canoe drift astern to the end of its line, climbed to the poop deck, and sat down in her particular corner by the gunwale.

She was sitting there when Morgan came on to the deck, yawning and bleary-eyed. He did not see her for a full minute and when he saw her he started.

"They told us you were gone! Where have you come from now?"

"The other islands," she answered, scanty with the truth as always. She looked at him with a faint unease.

"Mr. Tillman is angry."

"He is always angry," she answered indifferently. And then, smiling at him with a conscious effort of charm, she asked:

"Do you go back to Singapore?"

"We have just come from there."

"But you go east?"

He knew enough Indonesian now to accept the word 'timor.'

"No, we go west," he replied. "We go"—he paused for the smallest fraction of a second and her heart leapt in her; then he said the fatal words—"to England."

She let her hands, which had been raised in something that was almost supplication, fall dead into her lap.

He looked at her, grave and uneasy. "It would be no use, Maya! He will search every inch of the ship before we sail unless he has you under his eye. He has said so to the captain, to Flint, to me. He means it. There's no way he's going to let you go."

"This I know," she agreed. She was afraid to ask the other question that she had come to ask.

He had enough insight, enough knowledge of her, to know that she was afraid.

"You have grown since we left here, Maya. You are taller." He tried, knowing that it was folly, to attempt a compliment. "You have grown more beautiful."

"You have news for me?" she blurted out, disregarding his compliment altogether.

"I have no news—I do not speak Indonesian—but Flint has."

He went down the ladder before she could stop him, and she read all that was necessary for her to read into the manner of his going, but she still sat there, her face expressionless.

Flint came up the ladder swiftly. He strode over to her and dropped on one knee. "Maya, your father is dead. They found his body four miles off the shore." He stared into her enormous eyes.

"Who found him?" she asked quietly.

"The man you spoke of—Jin-qua."

"Jin-qua was a coward!" She looked at him fiercely. "He is a liar also. I do not believe this!"

"Nonetheless," Flint said very gently, "it is true. He has not been seen since that day. If he had been alive, he would have still been raiding along that coast."

For a moment her lips closed, pursing themselves in an effort to repress the pain.

"He would have still been raiding," she echoed at last, with a terrible reluctance. Getting up, she brushed past Flint where he still knelt on the deck and went blindly down the ladder.

The canoe came in with an almost live obedience. She climbed into it without purpose, found the paddle, and headed in towards the anchorage.

The two men on the poop could not see her face. Only in the droop of her shoulders and the angle of her small head could they sense the quality and depth of her grief.

BOOK FOUR

THE TEMPTRESS

21

They had almost completed the digging of the new well at the hour of the noon break. Gunn kept them at it, for once the water filled, the work would become twice as difficult. Only when it was all done, and the fresh water was seeping up into the newly dug well bottom, did he finally order the break. They went back across the island to the huts, Campbell, as always, leading.

It was Campbell who first saw Chris. He lay sprawled and naked on someone else's blanket, and the brilliance of the early afternoon sun, coming in at the door of the hut, lit him startlingly. He was bronzed. He looked fit, and the weariness that had been engraved in his face after the long swim across the channel had already disappeared in the brief sleep.

"Chris," Campbell said softly and delightedly, "ye sly wee buck, whar in God's name hae ye been?" The others crowded in behind him.

Campbell took a step closer, stuck out his foot, and kicked Chris in the ribs. "Chris," he said more loudly, "wake up!"

Chris rolled over, stretched, and grinned back at him with a confidence that was entirely new.

"Whar hae ye been an' whar's the lassie?"

"Travelin'," Chris replied almost insolently, and Campbell, sensing a new defiance in the boy, laughed aloud.

"Gunn's going to take the hide off you," Hunter warned him. "Where have you been all this time? What did you do for food?"

"It's no' food he's been worrying himsel' aboot!" Campbell burst out. "Whar's the lassie?" he demanded again.

"Gone up tae the ship," Chris answered slowly, suddenly aware that he need not attempt to keep secret the incredible thing that had happened to him, aware equally that he had acquired from it a new standing in their eyes.

Hunter refused to speculate further. "We'll hear of it when someone comes ashore from the ship. The thing is now"—he nodded at Chris, who was getting up slowly from the blanket—"what will Gunn do with him?"

"I'm getting tired o' Mister Gunn." Campbell said reflectively.

"We're all tired o' him!" a voice chimed in from the back.

"He's over-handy wi' that bull whip," another voice complained.

"An' we dinna like bein' beaten, eh?" Campbell went on, sensing like a good leader the anger of the men.

"He has not beaten you, Duncan," Hunter said sarcastically.

"I'm thinkin' o' the weaker brethren," Campbell

explained with mock piety.

"It's all very well for you," Hunter replied. "You're too big for him. But the rest of us have all been beaten one time and another."

"An' we're no' slaves." Campbell raised a hand, like a saint in a religious painting. "Mister Gunn is growin' out o' all proportion tae his proper station. Get up, Chris, an' put on yer trousers! Ye want to hae Mister Gunn see ye like that, sunburnt right down tae the end o' yer malehood—and ye awa' on a island with a lassie and ye livin' together alone for a' this time. Ye would not want tae be putting ideas into his saintly head now, wad ye?"

Christ felt himself blushing hotly, but the laughter that engulfed him was friendly, envious laughter.

"There'll be nae beatin'," Campbell declared when the laughter had died down, "neither Chris here nor any o' us. It's time for a stand."

"He ran away," an English voice from the back of the group said. "He's not had to do any of the work for a month. Mrs. Finch will say he's done wrong and needs to be punished."

Campbell smacked his lips. "I'd give a year's pay for a half o' the wrong he's done." His voice was full of gusty suggestion. "He's done a sight mair than that." His humorous eye took in the whole of the group. "He's shown us a' the way. There's several agreeable and unhappy females up tae Salomon Island. There a' sorts o' possibilities. Let's all go an' search for Mister Gunn an' remind him o' the scripture text that says there's more joy in heaven over one sinner that repenteth."

Chris put a lashing of rope round his trousers and walked out of the hut and stood ready.

Campbell stooped over to leave the hut and stared questioningly at Chris.

"Is it true that she wears a dagger between her legs?" he asked confidentially, but in a whisper that all the hut could hear.

"I never saw it," Chris answered with an absolute naivete, and was amazed at the weight of the roar of laughter that exploded around him.

Four of the women in the village were husking rice. The first boats had brought sacks ashore from the *Sea Wolf* with the excitement and the gaiety of a harvest festival. The loss of the rice to most of the women had been the direct result of the Devil Wind. They stood in a circle around the four at the rice mortars. The conventional, customary act had become a celebration, almost in a sense a sacrament to appease the wind gods for bringing the ship back safely. It signaled the full and final return of normal life to the colony.

And into the noise and the gaiety and the bustle of it, Nassurit's daughter, Maeti, came breathless and running.

"She is coming! The witch is coming!" And only afterwards did she gasp:

"The canoe! She comes in the canoe!"

Even before the final words were uttered, the other women knew by intuition that the girl meant Maya. The rhythm of the rice pounding hesitated and stopped. The noise of the talk ceased, began again and utterly changed its note.

Almira, sitting a little way away from the rest, raised a sardonic brow, and asked the crucial question.

"The boy from Egmont—is he with her?"

Maeti had recovered her breath a little. "No, she is alone. She comes from the ship."

"From the ship?" May Ling snapped the words as if they were a rebuke.

"Already she has been there!" Sabina exclaimed enviously.

"She goes where she wills," somebody said, and the envy this time was hopeless.

Almira considered the whole thing above the babble of women. When she spoke, they hushed quickly.

"It is that they have refused to shelter her upon the ship. There is nothing left for her to do except to come back here. This time he will assuredly beat her, he has said it."

"She must be beaten again," Nassurti's wife said virtuously. She was proud that her daughter was the bringer of the news.

"A month," a voice murmured behind her. And then, after a pause, her expression changed to a note of envy. "A month!"

"He will beat her this time as he beat you." May Ling looked at Zada.

"It is proper that she should be beaten again," another said. "It is only right. It is no more than justice."

Almira spoke again. "There is the matter this time of the boy. She will no longer have the favor of the Lord Tillman."

For a long while the women were silent, trying to judge what the hidden meaning of this was.

"Yet she has been a month away and with a man whom she chose herself," Sabina said thoughtfully at last.

Kim Chi lowered the lids of her beautiful eyes and stared down into the mortar bowl with its varicolored patterns of half-husked rice.

"It is something that is denied to us, though we have the favor of the Lord Tillman," she murmured softly.

"She has shown us the way," Zada said

defiantly. And a faint murmur of agreement rose from the younger women.

Almira reflected and pronounced her judgment. "That way is not for us. We are the wives of the Lord Tillman."

"The slaves!" Sabina declared, adding her defiance to that of Zada.

"There are many of us, but there is only one Lord Tillman," Kim Chi murmured softly again. "They say that the young men on Egmont are strong." This time she looked directly at Astram, and the girl flushed under the brown of her skin.

"She has shown us the way," Sabina said again.

"And for that," May Ling spoke out venomously, "the witch must be beaten and will be beaten. This time the Lord cannot pass the matter over lest"— her eye took in, quick succession Zada, Sabina, Astram, and Kim Chi—"others be corrupted by her evil ways."

"We are already corrupted. A month with a man she chose . . ." Kim Chi sighed as softly as a leaf in a gentle breeze.

Astram edged back a little into the crowd, away from Almira's eyes. "We could, any of us, do this thing," she announced proudly.

"We do not, any of us, have what she has." Kim Chi's delicate voice was clear.

Another breathless child came running up the path. "She is at the landing place!" she called, and all the women turned towards the beach, though they knew that they could not see the landing place from where they stood.

Mrs. Finch towered over her daughter like a figure of justice carved with an inadequate chisel. "He must be lashed," she announced with the absolute conviction of her authority.

"Not lashed." Mrs. Cooper spoke hesitantly. She was at a disadvantage, sitting and feeding her youngest child.

"Lashed," Mrs. Finch repeated firmly, "or all rule is lost on the island."

"He is so young," Mrs. Cooper said, a little less hesitantly.

"He is old enough," her mother answered positively. "A month alone on an island with that whore! You must give your support to Mr. Gunn. You must speak for the captain."

Mrs. Cooper shook her head.

"I saw his mother," she said irrelevantly. "A very small woman. I remember she had a black shawl." Across the contentment of her child's sucking on her breast, she saw in the eye of her imagination a long vista of palm trees, and in them two beautiful figures, golden-brown and naked. She acknowledged that they would be naked, though she would not have admitted it aloud.

"It is very necessary that Mr. Gunn should make an example of him," Mrs. Finch said sharply. "There are other women. . . ." She indicated Salomon with the faintest of movements of her head. "He has taught them that it is possible. For that alone he must be lashed—as a warning to them."

Mrs. Cooper had now regained her confidence. "I will not agree, Mother."

Mrs. Finch leant over her. "But you must! The whole discipline of the island is at stake."

"No," Kathleen Cooper answered calmly. "I will tell them that they must wait until Dirk returns. It is for him to judge. This is beyond Gunn's authority."

Her mother straightened herself. "Your husband placed him in charge."

"He is a brute."

"His personal qualities have no part in this. They have defied him. His authority is in the balance."

"It can wait until Dirk returns."

"It cannot! You will have a boatload away to Salomon at nightfall. They will rebel."

"That is not reason enough to lash the boy."

"His wickedness is reason enough."

"Not wickedness," Mrs. Cooper murmured dreamily, her eye deep again in her vision. The two beautiful golden figures were disappearing in the palms. "Not wickedness."

"You heard what the man said."

"What man?"

"The man Pitney from the other island. She carries a knife."

"Perhaps," Mrs. Cooper said softly in a bright flash of perception, "she needed it in the past to defend herself." When her mother looked at her, shocked, she smiled mischievously at her.

"Chris at least has no wounds," she added, trying to stifle her laughter.

Almira herself took the news to Roark. He lay unbuttoned and dishevelled in the great chair that had been re-created out of the recovered fragments. Ben Cooper sat opposite him with an almost empty glass in his hand. Pitney squatted on a rough stool.

"The witch comes," she said without preamble.

Like the women earlier, Roark had no need of further detail.

"Maya," he said instantly.

Pitney straightened himself so suddenly that he almost fell.

"She's come back," Roark said, in confirmation.

"I thought the ship would bring her."

"This time you will beat her properly," Almira whispered insinuatingly from the doorway.

"Go away!" Roark ordered brusquely.

"If you will not beat her, at least send her away!" Pitney almost gabbled out the words. "We've had almost a month of peace. Now there will be unceasing trouble again. Send her away!"

"Arrrh!" Roark growled at him.

Ben Cooper looked from one man to the other alternately as they spoke. Now he waited.

"Send her to me!" Roark called through the open doorway after a pause.

At once Pitney plucked at his courage.

"This time there was the boy," he muttered.

"Where does she come from?" Roark called out again.

"From the ship." Another voice, not Almira's, answered him.

"By God she does!" Cooper exclaimed. The look on Roark's face stilled him.

Roark lifted himself in his chair. "Someone will have told her."

"Someone will have told her," Cooper grunted in agreement.

Pitney was unable to understand their meaning. "If you will not send her away with the ship, Mr. Tillman, thrash her," he said. "Thrash her as a warning for the others."

Roark turned on him savagely. "Would you like to thrash her?"

"I?" Pitney queried, agitated. "It is not my place, Mr. Tillman, sir. It is not my place."

"Get the hell out!" Roark growled at him. "I will speak with her alone."

Ben Cooper got to his feet. "I'll start breaking out the rest o' the stores. Let me know what you need, Mr. Tillman."

Maya came in through the open doorway. She walked slowly, her shoulders stooped forward, her arms hanging limp, as he had seen her once before. Her eyes were stricken. He watched her, sitting upright in his great chair, and when she reached the center of the hut he spoke to her.

"Sit!"

Maya sat down as if sleep-walking.

"You have heard the word of your father?" he murmured, his voice soft and gentle.

"I have heard," she agreed sorrowfully, "but I do not believe." Her bearing belied the courage of her denial.

Roark lifted his shoulders almost imperceptibly. "It is a year. If he lived, it would be known on the sea. The merchantmen would have brought the news long since. If he lived, he would have had a ship by now and he would have struck somewhere."

"Jin-qua"—her voice acquired a doubtful defiance—"is a coward and a liar also. I do not believe his words."

Roark could see that she was uncertain. It could be that she had admitted the reality to herself but was not yet prepared to acknowledge it to the world outside. He waited while he turned this over in his mind.

"A year is a long time," he said only.

And she sighed so deeply that it was almost like a sob.

He lay back in his chair, still watching her, wondering how he could achieve an understanding with her, wondering how he could penetrate her mask. He had the feeling that it was all but within reach, the mask—that, if he discovered her secret, he could lift it, could make contact at last with her inner feelings. It was a mask that had a life of its own, that displayed emotions and desires that were not those of the real Maya beneath it.

"There is no longer any purpose in wishing to go east," he whispered very softly.

She flinched visibly and as visibly achieved control of herself again.

"I do not know," she answered him at last. "I have need to think."

His eyes were compassionate. What does a compass do when its lodestone is withdrawn?

Again she sighed in a deep admission of grief.

He allowed her time to think, watching her all the while, closely.

When at last she spoke it was almost to herself, whispering so faintly that he could scarcely make out the words. "If it is true, what remains to me?"

In two words he put the question that he had all but despaired of asking her.

"The boy?" he whispered, his tone matching hers.

She shrugged her delicate, beautiful shoulders in indifference, and in that movement told him almost all that he needed to know.

He kept silent, with a long-acquired wisdom. Then he rose from the chair at last.

"Sleep there!" he said. "I will send the women away." And then, amused, he added, "Pitney wishes to beat you."

"Tell him my dagger still remains to me," she said drowsily, and settled herself to sleep.

Roark gazed down on her sadly for a moment; then he stalked out of the long hut and marched into the sunlight, waving his arms.

"Away, away!" he called. "Crows, vultures— away!"

Pitney, from his own hut across the open space of the village, regarded him sourly.

Almira followed him down the path. She moved behind him silently and submissively so that Roark was not fully aware of her until he stopped in the shadow at the edge of the beach.

She waited a long time before she spoke.

"What will you do with her?" she said at last.

He waited almost as long before he answered her.

"Nothing. What is there to do?"

"And the boy?" she said hesitantly.

He made a little gesture, almost as if he were throwing something away. "That is over."

"Nonetheless, it happened."

He shrugged his huge shoulders. "It was necessary for her to prove that she can stand alone."

"Prove to whom?"

"To herself," Roark replied with an acute perceptiveness. He was trying, even as he answered the old woman's questions, to analyse his own feelings towards Maya. He had an immense, almost overwhelming, admiration for her defiance, for her iron will, for the strength of her determination to preserve her individuality. He knew that she was not moved by ordinary rebellions or the simple need for discipline. He guessed that she had inherited from her father a fierce pride of personality, and under the essential simplicity of his own amorality he could appreciate this quality in her character. His understanding of it was almost feminine in its delicacy. She was the one he had sought all his life.

For a long while, they were both silent while he thought and rethought the problem.

"You are in love with her," Almira said finally

with a weary scornfulness. "This I had never thought to see." And, remembering all the years she had loved him without question, she turned and walked slowly back down the path to the village, her eyes filling with tears.

Roark stood silently until nightfall on the edge of the beach, like some dark angel fallen from heaven's grace. An image suddenly appeared from the deepest core of his memory, blurring his vision and stirring the passion ever present within him. It was his soul-mate coming to him again. It was a girl, a madonna-like creature, lithe and lovely, with hair as dark as a raven's wing and eyes like indigo.

"I await you, my lord. Come, seek your desire in my arms. I am yours; you have only to reach out to touch me."

Inside his head, he heard her siren's song and remembered her dagger. He fought to remain strong. It was no longer merely a dream, he told himself. He knew the siren well now. For a hundred nights, when he slept, she would come. Somehow, she was inevitably linked to his future. But before, as quickly as it appeared, the vision had narrowed and vanished. Now the vision had a face and a name. It was Maya.

"I have become an outcast in paradise, lost because of her," he murmured huskily. "That is what I have become, but soon that will change."

Salomon was Roark's oasis from the madness of the world—his self-proclaimed kingdom. He would guard it well, and the waters surrounding it with a fierceness that few dared challenge. And Maya would be his queen.

22

Kim Chi had been upset. Everything had gone badly, and she was in desperate need to do something. She was far too overwrought to sit still with so many confusing emotions rolling around within her, and, in a sense, she had fled to Egmont as a result of her misdirection of sympathy. In a greater degree she had fled for reasons of revenge —Maya's revenge.

The change had begun at the moment of Maya's awakening on the mats in the center of the great hut. The sympathy of the women was real at first; inevitably, it was also temporary. Her loss, when Roark told them of it, had a particular effect on them, for they had no family ties. Not one of them could claim a loss like this. Their parents had disappeared in a process of indifference, of gift, of sale. None of them had anyone direct or immediate to lose, and therefore Maya's loss was the sharper and the more pitiable. They crowded into the great hut and sat around her, waiting for her to wake; and they began, talking softly among themselves, to take a new approach to her. They were gentle, they wiped the past out of their minds, they ignored the possibilities of the future, they overwhelmed her with kindness.

It was true, of course, that in any group there were always one or two who combined sympathy with satisfaction that punishment had at last fallen disastrously on her, that the gods had seen to her, but the general sympathy remained.

For a while, for perhaps a week, Maya allowed herself to be submerged in it. She had to adjust herself to the reaction from the weeks on the west island with Chris Lovel as well as to the reaction from the news of her father's death. These reactions interwove themselves, so that for the first time in her life she had feelings of guilt and punishment. Almost, but not quite, she arrived at a conception of sin; but before she fell into that dangerous trap she succeeded in blaming her punishment on the malice of the Tamil's head.

Rahmzi, listening to her when at last she achieved energy enough to go out from the women's quarters, had been confused by her words.

"It was not a holy cedar tree. An evil spirit must have lived in it—and yet not wholly evil, for at least I had happiness for a little."

It was beyond his comprehension and she did not choose to explain, and he could only be sorrowful for her.

Inescapably, before the end of the first week there was a change in the sympathy of the women. It began with the girls and the younger women. One or two of the more intelligent among them began to wonder why such an outflow of sympathy was necessary. She had, they recalled, spent a month alone with a man of her choosing on the west island, as Sabina had pointed out, and this was something to be set off against the news of the year-old death of her father, however beloved. A tinge of envy began to creep into their condolences. She was no longer given the best of the food in the meals. She was no longer accorded rank or privilege.

Sabina in the end was wholly frank about it. "He does not punish you," she complained. "If I were to go only to the ocean beach with a man, he would beat me until his arm was tired. What is the magic that you have and why should you have such magic?"

Maya was still too listless to become angry. She ignored Sabina's complaints and the increasing questions and the obscene interest in her relations with Chris. They wanted to know everything—the matter and the method of his accomplishment, his endurance while making love. They asked the questions unblushingly, and still Maya gave no answer.

When Maya bled, Zada went from woman to women complaining.

"There is no justice!" she spat, her eyes dark with anger and contempt. "She will not even have a child! And the great Lord no longer calls us to his bed. He has forgotten us. He loves only this witch! We were only whores to him."

Roark, who had been listening to her words, strode purposefully toward her and before she could contain her rebellious words, he was standing beside her.

He towered over her. "Whore?" he snarled. "Is that how you think you're treated?" He stared at her with eyes red with fury; then, in one lightning-quick move, he grabbed her hair with a vicious jerk, pulling her head back.

Zada screamed in furious indignation and clawed out at him. He easily caught her wrist in one hand. She struggled in vain. A bubble of a sob rose in her throat.

"Now you know exactly how it feels for me to treat you like a whore," he growled, thrusting her away from him with disgust.

Zada collapsed on the ground and curled her arms and legs into her body.

"Damn you," Zada heard him sigh raggedly. "Why do you always bring out the worst in me? Do you purposely goad me to punish you?"

She wanted to tell him that she would not be his slave anymore, that she wanted a man of her own.

Suddenly Roark regained his cool composure and was viewing her with a momentary flicker of compassion in his eyes. Then his anger returned.

"You are to do exactly as I tell you for the rest of your life," he commanded in a steel-edged voice. "And I swear to you, if you defy me once more, I'll punish you in a way that will make you wish you had never been born." He stood observing all the women who had gathered round them, his eyes narrowing dangerously, then spun about and strode off toward the beach. A glimmer of sadness flickered in his brooding gaze as he walked, and an overwhelming sense of loss and sorrow assailed his very soul. He wasn't proud of what he'd done to Zada, or of his treatment of the other women, and, as always, he felt unsettling twinges of guilt. But this had been his way for so many years. How could he change now? Roark had never taken a woman who wasn't willing, and he backed away if he sensed that she was not. He had never wished to marry and believed celibacy a sacrifice for saints. But a night with a woman like Maya might change all this.

Roark rubbed his eyes with his right thumb and forefinger, thinking, the hell with it! I'll watch Maya closely, in case the little hellion tries to cause any more trouble, but no more of these crazy thoughts of love and marriage. One woman could never satisfy me!

Through it all Maya moved like a wraith of herself. She hated him also. He trampled on people's lives and emotions as though they meant nothing to him. She was his slave, too, and at the moment, there was nothing she could do about it. Her will to fight was gone. But for some strange reason she found herself mesmerized by everything about him.

She walked without her old arrogance, and the strength seemed to have gone out of her spine. She disregarded the rising tide of small annoyances and spitefulness. She was gentle with the children and kind, but she offered no leadership. She led Rahmzi and the other boys into no mischief. She ignored Pitney and made no attempt to head conspiracies against him. She kept out of Roark's way.

By the end of a fortnight, the quality of the sympathy had changed again completely, this time among the older women. It was May Ling who voiced it. She sat in the middle of a flow of aimless, pointless comforting.

"Nonetheless, he is dead," she sneered. "It may be that he drowned, or it may be that Jin-qua cut his throat; all death is the same. The Lion of Ceylon is no more. He will not come here to rescue you, that at least is certain." She paused while Maya looked at her with somber eyes. "We no longer need to walk in fear."

It was after this that Maya began to shake off her lassitude—this and the words of Sabina.

"We are many, but you are by yourself."

It was a long time before Maya finally summoned the strength to think rationally again. It would be too much to say that she evolved a plan; rather, she achieved an intention.

Something of this she put to Rahmzi as she watched him fishing in the shallows one day.

"The Lord Tillman will not always protect me. He is a man." She did not bother to look at the boy to see how he took the insult. "The man Pitney will always try to do me harm. The other men do not matter, for they cannot help. There are all the women on the one side and myself on the other. Even you I cannot trust any more."

Rahmzi hauled the net in from the water and inspected a fish. It was true, there seemed no point in denying it. He could not fight with her against all the other women and Pitney.

"There is myself alone, and there is the Tamil's head," Maya said dreamily. "It is time that I went back to my head again."

It was Roark, however, who finally triggered the opening of the trouble—and that too was due to an excess of sympathy for Maya.

Late in the afternoon of her conversation with Rahmzi, he called her to the big hut.

He came to the point more directly than was customary with him.

"Are the women troubling you?" he asked.

Maya shrugged her shoulders. "They do not like me, and they are no longer afraid that my father will come." The memory of her father brought back, as it always did, the look of pain to her eyes.

Almost unconsciously, Roark stretched out and put his arm round her and drew her to him. He meant it as a gesture of tenderness, but, in the very act of making it, his desire overcame him.

She felt the change in the pressure of his hand against her bare back, she felt the physical rise of passion in him, and instantly, with precisely the movement of a mongoose facing a cobra, she sprang away from him and stood quivering, close to the door.

"It is enough!" she cried. "I must go."

With her head held high and arrogant, their eyes met in a clash of wills. When she was like this, so brazenly defiant and spitting like a wildcat, Roark thought she was quite easily the most exciting woman he'd ever encountered. She gave as good as she got. His mouth widened momentarily into a rakish smile.

She looked like a lithe young lioness, a fine sheen of moisture on her soft skin, her every gesture exciting his passion more. Her long black hair tumbled down her back and about her naked shoulders. He stared greedily at her full, high breasts.

But for the first time he yielded to a positive jealousy.

"To that damned boy!" he said, the words forced out of him against his will. "Nothing about me warrants your love, does it, Maya?" His upper lip curled into a sneer. "You go to this boy, don't you?"

She stared at him, her eyes wide and suddenly very frightened.

"No, to my island—to be alone," she answered. Then she turned and went out of the hut and, as she went, she was moved by some emotion that she could not understand; but feeling herself under some strange compulsion, she stopped before the hut. ''I will be back in two days, at the most three,'' she added.

Through the passage across the channel she thought of this and of other things—of her father's death, for it was necessary now to admit, at any rate to herself, that he was dead, of her defenselessness, of the weight and power of the other women, of the inconsistencies of Roark and of the weaknesses that showed in his blustering facade. Her proud eyes were enormous as her proud spirit struggled with these feelings for Roark. She did not wish to acknowledge them, refused to. Still, a little voice inside her would not be silent. He has a powerful hold on you, the voice said, and if you allow him to touch you one more time, you might be lost.

Roark sat in the big hut alone. As before in his dreams, he wanted to turn away, to run as fast and as far from her haunting eyes as he possibly could. Yet he knew it was useless. This bewitching girl with her haunting eyes was somehow linked with his future, and whether he liked it or not, he knew he could not simply walk away and let her go. He shook himself. Stop it, you damned fool, he raged inwardly, before this girl completely destroys you! Bloody hell! What is this power this girl has over me!

Maya began thinking of the head after the halfway point. What she had said to Rahmzi about the cedar tree was true. She debated the consequences of this. It could be that the spirit that had entered from the tree that she had used was a mischievous spirit. It could be, on the other hand, that it was a weak spirit and unable, there-

fore, completely to overcome the spirit of the
Tamil woman's head. Or it might be that there was
only the spirit of the Tamil and nothing had come
in from the tree at all. But she had power over the
Tamil woman's spirit—a potential power at least.

And through all this conjecture, she wondered
dispassionately if she really believed in the head.
It had sent ships when she asked it, but might not
those ships have come by themselves? Certainly it
was obvious that they had set sail long before the
head had been placed in the smoke-filled roof of
the hut. It was true that she had found happiness
with Chris, but equally it was true that she had
marked Chris as hers on the very first day of the
arrival of the *China Clipper*, and she could not be
certain whether it was the head or her own heart
that had brought them together. It was true that
the head had called down the birds on her, but
then the birds might have come to any fire in their
state of panic and weariness on their return to the
island. At least she had not built another fire in the
open.

Maya landed on the west island half an hour
before sunset, and, dragging the canoe up as far as
she could, she made it secure and walked in
towards the clearing of the hut. She no longer
walked arrogantly; her whole carriage was doubtful.

Overhead, the moon was rising higher in the
forbidding, twilight sky, full and blood-red. The
evening was still and foreboding. Even the roar of
the surf had abated to a whisper. No leaves moved
in the palm trees; no air came through between
the tree trunks. After Maya had made the necessary noise getting the wood together, the silence
became profound again. Now and then bird
sounds broke out or, rather, splayed themselves

across the silence. She could make out the
twittering of the terns and the grunt of a dis-
contented sea gull.

The fire under the head began to set up noises of
its own, the crackling and the spurt of flame, the
hissing sound of the damp wood. In its light, and
before the smoke swallowed it, the head looked
more grotesque than ever. The leaves, which
should have been holy leaves but were not, were
withered. The bird droppings—two sandpipers
had flitted through under the roof as she
approached—were thicker on it. The skin had
dried still further. The grin had changed to a leer.
The whole place had a shabby and depressed air.
Palm fronds had blown in on the coral slabs of the
floor. The roof itself was damaged, and she made a
note to mend it in the morning.

Slowly the smoke crept down. It swallowed the
uppermost leaves of the wrappings. It billowed
down, swallowed the head, released it, and crept
down again. In a little while the head was gone.

Maya sat in her customary place, her back
against the tree trunk. She had now to consider
the tasks that she had to ask of the Tamil head.

For almost three hours she sat quite still,
trance-like, going over and over her predicament
in her mind. She could plan for immediate
possibilities; she had an amazing power of fore-
thought, but she did not want a long, complicated
plan. All that she could think of now was the need
to re-establish her domination over the women, to
provide the possibility of an escape from Roark—
there was even an element of uncertainty about
her need for this—and to ask again for her
happiness back.

When at last the smoke cleared, and the head
grew animate and responsive in the fire's glow,

she had reached no decisions, but, because of her indecision, she began with an attack.

"There is an evil in you. How it came there I do not know. Perhaps it was that I brought the wrong tree to you, but there was no other way for me. Upon this small piece of dirt upon the sea, there are no cedar trees, nor could I do you the proper honor with holy leaves because there are none. This you must understand. I have done you all honor that is possible for me to do in this place, and no one else would have done this honor for you. Therefore you are mine and you must do the things that I wish you to do. Do you understand?"

She stared at the head, and a flame leapt and the mouth seemed to frame a word, but she could not tell whether the word was yes or no.

"Very well," she went on, "if you will not answer me clearly I will tell you what I will do. I will ask certain things of you, and if you do them I will continue to honor you and to light fires to you. But if you do not do them, or do again as you have done before and put mischief into them, I will take this fire and put it to the roof, and you will burn and be destroyed and have no more existence in this world. This is a power that I have in my hands always."

The glow of the fire remained steady, but the mask of the face was utterly still. Outside, in the night, bird noises, soft and distant, faltered around her.

After a long silence, and with the fire diminished to a dull red glow, she spoke again.

"You will return to me my power over the women. You will bring another ship. And you will give me back my happiness!"

At sunset two days later, on Egmont, she called

to Tom Hunter from the shelter of a clump of ironwood. She had waited all the afternoon for Chris, but he had not appeared.

The Englishman peered in through the ironwoods. "Chris's girl, by God! You'd better not let Gunn see you here."

Maya smiled beguilingly at him. "You tell Chris I here quick."

Hunter came closer into the ironwood trees. "Couldn't you do with an older man? Chris's no more than a boy, my sweet." He leaned against a twisted arch of ironwood and grinned down at her. Something about her eyes and her nakedness started the blood surging through his veins, tantalizing him and stirring his passions until they became a hot, sweet ache in his loins. She was like some beautifully savage sea nymph with those alluring, soulful eyes and those firm, golden breasts. His pulse jumped.

Maya knew exactly what was in his mind.

"You tell Chris," she repeated, her voice firm, positive.

He nodded approvingly. "I like a girl to have spirit. Chris—he's only beginning, like. I've had my pickings o' girls."

She got up from the ground and turned away from him. When she turned again, her right hand was behind her back.

"You tell Chris now," she said, watching him with enormous care and no vestige of apprehension whatever.

Hunter put out both arms and took the one step forward that was necessary, and instantly the blade of the dagger was between them like a silver flame.

Hunter's stomach knotted in panic as he saw the dagger, appearing even more threatening in size as he stared at it.

He stepped back hurriedly.

"It's true what they say; you are a small devil. And as quick as an adder." He laughed nervously. "I'll send Chris."

But it was dark before Chris found her, and he came to her hungry and full of love.

Maya reached eagerly upward, her hands clinging to his shoulders. She felt a need so great within her that it brought a small moan to her lips. She laced her fingers behind his head and drew his lips slowly down to hers.

"I want you . . . now," she murmured. She felt a quiver race through his body.

"Here?" he asked, his voice hoarse with desire. "Do you know what ye are saying?"

There was no need to reply. Maya kissed him with all the pent-up longing inside her.

She knew he'd take her wherever she let him. And she wanted to let him again. And again . . . and again.

Hands that had experienced her body for a month moved with effortless ease and exquisite delight up and down her spine, gripped her rounded buttocks, and pressed her hips to his. She could feel the heat of him luring her through the thin material of her sarong and moved her hips feverishly against him.

Her uninhibited passion surprised him as always and banished all thoughts save one from his head. Was this a sin? Of a sudden, it no longer mattered. He knew it should. But there was something about this woman that made him lose all sense of reason whenever she was near. Damn, her witch eyes had surely cast their spell. Deep within the dark recesses of his soul, primeval passion awakened and all thought of sin, or anything else, vanished. Just looking at her was enough to make desire flare within him. She was a beautiful temptress who threatened everything he believed in.

But here tonight, far from civilization, bounded only by a canopy of stars and the restless sea, Chris's tenuous control had snapped again, and with a muffled groan, he surrendered to the hardening fire in his loins. His lips moved over hers, his tongue pillaging her sweetness, seeking the honeyed warmth within. Sleek golden limbs molded to his body, drove all sanity from his mind. He wanted her.

Just as mindlessly, Maya returned his heated passion. She returned his ardent kisses, her tongue entwining with his, hands exploring him boldly, making him think only of taking her, wildly and passionately beneath the stars with the dark cloak of night around them.

She did not protest when he slipped the sarong from her waist. A breathless sigh and a slight tremble and the sarong lay in a wisp of colors at her feet. Her body quivered as his lips found her breasts and set her on fire.

"I want ye so damned much," he murmured against her satin skin.

She placed a finger to his lips. "Shh . . . don't talk . . . show me."

His lips slanted hard across hers. Desire rose in sweeping waves to blot out every emotion save one. Here, far from the agony of what was right or wrong, he was free to express himself.

As she lay with his arms around her later, she acknowledged that the head had at least done the last thing that she had asked of it and brought her happiness back to her. She listened to the soft rustle of the land crabs going down past them to

the water and wondered if the head would fulfill
her other askings. She wondered what Roark
would say. She had told him that she was not
going to Chris, and she had, in fact, gone to the
island first. Her conscience was secure; she had
come back to Chris, and the subtlety was quite
enough to satisfy her almost indiscernible sense of
right and wrong.

Chris rolled over on his back, folding his arm
beneath his head. He gave her a slow, careful
scrutiny that made her feel devoured.

"Lord, you're a witch," he half groaned, half
sighed in longing at the sight of her in the moonlight. "A beautiful, sweet witch."

"A witch, am I?" she chuckled wickedly, raking
him with a mischievous stare that nearly drew his
breath from him and rekindled the fires in his
loins.

Chris stretched out a finger and leisurely traced
an imaginary line over the firm, swelling curve of
her breasts, studying her face as he traveled the
peaks of her hard nipples, seeing her eyes grow
dark and limpid, like two bottomless pools staring
at him from behind lowered lids. Her soft mouth
parted with yearning, and Maya leaned down to
him and kissed his waiting lips, touching her
tongue to his. His arms came around her, pulling
her lithe body over his, and, once again, time
ceased to be, though on the eastern horizon the
sky lightened to a dark blue.

At dawn he made love to her again, still hungry,
and she watched his face in the glowing light.
Even to herself she could not say why, but in
Chris's arms she had thought of Roark for a
moment, and, thinking of both Roark and Chris, it
still seemed necessary to her to think of
controlling the pattern of her life. The three things

she had asked the head were in conflict; her mind was in turmoil. When Chris pleaded with her to stay on Egmont, she refused, though she knew it might be a solution.

Finally, she abandoned the argument and asked about Tom Hunter.

"Why d'ye want to know?" Chris demanded fiercely.

She laughed at his transparent jealousy.

"He would have made love to me"—Chris had taught her the words—"if I let."

Chris glared at her. "Bloody hell," he cursed softly, his face a cold, hard mask. "Ye wouldn't! Ye wouldn't!"

She laughed at him and shook her head.

"I was your first lover," he said fiercely, "and your last."

For some unknown reason, Maya felt gladdened by his reply; she smiled. She had felt a stab of jealousy herself. Chris was someone very special to her. But the realization that her jealousy was the visualization of another woman in Roark's arms, stunned her. She was momentarily shaken by an inexpicable sensation of yearning for Roark. Her thoughts swirled in confusion, coming under control again only through the sheer power of her iron will.

Chris lay beside her in deep thought. "Hunter wants a girl—bad," he said at last. "They've a'been after me since we came back. They're full o' envy."

Maya managed another smile, this time at the masculine self-satisfaction in his voice.

"Does Campbell like tapai?" she asked, a hint of a wicked smile barely evident.

"Wha's tapai?" He cocked his head.

Once again Maya went through her pantomime

of drinking, making the faithful gurgles in her throat, and once again he collapsed with laughter. She got to her feet and did her little imitation drunkenness, naked and happy, and full herself of laughter again.

"It's no' palm wine?" he asked.

Maya shook her head.

"Tapai," she repeated, and then remembered the English word 'rice.'

"Rice drink," she said silkily.

Chris smiled broadly. "Saki!" He remembered the Japanese name for rice wine coming up in one of the endless discussions on liquor that were held in the young men's hut in the darkness. "Ae ye want me tae tell Duncan?"

"Campbell, yes. Tell him . . ."

It was suddenly necessary to fix a time, a date. There was, of course, no saki. The whole plot had sprouted suddenly in her head, suggested in a sense by the sex hunger of Hunter, shaped by her memory of Campbell's love of drinking. But there was rice on the island now. Ameni could be induced or, if necessary, bullied into making saki. Maya had no plan yet, only a comprehension of possibilities.

"When the moon is thin," she said at length, and described in a small, elegant gesture of her hands the curve of the sickle moon.

Long since Chris had achieved complete understanding of her meanings.

"Ye want us tae come at the new moon?" He copied her hand gestures.

Maya held up one hand with the fingers and thumb stretched.

"Bring five? Right! To the same place as before?"

She nodded and grinned meaningfully.

"We'll come," he said positively. His new-found authority had not deserted him.

The stealing of the rice was simple. Rahmzi did most of the carrying. It was easy enough to slit a bag and let it spill out through a hole in the outer wall of the storage hut. They did it in the darkness, and over three nights moved the rice to Ameni's hut. As she had thought, he was wholly willing. Where he had acquired his skills, she did not know, but she knew that he was a drunkard when the stingy fates allowed, and drunkards were easy enough to handle. They stole a whole bag in the end, and Rahmzi was depressed and afraid for a week afterwards, thinking Pitney would find out.

It was at the end of this week that the problem of the other women came to a head. Something of it stemmed perhaps from the weather. It was cruelly hot. The sun glared like white fire against the huts in the village, heating the air to shimmering waves over the island. The trade winds had failed entirely. On the sand the vertical sun produced a baking heat. From the reef shallows and the lagoon shallows it produced a moist heat, clinging and intolerable. It crept through and under the cool palms like sea tides engulfing a sandbar during a typhoon.

Maya sat a little apart from the other women. They were washing clothes at the well that was reserved for them. It was full now because the tide was high, but it was not as cool as it was ordinarily. The women were ill-tempered and complaining, snarling at one another, and presently, as they always did, they began to talk over Maya—not at her, over her. In a sense Maya courted it. She spent more time with them these days—it was necessary that her battle against them should come to a head—but she had made no plans for it, for any plans would have involved alliance and any alliance was predestined to disruption. A harem, she knew from within, was a whole, an entity, but it was an entity composed of essentially different women. Alliance was impossible. She had watched the quick groupings of the women that came together like mercury, and separated as swiftly and as improbably. Maya sat quietly while they talked, listening patiently.

Out of the commotion, she heard May Ling echoing Sabin's words.

"What, then, are we afraid of?" she was saying unemotionally. "There are many of us and she is alone. Her father will not come. For a year we have feared him—and all that year he was dead! She is no more than a silly child."

Maya watched their every move from across the well. She knew that soon fate would intervene once more. And then, perhaps, her chance would come to restore her power over them.

"And the Lord Tillman?" someone asked timidly.

"He will beat us afterwards, but what is a beating? At least we will be free of her."

"There is still the dagger," someone else said.

"We can take it from her. After that, she will have nothing."

There was a little hush of admiration at the reasoning of May Ling.

"I have still my powers as a witch," Maya said softly into the hush.

"Do not listen to her!" May Ling screamed. "Do not listen to her!"

"I have my powers as a witch," Maya repeated more loudly, "and you are afraid that I will use them. Listen! I brought the first ship to the island

—it was my doing. I brought the second ship."

"Lies! Lies!" May ling burst out.

"Ask Ramhzi. I told him that I would call them up." Maya looked directly at Sutekh. "Ask Rahmzi —or do you fear to?"

Rahmzi's mother sat silently for a moment before speaking.

"It is true," she said, her voice reluctant. "The boy told me the story of the ships."

May Ling glared at Sutekh venomously, but the unease was already apparent in the harem.

"What I have done, I have done," Maya said, deliberately obscure. "What I will do, I will do. I have the power. I have the karma. Listen!" The inspiration had come to her in the very moment of her declaration. She held both arms out straight before her, her fingers in the imperious sign of command that belonged to the ritual of the Hindu belief of transmigration of souls. According to Maya's Hindu nurse, this rite allowed a head person's soul to pass into the body of the one who performed the ceremony. "Listen, and in a little it will speak."

Maya began to quiver, her movement starting her in hands, spreading up the golden, graceful arms and involving her whole body. Her head moved very slowly backwards, and her eyes rolled until the pupils were altogether lost, and they were white and sightless, and her face was set in a mask that was, because of the time she had spent with it, uncannily like the dried malignancy of the Tamil's head.

The women drew closer to her. She kept rigid except for the quivering. The heat seemed to help her, to create an aura of horror about her. The more timid of the women watched in terror.

The silence grew graver, more foreboding. Even

the reef was only whispering today. The birds were quiet and still. Roark's chickens had gone to sleep. The men were away fishing or working quietly on their fish nets, and the oppression of the heat held everything utterly still.

Maya began to babble formless words, syllables, mute sounds. It was easier than she had thought it would be. If I had stolen a little of the Lord Tillman's soap, she thought, returning for a moment to a pure, childish mischief, I could have foamed at the mouth. But it was not necessary; she had them hypnotized.

Suddenly she began to speak in an intensely strained voice, so like the Tamil's that Almira made her holy sign to ward off the evil eye.

"I will send another ship. I will send it soon."

"What else?" Maya demanded of the Tamil's spirit in her natural voice. "What else? What else?"

"One of the women will go," the Tamil woman's voice said.

"Where?" Maya demanded again.

"To Egmont," the voice answered and then relapsed into babble again.

For a little the quivering went on, and then Maya allowed her fingers to droop, her arms to slacken, her head to come back. But before the pupils came down, her eyelids shut, and she slumped, slowly and gracefully, to the ground on one side, her face pillowed on her upper arm.

The women stood around whispering in shock. She heard Almira's faint words of acceptance, "Allah is merciful." And in a moment, exhausted by the strain of her performance, snatched back into her childhood by the success of her mischievousness, and paying tribute to the heat, she slept. The women left her there.

There was no other attempt to challenge her directly.

Inevitably, of course, the young women came to her one by one to ask who would go to Egmont. She had been quite certain that they would do just that. At the third asking, she told Kim Chi. She told her of Hunter, describing him to her in terms that had at least an attachment to the truth. It was easy enough to work on Kim Chi, for it had long been Kim Chi's own hope that she would go to Egmont or, for that matter, to any island with a man—a young man. The others Maya cut off with mystifying sayings and twisted words; that too was easy enough.

Three days before the new moon, she went to the hut of Ameni in the evening. The making of the liquor was done. He produced it for her proudly, already a little drunk himself. It tasted like sulfur aged in the fires of hell. Maya gagged and screwed her face up on the first impact of it on her tongue. It was not ordinary saki. With a patient ingenuity, Ameni had built a primitive still on the other side of the island, working on it only at night. No one had smelt anything. This was a hell-brew of rice wine fortified by raw alcohol, potent and flammable. Maya went back, content with her plan, to see Kim Chi and to wait for the new moon.

When it rose, it shone thinly on a drinking party that was utterly different from the first orgy on Salomon. Campbell protested as they landed that there were no women, but, with Chris to help her, Maya explained that this was a time for drinking only, that the women were frightened of the Lord Tillman's beatings, that there was a watch now at night in the village. Her earnestness and the first half-shell of saki were sufficient. Women and drink was best of all, but drink alone was better than nothing. There was no fire this night either. Maya told them that the men would spot a fire at once.

When she had settled them to their drinking on the beach, she pulled at Chris's hand, and they moved slowly up the slope.

"Carefu', ye wee devil!" Campbell called after them, filling his half-nut cup again. "Remember th' moraleeties." And then, to the others, he spoke simply, but his tone revealed unspoken envy. "He doesna drink and he doesna go to th' brothels, but he's two jumps ahead o' us evra time since we com' to these island!"

Chris went with her, expectant, and found Kim Chi hidden in the shadows.

"This," Maya said, "is Kim Chi. It means beautiful lotus." She had no conception of the word lotus but somebody—Roark perhaps—had told her the translation. "When Campbell begins to be very drunk, you will go down to fetch Hunter. She is for him."

"I dinna know if this is rightly. . . ," he began, puzzled. But he felt her arm on his shoulders and he forgot what he was thinking, and Kim Chi watched them enviously in the darkness.

Presently he fetched Hunter. Campbell was already too deep in the devil's brew to care. The moon, the stars, the white sand gave just enough light for the Englishman to make her out.

"By God," they heard him say, "she's Chinese! And young and beautiful, for all that I can see."

They sat there, the four of them, deeply involved with each other. They did not know that Rahmzi, posted to keep a watch on the beach two hundred yards up from the boat, had crept down in the darkness to watch the love-making. For that reason, the crash of Roark's gun and the flash of the explosion were to them like the end of the world.

Hunter reacted more swiftly than any of them, even Maya.

"He will have to reload," he said softly and urgeny. "We'll have time to get to the boat. Take her arm, Chris!"

Chris turned, clinging to Maya. "Come wi' us, Maya! Come wi! us!"

But she shook herself free.

"I cannot." She was not sure why she was so positive. "Go," she urged, "go quickly!"

Where the men were drinking, there was a confused babble of cursing, of alarm, and of drunken laughter. Already they could hear feet splashing in the water and Campbell shouting enormous threats into the night.

For a moment longer, Chris hesitated, not wanting to leave Maya behind. She pushed at his back. "Go! Go! You must not be hurt!"

Then the three of them—Hunter, Kim Chi, and Chris—broke from the shadows of the palms and moved, silent as night birds, across the narrow sand strip. They fell into the boat together as it was pushed through the shallows. Nobody seemed very much hurt. The shot had scattered too widely.

"The bastard's done shot me in ma arse!" Campbell roared joyously, feeling no pain in his drunken state. "I'll have to stan' to row."

One of the men had a slug in his shoulder, another one had a scratch down his thigh, but these were discovered afterwards. The important thing was to get the boat through the shallows before Roark, dancing like a wounded bear on the white sand, could load his gun again.

Maya stood motionless for a while, watching
Roark jumping up and down in rage; then she
turned and walked coolly through the palms. She
did not even hurry, for he would be there still
when she was back at the village. She wondered
what, or who, had warned him. Rahmzi had run.
After she had gone a short distance, she began to
skip in her walk. The ranks of her enemies were
diminished by one. The second part of her
prophecy to the women had been made true. It
might even be that it would not be necessary for
her to do more. If Kim Chi settled with the
Englishmen, neither Roark nor Gunn could stop
the others from coming. She skipped again, her
bare feet skimming across the sand, the soft
breeze whipping her colorful sarong high about
her sleek thighs. She would have sung, but she
feared that some of the men, attracted by the shot,
might have come down, fearfully, to the beach.
She tossed her head in a playful scoff and, smiling,
disappeared into the darkness.

23

The *China Clipper* was already at the landing place at the first approach of daylight. Dirk Cooper had made out the gap between the coral reefs of Peras Banhas Island and Salomon with the last brilliance of the moon. The noise of her anchoring, the shouts, the squeaking of the blocks, came through the palm trees to their still-sleeping ears.

Maya, in her corner of the young girls' hut, stretched herself smugly in the half-light. She could hear the voices chattering around her. "A ship has come! A ship has come!" She could feel the girls drawing away from her in fear.

A woman had gone.

A ship had come.

Her power was secure.

She walked proudly down to the beach in time to follow Roark's boat out to the *China Clipper* in her canoe. Well down the channel she could see a boat coming up from Egmont through the reefs.

Somebody must have seen the *China Clipper* earlier than the people on Salomon, but Roark would win the race easily.

Roark did not go aboard the *China Clipper*. His longboat lay on her oars just clear of the ship's ladder.

"Dirk Cooper," he bellowed up, "Dirk Cooper! Call your raping bastards off!" He was beside himself with rage. For days he had been smoldering, now the flame of his rage leapt. "Call them off or I'll shoot them! I'll shoot every damned whoreson of them. They're a drunken, good-for-nothing pack of damned pirates, and you're no better yourself. God damn your hide, sir, you're not a whit better yourself! Keep them off my island, Dirk Cooper—keep them off!"

Dirk Cooper came to the rail, placed his two huge hands wide apart, and leaned forward, staring down at the angry man.

"What in the hell are you raving for, Tillman?" he shouted. "What in the God-damned hell are you raving for? I told you before, look after your own women! Young blood's young blood—there's no holding it."

Roark's voice rose maniacally as he shouted back.

"God blast your eyes! Keep your men away. I'll kill anything that comes from Egmont Island. I'll fire on every boat. I'll fire on every man whose foot touches my beach. I'll give guns to my men. You'll keep them clear, Dirk Cooper!"

The Egmont Island boat was almost up to them now, rowing furiously, the ocean spray leaping high from the oars.

Gunn rose suddenly in the bow. "You filthy murdering fool!" he bellowed at Roark. "I'll have the law on you if a British Navy ship comes here.

By God, I'll have you swung on a yardarm!"

Gunn turned and, cupping his hands, looked up to Cooper. "Mr. Cooper, Mr. Cooper, he's trying to murder our men, he is! He's trying to murder our men!"

Maya lay back restfully in the canoe, wriggling her toes with pleasure. This too was her doing.

Dirk Cooper shouted, Roark Tillman shouted, Gunn shouted, and the triangular argument went on and on. The Egmont boat swept past, and she could see the half-healed scar on the shoulder of one of the men. She saw the man now leaning forward like a beggar displaying his wounds to elicit sympathy and alms.

"Look here, Mr. Cooper, look here!" Gunn bawled. "A slug in his shoulder, by God! And Duncan Campbell has a slug in his arse!"

The crew of the *China Clipper* had come to the side, joyful and laughing in their entertainment.

Maya saw Chris watching her, puzzled and anxious, and she smiled at him so that his heart leapt and the anxiety went from his mind. She stayed where she was, drifting, utterly content.

Still the argument went on—Roark at a grievous disadvantage, one bull voice against two, one giant of a man against two other giants and a choir of support from the *China Clipper*. Finally hoarse and suddenly weary, he abandoned the stupidity of it. He spoke to the Indonesians in the boat and they dipped their oars.

"Next time, Dirk Cooper, I will load with ball," Roark shouted his final warning. "By God, sir, I will load with ball!"

A week later the boat from Egmont Island came up again. Roark met it at the beach with his gun.

Dirk Cooper himself was at the helm. He stood

off, backing water, ten yards from the beach.

"I wish to talk to you, Mr. Tillman," he said, his voice subdued and formal. "It is best that we should settle this thing."

Grudgingly, Roark allowed him to land, still holding the gun in the crook of his arm. They went up the path to the big hut, not speaking.

The women hung back in fear, but Maya went on to the doorway of the hut. There was a panel of well-woven leaves that one could hide behind to eavesdrop.

"Well?" she heard Roark say belligerently to Cooper.

"Aren't you going to offer me a drink? It's a thirsty run up."

There seemed to be a moment's hesitation. Then she heard the clink of the bottle against a glass.

"We're here, Roark," Cooper said when they had drunk. "There's no contradictin' that. We have got to live together. I'm a peaceful man by nature." His voice went silent for a moment; evidently he was drinking.

Most of his words Maya could understand. All of Roark's were clear.

"You may be a peaceful man, Dirk Cooper," Roark thundered, "though you were not a peaceful man when you faced the entire Dutch Navy with three gunboats. I will believe that you have changed, but, by God, you've got some unchained devils on your island! Chain them!"

"I have talked it over with my women," Cooper said reluctantly. "We will move down the channel." It was a clear enough admission of guilt for Roark, and Roark accepted it as such.

"You would be better off on the south island, Diego. It's a long way from the anchorage, but you have got all that you could want there and you will not be swept on the south island—the sand is thirty feet high in places."

"It's a long way from the anchorage," Cooper agreed, as if underlining the magnitude of his sacrifice.

They drank again. Roark reached for the bottle and refilled the glasses.

"Why did you make up your mind to move?" Roark asked suspiciously when he had started on the second drink.

"The women," Cooper replied morosely. "My wife most of all. She wants no fighting. We shall be six miles from you there. I will try to hold the men in check. By God"—his voice rose suddenly—"I'll sweat it out of them! They'll move every damned thing from Egmont on the boats, every damned thing! I'll take the rowdiness out of them if it takes me a year. They'll be too damned tired to be chasing your women!"

Roark grunted. His mind cast suspiciously round what was being said. He mistrusted Cooper; Cooper mistrusted him.

"Her mother," Cooper said after a moment or two. "Her mother wants it too. A determined woman, Mrs. Finch."

"My wives have no mothers, by God!" Roark bellowed, suddenly boisterous. "There's worse things than mothers-in-law, but I can't think of one at the moment." He was instantly expansive, bawdy, full of laughter.

Dirk Cooper chose the moment. "There is one condition—my wife insists upon it."

At once Roark's suspicious came back. "Condition?" he demanded.

"That the Chinese girl stays."

"Ha!" Roark expelled his breath like a pistol-shot. "You have found her, then?"

"They had hidden her on the west side of the island. Gunn is a lazy man."

"I know that," Roark growled angrily.

"He did not search the west side. She was there all the time. Hunter went to her at nightfall and sometimes in the day also. He brought her to my wife three days ago. She is quiet and gentle. My wife wishes to keep her."

"I will send a boat for her this afternoon," Roark said bluntly, brushing the appeal aside.

Cooper shook his head.

"You will have enough women if we move to the southward, Roark Tillman. You will not get her back. My wife is a stronger woman than her mother when it comes to these matters." He drained his glass. "You will not get her back."

Automatically Roark stretched for the bottle again and filled his glass. "She must come back," he said. But his conviction was noticeably uncertain.

Cooper drank before he spoke again. "My wife is very fond of her. There is nothing you can do about it"—he leaned forward confidently—"nor I either, Roark. We will move to the south island and I will do my best to keep the young men close. Gunn is a fool."

They both drank to that. Gunn was a fool. The brandy was an honest solvent. They sat and talked late into the afternoon.

The boat's crew, watched over suspiciously by Pitney, stared long and hard at the young women who strayed down close to the landing place.

24

At the end of the third month from the return of
the *China Clipper*, Sabina went. This was not
Maya's doing—at least, not wholly. In the hot
hours while the boat's crew waited for Cooper and
Tillman to finish their drinking, she had
established a rapport with Slim Darby, another of
the young men. Sabina had an odd beauty of her
own. Roark's taste in women was rare. Her nose
had a fine Arab cut about it; her eyes were
Oriental eyes, soft and deceptive; her forehead
was high and bespoke an intelligence that she hid
well—it would take Darby two years at least to
discover it. Darby made the plan himself. Maya
acted as no more than the go-between. He outlined
the plan to her one day when she took the canoe up
to one of Cooper's boats, which was fishing
against the west island.

Atfter she had agreed to the plan, she went
ashore for an hour with Chris, but in the hour it

was impossible to recapture the delicate
memories of the west island. The shadow of Roark
was between them.

That day she did not go near the head.

The seeds of jealousy are not often planted in
vain. It would be impossible to put a precise
moment upon their planting, as between the
women and Maya. Perhaps it was the day when
she was brought aboard the *Sea Wolf* at the Cape
of Good Hope. The day was not important; what
was important was that with everything she did,
with every move that she made, the seeds
germinated and sprouted and grew.

Jealousy permeated the whole of Roark's village
now. Kim Chi—the soft, willowy, the exquisite—
was gone, was safe on the south island with her
young man. Sabina—forceful, loud, irritating, and
irritable—was gone, safe on the south island with
her young man. Maya . . . Maya went as she willed,
and the younger women without exception were
jealous of the youth of Chris Lovel. What was this
strange power she had over the Lord Tillman that
he allowed her to have this youth?

The final manner of Sabina's escape was
simplicity itself. Slim Darby and Chris rowed the
lighter of the Diego boats all the way up by themselves. It had to be accurately timed because of the
tides and the endless reef shallows throughout the
channel.

Maya led her to the meeting place. Her own
moments with Chris were hurried and anxious.
There was no time for love. Again the presence of
Roark was almost palpable.

The urgent passion of it was ended by Rahmzi,
who had been posted up the beach as lookout and
had again crept in, to watch.

Rahmzi too had achieved an awareness of jealousy.

Roark was angry, but he was not as angry as Pitney had expected him to be, for he was tired of the constant whining of the girl.

"It does not matter," he said, as Pitney cursed softly over his drink. "She would have grown ill-favored, and she has the heart of a shrew."

Pitney disregarded Roark's words. "I said that where one went others would follow. You should have sent Maya with the *China Clipper*."

"You grow monotonous."

"It is the truth, the exact truth. First Kim Chi went—she would never have been a shrew." He slipped the retort in indirectly. "Now Sabina! There will be another in a week or two, as long as you fail to put a whip on that girl."

Roark watched him with his head tilted to one side, his eyes squinting as if in an effort to blur the gloomy-looking weasel of a man in front of him.

"I have told you before," he said after a long silence, "you are too stupid to understand her. You are a damned fool, Skinner Pitney. She is worth all of them, and in time she will come to me of herself and that will be worth waiting for. It is destiny, hers and mine."

Pitney crouched forward and stared up, trying to see into the eyes between the narrowed lids.

"By the horns of God," Pitney said dryly, "I think you're in love with the girl!"

In bittersweet despair, Roark envisioned a dark, tauntingly beautiful girl who held his heart in a powerful vise that he could not escape, even if it destroyed him.

"She will be mine!" he bellowed suddenly at Pitney. "She will be mine, by God!"

* * *

Astram went almost three months later. It took her most of that time to make up her hesitant mind. Again, this was not Maya's doing.

Almira died three days after the fury and anger at Astram's flight had ebbed. This too was not Maya's doing. She died as any old woman, of some nameless illness, more perhaps of a broken heart and spirit than of her body. She had loved Roark Tillman most of her life.

Maya grieved for her, for the old woman had been kind to her between the upsurges of the women's anger. And now the anger of the women surged up again, and there was no Almira to control it.

Maya heard them talking in the distance on the morning after Almira's death and disregarded it. She thought her power over them was complete, more complete now perhaps than ever.

Except that she forgot about the boy Rahmzi.

An hour later she heard the noise of them in the path that led to the village and then she heard shouting at the center of the village, somewhere about the big hut. The women had gone in a group to Roark, and Pitney tailed behind them. The boy Rahmzi was held almost as a prisoner in their center.

May Ling was their leader now, a May Ling grown harsher, more spiteful with the passing of time. She pushed in through the door with a solid wedge of women behind her.

"She is a witch!" she screamed. "She has done this thing!"

Roark snarled at her from the depths of his chair. "Be still, woman! What is this?"

"The girl is a witch!" May Ling flung back at him. "The girl Maya! She has powers. She has shown them to us. This we have seen with our own eyes, that she prophesied and that the prophecies came true. Is this not so?"

"It is true," the other women shouted behind her in chorus. "She prophesies. She is a witch. She has power over spirits. We are afraid of her."

May Ling's voice dominated the babble. "And she must go!"

The rest of the women had crowded now into the big hut. The whole frame of the doorway was full of them. They waved their arms; they moved; they surged; they swayed forward, seeming to have one mind, to be a single entity.

May Ling was the voice of that entity.

"She is a witch!" she kept on screaming. "She is a witch! She is a witch!"

Roark stood and towered over them.

"Be still!" he shouted angrily. "Damn you for fools, be still! I do not require to be screamed at. You!" He nodded sharply at May Ling.

"She sat on a hot day at the washing well, and when we told her that we no longer feared her because her father was dead, she answered that nonetheless she was still a witch."

"Is this true?" Roark barked.

"It is true, Lord," the women replied in a single voice.

"And she sat there and she put her hands forward"—May Ling imitated the action with her hands—"and she quivered, all her body quivered, and she passed from us into the spirit world. And when she spoke"—a deep shudder took May Ling, and Roark, watching her narrowly, knew that it was the truth—"when she spoke it was in the voice of the Tamil."

"It is true," the women behind her shouted. "It was the voice of the Tamil, Lord."

"And what were her prophecies?" Roark's voice

was growing harsher.

"She prophesied that one of us would go to Egmont."

"Was that all?"

"She prophesied that a ship would come."

"And what else?"

"It was enough, Lord." May Ling relaxed suddenly. "The ship came and the girl Kim Chi went."

"Bloody fools!" Roark relaxed a little. "What is there in this but children's talk? She knew that the ship would come, for it had to bring back Lord Cooper. All of you knew that the ship would come."

"But not when it would come," a voice said.

"That is nothing. She did not tell you when, only that it would come. As for the girl Kim Chi, she helped her go to Egmont; she knew that she would go. This is less than the talk of children. If this is all, you may go."

"It is not all," May Ling said. "Lord, it is not all. There is the matter of the head."

"What head, by God?" Roark took a fierce pace forward and overshadowed her. "What head, you witless fools?"

May Ling seemed to sense in his anger a tension that arose from fear. For the first time she attained control of herself. She watched him, her eyes unblinking, for a long moment.

"The head of the Tamil," she answered slowly, "which she took."

"By God!" Roark exclaimed uncertainly. "By Almighty God!" he went back to his chair. "This is more children's talk," he shouted, but his tone lacked conviction. "What proof have you?"

They brought forward the boy Rahmzi from the center of the group, like a magician producing an unimaginable prize.

"She told him! She told him!" All the women were shouting now because they were all overcome by fear in this final moment of crisis— fear of Roark, fear of Maya, fear of the head and of the incomprehensible evil spirits behind it. They were shouting at Rahmzi; they were shouting at May Ling; they were shouting at Roark. The hut was submerged in a torrent of sound.

Maya began to walk up the path to the village. Then she heard Roark's voice, quelling the madness of the women. He was bellowing curses, almost beside himself with anger.

"Speak, boy!" he roared when at last he had controlled them.

And Rahzmi spoke, so softly that Maya, coming up the path, could not hear his words.

"She told me that she had taken the head of the Tamil woman and that she had dealt with it according to her Hindu nurse's teachings." He hesitated.

"Go on, boy!" Maya heard Roark's voice roaring. "Go on!"

And again she could not hear Rahmzi's answer.

"She said that it did her bidding," he murmured softly.

It took Roark and the men two full days to find the place which sheltered the head. In a sense Rahmzi misled them, for Maya had told him of the blue pool and the hut, and that information he had also passed to Roark. They found the hut an hour after sunrise on the first morning and, while Roark drove them like a wild man, they pulled its thatched roof to pieces and stripped the mats of leaves and tore the palm frond screens. They searched the area about it, driven and anxious, afraid of Roark and afraid of the head. All that day they found nothing.

That night, they slept in the wet shelter of the palms—it had rained through the afternoon.

"If that boy has lied, I will beat him to the edge of his life!" Roark said. But he knew that Rahmzi had not lied, for Maya, charged with this monstrous thing, had denied nothing. Equally she had admitted nothing, but Roark knew that the accusation was true.

They found the place late in the afternoon of the second day. Roark was close to the man who gave the shout and he went forward alone. The men came hurriedly together, trembling like frightened rabbits, ready to run. The small hut was still solid. Maya had repaired the roof twice, and the extra thickness of the thatch had held. He regarded it sombrely from the outside, and at last he brought himself to stoop and crawl into the shelter.

For a long time his eyes would not adjust themselves to the gloom, but in the end he saw it. The head, inadequately smoked, had cracked and stretched still further. The bone showed through the bound-up lower jaw, and the mouth had split towards the left ear, giving the effect of a shriek of torment. The eyeless sockets were terrible, grotesquely covered by the droppings of the birds.

Nonetheless, he knew at once that it was the Tamil.

He sat, almost where Maya ordinarily sat, for a long while, thinking.

"I have remembered before that you were beautiful," he said at last, "but I know that you had malice and envy and a spirit of vengeance. It may be that she brought you back to break our peace." Once more he fell silent. When he spoke again, it was wearily. "No, I do not believe these things. I do not believe in the power of witches. All you have given to her was the power to frighten the other women, and it might be that she needed that power. She is still very young against them all."

When he came out of the hut he was no longer angry, but he turned, looking back at it.

"The rest of your body I burnt," he said quietly. "It is proper that your head too should join that smoke." And he called for firewood.

The men brought it fearfully. When there was enough he struck flint on tinder and again, remembering what he had done on the beach at Diego Garcia, he lit each of the four corners of the hut.

On the beach at the landing place below the village, Maya watched the smoke from that burning rise over the west island. For two days she had sat there. The children had brought food to her. Even the women had come, timidly and uncertain, afraid of the angers that they had aroused. Rahmzi watched her from a point a hundred yards up the beach, sitting with two or three of the smaller boys. The smoke rose in the still afternoon air as it had risen on Diego when Roark had burnt the body—a high, thin plume, blue just above the palm trees, brighter where it snatched the last of the sunlight, bending over at the top where it caught the wind.

Maya could feel her fear slowly returning. An anguished sob escaped her trembling lips.

Early in the darkness, Rahmzi left Salomon. He took his small fishing boat and started toward the south island. There was no longer any place for him with Maya, and though the fear of the head was gone, other fears remained. Maya did not see him go, nor did the small boys who earlier had sat with him—they had gone to sit with her now.

She sat on in the darkness, waiting for the return of the boats from the west island. One by one the children slipped away, until at last she was left alone. There were other women waiting, but they were farther down the beach.

It was difficult to think rationally. How important was that wisp of smoke? What did this day's events really mean? She asked the questions of herself in an extraordinary variety of ways before she realized that there was only one question. That the one thing that was truly vital was the reality of the head—not its physical reality, its structure of cracked skin and protruding bone, its empty sockets, and the terrible silent laughter of its mouth—but the reality of its power.

Was it the head that had brought the ships? She knew from her own common sense that it was not, that one of them at least had started before the Tamil woman died, and the other would have come in due time, dependent on no more than the decision of Cooper and the willingness of the winds.

Had the head brought her happiness? She was not sure now that she had ever been happy. The bright image of the days on the west island had faded. She was possessed by the need to establish herself against Roark, and because Roark was the focus of her possession, his shadow was dark between her and Chris's simplicity.

Had the head made it possible to break up the solidarity of the women? It was true that three of the young girls had gone, but they would have gone anyway. She knew enough of the heat of the blood now to be positive of that. They had gone and more would go, and though she had first shown them the way, it had been because of the heat in their own blood for the young men, and not because of the head, that they went.

Should she herself go south to Diego with the others? The question seemed to have no relation to the earlier ones that had been so urgent, but she was instinctively aware that it was the one that completely mystified her. The canoe was twenty yards up the beach, the paddle was lashed in it with the net, the flint and tinder, and the fish spear. Between her and escape there was no more than a minute and a half of time. Nonetheless, while she knew that she could not go, she did not know what made her stay.

Maya sat on with these things moving in her tortured mind. A little before midnight she heard the thud of oars of the returning boats.

Roark came ponderously from the boat, moving through the starlit shallows. His voice, when Maya heard it, was almost meditative.

"Where is her canoe?" he asked.

"It is here, Lord!" one of the women called. "It is here!"

He turned towards the voice and walked, still heavily. He was bowed, the steel gone out of his triumphant back. His shoulders sagged. He walked slowly towards the canoe, and some of the men busied themselves with the hauling of the boat and some followed him. The second boat was coming in now. They could hear the slow thud and return of the oars and the sound of the oar splash. When Roark reached the canoe, he stood for a moment or two in thought.

At last, reluctantly, as if the words were drawn out of him, he spoke. "Bring wood and palm leaves for a fire."

The men drifted into the night. Everyone moved slowly, like shadows passing with the drift of small fleece clouds against the moon.

Maya sat still.

They brought the palm leaves and dumped them on the ground. They brought small branches and driftwood and rubbish. They piled it together and when the pile was made he spoke again. "Bring the canoe."

Maya could see it all through the starlight, but the dimness of the light robbed the scene of reality. It had no meaning for her.

They lifted the canoe and placed it on top of the pile and Roark himself struck flint to the tinder once again. He blew and the small flame grew, and he put it to the leaves and a larger flame leapt upward. In a moment it was blazing. The night took on a different quality. The starlight was beaten back. The underside of the palms became scarlet and visible in the darkness, the trees attained form and solidity and stature. And on top of the fire the canoe was black and beautiful, floating, as it were, on a sea of flame.

Roark, standing back, watched it sullenly. The men of the second boat, coming in, gathered between Maya and the fire and stood, sharply silhouetted, against its dancing brilliance.

Maya sat quite still in the place that she had chosen. After a while, the canoe caught and began to burn also. It was the end of a chapter of her life, but it was the chapter that was important, not the ending. She had no real need now for a canoe. Before it had been a way of escape; but there was nowhere now to go. The head was burnt, and there was no longer any importance in the west island. There was still a way of escape—she could wade the reef shallows and swim from island to island until she reached Diego. She sat quite still, cold in spite of the leaping flames.

A long time afterwards, Roark stirred and went up the pathway to the village.

They heard Roark quarreling with Pitney over half the island. Maya heard it also, but she made no attempt to eavesdrop at the door. An awareness of fate had engulfed her. What would happen would happen. If she had believed in Allah, it might have been well, but she had no belief in anything—now.

At length the argument between Roark and Pitney died down, quenched with liquor. The two men sat opposite each other, as they had sat so many times before, faintly drunk.

Roark was reiterating his reasoning. "I have burnt her head. I have destroyed her canoe. The women know that she is not a witch, and there is no more that she can do. I will not send her away. I cannot!"

"You are a bloody damned fool!" Pitney said, emboldened with rum.

"Damn your filthy hide!" Roark returned, but without anger.

"You are a bloody fool because the women still believe that she is a witch."

"What do you mean?" Roark demanded.

"They still believe that she brought the Devil Wind."

Roark opened his arms in a gesture of hopelessness. "Bloody fools! There is nothing they cannot believe! Nonetheless, the head is burnt and she will change now." He leant forward confidentially. "She could have got clear months ago had she chosen. She did not. Now she will come to me of her own will, and it will be worth everything that I have lost. It is predestined. You are not able to understand it. You do not dream, Pitney. Your mind is a dungheap."

"Before that happens, she will have destroyed everything," Pitney retorted sourly. "Everything! Even the boy Rahmzi has gone."

"The boy? The boy! Before it was only the women." Roark sat upright with his glass poised halfway between his knees and his mouth.

He sat silent for so long that Pitney asked a question. "What will you do?"

Roark disregarded him, his mind working. He had thought this over in the boat coming back from the west island. When at last he was ready to speak, his voice was soft, slow, and reflective.

"This island is indefensible. It is too wide, with only a small reef. A boat can land anywhere along the shore. We cannot watch the whole of it."

"What do you plan?"

"To keep guards posted always would take too much of the men's time, nor would it serve. They can be bought." The contempt flooded into Roark's voice.

Pitney was possessed with curiosity. "But what will you do?"

"I could lock them up at night, but it would serve no purpose. Somehow they would get away, somehow she would help them." Quite suddenly, Roark's manner altered again. He drained the glass and put it down with a thud.

"The older women who do not wish to stay, they may leave," he said, his voice surprisingly gentle and sad. "And I shall see that they are well provided for. Zada will go south when she chooses anyway, and I shall not stop her. She is like a bird waiting for the migration to begin. But I shall build a stockade on Eagle Island and I shall move the younger women and the children and Maya there. I shall build a stockade at the summit of the rise; it is the highest place in the islands. A man can watch from there—there is no point on the island that you cannot see." There was a hard determination in his voice. "A stockade, by God! Yes! There is the answer, a stockade! They will not get them out of a stockade."

"And this island?"

"You will manage it," Roark replied distantly, "and I will oversee you. I will need more guns when the *Sea Wolf* comes again, but meanwhile I will build a castle."

Pitney stared at him doubtfully.

Roark's blood thudded in his ears. Never in his life had he felt this way about a woman. This bewitching girl with her haunting eyes was somehow linked with his future, and he knew he could never let her go.

25

Eagle Island lay midway between Salomon and Diego Garcia, just south of the eerie, evacuated half-ruin of Egmont Island. The scrub there was already pressing back on the clearing that Dirk Cooper had made. The wells were shallow and silting.

Roark planned the stockade with extraordinary energy and vigor. The man seemed to have an incomprehensible resilience. After finding the head, he had been for a brief time weary and exhausted, but now he rampaged round the island searching for sound timber, driving the men along the high-tide mark, hunting for strong trees. They dug furiously for a well. The whole settlement was driven to the task, Roark's enormous voice booming through them like that of an ancient slave-master of Egypt.

With the passing days, the heat became unbearable. The sun gathered strength and the air

332

became heavy with moisture. The men suffered intensely. Sweat dried in the armpits and groin, and festering sores erupted; many became sick.

Maya watched it all, indifferent and catlike. With the burning of the canoe, she had ceased to do anything of practical value for the community, and Roark accepted her idleness as if he understood the inner state of her mind.

Eagle Island was wind-blown sand built up by a succession of gales to a height of almost twenty feet at the inner edge, where it fell steeply, like a cliff, veined and bonded with the creeping plants and the thin, coarse grass of the islands, crowned with palms. It was also the home of several sea eagles, which gave it its name.

Roark measured and thought and planned. When he was ready, he cut off the tops of the trees nearest to the edge of the sand cliff and used them to brace the high edge of his stockade wall. He ran the wall for forty feet along the cliff and brought it down the incline of the hill, using a steep slope to guard one edge. Outside he cleared the nearer palms to give him an open field of fire, and used their trunks, which he buried deep, to add to the strength of the stockade.

The shape of the stockade was determined by the contour of the hill. To the north, towards Egmont, it followed an eroded gully that climbed up through the cliff. To the south, towards Diego, it followed the straight line of the slope, and before they had finished the building of the stockade itself, Roark had set men to work to cut back the face of this slope to make it steeper.

It was in the main building, the keep, that he used his greatest ingenuity. With careful measurement he selected a dozen palms and made a fortification close to the cliff edge, leaving just enough room for a field of fire between it and the stockade itself. The whole of the lower part of the fortification became an immensely strong box. When it was finished, it was airy, cool, and enormous. On the floor above, he built a light pavilion, strongly roofed. It stood above the stockade so that a man sitting in a great chair with a long glass in his hand could watch the lagoon, could see over the channel between Eagle and Diego and even to the sparkle and blue of its reef.

"The first gale will take it away," Pitney said with a tone of sarcasm.

"It will go with a typhoon," Roark growled at him, "not otherwise."

The lower room was for the children and the young women. The steps, half ladder, half stairs, that led from it came up through the pavilion that was Roark's own living-quarters.

Maya watched its erection cynically, drifting through the work. But for the most part she played with the children; she had reestablished her friendship and power over them—if, indeed, she had ever lost it.

Roark came upon her on the ocean beach one morning. Whether she had seen him coming he could not say, but she was telling them a story and they were clustered in a fan of golden nakedness in front of her. Her voice reached him, clear and gay, as he stood in the shadow of the seaward palms.

She was telling them the story of the time when the mongoose Maya had been enticed into a wooden fence by the dragon in punishment for his trickeries.

". . . for a whole week Maya was held there and the pig was his jailer. Then one night, when he was full of anger, he heard the snake slithering round the wooden fence.''

Her arms lifted and with her invariable grace she made the motion of the great snake and hissed realistically.

The children shuddered.

''And Maya made a plan. There was a weak place in the fence that was too small for his body but, as the snake passed round for the thirteenth time, Maya whispered to the snake.

'' 'Sir Snake, what do you seek?'

''The snake said, 'I seek you.'

''Maya said, 'Sir Snake, the pig is here with me.

''The snake said, 'But the pig is fast and he has sharp hooves and he is strong. You are weak.'

''And Maya said, 'The pig sleeps but I am awake. If I make a hole for you so that you can come and eat the pig, what will you do to me?'

''The great snake said, 'My hunger will be satisfied. Why should I do anything with you?'

'' 'So,' Maya said. And he made a small hole in a weak place that he knew, and the snake entered and killed the pig and swallowed it.

'' 'Now,' the snake said, 'I must escape before the dragon finds me and eats me.'

'' 'Go then! Maya said. And the snake went to the hole, but because of the size of the pig in its body it could not get through it.

''Then Maya said, 'I will make you another hole higher,' And he made another hole between two strong tree trunks, and he said, 'Thrust through it with all your force!' And the snake thrust and jammed itself where the body of the pig was, and it thrashed mightily with its tail.

''The dragon heard the thrashing and came in roaring. It remembered to shut the gates behind it and it said, 'What is this thrashing?'

''Maya said, 'It is the snake which has eaten the

pig and is escaping through the fence.'

"And the dragon said, 'Where? Where?'

"Maya said, 'Charge it now before it wins clear! Crush it with your mighty fangs. It is where the peeled logs are.'

"And the dragon charged with its mouth open, roaring, and its great fangs went into the peeled logs and were stuck in the tree trunks of the fence, and the dragon roared, but it could not pull loose its fangs. Maya sprang onto the body of the pig inside the snake, which made a step, and he sprang from the body of the pig on to the head of the dragon, which made another step, and he sprang from the head of the dragon over the top and escaped."

She ended the story and the children broke, laughing.

She left then, and turned into the palms and gave a little start at seeing Roark. The exaggeration of the start was perhaps a fraction overdone. Roark regarded her cynically. He was sure that the story was by way of being a warning to him, sure now that she had seen him from the first moment of his arrival. But he was also sure of his own intentions. The stockade was to keep the children and his young women from escaping; Maya would not leave him.

"There will be no need for Sir Snake here," he said, laughing.

"But the dragon must be forever watchful." She laughed at him without malice in her laughter.

Dirk Cooper came when the stockade was complete and the keep almost finished. He came up by the normal boat passage toward the anchorage and turned in towards Eagle, with Chris Lovel sounding the water depth over the bow with the blunt end of a boat-hook.

Roark greeted him on the beach with the gun cradled in his arm.

"You can put that away, Roark Tillman," Cooper said. "I have come to ask why you have moved down towards us."

"I have come here because I can hold this island against your raping bastards," Roark answered, quietly for him. "I have put up a stockade that even they'll not scale, and I have made a house inside it that even they'll not break into, and there will be a gun at every corner of it and they will be loaded with ball. All those who had wished to leave, Dirk Cooper, have left."

"We have kept clear of you since we moved to Diego," Cooper said reasonably. "The girls came to us of their own accord."

"The black one two weeks ago?"

Zada had disappeared almost unnoticed in the turmoil of the building of the stockade.

"Yes, the black one too. There is nothing that I can do if the girls are willing—you know that. Do you mean to use Egmont also?"

"What would I do with Egmont?" Roark asked sourly. "I have enough to do to keep them at work on Salomon with that fool Pitney. You keep to your island. I'll keep to mine."

There was sense in what Roark said. Cooper saw that.

"I will do my best to keep clear," he answered. "I chain my boats at night now."

"You should have done that long ago!"

Cooper was angered by Roark's words, for he had come in peace.

"I will go, then."

"Before you go," Roark said grimly, "come and look at what I have done and tell your bastard young men. From my chair I can watch everything that moves in the channel. I can watch the sea reef, and there is no place that they can break through. There is a double fence at the gate. It would take a regiment to come in against my guns. Tell your hot bloods that! But see for yourself." He turned, still nursing the gun, and stalked up the path they had made through the gully.

Chris, standing at the boat, waited till they were out of earshot.

"Maya!" he called quietly.

Maya came, as he had expected, out of the shade of the palms. He could hear the laughter of children behind her.

"Will you come wi' us?"

"He would not let me," Maya said softly, "and he has a gun. Even if I did, he would come after me."

Chris walked into the cool of the palms' shadows. The children moved back before him. He put his arm round Maya's shoulders, and she momentarily yielded to him.

"Come awa' wi' me, Maya," he urged.

"No, I must stay here. Your island is full of the other women now."

For the first time he realized the implications of that fact. He had heard everything that the other women had said of Maya. He knew the measure of their jealousies and their fears.

"Aye, there's the other women," he agreed. "There would be trouble."

They sat silent.

"If I come, the quarrel between them and me would begin from the beginning again," she said after a long interval. "It is best to stay here for now."

"In there?" He jerked his head up at the stockade.

"I go where I will," she answered with an echo of her old arrogant independence.

He considered this for a while before he finally spoke. "It was hot work comin' up the channel. Ha' ye a well on the island?"

"Ana!" Maya called and clapped her hands.

The eldest of the young girls who remained to Roark came through the trees to the water's edge. She stood in front of them, her eyes downcast, her face expressionless.

"Take the Lord Chris," Maya said, giving him the title naturally, "and give him drink."

She watched them as they disappeared between the palms. Chris was staring down at Ana's young slender body. Maya allowed herself a little laugh of total wickedness.

The stockade was completed. The thatching for the roof of the house was finished, and its completion made the occasion for a celebration. The people came down from Salomon. There was a feast, there was drink. There was dancing and music.

Roark wished to make clear the security that he had constructed for himself. It looked formidable on the crest of the sand hill of Eagle Island, the still-new thatch roof richly golden, the grey tree trunks sinister. Little by little, however, the sun scorched it, and the rain and the winds worked at it, and it took on something of the natural appearance of the island. Vines grew through the trunks where Roark had planted them. The green inside the stockade spread and covered it as with wings. And in the great room that took the whole of the top half of the keep, Roark watched and

waited. He hardly ventured out of it now. He sat
there with the telescope on a stand that they had
made for it. He could see the whole of the channel.
He could watch the sea in every direction. The
place was his nest and he achieved the patient
watchfulness of a sea eagle.

The boys had a camp and huts between the keep
and the gate; the girls and the young women had
the huge chamber of the under part of the house.
There was no door to the chamber, only the stairs
that led through Roark's room. Maya slept where
she chose, sometimes outside the stockade in the
huts of the two families Roark had brought down
from Salomon to cook for him and to keep the
stockade clean, sometimes in a small shelter
inside the stockade, whose doors were barred and
padlocked after sunset.

The young men came up from the south from
time to time—Roark knew that. They had canoes
now, three of them; he saw them out fishing with
the Diego boats.

He did not know that with patient ingenuity, they
had built a fourth at the same time as the three
that Cooper had ordered, interchanging it night
after night with the other canoes so that the work
proceeded in an orderly fashion. He did not know
that it was kept hidden in a deep pool in the
middle section of the south island after the
manner of the hiding of Maya's first canoe on the
west island.

He spoke of them occasionally to Pitney when
he came down from Salomon to get his orders.

"They prowl and prowl around," he snarled.
"But I shall kill the first one who sets foot on this
island!"

To Mrs. Cooper the existence of the stockade

was an offense and sinful. Cooper had told her of
Roark's practices, but she had not absorbed the
realities of them at first, for he had never been
explicit. Roark Tillman had a harem. She had the
accepted Western notion of a harem, never having
explored it in her own mind. But this thing, this
building that she could see crowning the hill of
Eagle when she went out occasionally with the
boats, was an outrage to her morality, for it was a
prison of children; it was a brothel prison for the
enjoyment of this wicked man, Tillman. It was
unspeakable—he was unspeakable.

Had the boats gone closer in to Eagle she would
have seen the children playing naked and happy
on the beach. They were fond of the keep, for to
them it had a romantic and fairy tale-like air. They
were wholly unconcerned about Roark. This also
was their custom.

From time to time she harassed Cooper about it.
"We cannot leave them there. Think of them—
children with that man! I lie awake at night."

"They're used to it," Cooper answered bluntly.
"They've never known anythin' else. And Roark's
quiet. These hot bloods of ours can't get at him, so
there's peace at last."

"Slavery is too high a price to pay for peace,"
she returned sharply.

The whaler came towards the end of the sixth
month from the day that Roark moved into the
stockade. Roark sent for the rest of the women
from Salomon Island. He held them in the
stockade while the whaler was at anchorage. The
men came ashore to look for drink and women and
found neither. Even Maya stayed in the stockade
these nights. The whaler left after ten days, her
water-barrels filled. Roark saw to the priming of

his guns and watched day and night until the whaler went.

A month later the *China Clipper* came back, and Cooper went with her east to Singapore.

Before he went, Mrs. Cooper pleaded with him again.

"Rescue the children!"

"We have peace," he said once again. "Leave the sleeping dog."

But Dirk Cooper, like many masterful men, underrated the determination of his wife. She left Gunn alone. Instead, she made her first appeal to Duncan Campbell. She had no success. Campbell was still busy discovering the not too elaborately hidden possibilities of Zada. He was neither physically nor mentally alert. She tried Tom Hunter next, but Tom Hunter had married Kim Chi and was wholly satisfied with her, and still the envy of the other young men.

She tried them one after the other, appealing to them delicately, until she came to Chris Lovel. She came to him reluctantly, for in measure Chris Lovel was already a part of this thing and she was not sure of her own attitude towards him. She spoke to him indirectly at first, of the meaning of chivalry. She talked of knights' adventures and princesses in towers and damsels in distress. In her own way it was subtle enough, but it did not require repeating. Chris was ready at the first hint to rescue a certain princess from Roark's tower.

It was Chris, therefore, who made the plan. Duncan Campbell was the actual leader, because it was customary for him to be the leader, as he was bigger than the rest; but he was also one of the led this time. Chris worked out the plan in his own mind during the days on Eagle, watching the stockade through a glass that Mrs. Cooper had given him. It took a fortnight to polish the details. It needed the third quarter of the moon for perfection and all the boats that Diego had.

The arrival of the *India* could have wrecked their plans. The *India* was a two-masted brig. She was bound for Singapore and then Hong Kong with piece goods. Her captain had heard of the new settlement on the Chagos Archipelago—as by now everyone in ports throughout the Orient had heard of it. Chris altered his plans to take in her presence in the anchorage.

He was able to create an immense enthusiasm among the other young men—those who had not yet snatched women from Salomon. He had the complete support of Kathleen Cooper. There were times, as he worked at the planning, when he allowed himself to think that if after this last attempt Maya would not come to him, there was still the girl Ana. Gradually, the memory of her golden body acquired solidity.

On the night that he had planned, the Diego boats went up the channel singing. From very far off Roark recognized the tune. He picked them out with his long glass almost at once. The night was quiet, though it was not wholly windless. They came one astern of the other, and he thought at first that they were from the *India* returning to the ship. Then he remembered that her boats had gone in long before and that nothing else had gone down to Diego throughout the day.

He looked to the guns methodically, one after the other, though he was almost certain that this was not a threat to him. Cooper's young men were going up to the *India* for some drunken reason of their own—she was to sail on the morrow. He watched the boats, nonetheless, as they came across in the moonlight, black and crawling like insects across the water.

It was not until they had turned out of the boat
channel towards the island that he knew it would,
after all, be necessary to fight. For months he had
dismissed the possibility, but now he went swiftly
to the gate and shouted, and behind him he heard
the stockade awake and the shrill chatter of voices
and the quick increase of excitement. He ordered
one of the two Indonesians to take the light boat to
Salomon to find Pitney and bring help; as soon as
his back was turned, both men went. They took
their women and their own children with them.
Roark returned and barred the heavy gate, and as
he ran back he wondered where Maya was. He
found her immediately, at the firing platform on
the southeast corner of the stockade. She was
standing quite still, peering intently down to the
moonlit water.

The singing of the young men in the boats was
reaching them very clearly now.

> "Five and twenty ladies
>   Came to we young lads.
> Only one cam' home again,
>   An' she was nae so pure."

The loud, vulgar song came up to Roark like a
challenge, like an obscene battle hymn. There was
laughter with the song and excitement, fellowship,
and threat.

But Roark listened intently, and after he had
listened he spoke viciously.

"The bastards would not come singing like this
if this were all they were up to." And he turned
away from them to watch the shallows of the reef.
There were three canoes, the three canoes that
Cooper had built. Like Cooper, Roark did not

know about the fourth. He watched them grimly for a while, and then he took one of the guns and, sighting carefully on the lead canoe, fired.

"That'll let the young fools know we're aware of them," he said, more to himself than Maya, and, turning, he fired again at the leading boat.

A splash of water well to the right of the boat showed in a sudden brightness in the moonlight. From the boats a roar of curses answered him.

He did not know of the fourth canoe as it came, drifting and silent, across the narrow channel between Diego and Eagle. There were many things that he did not know—of the deep hole, for example, that had been dug in the floor of the children's room, and of the weakened lashing of the stockade on the north face. Maya had cut the lashings herself and ordered the digging of the hole; the children had done it with their bare hands, using no more than a knife to loosen the dirt; it went under the footing of the palm trunks to the outside of the stockade wall.

Chris had asked Maya to do these things, waiting for an opportunity to speak to her on Eagle. She stood beside Roark now, remembering the plan of the attack as Chris had told it to her.

By the time Roark was ready to fire again, the boats were in the shallows, the men splashing ashore. There were too many targets. But coolly and deliberately, he put two balls into the bottom of the first boat to hamper their return. Once again there was a roar as he fired, followed by laughter and shouting and threats. Kathleen Cooper had not allowed the young men to bring guns with them.

Behind Roark in the great room, the children were in a fury of excitement. The boys were running in a small, compact, agitated group

around the keep. The night was furious with
sound, and the birds, woken out of the palm tops,
were thrashing through the leaves and rising clear
and shrieking and turning to shriek again. It was
an insane, humorous imitation of battle. All
through the leaves below the trees Roark could
hear sounds, as if the young men were making
noise deliberately, trying to intimidate him with
noise. They were shouting their unflattering
opinions on him into the rustle of the night air.
They were threatening him with unimaginable
indignities to various parts of his body.

Roark turned and fired again at the last of the
three canoes. The first two were already in the
shelter of the palm trees.

"I should have cut all the trees," he said to Maya
once, but he knew, as he said it, that the heat
would have been intolerable. He fired down into
them now, not aiming his shot, but using it as a
warning.

All during this time Chris and Tom Hunter were
freeing the lashings on the north face and moving
the timber and tree trunks aside.

Roark's own mood matched the noise. He went
to the northern firing platform, took up the guns
there and fired them blindly into the green below
him. He reloaded and fired again. The shouting
and the taunts and the laughter came closer and
closer, but he saw nothing now; there was only
noise to shoot at—and noise was not enough.

In the keep the children were screaming.

"Go in and quiet them!" Roark bellowed at
Maya, who still stood quite still on the southern
firing platform.

"If it is your wish," she said softly, and went.

The escape was going to be easier than it had
promised to be. Maya went up the outer stairs to

Roark's pavilion and opened the hatch that led
below. The children's hysteria had risen. She dealt
with it firmly and effectively, slapping faces,
shaking, pushing. She forced order on them and
then, when they were under control and had
overcome the outbreaks of panic that followed
each successive shot that Roark fired, she led
them to the hole in the wall. The boys joined them;
in five minutes they were all gone.

All around them, the noise of the attackers
continued outside the stockade—the shouts of the
young, hilarious voices, the shaking of bushes, the
snap of breaking branches.

Still Roark could not see them, could not see
enough to aim at. The light of the moon was
deceptive, its shadows concealing. He was
surrounded by laughter and shouted curses and
threats that seemed to have no meaning and
insults that had no purpose. The moment seemed
to have come when there was no point in
attempting to defend the stockade itself. No
reinforcements had reached him from Salomon.
He withdrew to join Maya in the keep—at least it
would be easy to defend the keep.

Maya stood silently at the hatch that led down
into the children's quarters. The hatch itself was
closed again.

"They are quiet now," he said hurriedly.

"Yes, they are quiet," she answered truthfully.

He began to reload all four guns, placing one at
each corner as he did so.

The shouting was now louder around the
stockade wall. They were beating at it, hammering
at it, attempting to break it down.

Roark thought he saw movement beyond the
huts of the boys and fired at it. He fired at a
shadow at the main gate. He ran from corner to

corner like a crazy man, firing, reloading, firing. The room filled with smoke that drifted slowly with the night breeze, the smell of it pungent in his nostrils.

He developed a method. There was a ramrod for each gun, a powder-horn for each gun, balls for each gun; he fired and fired and fired. He ran from one side of the room to the other. He was no longer attempting to persuade the attackers that the place was defended by a force of men. The important thing was to fire the guns. He also had progressed into hysteria.

Roark finally set fire to the stockade himself, knocking over the whale-oil lamp as he rushed from one corner to another. There was a powder-horn close to it, and it flared and exploded, knocking Roark to the floor. The flames leapt to the palm-screen walls and from there to the roof thatching, and at once the place was ablaze. From the roof it leapt to the dried leaves under the palm-tree walls of the stockade. The trees themselves burnt like dry torches in the wind and the laughter of the young men died as the flames rose against the dark sky.

Roark rose slowly and stood in shock, still for the first time since the sighting of the boats. The sweat was running from him, his eyes were distraught. Then he shouted in terror.

"The children! The children!" Then he struggled with the bolt of the hatch.

Beside him Maya stood motionless.

"There are no children," she said calmly.

Roark, on his knees beside the hatch, looked up at her, overcome by his weariness.

"They have gone," she said simply. "it is time for us to go."

Without question Roark turned and followed

her down the stairs. She led the way towards the gate, but halfway there he staggered, caught himself, stood propped with his arm against a tree trunk, and then moved slowly around to face the burning keep. It was eerily beautiful through the slender columns of the palms.

Maya thought, watching him and watching the flames, that everything that she had done, everything that was of significance since she came to this man, had been marked with fire—the fire in his cabin on the first day, the fire that burnt the body of the Tamil, the fire under the head, the fire that brought the birds, the fire that ended the power of the head, the fire that burnt her canoe, and now the splendor of this transcendent flame engulfing the stockade.

Maya's eyes went back to Roark. He stood awkwardly, leaning his weight against a tree. There was in his face an expression of bewilderment and of pain, physical pain.

"The fire comes this way," she said at last. "We must leave this place."

But he made no attempt to go.

The heat of the flames reached them now and she half turned to go by herself. Still Roark made no move. Finally she went to him and took his arm. He came without protest, but slowly, walking with a heavy, uncertain gait. At the third step he staggered and put his arm across her shoulder. It was obvious even to Maya that it was done without other intent, but simply to save himself. The strength had been knocked out of him by the explosion. They followed the curve of the path to the head of the gully that led to the beach, and again he stumbled. His right foot dragged. He did not speak at all.

In the gully they lost the light of the flames.

Maya groped in the darkness. Increasingly she was aware that she was leading him, that he had lost his mastership. When they came to the clearing just before the beach, the flames in a new uprush lit them again, and she turned to look at his face. She could see that he was exhausted to the point of physical collapse.

"Sit here and wait," she said. "The boats from Salomon will come for you."

Roark spoke for the first time—thickly, the words hesitant. "Don't leave me, Maya!" Very heavily he lowered himself to the ground, sat for a moment in almost childish obedience, and then lay slowly back.

Maya stood looking down at him. Seeing him like this, bathed in the soft light of the flames, her eyes could not help but study him. She found herself recalling that this was one man who knew no authority higher than his own. He survived by his own set of rules. What he did, he did because it suited him; what he wanted, he simply took. But now he seemed different, in a sense sad. She herself stood free and strong. This was the climax of all her plots and her scheming, the moment that she had worked for, the moment when their roles were reversed. Strangely, she felt no satisfaction.

This man had shown her respect and honor in his own strange way, and now she was confused. Her victory had a sour taste to it. So she stood, waiting for some sign that would guide her, but no sign came. She still felt that her destiny was tied to this man, and the sudden realization that he'd never hold her, never make love to her, made her cry out even as her ire rose thinking of his callous treatment of those around him. Damn him! Damn him! Her thoughts continued to rage silently as she realized the sheer hopelessness of her confusion. She was free, at last free . . . yet still a prisoner of her feelings for this giant of a man.

The young men had come away from the fire. They were shouting to one another through the darkness of the palms.

She could hear Campbell's loud voice coming from the beach. "There wasna a sign o' the bastard. He musta got clean awa'."

"We searched the place," another voice called. "There was light enough. We'd 'a' seen him if he'd bin there."

"And the girl?" a third voice asked.

"I wasna worrit aboot the wee devil," Campbell replied. "She'd win clear o' the Day o' Judgment. Come awa' tae the boats!"

The shouting went on, and she heard the thud of oars and the splashing in the water, but she did not change her position. She felt an overwhelming confusion again as her hate and desire for this man stirred together. Her unbidden thoughts broke through her haze of frustration. Did she hate this man—or love him? Did she hate him, or love him?

At last, when the noise had diminished imperceptibly into silence, Maya dropped to her knees beside him.

"I must go," she whispered softly. "Your men will come soon."

"No!" Roark's voice answered huskily. He grabbed her wrists, imprisoning them easily with one great hand until the tendons felt crushed. With infuriating dominance, he pulled her to him, crushing her breasts against his chest. "You are mine, goddess of my dreams."

Maya could feel every inch of him pressed against her. Startled into action, she rolled swiftly away from his grasp and tried vainly to scramble away. Roark grasped her easily about the hips, dragging her flailing body back into the circle of his arms, then slid his tall, steel-hard body over hers.

As soon as his mouth pressed against her golden skin, Roark was lost in the fire of his passion. His lips parted, tasting her, savoring her upon his tongue. It was an instinctive action, brought about by his first glimpse into those mysterious indigo eyes, so captivating that they seemed to draw him into her very soul. His emotions and reasoning were shattered by her.

There was nothing in heaven or hell that could have stopped him from taking her, for he knew that she was his, and that very soon she would realize it, too. No one could not stop what the fates had decreed. They were of one mind, one desire, one destiny.

"Stop. . . ." Maya whispered even as she felt her desire awakening deep within her.

Roark felt her slowly responding. "Ah, love, even if hell beckons, it will not stop us. You were made for this moment, and for me. I am your master."

His words so overwhelmed Maya with contempt that her desire turned as cold as ice, and she spat directly into his face.

"I am my own!" she cried out in a choked voice.

Spittle ran down Roark's cheek, yet he paid it no heed. He shook his head as if to clear the red mist before his eyes. Long-suppressed hatred burst from him in sudden blinding fury. No longer was Maya the beloved temptress he sought to capture, but an enemy, a reminder of past failures that even now tormented his soul. Rising swiftly to his knees, he grabbed her legs and pulled her hips to him. Maya's temper soared the higher at this treat-

ment, and she tried to reach the dagger on her leg,
but his hand jerked away her sarong and the silk
binding of the dagger, dropping them into the
sand. She screamed, trying to entangle her legs
within his to keep him from her. She fought like a
lioness, with teeth and nails and spirit. Roark
only sneered at her futile efforts, enjoying the
battle and the lusty awakening of other senses.
Then, tiring of the game, he grasped her beneath
the arms and pulled her thrashing body against
his, dark, hard eyes staring straight into hers,
which were slittled like a cat's and filled with
rage.

"Place your legs about my waist," Roark
growled, and when she did not respond, grabbed
her beneath the buttocks and forced her slender
legs there himself.

The relentless pressure from his hand
encompassed the back of her head and pushed her
face forward until their lips touched, and caught
fire.

Hungrily, Roark's mouth moved over hers,
seeming to draw every drop of fight from her.
Maya was shocked to feel the pleasure amidst her
rage as their lips clung in a fiery kiss. What was
wrong with her? she screamed inwardly. Never
had a man's kiss excited her this way before. And
this man was an unfeeling monster who was hell-
bent on using her, not making love to her. Roark's
tongue darted in and out of her mouth, plundering
the passion within, until she moaned in despair.
Her body shuddered against him. It was as if she
finally realized that she could not fight him and
hope to win. She lay limply in his arms, tears
streaming down her face.

That small indication of defeat should have
made Roark feel triumphant. After all, that was

what he had sought from her, wasn't it? He wanted to ravish her, punish her flesh until she was broken and submissive and lay sobbing in his arms while he took her. Yes, that was exactly how it was to be! His lips and hands continued their arrogant assault, but buried in the back of his mind lay a strong conviction that to do this was wrong, and that he would, for some reason, regret it.

"My beautiful indigo-eyed tremptress," he whispered, chokingly. Raising his head, Roark's eyes locked on hers, their depths shimmering with emotion. "I want you to share my life and that which belongs to me. I want to build you a mansion in these islands. I want to give you children and watch them grow. Stay with me, Maya."

Eyes blurred by tears, Maya looked up at him, stunned by his words and by the pain she glimpsed in his dark gaze. Neither moved for a moment; they only clung to each other, studying, searching, raw emotions plainly visible.

Mockingly over the water came the words of the young men's song:

> "When the party was over,
>   They took a' the women,
>   And went hame tae rest.
> They said they liked th' music
>   But. . . ."

Hearing the song, Maya's nerve suddenly broke and she pulled free and ran, silent and confused, to the sea. At its edge she sank down, half sitting, half kneeling, one hand on the sand. For a moment she breathed heavily, as if she had run a race. Then, venting a long sigh, she looked out at the dark sea, trying to summon some reason out of the chaos in her mind. For all her earlier satisfaction in destroying Roark, she felt pensive and lonely now, as if the victory had lost its savor. The young men's song had snatched a beautiful moment, and she could only wonder what it would have been like to share the night with him.

Her mind argued, this is madness! Her heart answered softly, I love him. Shaking, Maya bit the back of her hand, seeking pain to awaken her will. But it brought only fear, not of him but of herself, for she still wanted to draw him down with her upon the sand and show him once and for all time that she was more than enough woman for him.

Miserably, she stared into the dark sea. Had he seen? Did he know the sudden naked desire that must have shone in her eyes? Her face still burned where his lips had touched her tender flesh.

Clenching her eyes tightly, she covered her ears with her hands. But the image of Roark's face was scored into her brain, and nothing could force the image to flee.

Chris Lovel watched her from the shadows of the trees. The moon was setting. Maya was not in the path of its light, but she was silhouetted against the lesser darkness of the water.

Far down the channel, the young men were still singing at the oars. It was no longer possible to hear the words of the ancient, bawdy song.

His own mind was moving swiftly. He had been shocked into honesty by the actions of the night. He was aware at last that Maya would never be his, that she was tied to Tillman by some mysterious power. He still felt overwhelmed by the strength and purpose of Tillman, even though Tillman was now broken. He knew that Tillman was not wounded—the young men had brought no

guns to the island—and he was not burnt; but by
some miracle the power had been taken from him.
Chris had heard the murmured words between
him and Maya; he had seen dimly the struggle and
the embrace between them. Then Maya had run
towards the beach. He knew at that moment that
Tillman's reign was over for ever. Maya had
beaten him.

On that thought, he walked down the beach,
silent on the sand, and stood behind Maya.

"You want tae stay with him, don't you?" he
asked softly.

"Yes," she said simply, without turning. "Now
he needs me."

The days and nights aged into weeks on Eagle
Island, and still the battle raged inside Maya. Her
mind was exhausted from the struggle and seemed
to lie within her head without movement. Every
time she closed her eyes a vision of Roark's face
tormented her; she could no longer bear the
struggle.

I am now my own enemy, she thought. There is
little I will not do for him, or give him if he asks.
My mind is not turned toward Chris, escape or
revenge, but to him. I must master myself again,
or I will be consumed in my own passions. I must
free myself of this madness. I must face Roark
Tillman.

With her decision finally made, Maya closed her
eyes almost fearfully, but only a soft, warm half
darkness was there. Then sleep drifted like a
soundless wave over her, and she was engulfed in
its peace.

26

It was early in the morning nearly a month later on the island of Salomon. The lagoon and the channel were full of fishing boats. A small schooner rode high in the water at anchorage. At the landing place were piled mountains of trade goods.

Roark Tillman sat alone in his great chair in the big hut. The village was quiet except for the soft chatter of women's voices and the occasional sound of laughter drifting in from outside the hut. His mind was not on these sounds.

The island was unbearably lonely of late. There was something missing deep inside him. Life seemed to move on as usual, slowing in the heat of the day, hastening with the harvest of coconuts or a ship calling. It accommodated the rush of the oil presses and the trading of goods, and the new wealth and peace on the island was enjoyed by all. The island was starting to prosper again. It was

what he had always dreamed of, his own kingdom.
But now the edge was gone from the achievement.

Roark frowned and rose slowly from his chair.
His nostrils flared slightly, sniffing the tangy
crispness of the salt air, cursing the heat and
wishing he was miles away. It was difficult for
him to keep his mind on the business of the island,
for his every thought was of the woman he loved
and had lost.

He cursed himself unmercifully for the
countless months he'd wasted, refusing so many
times, because of his pride and his arrogance, to
say the words that might have made her his.

"I love you, Maya . . . I love you more than life
itself," he whispered to the empty hut. A glimmer
of sadness flickered across his handsome face.

Roark began to pace back and forth inside the
hut in agitation, a silver object clutched tightly in
his huge hand.

He paused in his thoughts to glance down at the
dagger in his hand. Even now, after so many
weeks, the memory of her still haunted him.

A searing burst of anger almost overwhelmed
him.

He stared down again and could not for the life
of him bring forth words to express his pain. He
gazed lovingly at the silver blade, bewildered by
the disturbing memories that seared through his
brain, flooding his body with a pulsing, warm
excitement.

A small sound intruded upon the quiet of the big
hut. Roark turned and stared in amazement. It
was Maya, and her name escaped his lips in a
whispered question. Like the temptress of his
dreams, she came forward. Her voice was husky
as she spoke.

"Roark Tillman. You have vexed me much these

past months. But now—now we are equals!"

Roark stared at her in disbelief. He came to stand close beside her, and Maya returned his stare as boldly as he gave it.

"I will not be your brood mare," she continued firmly. "I will be your wife. Your only wife. The rest must go, or I will leave this place forever!"

"They have all been freed," Roark replied. "Only the wives of my men remain."

"And the pig, Pitney?" she questioned. "Where is his lair?"

"He left with the last ship. I am alone. You have my word."

Suddenly remembering his haunting dreams, Roark turned his back upon her beauty. It was in his mind to flee the place before this temptress destroyed him completely. But his feet were leaden.

"I fear you are playing games with me once more," he said harshly. "And I have survived so much that I am leery of what deeper fate you have in store for me."

Maya's laughter softly entwined him as she reached out and caressed his back, tracing the long swell of his muscles through his shirt. Roark's knees went suddenly weak as her cool hand touched him and wandered with its soft, silken smoothness, stirring his emotions until they boiled in the pit of his stomach.

He faced her suddenly, and her hand stayed to lightly rub his chest. She felt his hands on her shoulders, forcing a distance between them again. His eyes met hers. "What about the boy, Chris Lovel?"

"Chris was—" Maya's mouth suddenly broke into a smile, and then she laughed, stopping only when she saw that Roark's eyes were still totally serious. "Chris was my revenge," she forced out soberly.

Roark frowned. "Your what?"

"My revenge." Maya closed her eyes and sighed, her mouth curving into a mischievous smile. "Something I wanted for so long, that a part of me didn't know when it was over." Her smile vanished as she opened her indigo eyes, and when she spoke again her words were from the deepest part of her heart. "He is gone from my life, Roark. My life is with you. Do you still want me?" She clung to him tightly for a long moment, then kissed him with all the passion and warmth that had suddenly blossomed inside her.

Roark's lips hovered over hers, and his voice was gentle as he spoke, like a small boy pleading for attention.

"Maya, love me. Maya, love me."

With a small, welcoming cry, she reached slender, golden arms to lead him to the bed, her heart flooding her body with warm gladness.

Roark's arms slipped with infinite care about her, and she forgot all else. His face brushed against her hair, stirring from it the sweet fragrance of her body, until his mind reeled with the heady scent of it. Roark knew he must be gentle with her for fear of destroying the moment, but it took an extreme exercise of will to control his desire.

Lifting her heavy raven-black hair aside, she offered him her shoulder, and his long fingers nimbly worked the silken sarong until it was free and slid to her feet. Loosening his linen shirt and slipping it over his head, Roark once more embraced her, bringing her back into close contact with his muscular frame. Maya felt the hard, manly boldness of him, and she closed her eyes as his searing lips slowly traced her throat and shoulder. His hands caressed her, leisurely arousing her, stroking her breasts, and moving downward over her flat stomach. A warm tide of tingling passion flooded her. The whisper of a sigh escaped her as she lifted her face to meet his, her trembling lips slackened and parted as his mouth possessed hers. They came together like the forging of iron, their kisses now savage and fierce, devouring as tongues met and their mouths slanted across each other's with hungry impatience. His hand wandered down her back, pressing her hips tighter against him. His passion raged within him, and the fire in his loins was raging out of control.

Roark bent a knee upon the bed, pulling her with him. His open mouth, hot and wet, seared her breasts, and his white teeth lightly nibbled her curving waist and the smooth golden skin of her stomach. Maya closed her eyes, panting and breathless, pliable beneath his caresses. His eyes aflame, Roark lowered his weight upon her, parting her thighs, her woman's body reacting instinctively to this indescribable, bursting, splintering feeling that built with pulsing leaps and bounds deep within her. The pleasure mounted so intensely that she wondered wildly if she could bear it.

With Chris it had been an innocent awakening of her desires. But with Roark it was magic, a stunning, beautiful, exploding bloom of ravaging rapture that made her arch against him with a fierce ardor matching his. The wild, soaring ecstasy burst upon them, fusing them together in the all-consuming fire of their passion. Clasped tightly to him as if he would draw her into himself, Maya felt the thunderous beating of his heart against her naked breasts and heard his hoarse, ragged breathing in her ear.

It was like a time for things meant to be, like the trees, the sand, the emerald sea, the sun, and the stars. It was all the stars in the heavens blending into a single sun, the naked hunger that caught them both in an eternal, violent whirlwind. They were one, belonging and possessing, giving and taking.

Sated, they lay entwined, Maya warm and secure in his arms, knowing the strange peace she had found nowhere else.

A moment of silence passed as they nestled in each other's arms. Roark met Maya's eyes, and their love glowed in unspoken words.

"Have you slain your mighty dragon, my love?" Roark asked softly.

"Slain my dragon? No, and I will hear no more such talk." Maya laughed and slipped her arms about his neck. "Come, my mighty dragon, breathe your fire and warm me. The day is just beginning for us."

"God, but I love you," Roark murmured thickly, burying his lips in her hair.

"Always and forever," Maya replied in a whisper-soft voice.

"Yes, my love, always and forever, beyond all else."

Deep within the spiritual passages of their souls the promise was conveyed and accepted.

On the day of Roark and Maya's wedding, Diego Island was awash with evanescent sunshine. Dirk Cooper had succumbed to Kathleen's pleas and agreed to marry them in their flower-drenched garden, surrounded only by their loved ones and friends.

They stood together now before Dirk Cooper, reciting their vows. Maya was an exquisite vision in a simple, high-waisted gown of gossamer white muslin that Kathleen had given her. Her raven-black hair tumbled free over her shoulders, adorned only with a garland of flowers. Against her bare throat sparkled diamonds in the shape of a heart; it was Roark's wedding gift to her.

Roark's eyebrow cocked slightly as he listened to Maya promise to obey him, and the humor wasn't lost on Kathleen Cooper either.

The boy, Rahmzi, stepped forward smiling to present the ring to Roark. It was one more sign of the transformation from the past since Roark and Maya had made their peace. The boy was back with them now, and happy, and Roark was no longer the Lord Tillman. Gone were the slaves, the whip, and his raging anger. He was impeccably handsome on his wedding day, clad in snug black-velvet trousers, a dark blue frock coat, an ivory silk waistcoat, a white silk shirt, and a skillfully tied cravat. His hair gleamed in the golden sunlight, accentuating the rakish lines of his profile as he slipped the ring onto Maya's slim finger, then bent to kiss her.

"I have loved you from the beginning of my dreams, my temptress," he whispered softly to her, "and I shall love you long after those dreams have faded from this mortal body."

Maya twined her arms about his broad shoulders, stood on tiptoe, and returned his kiss with unabashed rapture.

Then, arm in arm, they turned to greet their guests. The warm informality of the ceremony lent it the air of a true celebration. Silvery tears glistened in Maya's eyes as she embraced Kathleen and Roark followed suit, careful not to press against Mrs. Finch.

"Oh, Kathleen," Maya whispered huskily, "I am so happy!"

"I know you are, darling, and we're happy for you. I'm so glad everything worked out peacefully. We were worried sick about you when you disappeared after the battle."

"Now Roark can do the worrying," Dirk Cooper interjected wryly, grinning at his new partner.

"By God, she's just taken a vow to obey me!" Roark laughed. "Didn't you hear her?"

"I don't remember saying that," Maya teased. "I think you must have dreamed it, dear husband."

"Well, I can promise you one thing, Roark. You'll never be bored," Dirk assured him.

Servants appeared from the Cooper house to serve brandy.

"I would like to propose a toast to the bride," Dirk announced, smiling at Maya. "A most singular woman! You're a lucky man, Roark."

"I'm aware of that," Roark nodded, a huge smile on his face.

The wind blew a siren's song through the rigging of the longboat as Maya and Roark sailed over the gently rolling sea breakers of the channel toward Salomon Island.

Maya glanced shoreward to watch the islands slip by, and was thrilled by the sight of a flock of great white herons rising from one of the islands and lumbering lazily across the green treetops, to disappear on the far side of the horizon. "They're beautiful, Roark, beautiful!"

"Aye, my love. But I have eyes for only you."

Maya snorted. "You have eyes for only me, my husband? Will you be as faithful to me as the day is long," she questioned, holding back her laughter, "or will your eyes follow each young pretty girl that passes?"

"Nay, my temptress, I will have eyes for you only! Why else do you think I let Cooper's men take all the women? I will love you, honor you, cherish and keep you always," he said softly and drew her into his embrace. He kissed her softly parted lips, then his mouth traveled along the curve of her cheek to her ear. "Always," he repeated huskily, his breath warm and exciting.

Maya melted into his arms and snuggled against his broad chest with a deep sigh of contentment.

"Just as I will love and honor and cherish you always," Maya murmured dreamily.

"And obey me?" Roark demanded hopefully.

Maya laughed merrily. "Is loving and honoring and cherishing not enough for you, mighty dragon? We will speak more of obeying at some other time."

Roark nodded. He loved her just as she was, proud, rebellious and strong-willed, but with an inner core of softness and vulnerability that needed his strength to draw upon as much as he needed hers.

"This is the happiest moment of my life," she murmured.

Roark touched her lips softly with his, then drew back to smile and to arch a suggestive eyebrow. "So far, you mean!"

Maya's heart swelled as she tasted him on her lips and considered that promise. How wonderful it was to devote life and soul to one love, one person forever, and to share equally, receiving the same in return.

Epilogue

Together, Maya and Roark built a great house on Salomon Island. The house was designed with an entry that had staircases on either side, and beyond, a large hall. There were wings on each side of the main living area, one containing the bath, the other the kitchen and servants' quarters. The second story of the great house contained six large bedchambers, all looking out to the sea. Between the wings of the house was a lovely, sheltered garden of herbs and spices, where Maya and Roark would sit in the evening. Beyond the garden stretched a long building whose lower story housed the farm animals they had imported to the island.

Branching out, they grew crops of sugar cane, cotton and vegetables. The citrus orchards and vineyards came later. This new diversification was Maya's idea, and meant that the islands were not strictly dependent on the trade from passing merchant ships and they were able to become self-sufficient.

Their first son was followed by five brothers and three sisters. Then nine children grew up watching their parents work long hours, fighting storms, droughts, insects and pirates. But through it all, the family remained happy and prospered.

Roark and Maya walked arm in arm down the streets of the settlement. The whole of Salomon Island was pulsating with activity, and they felt not a little pride. The market was filled with people—colorfully dressed European traders, gentlemen and ladies in pretty silks and satins, as well as the Indonesian workers in their native dress. The air was warm and rich with the strange, exciting aroma of Chinese tea, spices, and the tang of citrus fruits.

There were the beginnings of many buildings. The biggest two were the huge two-story buildings of the Tillman and Cooper Trading Company, the vast buildings containing the kind of warehouses, offices and living quarters favored by the European traders and similar to those in Singapore. At present they were just shells of peripheral bamboo and imported timber scaffoldings soaring skyward, dozens of Indonesian laborers swarming around on them. And around these dominating structures were several other buildings, stores, dwellings and wharves.

In the distance, halfway to the landing place, Maya and Roark could see that work had already begun on the dockyard; a never-ending stream of workers was dumping stones and rocks to form the first of the deep-water wharves. Opposite the harbor master's small house, complete but for its roof, were the stone walls of the church, three-quarters finished. And beyond the dockyard was the beginning of a school.

Later that day, during the early evening hours, a gentle sea breeze filled the air, and the earth, wet from a brief rain, was redolent with the scent of spices from the garden. The emerald-green waters of the sea shimmered under the towering piles of clouds, magestic in their splendid colors of lavender, orange, red, and gold, as the sun settled into the sea.

Roark stood behind Maya in the garden, watching the beautiful sunset. His hands rested lightly upon her shoulders, and looking down at her, he said again the words that he had first spoken to her at their wedding so many years ago. "I have loved you from the beginning of my dreams, my temptress, and I shall love you long after those dreams have faded from this mortal body."

Maya's heart swelled within her chest. It swelled until she thought it might burst with the happiness she felt spreading through her entire being. As Roark turned her gently towards him and lowered his head to capture her lips in a tender yet passionate kiss, her last rational thought before she gave herself up to him was that no matter what happened now she was whole in body and spirit forever, for she had Roark Tillman for all eternity. It is enough, Maya thought. It is more than enough.

In the years that followed, Maya and Roark knew a happiness that neither had dreamt possible. The old hurts faded, leaving in their wake a sense of peace, contentment, and love. They drew strength from each other, and neither feared what the future might hold, for they knew they would face it together.

Their world was peaceful at last, and Maya and Roark had found their place in it.